PRAISE FOR FRANCINE RIVERS

And the Shofar Blew
"Meticulously plotted, Francine Rivers's new masterpiece, **And the Shofar Blew**, brims with unforgettable characters."
—Romantic Times

The Atonement Child
"**The Atonement Child** is well written, presenting the truth about abortion in a compassionate, nonjudgmental way."
—The Post-Abortion Review

The Last Sin Eater
"Rivers skillfully combines character and mood to create a haunting story that effectively depicts the horror of sin and the beauty of forgiveness."
—CBA *Marketplace*

Leota's Garden
"Francine Rivers is a master gardener, deftly pruning brush and deadwood, using poignant humor and bittersweet revelation to open hearts to reconciliation."
—Romantic Times

Lineage of Grace series
"Readers will find this book worth reading more than once. . . . Masterfully written."
—Romantic Times

"Rivers's writing is excellent."
—Publishers Weekly

"Rivers is such an excellent author. Her people are vibrantly alive, with all the strengths and weaknesses that make them so human."
—Historical Novels Review

Mark of the Lion series
"Francine Rivers puts readers right into the history of the moment. . . ."
—Romantic Times

Redeeming Love
". . . a splendid piece of work."
—*Library Journal*

"Rivers shines in her ability to weave together spiritual themes and sexual tension in a well-told story, a talent that has propelled her into the spotlight as one of the most popular novelists in the genre of Christian fiction. This is one of her best."
—Amazon.com

"The truth that ran through that book [**Redeeming Love**] absolutely brought me to my knees. I was a changed person after reading that book."
—Amy Grant, singer/songwriter, in an interview with Ted Koppel, ABC Nightly News

". . . a thought-provoking novel that you will not easily forget."
—*Romantic Times*

Sons of Encouragement series
". . . packs a powerful punch through characters that resonate in the soul. Fast-paced and seamless, this is a magnificent tale of courage, faithfulness, woe, and great joy."
—*Romantic Times*

MARK OF THE LION ❖ BOOK III

AS *SURE*

AS THE DAWN

FRANCINE RIVERS

Tyndale House Publishers, Inc.
CAROL STREAM, ILLINOIS

Visit Tyndale online at www.tyndale.com.

Check out the latest about Francine Rivers at www.francinerivers.com.

TYNDALE and Tyndale's quill logo are registered trademarks of Tyndale House Publishers, Inc.

As Sure as the Dawn

Copyright © 1995, 2002 by Francine Rivers. All rights reserved.

Roman Empire map on page xvii copyright © Leen Ritmeyer. All rights reserved.

Maps on pages xviii–xix copyright © 1995 by Hugh Claycombe. All rights reserved.

Discussion Guide section written by Peggy Lynch.

Cover illustration copyright © 2008 by Robert Papp. All rights reserved.

Author photo by Elaina Burdo copyright © 2014. All rights reserved.

Cover designed by Ron Kaufmann

Interior designed by Zandrah Maguigad

Scripture quotations marked NIV are taken from the Holy Bible, *New International Version,*® NIV.® Copyright © 1973, 1978, 1984 by Biblica, Inc.® Used by permission. All rights reserved worldwide.

Scripture quotations used in Discussion Guide are taken from the *Holy Bible,* New Living Translation, copyright © 1996 by Tyndale House Foundation. Used by permission of Tyndale House Publishers, Inc., Carol Stream, Illinois 60188. All rights reserved.

As Sure as the Dawn is a work of fiction. Where real people, events, establishments, organizations, or locales appear, they are used fictitiously. All other elements of the novel are drawn from the author's imagination.

Library of Congress Cataloging-in-Publication Data

Rivers, Francine, date
  As sure as the dawn / Francine Rivers.
    p. cm. — (Mark of the lion)
  ISBN 978-0-8423-3976-6
  1. Church history—Primitive and early church, ca. 30-600—Fiction.
2. Rome—History—Empire, 30 B.C.-476 A.D.—Fiction. I. Title. II. Series: Rivers, Francine, date   Mark of the lion.
PS3568.I83165A9   1995
813'.54—dc20   95-1034

Printed in the United States of America

20   19   18   17   16
31   30   29   28   27

To my brother,
EVERETT MELBOURNE KING, JR.,
and his wife, EVELYN,
I love you both and thank God we were
together through the hard times.

CONTENTS

Foreword by Mark D. Taylor   xi

Preface   xiii

Acknowledgments   xv

Maps: The Roman Empire c. A.D. 117   xvii
The Journey to Germania c. A.D. 72;
The Ocean Route from Ephesus to Rome   xviii
The Overland Route from Rome to Germania   xix

Prologue   xxi

PART I: THE SEED   1

PART II: THE SOIL   121

PART III: THE GROWTH   281

PART IV: THE THORNS   303

PART V: THE SACRIFICE   419

PART VI: THE HARVEST   455

Epilogue   471

Glossary of Terms   475

Discussion Guide   478

FOREWORD

In 1992, Tyndale House made a conscious decision to begin publishing excellent fiction that would help us fulfill our corporate purpose—to "minister to the spiritual needs of people, primarily through literature consistent with biblical principles." Before that time, Tyndale House had been known for many years as a publisher of Bibles and of nonfiction books by well-known authors like Tim LaHaye and James Dobson. We had dabbled in fiction before "Christian fiction" became popular, but it was not a major part of our publishing plan.

We began to recognize, however, that we could carry out our purpose very effectively through fiction, since fiction speaks to the heart rather than to the head.

Fiction is entertaining. Well-written fiction is gripping. As readers, we'll stay up until 2:00 a.m. to finish a good novel. But Tyndale has a greater goal than simply entertaining our readers. We want to help our readers grow!

We recognize that authors have something of a bully pulpit for communicating their worldview and values to their readers. But with that opportunity comes a danger. Just what worldview and values is an author communicating? At best, most contemporary novelists present a squishy worldview. At worst, they sow negative values and unhealthy attitudes in the hearts of their readers. We wanted to set a whole new standard for fiction.

So we began looking for novelists who had a heart message that would help our readers grow. And we met Francine Rivers.

Francine had been extremely successful as a writer of romance novels for the general market early in her career. But when she became a Christian, she wanted to use her talents to communicate faith values to her readers. One of her early projects was the Mark of the Lion trilogy.

When I read the manuscript for the first book in the series, *A Voice in the Wind*, I was blown away by the power of the story. I was transported back to the first century—to Jerusalem, Germania, Rome, and Ephesus. I lived with Hadassah as she struggled to live out her faith in the midst of a pagan Roman household. I felt the terror of the gladiator as he faced his foes in the arena. Above all, through their experiences I learned lessons in courage.

We are proud to present this new edition of the Mark of the Lion. I trust it will speak to your heart, as it has to mine and to hundreds of thousands of other readers.

MARK D. TAYLOR
President, Tyndale House Publishers

PREFACE

When I became a born-again Christian in 1986, I wanted to share my faith with others. However, I didn't want to offend anyone and risk "losing" old friends and family members who didn't share my belief in Jesus as Lord and Savior. I found myself hesitating and keeping silent. Ashamed of my cowardice and frustrated by it, I went on a quest, seeking the faith of a martyr. *A Voice in the Wind* was the result.

While writing Hadassah's story, I learned that courage is not something we can manufacture by our own efforts. But when we surrender wholeheartedly to God, He gives us the courage to face whatever comes. He gives us the words to speak when we are called to stand and voice our faith.

I still consider myself a struggling Christian, fraught with faults and failures, but Jesus has given me the tool of writing to use in seeking answers from Him. Each of my characters plays out a different point of view as I search for God's perspective, and every day I find something in Scripture that speaks to me. God is patient with me, and through the study of His Word, I am learning what He wants to teach me. When I hear from a reader who is touched by one of my stories, it is God alone who is to be praised. All good things come from the Father above, and He can use anything to reach and teach His children—even a work of fiction.

My main desire when I started writing Christian fiction was to find answers to personal questions, and to share those answers in story form with others. Now, I want so much more. I yearn for the Lord to use my stories in making people thirst for His Word, the Bible. I hope that reading Hadassah's story will make you hunger for the real Word, Jesus Christ, the Bread of Life. I pray that you will finish my book and pick up the Bible with a new excitement and anticipation of a real encounter with the Lord Himself. May you search Scripture for the sheer joy of being in God's presence.

Beloved, surrender wholeheartedly to Jesus Christ, who loves you. As you drink from the deep well of Scripture, the Lord will refresh and cleanse you, mold you and re-create you through His Living Word. For the Bible is the very breath of God, giving life eternal to those who seek Him.

Francine Rivers, 2002

ACKNOWLEDGMENTS

I want to thank my husband, Rick, for his continuing support and encouragement to stretch my wings and fly. I also thank God for my children, Trevor, Shannon, and Travis, who have taught me many invaluable lessons about life and love.

I also thank my editor, Karen Ball, for the use of her talents and expertise in fine-tuning ideas and improving my work. More important, I thank God for leading me to an editor who shares my vision and has faith exceeding my own.

The Roman Empire c. 117 AD

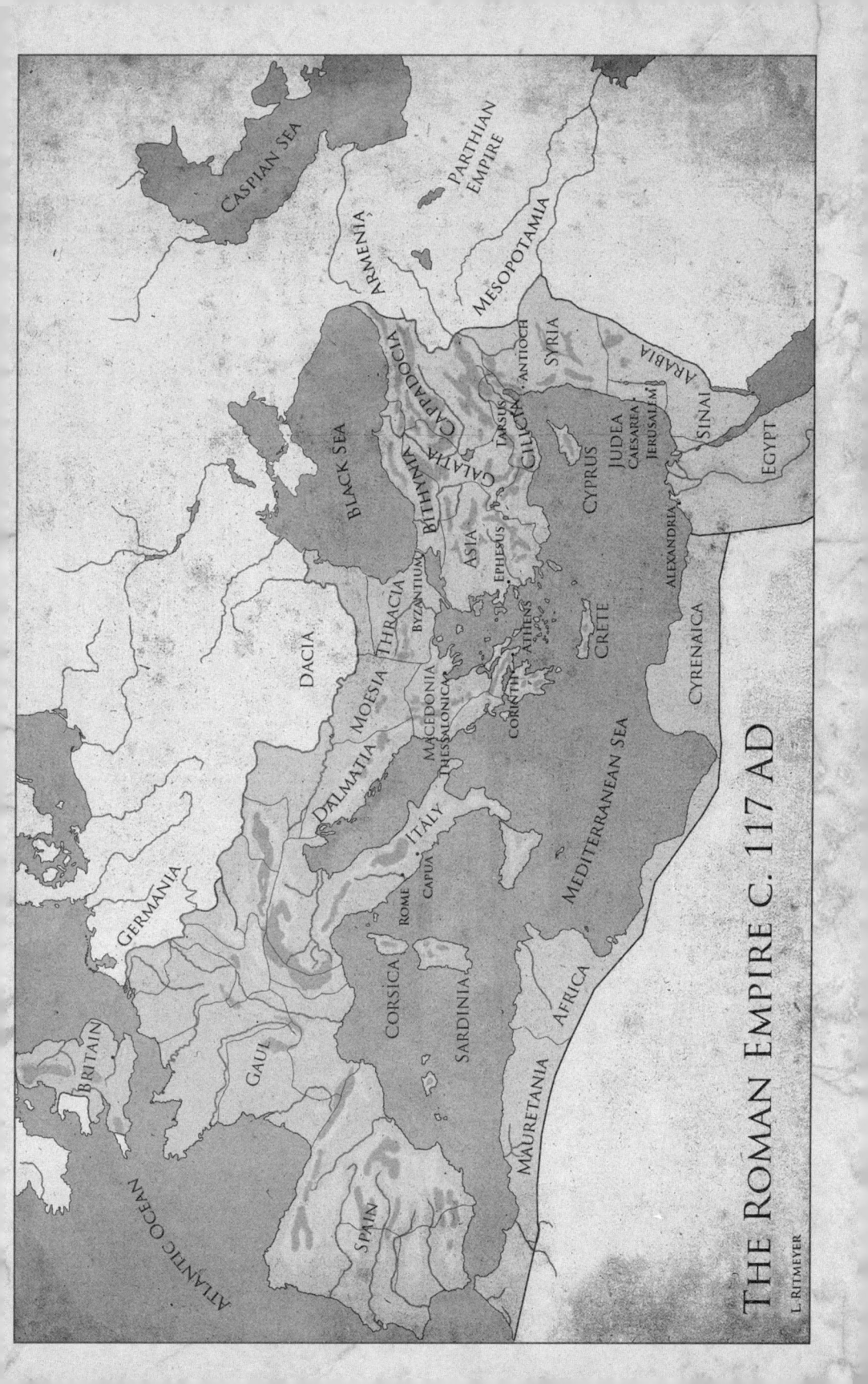

L. Ritmeyer

The Journey to Germania c. A.D. 72

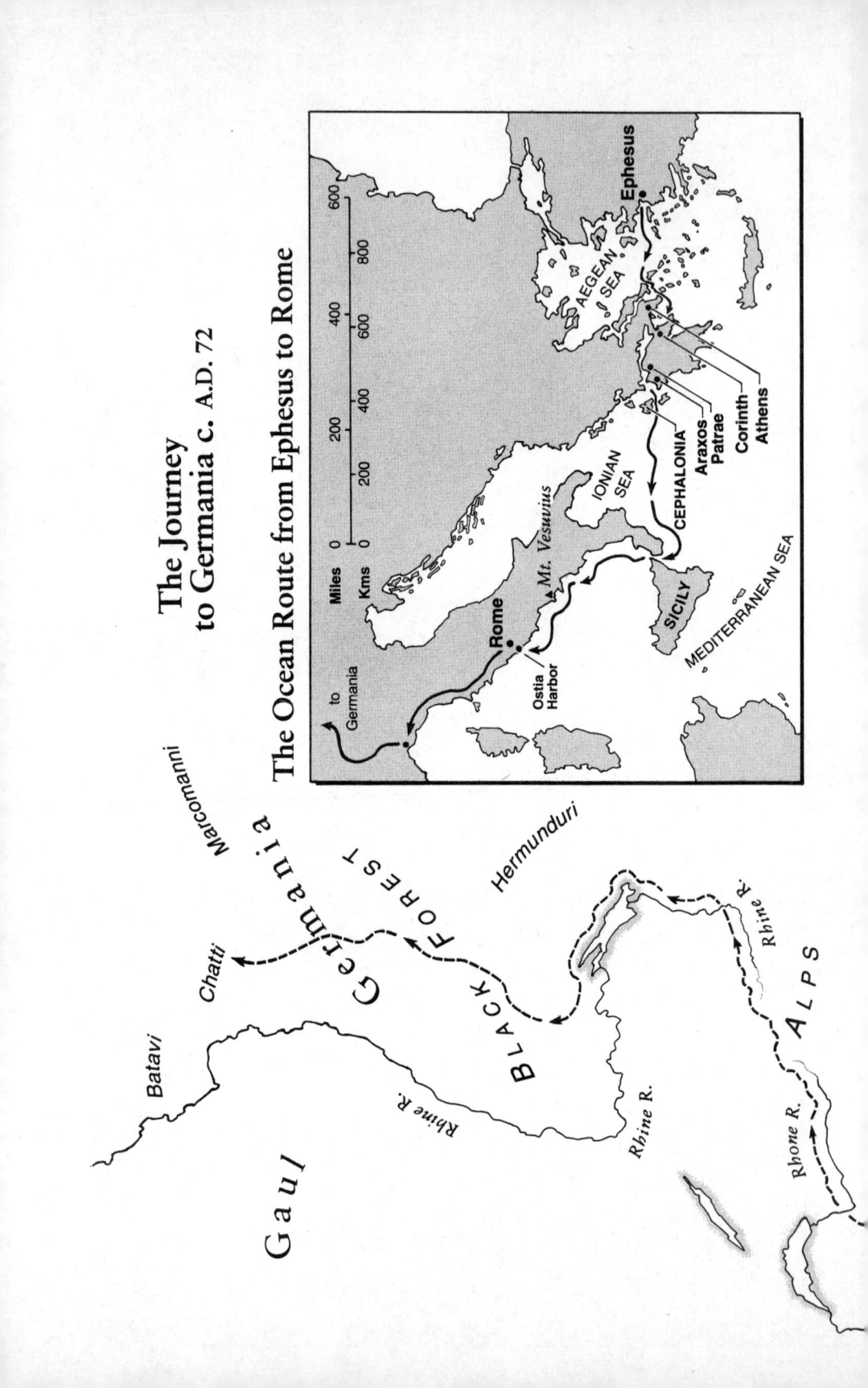

The Ocean Route from Ephesus to Rome

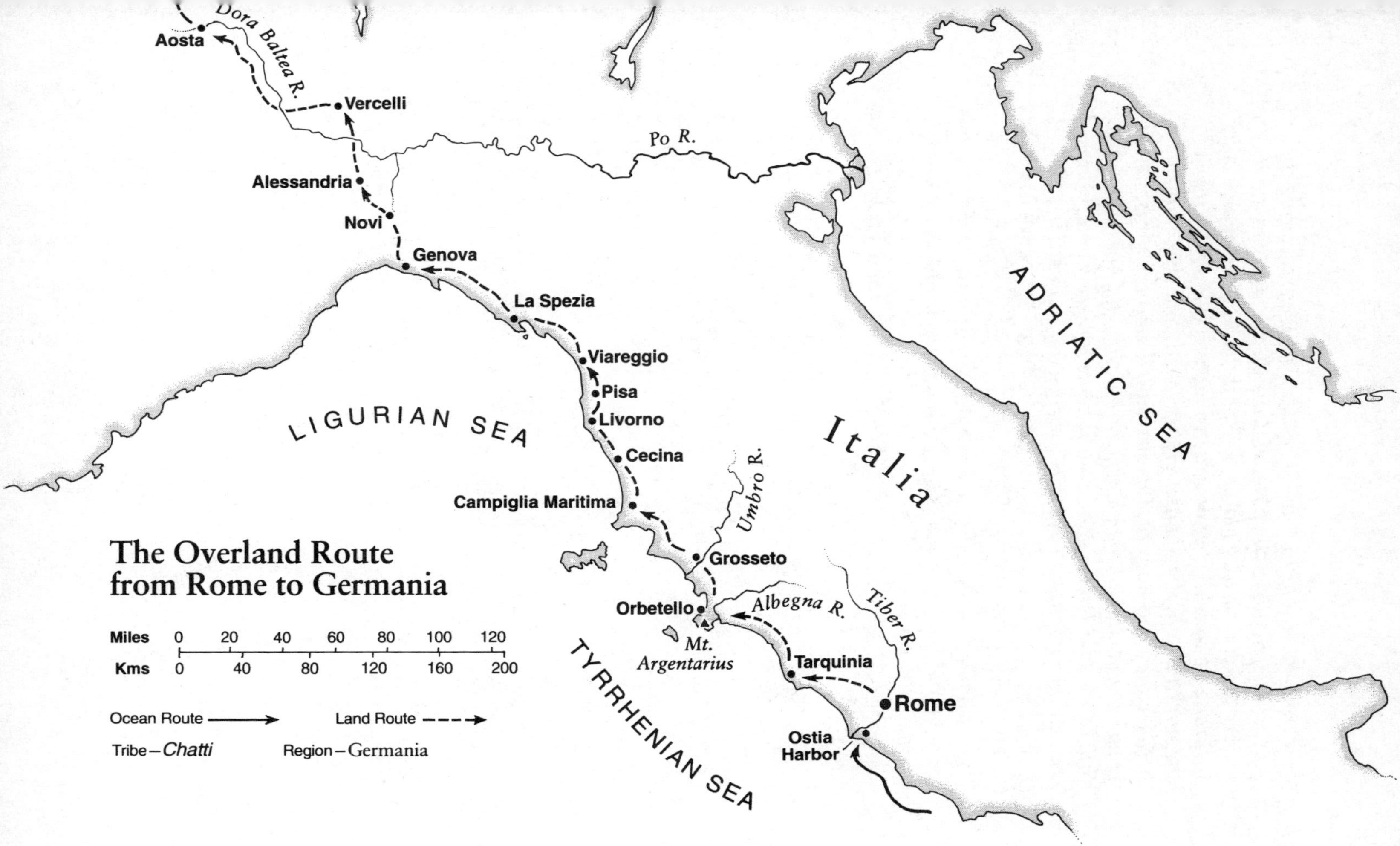
The Overland Route
from Rome to Germania
Miles 0 20 40 60 80 100 120
Kms 0 40 80 120 160 200
Ocean Route
Land Route
Tribe—Chatti
Region—Germania
Aosta
Dora Baltea R.
Vercelli
Po R.
Alessandria
Novi
Genova
La Spezia
Viareggio
Pisa
Livorno
Cecina
Campiglia Maritima
LIGURIAN SEA
Umbro R.
Grosseto
Orbetello
Mt. Argentarius
Albegna R.
Tiber R.
Tarquinia
Rome
Ostia Harbor
TYRRHENIAN SEA
Italia
ADRIATIC SEA

"A farmer went out to sow his seed. As he was scattering the seed, some fell along the path, and the birds came and ate it up. Some fell on rocky places, where it did not have much soil. It sprang up quickly, because the soil was shallow. But when the sun came up, the plants were scorched, and they withered because they had no root. Other seed fell among thorns, which grew up and choked the plants, so that they did not bear grain. Still other seed fell on good soil. It came up, grew and produced a crop, multiplying thirty, sixty, or even a hundred times."
Mark 4:3-8, NIV

"Jesus replied . . . 'I tell you the truth, unless a [seed] falls to the ground and dies, it remains only a single seed. But if it dies, it produces many seeds.'"
John 12:23-24, NIV

PROLOGUE

A.D. 79

The guard of the lower dungeon threw the bolt and led the way. The sound of the Roman's hobnailed sandals sent Atretes back to Capua. As he followed the guard, the smell of cold stone and human fear made the sweat break out on his skin. Someone cried out from behind a locked door. Others moaned in despair. Then, as they kept walking, Atretes heard something coming from the far end of the dank environs—a sound so sweet that it drew him. Somewhere in the darkness a woman was singing.

The guard slowed, tilting his head slightly. "Have you ever heard a voice like that in all your life?" he said. The singing stopped, and the guard walked more briskly. "She's been in here for months, yet it doesn't seem to affect her. Not like it does the others. A pity she's going to die with the rest of them tomorrow," he said. He paused before a heavy door, then threw the bolt.

Atretes stood on the threshold and looked from face to face inside the dim room. A single torch flickered in the mount on the sidewall, but the huddled forms in back were cast in shadows. Most of the prisoners were women and children. There were less than half a dozen old bearded men. Atretes wasn't surprised. The younger men would have been saved for fighting in the arena.

Someone said his name and he saw a thin woman in rags rise from the mass of filthy captives.

Hadassah.

"Is that the one?" the guard said.

"Yes."

"The singer," he said. "You there! Come out!"

Atretes watched her as she picked her way across the room. People reached up to touch her. Some took her hand, and she smiled and whispered a word of encouragement before she passed by. When she reached the open doorway, she peered up at him with luminous eyes. "What are you doing here, Atretes?"

Unwilling to say anything in front of the Roman guard, he took her arm and drew her out into the corridor. The guard closed the door and set the bolt. He opened another door across the corridor and lit the torch, then went to stand at the end of the corridor.

As Atretes followed Hadassah into the room the guard had opened, he listened to the sound of the hobnailed sandals on stone and clenched his fist. He had vowed never to enter a place like this again, yet here he was—and by his own choice.

Hadassah turned to him and saw his torment. "You must hate this place," she said softly. "What brought you here to me?"

"I've had a dream. I don't know what it means."

She felt his desperation and prayed God would give her the answers he needed. "Sit with me and tell me," she said, weak from confinement and days without food. "I may not know the answers, but God does."

"I'm walking through blackness, a blackness so heavy I can feel it pressing against my body. All I can see are my hands. I walk for a long time, not feeling anything, searching for what seems forever, and then I see a sculptor. And before him is his work, a statue of me. It's one like those they sell in the shops around the arena, only this one is so real it seems to breathe. The man takes a hammer and I know what he's going to do. I cry out for him not to do it, but he strikes the image once and it shatters into a million pieces."

Shaking, Atretes rose. "I feel pain, pain like I've never felt before. I can't move. Around me I see the forest of my homeland and I'm sinking into the bog. Everyone is standing around me, my father, my mother, my wife, friends long dead. I cry out, but they all just stare at me as I'm being sucked down. The bog presses around me like the blackness. And then a man is there, holding out both hands to me. His palms are bleeding."

Hadassah watched Atretes sink wearily down against the stone wall on the other side of the cell. "Do you take his hand?" she asked.

"I don't know," he said bleakly. "I can't remember."

"You awaken?"

"No." He breathed in slowly, struggling to keep his voice steady. "Not yet." He shut his eyes and swallowed convulsively. "I hear a baby crying. He's lying naked on the rocks by the sea. I see a wave coming in from the sea and know it'll sweep him away. I try to get to him, but the wave goes over him. Then I awaken."

Hadassah closed her eyes.

Atretes leaned his head back. "So tell me. What does it all mean?"

Hadassah prayed the Lord would give her wisdom. She sat for a long time, her head bowed. Then she raised her head again. "I'm not a seer," she said. "Only God can interpret dreams. But I do know certain things to be true, Atretes."

"What things?"

"The man holding his hands out to you is Jesus. I told you how he died, nailed to a cross, and how he arose again. He's reaching out to you with both hands. Take hold and hang on. Your salvation is at hand." She hesitated. "And the child . . ."

"I know about the child." Atretes' face tautened with barely controlled emotion. "He's my son. I thought about what you said to me that night you came to the hills, when I told you to let the child die, that I did not care." He paused, then went on. "I sent word I wanted the child when it was born."

Seeing Hadassah's startled look, Atretes stood abruptly and paced restlessly. "At first, it was to hurt Julia, to take her child from her. Then I truly wanted him. I decided I'd take the child and return to Germania. I waited, and then word came. The child was stillborn."

Atretes gave a broken laugh filled with bitterness. "But she lied. The child wasn't stillborn. She ordered it left on the rocks to die." His voice choked with tears, and he raked his fingers through his hair. "I told you if Julia laid him at my feet, I'd turn and walk away. And that's exactly what she did, isn't it? Placed him on the rocks and walked away. I hated her. I hated myself. God have mercy on me, you said once. God have mercy."

Hadassah rose and went to him. "Your son is alive."

He stiffened and looked down at her.

She put her hand on his arm. "I didn't know you'd sent word you wanted him, Atretes. Had I known, I would have brought him directly to you. Please forgive me for the pain I've caused you." Her hand fell limply to her side.

He took her arm. "You said he's alive? Where is he?"

Hadassah prayed God would make right what she had done. "I took your son to the apostle John, and he placed him in the arms of Rizpah, a young widow who'd lost her child. She loved your son the moment she looked upon his face."

His hand loosened and fell away from her. "My son is alive," he said in wonder, and the burden of pain and guilt fell away from him. He closed his eyes in relief. "My son is alive." His back against the stone wall, he slid down it, his knees weakened by what she told him. "My son is *alive*!" he said in a choked voice.

"God is merciful," she said softly and lightly touched his hair.

The light caress reminded Atretes of his mother. He took Hadassah's hand and held it against his cheek. Looking up at her, he saw again the bruises that marked her kind face, the thinness of her body beneath the ragged, dirty tunic. She had saved his son. How could he walk away and let her die?

He stood, filled with purpose. "I'll go to Sertes," he said.

"No."

"Yes," he countered, determined. Though he'd never fought lions—and knew there was little chance he would survive—he had to try. "A word in the right ear, and I'll be in the arena as your champion."

"I have a champion already, Atretes. The battle is *over*. He's already won." She held his hand firmly between her own. "Don't you see? If you went back into the arena now, you'd die without ever fully knowing the Lord."

"But what of you?" Tomorrow she would face the lions.

"God's hand is in this, Atretes. His will be done."

"You'll die."

"'Though he slay me, yet will I trust him,'" she said. She smiled up at him. "Whatever happens is to God's good purpose and for his glory. I'm not afraid."

Looking upon her, Atretes felt an aching hunger for a faith like hers, a faith that could give him peace. He searched her face for a long moment and then nodded, struggling against the emotions raging within him. "It will be as you say."

"It will be as the Lord wills."

"I will never forget you."

"Nor I you," she said. She told him where to find the apostle John, then laid her hand on his arm and looked at him, peace in her eyes. "Now, go from this place of death and don't look back."

She went out into the dark corridor and called to the guard.

Atretes stood holding the torch as the guard came and unbolted the cell door. As he opened it, Hadassah turned and looked up at Atretes, and her eyes shone with warmth.

"May the Lord bless you and keep you. May the Lord make his face shine upon you and be gracious to you. May the Lord turn his face toward you and give you peace," she said with a gentle smile. Turning away, she entered the cell.

A soft murmuring of voices greeted her, and the door was closed with a hard thud of finality.

THE SEED

"*A farmer went out to sow his seed. . . .*"

1

Physically exhausted, pride bruised, Atretes had had enough. His patience was at an end.

As soon as Hadassah had told him his son was alive and that the apostle John knew where to find him, he had begun making plans. Because the mob adored him, he couldn't enter the city of Ephesus at will, but had to wait for the cover of darkness. And so he had. Finding the apostle's house hadn't been too difficult—Hadassah had given good directions—but even in the dead of night the man of God had been about his business, comforting a sick child and then hearing someone's deathbed confession.

Atretes had waited for John and then been told after hours of doing so that the apostle had sent word he was going directly to a dawn worship service along the riverbank. Angry, Atretes had pursued him, arriving just after a great crowd had gathered to hear John speak of Jesus Christ, their risen God. A carpenter from Galilee? A god? Atretes had closed his ears to the words being proclaimed and retired to a quiet place beneath a terebinth tree, resolved to wait.

Now, however, he would wait no longer! Dawn had come and gone, and still these worshipers sang praises to their heavenly king and told their stories of personal deliverance from disease, heartbreak, habits, and even demons! He was sick of listening to them. Some, fully clothed, were now being dunked in the river! Had they all gone mad?

Getting up, Atretes walked down to the back of the crowds and prodded a man. "How long do these meetings go on?"

"As long as the Spirit moves us," the man said, giving him a cursory look before singing again.

The spirit? What did that mean? Atretes was used to the discipline of training schedules and regimes, to dealing with solid fact; the man's answer was incomprehensible.

"Is this your first time hearing—"

"And my last," Atretes cut the man off, eager to be gone.

The man glanced back at him, and the smile fixed on his face. His eyes widened. "You're *Atretes*!"

A jolt of adrenaline flooded Atretes, stiffening his muscles. He could flee or fight. Mouth set, he stood his ground. The first choice went against his grain; the long night of waiting had made him ready for the latter.

Fool! he berated himself. He should have kept silent and waited unobtrusively beneath the shade of a tree rather than draw attention to himself. But it was too late now.

He made excuses for his mistake. How could he guess people would still remember him? It had been eight months since he left the arena. He had thought he would have been forgotten by now.

Apparently, Ephesians had a long memory.

Others turned at the mention of his name. A woman gasped and swung around, whispering to those near her. News of his pre-sence spread like a wind riffling dry leaves. People glanced back to see what the stir was about and spotted him, head above the rest, his accursed blonde hair serving as a beacon for their attention.

He swore under his breath.

"It *is* Atretes," someone said, and the hair on the back of his neck rose. He knew it would be wise to leave as quickly as possible, but stubbornness and the fiercer part of his nature took control. He was no longer a slave of Rome, no longer a gladiator fighting in the arena. His life should belong to him again! What was the difference between the walls of a luxurious villa and those of the *ludus*? Both imprisoned him.

The time has come! he thought in frustrated anger. He would find out what he needed to know and leave. Any man who tried to stop him would have grave cause to regret it.

Shoving the still-gaping man aside, he began pressing his way forward through the crowd.

Excited whispers rippled through the sea of people as he moved through it.

"Make room! It's Atretes. He's going forward!" someone called out, and those at the front stopped singing praises to turn and stare.

"Praise the Lord!"

Atretes' mouth set as the buzz of excitement surrounded him. Even after ten years of fighting in the arena, the German had never become accustomed to the furor his presence inevitably brought to any gathering.

Sertes, editor of the Ephesian games and the man who had

bought him from the Great Ludus of Rome, had reveled in the mob's reaction to his prized gladiator and exploited Atretes at every opportunity, gleaning gold for himself. The Ephesian had accepted bribes from wealthy patrons and brought him to feasts to be pampered and petted. Other gladiators enjoyed such royal treatment, taking whatever pleasures were offered, relishing their last hours before they faced death in the arena. Atretes ate and drank sparingly. He intended to survive. He had always stood aloof, ignoring his hosts, glaring at the guests with such ferocity and contemptuous disdain that they had walked a wide circle around him.

"You behave like a beast in a cage!" Sertes had complained once.

"As you and the rest have made me."

The memory of that time only fueled his anger now as he forced his way through the crowd beside the river. Hadassah had told him to go to John the apostle. These gaping, mumbling fools were no longer going to stop him from doing just that.

The drone of excited voices grew. Despite his greater height, the warrior still felt the crowd pressing in on him. People touched him as he pushed his way forward. He tensed instinctively, pushing them back. He waited for them to grab or tear at him like the *amoratae* who had often pursued him through the streets of Rome, but these people, excited at his presence, only laid hands on him to urge him forward.

"Praise the Lord . . ."

"He was a gladiator . . ."

". . . saw him fight once before I became a Christian . . ."

The people closed in on him from behind, and his heart began to drum heavily. Cold sweat broke out on his forehead. He didn't like having anyone behind him.

"Make way," a man said. "Let him through!"

"John! *John!* Atretes is coming forward!"

Did they already know why he had come to this meeting of the Way? Had Hadassah somehow sent word ahead?

"Another! Another for the Lord!"

Someone started singing again, and the swell of sound rose around him, raising gooseflesh down his back. A passage opened before him. He didn't wait to wonder why, but strode the remaining short distance to the riverbank.

Several men and women were standing in the water. One was

being dunked. Another, sopping wet, was throwing water into the air and crying and laughing at the same time while others waded in to embrace him.

An old man dressed in a woven tunic and striped sash helped another person rise from the water, saying as he did so, "You've been washed clean by the blood of the Lamb." The singing grew louder and more joyful. The man waded quickly toward friends. One embraced him, weeping, and the others surrounded him.

Atretes wanted desperately to be gone from this place, to be far away from this gathering of crazed men and women. "You there!" he shouted at the man who wore the striped sash. "Are you John? The one they call 'the apostle'?"

"I am he."

Atretes waded into the river, wondering at the eruption of excitement behind him. Sertes had once said John the apostle was a greater threat to the Roman Empire than all the frontier rebellions put together, but measuring the man standing before him, Atretes saw nothing to fear. In fact, John seemed singularly unremarkable.

However, Atretes had learned never to assume that things were what they appeared; grim experience had taught him never to underestimate any man. A coward sometimes had more deadly cunning than a man with courage, and even someone who was seemingly defenseless could inflict wounds too deep to heal. Hadn't Julia ripped his heart from him with her treachery and lies?

This man held one weapon against him, a weapon Atretes meant to take from him. He planted his feet firmly, his face and tone hard as stone.

"You have my son. Hadassah brought him to you about four months ago. I want him back."

"Hadassah," John said, his expression softening. "I was concerned about her. We have not seen our little sister in several months."

"Nor will you. She's among the condemned in the dungeons below the arena."

John let out his breath as though he had taken a blow and then murmured softly under his breath.

"She said you gave my son to a widow named Rizpah," Atretes said. "Where do I find her?"

"Rizpah lives in the city."

"Where exactly?"

John came forward and put his hand on Atretes' arm. "Come. We will talk."

He shrugged the man's hand away. "Just tell me where to find the woman who has my son."

John faced him again. "When Hadassah came to me with the child, she said she had been commanded to place him on the rocks to die."

"*I* gave no such command."

"She told me the father didn't want the child."

Heat poured into Atretes' face. His mouth set. "The child is mine. That's all you have to know."

John frowned. "Is it because she brought the child to me that Hadassah now stands condemned?"

"No." Hadassah's act of disobedience in not placing the baby on the rocks would have been enough to condemn her, but it hadn't been for that reason that Julia had sent her to die. Atretes was sure of it. As far as he knew, Julia wasn't even aware that her child still lived. But then, Julia could have condemned Hadassah for any whim that struck her fancy. He only knew one fact regarding what had happened to Hadassah.

"One of the servants told me Hadassah was commanded to burn incense in honor of the emperor. She refused and proclaimed your Christ the only true god."

John's eyes shone. "Praise God."

"She was a fool."

"A fool for Christ."

"You are pleased?" Atretes said in disbelief. "She will die for those few words."

"No, Atretes. Whosoever believes in Jesus shall not perish, but will have eternal life."

Atretes grew impatient. "I didn't come to discuss your gods or your belief in life after death. I came for my son. If it's proof you want that I fathered him, would the word of his harlot mother satisfy you? I'll drag Julia Valerian here and put her on her knees before you to make her confession. Will that suffice? You can drown her, then, if you want, for the harlot she is. I might even help you."

John met the barbarian's wrath with gentleness. "I don't doubt you are the father. I was thinking of the child's needs, Atretes. This is not a situation without grave consequences. What of Rizpah?"

"What needs has a babe but to be fed and kept warm? As for the woman, give her another child. Someone else's. She has no right to mine."

"The Lord intervened on your son's behalf. If not—"

"*Hadassah* intervened."

"It was no coincidence that she brought the child to me at the moment she did."

"Hadassah said herself that had she known I wanted the child, she would have brought him to me!"

"Why didn't she know?"

Atretes clenched his teeth. If not for the crowd watching, he would have used force to get the information he wanted. "Where is he?"

"He's safe. Hadassah thought the only course to save your son was to give him to me."

Atretes' eyes narrowed coldly. A muscle jerked in his jaw as heat poured into his face. He tried to hide his shame behind a wall of anger, but knew he had failed. Only one person had ever looked at him as though she saw beneath his skin, into his very heart and mind: Hadassah. Until now, that is. For now this man did the same.

Memories flooded Atretes' mind. When the slave girl had come to him and told him that the child Julia carried was his, he'd said he didn't care. What assurance did he have that the child was even his own? Despite Hadassah's assurances, Atretes had been raw from Julia's betrayal with another man and too angry to think clearly. He had told Hadassah that if Julia Valerian laid the baby at his feet, he would walk away and never look back. He would never forget the sorrow his words had brought to the slave girl's face . . . nor the regret that had flooded him even as she left. But he was Atretes! He would not call her back.

How could he have expected any woman to be so unfeeling about her child as Julia had been? No German woman would think of commanding that her baby be abandoned on the rocks to die. No German. Only a *civilized* Roman woman would carry out such a deed.

If not for Hadassah's intervention, his son would be dead.

Once again he focused on the present, on the man standing so patiently before him. "The child is *mine*. Whatever I may or may not have said before no longer matters. Hadassah sent me here, and I will have my son."

John nodded. "I'll send for Rizpah and speak with her. Tell me where you reside, and I'll bring your son to you."

"Tell me where she is, and I'll go for him myself."

John frowned. "Atretes, this will be very difficult. Rizpah loves the child as her own. It won't be easy for her to give him up."

"All the more reason I go. It'd hardly be wise to allow you to warn this woman of my intentions ahead of time so she can leave the city."

"Neither I nor Rizpah will keep your son from you."

"I've only your word on that, and who are you to me but a stranger? And a mad one, at that!" he said with a telling glance at the worshipers. "I have no reason to trust you." He gave a sneering laugh. "And even less reason to trust any woman."

"You trusted Hadassah."

His face darkened.

John studied him for a moment, then told him how to find Rizpah. "I pray your heart will be moved by the compassion and mercy God has shown you by sparing your son's life. Rizpah is a woman of tried faith."

"Meaning what?"

"She has endured many tragedies in her young life."

"This one is not of my doing."

"No, but I ask that you lay no blame upon her for what has happened."

"The fault was with his mother. I lay no blame upon Hadassah or you or this widow," Atretes said, relenting now that he had the information for which he had come. "Besides," he added with a wry smile, "I've no doubt this widow of yours will feel much better when she is generously recompensed for her trouble." He ignored John's wince at his words. Turning away, he saw the crowd had grown quiet. "What are they waiting for?"

"They thought you came to be baptized."

With a sneering laugh, Atretes strode up the hill, not sparing another glance at those who gathered at the river.

✶

Atretes returned to his villa by way of the outer road and waited again. It would be safer to enter the city after dark, and there were other matters that, in his haste, he had neglected to consider.

"Lagos!" His booming voice echoed up the marble staircase. *"Lagos!"*

A man ran along the upper corridor. "My lord!"

"Go to the slave market and buy me a wet nurse."

Lagos hurried down the stairs. "A . . . wet nurse, my lord?"

"Make sure she's German." He strode through the courtyard toward the baths.

Lagos followed, distressed. He had had several masters, and this one had by far been the most mercurial. Lagos had been greatly honored to be counted among the slaves belonging to Atretes, the foremost gladiator in all of the Roman Empire, but he'd never expected the man to be on the verge of madness. During the first week he'd spent in this villa, Atretes had smashed all the furnishings, set fire to his bedroom, then disappeared. After a month, Silus and Appelles, two gladiators Atretes had purchased from Sertes as guards, had gone out looking for him.

"He's living in the hill caves," Silus reported upon their return.

"You must bring him back!"

"And risk getting killed? Forget it! You go, old man. Not me. I value my life."

"He'll starve."

"He's eating the flesh of animals he hunts down with one of those bloody *framea* Germans use," Appelles informed him. "He's gone *feri* again."

"Shouldn't we do something?" Saturnina said. The slave girl was clearly distressed that her master had reverted to a barbarian savage and was living like a wild beast.

"What would you suggest we do, sweeting? Send you into his cave to improve his mood? You'd have better luck with me." Silus said, pinching her cheek. She slapped his hand away and he laughed. "You know you're secretly happy the Lady Julia spurned your master. If he ever regains his mind and comes back, you'll be waiting in the doorway."

While Silus and Appelles lolled around, drinking and talking about old battles in the arena, Lagos had taken charge of the household. All was kept in order and readiness should the master regain his mind and return.

Which he had, without warning. After being gone for five months, he simply strode into the villa one day, threw off the furs he was wearing, bathed, shaved, and donned a tunic. Then he sent one of the servants for Sertes, and when the editor of the games came, they were briefly closeted together. The following afternoon, a messenger came telling Atretes the woman he sought was in the dungeon. Atretes left as soon as it was dark.

Now, he was back asking for a wet nurse. A *German* wet nurse, as though they grew like grapes on a vine! There was no child in the household, and Lagos didn't even want to contemplate his master's reasons for the demand he was making. He had one main concern paramount in his mind: survival.

Steeling himself, he gathered his courage and opened his mouth to make his master aware of certain unavoidable facts. "It may not be possible, my lord."

"Pay whatever the going price is. I don't care how high it is." Atretes tossed his belt aside.

"It's not always a matter of price, my lord. Germans are in great demand, especially if they're blonde, and the supply is sporadic. . . ." He felt the blood draining from his face at the sardonic look Atretes gave him. If anyone knew these facts, he would. Lagos wondered if Atretes was even aware that a new statue of Mars had been erected, and its resemblance to the gladiator who stood looking at him so impatiently was remarkable. Statuettes of Atretes were still being sold outside the arena. Just the other day, at the marketplace, Lagos had seen idolmaker shops selling figures of an Apollo that looked like Atretes, though it was slightly more well endowed than nature made any man.

"I'm sorry, my lord, but there may not be a German wet nurse available."

"You're a Greek. Greeks are resourceful. Find one! She doesn't have to be blonde, but make sure she's *healthy*." He stripped off his tunic, revealing the body that countless amoratae worshiped. "And have her here by tomorrow morning." He stepped to the edge of the pool.

"Yes, my lord," Lagos said grimly, deciding it was best to work quickly rather than waste time trying to reason with a mad barbarian. If he failed, Atretes would no doubt eat his liver like the raven that feasted perpetually upon the god Prometheus.

Atretes dove into the pool, the cool water a relief to his feverish mind. He came up and shook the water from his hair. He would go back to the city tonight. Alone. If he took Silus and Appelles with him, they would draw attention. Besides, even two trained guards were no match against a mob. It would be far better if he went into the city by himself. He would wear commoner's clothing and keep his hair covered. Thus disguised, he should have no difficulty.

When he finished bathing, he roamed through the house. Restless and tense, he strayed from room to room until he came to the largest on the second floor. He hadn't set foot in this chamber since setting it on fire over five months ago. He glanced around, seeing that the servants had taken it upon themselves to remove the charred furnishings, wall hangings, and shattered Corinthian vases. Though they had certainly scrubbed the marble, there was still physical evidence of his rage and the destruction he had intended. He had purchased this villa for Julia, intending to bring her here as his wife. He had been well aware of how Julia reveled in luxury and remembered how proud he had been when he had furnished it with the most expensive things. They would have shared this room.

Instead, she had married someone else.

He could still hear her crying out her lies and paltry excuses when he came to claim her a few months after he had gained his freedom. She said her husband was a homosexual with a catamite and had no interest in her. She said she had married him to protect her financial independence, her *freedom*.

Lying witch!

He should have known what she was from the beginning. Hadn't she, with a heart of pure cunning, gone to the Artemision dressed as a temple prostitute in order to capture his interest? Hadn't she bribed Sertes in order to summon him from the ludus any time she wanted? As long as it didn't interfere with Sertes' training schedule for him, the time had been granted. Ah, but like a fool, he had gone to her at the mere crook of her bejeweled finger. Besotted by her beauty, craving her wanton passion, he had gone—and she'd slaughtered him.

What a fool!

When he'd taken Julia Valerian into his arms, he'd thrown pride to the wind and self-respect into the dust. He had embraced shame. All during the months of their clandestine affair, he'd return to his cell in the ludus, depressed and discomforted, not wanting to face the truth. He'd known her for what she was, even then. Yet he had allowed her to use him, like everyone else had used him since he'd been taken prisoner, torn from his beloved

Germania. Julia's soft, silken arms had been stronger around his body than any chains that had ever held him.

The last time he'd seen her, she'd cried out that she loved him. Love! She'd known so little about love—and about him—that she had actually thought her marriage to someone else would make no difference. She'd thought he would gladly continue to come to her whenever the mood suited her.

By the gods, he knew he could wash for years and never get the taint of her off of him! Now, looking at the barren, devastated room before him, he swore no woman would ever have that kind of hold on him again!

As the sun set, Atretes donned a woolen cloak, tucked a dagger into his belt, and left for Ephesus. He headed northwest along the hills, using a path he knew well before seeking the road. Small houses dotted the countryside, but grew more numerous and closer together as he came nearer the city. Wagons laden with goods traveled the main road toward the gates. He walked unnoticed in the dark shadows of one, seeking cover from the growing throng.

The driver noticed him. "You there! Get away from the wagon!"

Atretes made a rude hand gesture.

"You want a fight?!" the driver shouted, rising from the seat. Atretes laughed derisively, but said nothing. His accent would be noted—Germans weren't common in this part of the Empire. He left the darkness and strode by the torches and Roman sentries. One soldier glanced at him and their eyes met for the briefest second. Atretes saw a quickening of interest in the Roman's eyes and lowered his head so his face wouldn't be seen clearly. The guard spoke to a comrade, and Atretes moved in among a group of travelers, then ducked down the first available street. He waited in the darkness, but the sentry didn't send anyone to follow.

Atretes started off again, thankful the moon was full enough to reflect off the white stones inset on the granite slab road.

John had explained that the woman who had his son lived on the second level of a rundown *insula* in the poor district, southeast of the complex of libraries near the Artemision. Atretes knew he could find the right building if he went through the heart of the city.

As he neared the temple, the crowds increased. Following a

maze of alleyways in an effort to avoid them, he stumbled over a man sleeping against a wall. The man groaned, cursed, pulled his cloak over his head, and curled onto his side.

Hearing voices behind him, Atretes hastened his steps. As he rounded a corner, someone from a third floor window poured night soil down into the street. He jumped back in disgust and shouted up at the open window.

The voices fell silent, but he heard movement in the darkness of the alleyway behind him. Turning, he narrowed his eyes. Six shapes came toward him, moving stealthily. He turned fully, ready. Realizing they had been seen, the stalkers' manner changed to boldness. Several made mocking sounds meant to frighten him. Spreading out, they came on, circling the front of him. One was clearly the leader, for he motioned and the other five moved into carefully plotted positions intended to block a victim's escape.

Seeing the glint of a blade, Atretes smiled coldly. "You will not find me easy."

"Your money pouch," the leader said. From the voice, Atretes knew he was young.

"Go home to your bed, boy, and you might live through the night."

The youth gave a derisive laugh, still advancing on him.

"Wait, Palus," one said, sounding nervous.

"I don't have a good feeling," another said in the darkness. "He's a head taller—"

"Shut up, Tomas! There are six of us and only one of him."

"Maybe he has no money."

"He has money. I heard the coins jingle. Heavy coins." Palus stepped closer. The others followed his lead. "The pouch!" He snapped his fingers. "Toss it to me."

"Come and take it."

No one moved. Palus called him a foul name, his young voice shaking with enraged pride.

"I didn't think you'd do it," Atretes said, scraping his attacker's pride again. The youth with the knife lunged at him.

It had been months since Atretes had fought, but it didn't matter. All the training and finely honed instincts came back in an instant. He moved sharply, dodging the thrust of the dagger. Catching the boy's wrist, he drew the arm down and around, snapping it from the shoulder socket. Palus went down screaming.

The others didn't know whether to run or attack, until one fool did the latter, and the rest followed. One of them punched Atretes in the face, while another jumped on his back. Atretes slammed his full weight back against the wall and kicked the one in front low and hard.

Atretes took two punches in the side of the head as he brought his elbow up sharply and connected a blow to an attacker's chest. The thief dropped, gasping for breath.

In the scuffle, Atretes' mantle came loose and fell back off his head, leaving his hair to shine blonde in the moonlight.

"Zeus! It's *Atretes*!" Those still able scattered like rats into the darkness.

"Help me!" Palus cried out, but his friends had deserted him. Moaning in pain and cradling his broken arm against his chest, Palus scooted backwards until he was against the wall. "Don't kill me," he sobbed. "Don't kill me. Please! We didn't know it was you."

"Boy, the least in the arena had more courage than you." He stepped past him and headed down the alleyway.

He heard voices ahead of him. "I swear! It was him! He was *big* and his hair was white in the moonlight. It was Atretes!"

"Where?"

"Down there! He's probably killed Palus."

Swearing under his breath, Atretes ran down a narrow street that took him in the opposite direction from where he wanted to go. Jogging along a street between insulae, he turned up another avenue and came around a corner that put him back on track. Ahead was a main thoroughfare not far from the Artemision. He slowed as he neared it, not wanting to attract attention by his haste. He drew the mantle up over his head to cover his hair again and lowered his chin as he entered the evening bazaar.

The street was lined with booths and street vendors hawking their wares. As Atretes wove his way among the crowd, he saw miniature temples and statuettes of Artemis, trays of amulets, and pouches of incense. He came to an idolmaker's shop and glanced at the counter laden with marble statuettes. Someone bumped into him and he stepped closer, pretending interest in the wares on display. He needed to blend in with the crowd of evening shoppers. Visitors from every part of the Empire milled around, looking for bargains. Atretes froze as he looked at the detailed statuettes.

The merchant thought him interested. "Take a closer look, my lord! These are replicas of the new statue just erected in honor of Mars. You won't find better workmanship anywhere."

Atretes stepped closer and picked one up. He hadn't imagined it. It was *him*! He glared at the offensive idol. "Mars?" he said in an accusing growl, wanting to crush the marble into dust.

"You must be new to the city. Are you making a pilgrimage to our goddess?" The vendor produced a small statue festooned with breasts and wearing a headdress punctuated with symbols, one of which was the rune of the god Tiwaz, whom Atretes had once worshiped.

"There he is! Over there by the idolmaker's shop."

Atretes glanced around sharply and saw a dozen young men pushing their way through the crowd toward him. "I told you it was Atretes!"

"Atretes! Where?"

People on the left and right of him turned to stare. The idolmaker stood, mouth agape, staring at him. "It *is* you. By the gods!"

Sweeping his arm across the table, Atretes grasped the edge and upended the table. Shoving several people aside, he tried to run. A man grasped his tunic. Uttering an enraged shout, Atretes hit him in the face. As the man went down, he took three others with him.

Excitement erupted up and down the street. "Atretes! Atretes is here!"

More hands fell upon him; voices cried his name out feverishly.

Atretes was unaccustomed to real fear, but knew it now as the furor in the marketplace grew. In another moment there would be a riot, with him at the center. He plowed through half a dozen clawing bodies, knowing he had to get away. Now.

"*Atretes!*" A woman screamed, flinging herself upon him. As he shook her off, her nails scraped his neck. Someone else yanked out a hank of his hair. The mantle was torn from his shoulders. People were screaming.

Breaking free, he ran, knocking people aside as they got in his way. Amoratae shouted and followed him like a pack of wild dogs. Ducking into the narrow avenue of shops, he knocked over another table. Fruit and vegetables spilled across the walkway. He upended another counter of copperware, scattering more obstacles in the mob's path. There were cries behind him as several went down. Leaping over a small cart, he turned sharply and ran down an alleyway between two insulae. When he saw it was a dead end, he came nearer to panic than he had in his life. He had once seen a pack of wild dogs chase down a man in the arena. When the dogs caught him, they'd torn him apart. These amoratae, in their frenzied passion, might well do the same to him if they caught him.

Turning frantically, Atretes sought escape. When he saw a door, he ran to it. It was locked. Ramming it with his shoulder, he broke it open and ran up a darkened passageway of steps. One floor, then two. Stopping on a landing, he waited. Catching his breath, he listened.

Muted sounds of voices came from outside on the street. "He must have gone in one of the insulae."

"Look over there!"

"No, wait! This door's been broken in."

Hurried footsteps headed up the stairs. "He's in here."

Atretes ran along the corridor as quietly as he could. Even with tenement doors closed, the place reeked of humanity. A door opened behind him and someone peered out just as he ducked up a narrow, dank passageway. He reached the third floor and then the fourth. Still shouting, his pursuers were awakening everyone in the building. When he reached the roof, he was in the open with no place to hide.

Voices came up the stairs.

Seeing only one way to escape, he took it. Running full-out, Atretes took a flying leap across the yawning distance to another building. He hit hard and rolled. Coming to his feet, he scrambled across to another doorway, dove into it, and hid in the shadows of another stairwell just as a dozen people spilled out onto the rooftop from which he had just leapt.

Atretes drew back sharply, heaving for air, heart pounding.

The voices receded as one by one, they ran down the stairs again, searching for him in the dim environs of the insula. Atretes sank back against the wall and closed his eyes, trying to regain his breath.

How was he going to cross the city, find a widow with his son, and get the child and himself out of the city without losing both their lives in the process?

Cursing the idolmakers for making him a graven image to

these idol-hungry people, he closed down his mind to anything else but getting out of the city in one piece. That accomplished, he would find another way to get his son.

He waited for an hour before venturing down the stairs and hallways into the insula. Every sound made him flinch. When he reached the street, he kept close to the walls, using the veil of dark shadows for protection. He got lost. Using up precious hours of darkness, he found his way like a rat in the maze of alleys and narrow streets.

He reached the city gates just as the sun was coming up.

2

Lagos heard the door slam and knew his master had returned. He'd only just returned a few hours ago himself, having spent the afternoon, evening, and better part of the night searching slave markets for a German wet nurse. He'd finally found one and was certain Atretes would be pleased with her. She was robust and ruddy and had hair the same color as his.

He came into the entry hall feeling somewhat confident and saw Atretes' blackened eye and even blacker temper. Deep, bloody scratches still oozed on his neck, staining his ripped tunic with blood. The German looked ready to kill someone. Anyone.

"Did you find a wet nurse?"

Heart thundering, Lagos thanked the gods he had. "Yes, my lord," he said quickly, perspiration beading on his forehead. "She's in residence." He was certain if he had failed, his life would have been forfeit. "Would you like to see her, my lord?"

"No!" Atretes strode into the inner courtyard. Bending, he put his whole head under the water in the fountain. Lagos wondered if the man meant to drown himself. After a long moment, Atretes straightened and shook his head, flinging water in all directions like a dog. Lagos had never before witnessed such uncivilized behavior from a master.

"Can you write?" Atretes demanded coldly, his expression no less fierce.

"Only in Greek, my lord."

Atretes ran a hand down his face and shook the water off his hand. "Then write this," he commanded bitterly. "'I accede to your suggestion. Bring my son to me as soon as possible.' Sign my name and take the message to the apostle John. Tell him how to get here!" He gave him directions to the small house near a stream on the outer fringe of the city. "If he's not there, look for him by the river." He strode out of the courtyard.

Lagos let out his breath and thanked the gods he was still alive.

✶

The heavy stick in Silus' hands splintered as Atretes brought his own down. The servant fell back sharply to avoid the blow and staggered, barely managing to keep his feet. Swearing, Atretes stepped back. Mouth grim, Silus regained his balance and tossed the useless weapon aside.

Atretes made an impatient gesture. "Again!"

Gallus took another pugil stick from a barrel against the wall and tossed it. Silus caught it and took a fighting stance once more. The man would not let up!

Standing near the archway to the baths, Gallus watched with hidden empathy. Silus was sweating profusely, his face red from exertion. Their master, on the other hand, was breathing as easily as when the sparring match had begun.

Crack!

"Take the offensive!" Atretes shouted.

Crack!

Silus managed to block again, but seemed to be losing his strength.

Crack! "I would . . ." *Crack!* ". . . if I could," Silus gasped. He swung his stick wide, but missed entirely. He felt an explosion of pain behind his knees. For an instant, nothing but air was beneath him, and then his back hit the marble floor. He grunted and lay helpless, trying to get his breath back as Atretes stood over him. He saw the pugil stick coming down at his throat and thought he was about to die. It stopped a fraction of an inch away.

Atretes made a sound of disgust. "How did you ever survive the arena?" He sent the stick clattering across the floor and bouncing off the wall.

Silus grimaced, embarrassed. He watched Atretes warily, wondering if he was fated to another round with him.

Swearing in German, Atretes kicked over the barrel, scattering pugil sticks across the marble. He gave a shout of spine-tingling frustration and let out a string of unintelligible German.

Having regained his breath, Silus rose slowly, wincing in pain. He prayed to Artemis that Atretes would wear himself out breaking sticks over his knee and not decide to break him instead. He saw Lagos peering nervously into the room and saw a way to avoid further humiliation. "Well, well. The warthog returns."

Atretes swung around, expression fierce. "What took you so long?!"

Lagos entered the gymnasium as though he were entering a lion's den. "It was—"

"Never mind the excuses. Did you find him?"

"Yes, my lord. Late last night."

"And?"

"Your message is delivered, my lord."

"What did he say?"

"He said it will be done, my lord."

"The instant he arrives, notify me." Atretes jerked his head in dismissal. Grabbing a towel from the shelf near the door, he wiped his face and neck. He tossed it on the floor and glanced balefully at Silus and Gallus. They awaited his command. "Enough for today," he said tonelessly. "Go!"

Alone in the gymnasium, Atretes sat down on a bench. He pushed his hands back through his hair in frustration. He'd give John a few days to keep his word, and if he didn't, he'd hunt the apostle down and break his neck!

Restless, Atretes rose and strode out of the gymnasium, through the baths, and entered a corridor leading to a heavy door at the back of the villa. He banged it open and strode across the smooth dirt to another door in the wall. It was open. A guard stepped through it and nodded. "Clear, my lord," he said, having already checked for amoratae who, in hopes that Atretes would appear, might have stationed themselves outside the walls. People often came in hopes of a glimpse of him.

Atretes jogged in the hills until his body was slick with sweat. He slowed to a fast walk until he reached the crest of a hill facing west. In the distance was Ephesus, the great city, which spread like a disease along the northern, southern, and eastern hills. From where he stood, Atretes could see the Artemision, the complex of libraries near the harbor. Turning his head slightly, he could see the arena.

He frowned. Odd that he found himself always coming to this hill and looking back. As a gladiator, his life had had a purpose: to survive. Now his life was aimless. He filled his days with training, but to what purpose?

He remembered Pugnax, an ex-gladiator who owned an inn in Rome, saying to him, "You'll never be as alive as when you face death every day." Atretes had thought him a fool then. Now, he wondered. At odd times, he found himself craving the excitement of a fight to the death. *Survival.* Nothing short of the struggle for it had given him that rush, the sense of real meaning in life. *Survival.*

Now, he merely *existed*. He ate, drank, exercised. He slept. Sometimes he enjoyed the pleasures of a woman. Yet, all in all, the days rolled one into another, each empty, insignificant.

His son was somewhere in that foul city and he was the lone reason Atretes remained in Ionia. Somewhere beyond the expanse of cerulean blue was Italy, and north was his homeland. The longing to return to Germania was so strong his throat closed. He had his freedom. He had money. Once he'd taken possession of his son, there'd be nothing to keep him here. The villa would be sold, and he would buy passage on the first ship that set sail west.

And when he reached his homeland, he would teach his people better ways of fighting the Roman war machine.

Returning to the villa, he passed the evening drinking wine in the *triclinium*. Pilia brought in a tray of fruit. He watched her set it upon the marble table before him. She had loosened her hair. Her eyes grazed his, hopeful, hungry. "Would you care for a peach, my lord?"

Julia had wanted beauty in the things around her, including the slaves who served her. Except for Hadassah, all of her servants had been comely, like this one. His eyes moved slowly down over Pilia's body. His blood stirred. He had purchased her to serve Julia, but now she would serve him instead.

Remembering the women who had been ordered to his cell in the ludus, he gave Pilia the choice. "You wish to serve me?" he said, his brow raising slightly.

"Yes, my lord."

"Look at me, Pilia." When she did, he smiled faintly. "I'm not hungry for a peach."

She put it back on the tray. Her hand trembled slightly, but her eyes were dark and telling. When he held his hand out, she came to him without compulsion.

He was pleasantly surprised at her skill and eagerness.

"Did you serve your last master so well?" he asked much later.

She smiled slyly. "That's the reason his wife sold me!"

Atretes' expression hardened and he turned from her.

Pilia frowned slightly, perplexed. "Have I displeased you, my lord?"

He turned and looked at her coolly. "You served me very well," he said dryly.

She rose uncertainly. "Do you want me to accompany you to your chambers?"

"No."

She blinked in surprise. "No, my lord?" She attempted a seductive smile.

He looked her straight in the eyes. "You may go."

She paled at his coldness, her gaze dropping from his. "Yes, my lord," she said and left the room quickly.

Atretes wiped a hand across his mouth as though to remove the feel of her. Taking up the wineskin, he drank deeply. He left the triclinium. His footsteps echoed softly across the marble tiles of the antechamber. Loneliness closed around him, squeezing him until his heart ached. For what? A harlot like Julia?

He climbed the steps and went to his chambers. Sitting on the edge of his bed, he tipped the wineskin again, wanting to get drunk—so drunk he'd fall into black oblivion and sleep without dreaming.

Dropping the wineskin, he lay back on his bed, his vision blurred, his head light. It was a good feeling, a familiar feeling. Tomorrow it wouldn't feel so good, but for right now it was just right. He closed his eyes, drifting, and thought about the black forests of Germania and bathing in the river. Then there was nothing.

*

He awakened in darkness, hot and uncomfortable. Groaning, he rolled over and sat up, not used to the softness of a mattress. Dragging one of the furs with him, he lay down on the floor and sighed. The cold marble was like the granite bench on which he had slept in the ludus cell.

Lagos found him there in the morning. Had he choice, he would have left. As it was, he couldn't without incurring the master's wrath later and perhaps more dire consequences. Swallowing hard, he crossed the muraled floor and bent down. "My lord," he said, but Atretes snored loudly. Summoning his nerve, Lagos tried again. "My lord!"

Atretes opened one eye and focused slowly on the sandaled feet near his head. Muttering a curse, he covered his head with the fur. "Get out."

"You said to notify you the moment the apostle arrived."

Atretes muttered a foul curse in Greek and shoved the fur aside. "He's here?"

"No, my lord, but Silus sent word a woman is at the gate. Her name is Rizpah and she says you are expecting her."

Atretes threw off the fur. Squinting at the sunlight streaming in from the balcony, he rose.

"She has a babe in arms, my lord."

Atretes gestured impatiently. "Tell Silus to take the child from her."

"My lord?"

"You heard me!" he bellowed and winced in pain. "The child is *mine*, not hers. Give her a hundred *denarii* and send her on her way, then take the child to the wet nurse." When Lagos just stood staring at him, he shouted, "Do it!" He winced again.

"It shall be as you command, my lord."

Head pounding, mouth dry, Atretes looked for something to drink. Kicking the flaccid wineskin out of his way, he went to an elegantly carved table. Scorning the silver cup, he drank from the pitcher. Setting it down, he rubbed his face, feeling the stubble of several days' growth of beard. He walked back to his bed and fell on it, intending to sleep until nature awakened him.

"My lord?"

Atretes roused enough to ask, "Is it done?"

Lagos cleared his throat nervously. "The woman said the child is hers."

"I told you he's *mine*," he ground out, his throbbing head still on the soft furs.

"Yes, my lord, but she's unwilling to hand him over, and Silus hesitates to use force. She said she came to speak with you on her son's behalf."

Her son? Atretes rolled over and sat up, temper rising as he did. "Did the woman say anything else?" he said sarcastically.

Lagos swallowed. "Yes, my lord."

"You seem less than eager to impart her words," Atretes growled. "Out with them!"

"She said to give the denarii back to you and tell you to eat them." He held the offending pouch of coins out.

Atretes' face paled in rage. He walked over, snatched the pouch, and glared at Lagos. "Invite her in," he said through clenched teeth.

If the woman wanted to do battle, he'd oblige her.

✶

Silus glanced at Lagos as he crossed the yard. He could tell by the Greek's lackluster smile that all had *not* gone well with Atretes.

"The master will speak with you, my lady," Lagos said and gestured. "Please, follow me."

Rizpah felt faint relief as she did as he bade. She sent a silent prayer of thanks to the Lord and followed the servant. She'd regretted her cross words about the coins as soon as they parted her lips but hadn't had the opportunity to take them back. Perhaps the servant was far wiser than she and hadn't imparted her impetuously spoken insult.

She glanced around, disquieted by her surroundings. Despite the grandeur of the villa itself, there were no gardens. The entire area around the house was bare. She felt as though she'd entered the gates of a fortress rather than a home.

As she went up the steps, she tried to still the trembling in her stomach. The little she knew about Atretes she'd learned from John, and he'd only been able to tell her that the man was a captive from Germania who had been trained as a gladiator and freed when he survived an elimination match during the Ephesian games. A great deal of grief and violence were embodied in those few words. A barbarian from the frontier; a man trained to kill men.

"Is he a Christian?" she had asked John weakly, clinging to that small hope against a mountain of despair. Christ could transform a man. And a transformed man might have compassion upon her!

"No," he said sadly, "but he is Caleb's father."

"What sort of father would command his son be left on the rocks to die?"

"It was Caleb's mother who commanded it, Rizpah. He says he didn't know."

"And you believe him?"

"Hadassah sent him to find his son," John answered simply, and she had wept.

"I can't give him back. I can't. Haven't I lost enough? Oh, John, I can't give him up. He's my life now. All the life I shall ever have . . ."

"Be still, beloved." John had talked with her far into the night, comforting her and praying with her. "I will take the child to his father," he had said when dawn came.

"No," she said. "I will go." Perhaps he would relent and allow her to keep the baby.

John hesitated, troubled. "Do you want me to accompany you?"

"No," she said, her throat tight with tears. "I'll go alone." As she had seen John out of her small tenement apartment, a fleeting thought had entered her mind: She could take Caleb and run away where no one could find them.

And will you hide from me also, beloved?

The question had come so clear, she knew she couldn't pretend she didn't know the will of God. She put her forehead against the door, tears running down her cheeks. She knew if she waited at all, she'd give in to temptation and never go.

Caleb always roused hungry. Lifting the babe from his box-bed, she had nursed him before setting out to meet his father. All along the long walk, she prayed God would soften Atretes' heart and that Caleb would be left in her care.

Now, walking across this barren yard and into the silent house, she felt the cold remoteness of the place. Did it reflect the man?

Lord, help me. Help me!

She followed the servant through the front door and entered a large *atrium*, which was designed for receiving guests. Light streamed down from the opening in the roof, making the fountain pool shimmer with reflected light. A soft mist rose from the spilling water, cooling the chamber. It was a welcome relief after so many hours on the dusty road.

"Wait here, my lady," the servant said. Rizpah watched him walk beneath an archway and disappear around the corner.

Pacing nervously, she rubbed Caleb's back. He was stirring and would be hungry soon. Her breasts were full in readiness.

She heard footsteps coming, and her heart thumped. Closing

her eyes, she prayed fervently that Atretes would consider his son's needs above all else.

Lord, help me. O Father, how can I give up my son? How can you ask it of me? Isn't it enough that I have lost Shimei and Rachel? You gave Caleb to me. Surely you do not give that you might take away again?

"The Lady Rizpah, my lord," the servant said, and she opened her eyes. Alarm spread through her as she saw the man with him. Tall and powerfully built, his hair long, blonde, and unkempt, he stared at her, his blue eyes blazing with fury. She'd never seen so fierce a countenance. She felt the power of his anger from across the chamber.

"Leave us," Atretes said, and the servant departed with an alacrity that was even more alarming.

Her trepidation grew as she found herself alone with the imposing master of the house. The only sound was that of the running water in the fountain. Her heart beat wildly as Atretes walked toward her, slowly, his blue eyes narrowing coldly as they drifted over her from head to foot, pausing with an almost cursory interest on his son, and then returning to her eyes. She sensed the violence in him. She could feel the dark force of it emanating from him.

This man was her sweet little Caleb's father? How could it be?

She held her son closer, enfolding him in her arms.

Atretes felt the anger grow in him with each step he took. The woman who held his son so possessively reminded him of Julia. She was small and the drab woven shawl that covered her hair failed to conceal the fact that she was exquisitely beautiful. Strands of damp, curling black hair framed a smooth, oval, olive-skinned face. Her mouth was full and soft, like Julia's. Her eyes were brown, like Julia's. Her body lush, like Julia's.

He would have torn his son from her arms were the boy not wound into her shawl.

He tossed the pouch of coins at her feet. "*Two* hundred denarii," he snarled.

Rizpah's lips parted in shock at the gesture. She stepped back. She'd never seen such a hard, cold, implacable face.

"Not enough?" he said coldly.

"You think to buy the boy back from me?"

"No! I'm paying you for services rendered."

The hurtful words roused a fierce anger within her. "Money?

What recompense is that for tearing a child she loves from a woman's arms? You don't seem to understand. I *love* Caleb."

"Caleb?" he said, remembering a Jewish gladiator long ago in Rome, a man he'd respected—and killed.

"His given name."

"Not a name *I* gave him."

"You were not *there* to name him!"

"I was told he was dead," Atretes said coldly, cursing himself for offering any explanation. It was none of her business. "The child is mine, woman. Untie him and give him to me."

Rizpah tried to fight back the tears, but they overflowed her. "No."

"No?"

"Please. We must talk."

Atretes was unmoved. Julia had used tears against him to get whatever she wanted, too. "Nothing you can say will make a difference."

"Perhaps there's been a mistake. Caleb has dark hair and eyes. . . ." Her voice trailed off when his eyes darkened with an anger she did not understand.

"His mother had dark hair and eyes," he said curtly. He took a step closer, and she drew back an equal distance. "Though I may have doubted the word of his *mother*," he said cynically, "I have no cause to doubt the word of her handmaiden, Hadassah. The child is *mine*!"

"You speak of him as though he were a possession! He isn't a horse to be traded or a villa to be sold." She looked around. "This isn't a home. It's a fortress. What sort of life can you offer him?"

"That doesn't concern you."

"It concerns me greatly. He's my son."

"He was never your son, woman. Just because a child is placed in your arms doesn't make him yours."

"He became part of me the moment John placed him in my arms," she said.

"All women have the heart of a harlot, and I will not leave my son in the hands of one!"

Tears filling her eyes again. "You're wrong to judge all women because of what one did to you."

"Your opinion matters little when weighed against my legal right to him." He nodded at the babe, and her back stiffened.

"You speak of legal rights. What of *love*? Where were you when his mother was commanding that he be abandoned? Why didn't she send him to you? You didn't want him either, did you? You turned your back on him. And you speak of womankind? Where would Caleb be now had Hadassah not rescued him? Why do you want him back now when you cared nothing about him before?"

He wanted to throttle her for such questions, for they roused guilt and pain. They also roused a fierce possessiveness. "He is flesh of my flesh," he said coldly.

"Just because you spent a few hours in a woman's bed doesn't make you his father!"

A muscle locked in his jaw.

"You've scarcely looked at him," she said, struggling against anger and grief. "Why do you want him, Atretes? What do you intend to do with him?"

"I intend to take him back with me to Germania."

She let out a soft gasp. "Germania!" she said in anguish. "How will you, a man alone, tend a four-month-old nursing baby on such a long and arduous journey? Have you no thought of his welfare? He won't survive!"

"He will survive," he said with fierce determination. "Now, give him to me."

"He's too young—"

"*Give him to me, or by the gods, I will take him from you by force!*"

Caleb awakened and began to cry softly. Rizpah felt his small fists pressing against her breasts. Eyes filled with tears, she looked up at Atretes and knew he would do exactly as he threatened. She could not risk Caleb being harmed. Loosening her shawl, she held Caleb out to him. The baby cried harder, his small arms flailing. Her milk came, increasing her anguish. "He's hungry."

Atretes hesitated. His son looked small and fragile. He looked at Rizpah and saw her anguish. Tears poured silently down her cheeks. Face rigid, he reached out and took his son. The infant cried harder.

Rizpah crossed her arms over her heart. She looked up at him. "Please, Atretes, don't do this." Never had he seen such a look of anguish on a woman's face.

"Get out," he said hoarsely.

"Please—"

"Get out!" he shouted, and the baby began to scream.

Uttering a sob, Rizpah turned away.

"Don't forget this," he said and kicked the pouch of money after her.

She swung around at the door. Picking up the pouch, she flung it into the fountain, glaring at him through her tears. "May God forgive you, for I cannot!" With one last look at the child, she fled, sobbing.

Atretes strode over and watched her run down the steps and across the courtyard. He kicked the door shut before she reached the gate.

Discomforted, he looked down at his son's reddening face and felt a moment's doubt. He touched the black hair and smooth cheek. The baby stiffened in his arms and screamed louder. "Scream all you want. You're *mine*," he said gruffly. "Not hers. You're mine!" He held his son closer, rocking him and pacing the floor. The child didn't cease crying.

"Lagos!"

The servant appeared almost immediately. "Yes, my lord." Atretes wondered if he had been lurking around the corner, listening to every word.

"Summon the wet nurse."

"Yes, my lord." Lagos had never seen his master look ill at ease, but now, with a squalling baby in his arms, he looked almost comically devoid of confidence.

When the servant brought the woman to the atrium, Atretes was all too eager to hand the wailing infant to her. "Take him. The woman said he's hungry." She took him from the chamber, and Atretes breathed a sigh of relief as the sound of his screaming son receded.

Lagos saw the pouch of coins in the water. "She would not take them, my lord?"

"Obviously not."

Lagos moved to fish the pouch out, but jerked his hand back quickly when Atretes barked at him, "Leave it!" The servant knew by the dark look on Atretes' face as he turned and strode away that his master would spend the day in the gymnasium.

3

A servant awakened Lagos late that night. "It's Atretes' son. The nurse is worried." He rose groggily and followed the serving girl down the corridor. As he came nearer the kitchen he could hear the baby crying. He entered and saw the wet nurse pacing with a bundle in her arms.

"He will not nurse," she said, her face filled with anxiety.

"What do you want me to do about it?" he retorted, testy from being awakened in the middle of night.

"You must tell the master, Lagos."

"Oh no. Not I," he said, shaking his head. "It's enough that you've awakened me in the middle of the night. I won't knowingly put my head in the lion's mouth." Yawning, he scratched his head. "The babe will nurse when he gets hungry enough." He turned away.

The baby was her responsibility now.

"You don't understand. He's been crying since the master gave him to me!"

Lagos paused in the doorway and turned around. "So long?"

"Yes, and I tell you, I can feel him growing weaker in my arms. If he goes on like this, he could die."

"Then you had better *do something*!"

"That's what I've been telling you! I've done everything I know how to do. An infant this small needs milk."

"Has yours gone sour, woman?" he said angrily, knowing nothing of these matters. How was he going to tell the master the wet nurse was dry?

Vexed, the woman responded testily. "There's nothing wrong with my milk. He's pining for his mother."

"Oh," he said grimly. "His mother doesn't want him."

"Pilia said she was waiting outside the gate."

"The woman who brought the child to Atretes is not his mother," he said, having overheard the conversation in the atrium. "And the master wants her to have nothing to do with the child."

"Oh," she said and then gave a sad sigh. She placed the baby in a box-bed near the cookfire. "Then perhaps it's the will of the gods that he die. A pity. He's beautiful."

Lagos felt a cold chill. "Do you mean to leave him there?"

"I've done everything I can."

Considering the efforts and risks Atretes had taken to reclaim his son, Lagos doubted he would accept the babe's death in so calm a manner. "I'll tell the master of the situation as soon as he awakens. As for you, woman, if you value your life, I suggest in earnest that you keep trying to get that baby to eat."

※

Atretes couldn't sleep. He stood on his balcony looking out at the moonlit hills.

It had been ten long years since he led the Chatti in a rebellion against Rome. Defeated, he'd been taken prisoner and sold to a ludus in Capua, then to the Great Ludus of Rome. Ten years! Another lifetime.

Were any of his people still alive? Had his brother, Varus, survived the battle? What of Marta, his sister, and her husband, Usipi? What had happened to his mother? He ached to go home to Germania and find out if any of his loved ones were still alive. Reclining on a couch, he stared up at the star-studded sky, hardly feeling the still of the night air. He wanted to breathe in the pungent scent of pine, drink sweet honeyed ale and beer. He wanted to sit with the warriors around a council fire in the sacred grove. He wanted to be at peace with himself again.

Sighing, he closed his eyes, wondering how that would ever be possible. He wanted to sleep, to forget, to go back, far back to when he was a child running with his father through the black forests of Germania. Life had been so full and rich then, stretching out before him, ready for the taking. He wanted his son to grow up in the forest, wild and free as he had been, untainted by Rome.

Frowning, he listened intently. He swore he could still hear his son crying as he had when he'd taken him from the widow's arms. But that had been hours ago.

Letting out his breath slowly, he tried to turn his mind to the future and away from the past. Yet what came to him was a vivid image of Rizpah's face, tears streaming down smooth cheeks, eyes dark with anguish.

"*May God forgive you, for I cannot!*"

He shut his eyes tightly, remembering the night Hadassah had come to him in the hills and said similar words to him. *"May God have mercy on you."*

He swore, his head spinning with wild thoughts that tangled like arms and legs in combat. *"May God forgive you."* The sound that came from his throat was a growl of pain. He came off the couch with the swiftness of a powerful animal and gripped the wall as though he would leap over it to the dirt compound below. His heart was pounding heavily, his breath rasping in his throat.

He heard the baby crying again.

Turning away from the balcony, he went back inside his bedroom. Silence.

Stretching out on his bed, he lay wide awake. Still, he heard nothing.

Tension filled him until he lunged off the bed and strode to the door. Banging it back against a wall, he went along the corridor and stopped above the inner courtyard. Head cocked, he listened intently, trying to hear anything amiss. The fountain in the atrium was running. Other than that, no other sound was discernible in the large villa.

It was the middle of the night. Babies in his village had often awakened hungry and needed to be suckled. Perhaps that was all it was.

Yet the uneasy feeling persisted. Something was wrong. He didn't know what it was, but sensed it. He'd learned to trust his instincts while fighting in the arena and he couldn't ignore them now.

Muttering a curse, he went along the upper corridor and down the steps. He would see his son and set his mind at rest. Where had Lagos put the wet nurse?

He opened doors and peered into empty rooms, heading toward the back of the villa. Hearing footsteps, he turned a corner and saw Lagos with a small clay lamp in his hand. The servant jumped in surprise, then came quickly toward him. "My lord, I was just coming—"

"Where's my son?"

"In the kitchen. I was just coming to see if you were awake."

"Where's the kitchen?"

"This way, my lord," Lagos said, going ahead of him with the lamp.

"What's wrong?" Atretes demanded, wanting to push the man into a faster pace.

"He won't nurse. He's been crying since . . . since this morning."

Atretes said nothing. He could hear the child now, and the sound pierced his heart. He followed Lagos into the kitchen and was immediately struck by the stench of a latrine. The baby was in a box-bed near it. As it was near dawn, the cook was working bread dough.

He walked over to the baby and peered down at him. "Is he sick?"

"I don't think so, my lord," the wet nurse said nervously, standing nearby wringing her hands.

"What *do* you think?" he demanded angrily.

She was trembling with fear. Her master looked even more fierce than his reputation had painted him. She remembered Lagos' warning to her and was afraid he'd lay the blame for the child's decline solely upon her. She didn't dare tell him that the child might die because he'd taken him from his foster mother.

"Babies are very fragile, my lord. Sometimes they sicken and die for no reason."

"He was well this morning."

When he turned toward her, she drew back in fear. "He hasn't stopped crying since Lagos put him in my arms, my lord. I've done everything I can, and still he won't suckle."

He frowned and looked down at his son again. Bending, he picked him up. The soft, pathetic cries turned to wails that cut him worse than any sword ever had.

Lagos had never seen his master look more vulnerable.

"What do we do?" Atretes said, holding the babe in the crook of his arm as he began to pace. "I won't let him die."

"We could send for his mother," Lagos said and immediately regretted the words at the look Atretes gave him. "I mean the woman who brought him to you, my lord," he amended quickly.

Atretes continued to pace. He brushed his son's cheek, and the baby's head turned sharply, mouth open. "Here," he said harshly. "He's hungry now. Feed him."

The wet nurse saw there was no other way to convince him. She took the child, sat down, and bared her ample breast. The baby grasped the nipple and then drew back sharply, crying louder, milk running unwanted from his mouth. She looked up at Atretes. "You see, my lord?"

Atretes ran a hand back through his hair. He was responsible for the deaths of over a hundred and fifty men. Would he be responsible for the death of his infant son as well? He shut his eyes and turned away, rubbing the back of his neck. There was only one thing he could think to do. "Awaken Silus," he commanded grimly.

The wet nurse covered herself and put the baby back to bed. "Give him to me," Atretes said angrily, seeing how quick she was to dispense with her duties. "Perhaps you've bound him too tightly." He sat down and laid the baby on his thighs, untying the swaddling clothes that were wound around him, making him look like a mummy. The baby's skin was pale and blotchy. The cool air brought a stream of urine that splattered against Atretes' chest. Drawing back in surprise, he cursed.

"It happens all the time, my lord," the wet nurse said quickly. "Do you wish me to take him?"

Atretes gazed down at his son. "No," he said with a wry smile. "I think he's telling me what he thinks of me."

Silus entered the room looking bleary-eyed from drink and lack of sleep. "Lagos said you sent for me, my lord."

"Go to Ephesus. Southeast of the Artemision and library is a street with insulae on both sides," Atretes said. "Enter the one on the west. Second floor, fourth door on the right is the widow, Rizpah."

"The woman who brought the baby this morning?"

"Yes. Bring her back here as quickly as possible."

"She never left, my lord."

"What?" Atretes' face darkened. "What do you mean she never left? I ordered her out!"

"She left the villa, my lord. She went outside the gate and sat by the side of the road. She's been there ever since."

Atretes frowned, annoyed and relieved at the same time. "Get her."

Silus left quickly.

The baby's crying made his nerves raw. Atretes paced and then sat down, the child in his lap. "What's taking so long?" he muttered, feeling like he had a hot coal in his hands. Light footsteps hurried along the outer corridor, and the widow appeared in the doorway.

Face pale with cold and puffy from crying, she entered the kitchen. Atretes waited for her to rail at him with accusations.

She didn't. She said nothing except "Caleb" in a broken whisper as she came across the room. Grim-lipped, Atretes took his hands from his son, and she lifted the baby from his lap. As she cradled the infant close, he continued to cry, but the sound was different. Turning away, she shifted her shawl and untied the right shoulder of her tunic. Atretes saw her shoulders jerk once as his son began to nurse.

The kitchen fell silent.

The wet nurse gave a deep sigh, echoing his own relief. "A babe knows his mother."

Atretes rose sharply. "Get out!"

With a frightened gasp, the wet nurse fled the room. Atretes turned his angry glare on Lagos and Silus, dismissing both with a jerk of his head.

Again, silence fell over the kitchen as he stood alone in the room with the widow nursing his son. Hooking the stool with his foot, he scraped it closer to the fire. "Sit." The woman did so without looking at him. Her head was bent over the child, and she murmured softly to him as he nursed.

Atretes moved restlessly around the kitchen, finally stopping and leaning his hip against a counter. Clenching his teeth, he turned again. She had draped the shawl modestly over her shoulder; the babe nestled against her breast beneath it. He noticed the dampness seeping through the left side of her tunic.

Rizpah shifted Caleb tenderly, remaining covered as she loosened the ties on her left shoulder. She felt Atretes watching her and was embarrassed. Her eyes flickered to him.

Surprised, Atretes saw the color mount her cheeks. How many years had it been since he'd seen a woman embarrassed by anything? She turned herself on the stool so her back was to him, clearly disturbed by his presence. She could suffer it; he wasn't leaving her alone with his son.

Rizpah could sense his gaze boring into her back. She could feel the heat of his anger.

"I told you to leave," he said darkly.

"You don't own the road."

He gave a bleak laugh. "It would seem you own my son."

Rizpah glanced back over her shoulder and saw something in his face she knew he would prefer to have hidden. His mouth flattened and his eyes glittered as they held hers. "I had a long time to think," she said softly.

"About what?"

"I know very little about you. Only grim details about the violent life you've led."

His smile was cold and derisive.

Disturbed, she looked down at Caleb. He would soon be asleep at her breast. He was so beautiful, so precious to her, and yet she knew the harder she clung, the more fiercely determined Atretes would be to take him from her.

When she moved Caleb slightly, his mouth worked again, almost frantically, holding to her. Touching a finger against her breast, she broke the suction. A dollop of milk trickled from his mouth and she smoothed it away. Kissing him lightly, she laid him tenderly on her thighs and retied her tunic. She could still feel Atretes watching her.

She adjusted the shawl to cover the dampened bodice of her tunic, remembering how, the moment she entered the hall and heard Caleb crying, her milk had come forth. God was truly marvelous! Lifting Caleb to her shoulder, she rubbed his back gently as she stood. She paced slowly, patting him softly. He was warm and relaxed against her. She glanced at Atretes and saw his troubled frown.

Seeing the set of his jaw, Rizpah remembered the story of King Solomon and the two women fighting over a child. The one who had been the true mother had been willing to give up the child in order to preserve his life.

Caleb's mother had wanted him dead. And this man! She'd never seen anyone so ruthless and beautiful. His features seemed chiseled by a master sculptor. Everything about him exuded a profound, overpowering masculinity. There was not even the hint of softness. His expression was utterly implacable. But was he?

O Lord, God, soften his heart toward me.

Heart beating dully, Rizpah came and stood before him. She held his sleeping son out to him. "Take him." Frowning, he straightened. His eyes narrowed warily on her as he took his son. Caleb awakened immediately and began to cry, and Rizpah saw a flinch of raw pain flicker across Atretes' face.

"Hold him next to your heart," she said gently, fighting tears. "Yes, like that. Now rub his back gently." His hand was huge against Caleb's back.

Atretes held his son uneasily, half-expecting the soft pitiful cries to turn to screaming.

"I beg your forgiveness, Atretes," Rizpah said, meaning it. "My tongue is like a fire sometimes. I'm sorry for the cruel things I said to you. I had no right to judge."

Surprise flickered in his bleak face and then a cynical smile twisted his mouth. "Sweet," he sneered.

Why should he believe her after the way she had acted?

She looked at Caleb nestled in Atretes' powerful arms and thought how fragile he looked there. Her throat closed and she nodded slowly, blinking back tears.

Atretes studied her intently, disturbed by the feelings stirring in him. Her brown eyes were dark with exhaustion, her cheeks smudged with dirt and streaked where tears had run. She looked up at him now, her expression full of appeal.

"I know by all the laws of Rome, Caleb is yours to do with as you will," she said shakily, "but I ask you to think of his needs." When he said nothing, her heart sank. "Caleb and I are bonded as strongly as if he had issued from my own womb."

"You are not his mother."

"I am the only mother he's known."

"Every woman I've known since being taken in chains from Germania has been a harlot, save one. You appear no different from the majority."

She drew the shawl more closely around her shoulders, chilled by the anger she saw in his blue eyes. It made no difference that he condemned her without even knowing her. Other things mattered more. "Caleb will awaken in a few hours. If he still won't accept the wet nurse, send the guard again. I'll be outside the gate."

Surprised, Atretes watched her leave. Frowning, he listened as her soft footsteps receded down the darkened corridor. He felt a vague disquiet as he sat down and looked at his sleeping son.

✶

Mouth grim, Atretes strode across the barren courtyard, dismissed Gallus with a jerk of his chin, slammed the bar back, and opened the gate. He went out and looked around. The widow was exactly where she'd said she would be, sitting with her back against the wall. Her knees were drawn up against her chest, her shawl drawn around her for warmth.

When his shadow fell across her, she awakened and lifted her head. Her eyes had dark circles beneath them.

He stood over her, arms akimbo. "The wet nurse tried again with no more success than last night," he said, feeling it was somehow her fault. "Come feed him."

Rizpah noticed that he'd come to issue a command and not make a request. She rose stiffly, her body aching from her long vigil in the cold. Caleb was not the only one who was hungry. She'd not eaten since leaving Ephesus yesterday morning.

"You will stay," Atretes said in a tone that said the decision was made whether she liked it or not. Smiling in relief, she said a silent prayer of thanksgiving as she followed him up the steps and into the villa. "Silus will go for your belongings," Atretes said. "You'll have quarters near the kitchen." He glanced back and saw her smile. "Don't think you've won."

"I will not pull at Caleb as though he were a bone between two dogs," she said, following him through the atrium. She could hear the baby's cries. "It would be better if he was with me."

Atretes stopped and glowered at her. "You'll not take him outside these walls."

"I didn't mean that. I mean it would be better if he was with me in my quarters where I can watch over him and answer his needs as they arise."

He hesitated. "As you wish," he said grimly. "Satisfied?"

She looked at his hard face and knew his pride was hurt. Swallowing her own, she made a simple request that made her feel a beggar. "May I have something to eat and drink?"

His brows rose slightly in realization. "Tell Lagos what you want and he'll see it's prepared for you." His mouth curved sardonically. "Goose livers, oak-fed beef, ostrich, wine from Northern Italy? Whatever is your taste. I'm sure whatever you crave can be obtained."

Rizpah pressed her lips together, holding back an angry retort. Any harsh reply would only serve to stir his anger further, and she had already done damage enough with her wayward tongue. "Seven-grain bread, lentils, fruit, and watered wine will more than satisfy me, my lord. Other than that, I ask for nothing."

"You will receive a denarius each day for as long as you remain in my household," he said, starting down the corridor toward the kitchen.

"I will not be paid for—"

She broke off when Atretes stopped and came back toward her. Bending down, he brought his face close to hers. "A denarius a day," he said through his teeth, his blue eyes blazing. "Just so you understand you are here *by hire*. When my son is weaned, you *go*!"

She refused to be intimidated. *A year, at least, with Caleb,* she thought, thanking God again. She was done with crying. She would cling to the knowledge that many things could change in a year, not the least of which was a man's heart.

Atretes' eyes narrowed. When the woman made no further comment, he straightened slowly. He had cowed men with less anger than he had shown her, and yet she stood quiet, clear-eyed, gazing up at him without the least concern. "You know the way," he said, wary.

Rizpah stepped past him and walked down the hall.

Struck by her grace and dignity, Atretes stared after her until she entered the kitchen.

A moment later, the baby stopped crying.

4

Sertes leaned against a door in the east wall of the villa, smiling as he watched Atretes in the distance. "He's staying in condition," he said, watching the German run down a rocky slope.

Gallus gave a brittle laugh. "Don't assume too much, Sertes. Atretes labors to drive demons from his head."

"May the gods prevent him from succeeding," Sertes said with a slight smile. "The mob misses him. No man has excited them as he did."

"You can forget what you're thinking. He won't go back."

The Ionian laughed softly. "He misses it. Perhaps he won't yet admit it, even to himself, but one day he will." Soon, Sertes hoped. Otherwise, he'd have to devise a way of making him want to return, which was always easier when the man was so conditioned as a gladiator that he couldn't function in any other realm. And a gladiator with Atretes' passion and charisma was worth a fortune.

Sertes watched Atretes run up the last hill before the villa. The German's face darkened when he saw him, but Sertes was not offended. Rather, he smiled.

Slowing to a fast walk, Atretes shrugged off the weights, tossing them aside as he strode past Sertes into the villa's barren yard. "What are you doing here, Sertes?" he said without stopping.

Sertes followed at a more leisurely pace. "I came to see how you fare with your freedom," he said in good humor. He had been dealing in gladiators for twenty years and could see the quiet life was already chafing. Once a man had experienced the excitement and bloodlust of the arena, he couldn't leave the life without denying an essential part of his nature. He saw that very nature was goading the German, driving him, though Atretes himself didn't yet know it. Sertes had watched a tiger pace in its cage once. Atretes had the same air about him now.

Entering the baths, Atretes stripped off his tunic and dove into the *frigidarium*. Sertes strolled in and stood on the marble walk against the wall, watching him in admiration. He was the embodiment of power and masculine grace. No wonder women cried out for him. Atretes came up out of the pool at the other end with a single fluid movement of strength, water cascading from his magnificent body. Sertes was proud of him. "They still call your name, you know."

Atretes took a towel and wrapped it around his waist. "My fighting days are over."

Sertes smiled slightly, a tinge of mockery entering his black eyes. "No offer of wine for a friend?"

"Lagos," Atretes said and gestured. Lagos poured wine into a silver goblet and brought it to Sertes.

He lifted the goblet in a toast. "To your return to the arena," he said and drank, undisturbed by the tight-lipped glance Atretes cast him. He lowered the goblet. "I've come with an offer."

"Save it."

"Hear me out."

"Save it!"

Sertes swirled the wine. "Afraid you might change your mind?"

"Nothing could induce me to fight in the arena again."

"Nothing? You challenge the very gods, Atretes. That's never wise. Don't forget it was Artemis who called you to Ephesus."

Atretes gave a cynical laugh. "You paid Vespasian's price. That's what brought me here."

Sertes was affronted, but thought better than to remark on such blasphemy. "You will welcome the news that Vespasian is dead."

Atretes glanced at him. "Murdered, I hope." He snapped his fingers. "Wine, Lagos. Fill the goblet to the brim. I feel like celebrating."

Sertes laughed softly. "You will be sorry to hear he died of natural causes. Not that there weren't those, like you, who wished him ill, especially the old aristocracy who found themselves sharing the senate with provincials recruited from Espania. Vespasian's father was rumored to be a Spanish tax collector, but then, who knows?"

"Who cares?"

"I imagine those in Espania. He did seem to favor them. He granted Latin rights to them as well as Roman citizenship to all the magistrates." He laughed. "Something that hardly sat well with the old families who considered Vespasian a plebeian." He raised his goblet again. "Despite his bloodlines, he was a great emperor."

"Great?" He muttered a foul word and spit on the marble tiles.

"Yes, great. Perhaps the greatest since Julius Caesar. Despite his reputation for avarice, Vespasian's tax reforms saved Rome from financial ruin. His philosophy was to first restore stability to the tottering state, then adorn it. He accomplished much of that. The Forum and Temple of Peace stand in Rome as tribute to his efforts. A pity he was not able to finish the colossal arena he began building on the foundations of Nero's Golden House."

"Yes, what a pity," Atretes said sarcastically.

"Oh, I know you hated him. With good reason. After all, wasn't it his cousin that crushed the rebellion in Germania?"

Atretes cast him a dark look. "The rebellion lives."

"No longer, Atretes. You've been away from your homeland a long, long time. Vespasian annexed Agri Decumates in Southern Germania and cut off the reentrant angle formed by the Rhine at Basel. Germans are too fragmented to be of any threat to Rome now. Vespasian was a military genius." He could see Atretes did not like hearing plaudits for his nemesis. It fanned the hatred within him. Exactly what Sertes wanted. Keep the fire hot.

"You will remember his younger son, Domitian."

Atretes remembered all too well.

"I believe he arranged your last match in Rome," Sertes said casually, driving the knife in deeper. "His older brother, Titus, is now emperor."

Atretes downed the rest of his wine.

"His military career is as illustrious as his father's," Sertes said. "It was Titus who crushed the rebellion in Judea and destroyed Jerusalem. Other than his unfortunate attachment to the Jewish princess Berenice, his career is flawless. *Pax Romana* at any price. We can only hope his talents extend to administration as well."

Atretes set his empty goblet aside and took another towel from the shelf. He dried his hair and upper body, his blue eyes glittering.

Sertes studied him with veiled satisfaction. "Rumors abound that you were in the city a few nights ago," he said, as though remarking on some casual occurrence. He didn't add that Gallus had confirmed the rumors, though he had not known the reason for Atretes' clandestine visit. Something important must have been transacted, and Sertes wanted to know what it was. It might prove useful in getting Atretes back into the arena.

"I went to pay my respects to the goddess and found myself mobbed instead," Atretes said, the lie coming easily.

Seeing an opportunity, Sertes grasped it. "I know the proconsul very well. I'm sure, with a word, he'll put a company of legionnaires at your disposal. You can enter the city anytime you want and pay proper homage to our goddess whenever you choose without worrying about whether you'll live through it."

Sertes smiled inwardly. Such measures as he was suggesting would draw attention. Once Atretes was recognized, the excitement would spread like a fever, and such a fever could heat Atretes' cold blood. Let him hear the masses screaming his name. Let him see how they still worshiped him.

"I'd like the mob to forget I ever existed," Atretes said. He wasn't fooled by Sertes' machinations. "And your measures would merely serve to whet their appetite, wouldn't they?" he said, raising one brow sardonically.

Sertes smiled drolly and shook his head. "Atretes, dear friend, I'm dismayed to find you don't trust me. Have I not always had your best interests in mind?"

Atretes gave a cold laugh. "As long as they coincided with yours."

Sertes hid his annoyance. Atretes' perceptiveness had always been a problem. His success in the arena hadn't hinged merely on physical prowess and courage. Atretes was surprisingly intelligent for a German barbarian. The combination of hatred and sagacity was dangerous, but made him that much more exciting.

"Perhaps we can make arrangements more suitable to your desires," Sertes said.

"My desire is to be left alone."

Sertes was undaunted. He knew Atretes better than the gladiator knew himself. He had observed him in captivity and out. "You have been left alone," he said, watching Atretes drop the towel from around his waist and pull on a fresh, richly woven tunic. He was the most magnificently built man Sertes had ever seen. "For several months. You seem little satisfied by your solitude."

Putting on a thick leather belt with brass studs, Atretes looked at him with eyes so cold Sertes knew he had pressed him far enough for today. He wasn't distressed by his failure to gain Atretes' agreement to reenter the arena. There would be other opportunities. He would make use of them as they came. He waved his hand in a gesture of dismissal. "Very well," he said with a smile. "We'll talk of other things." And he proceeded to do so. Sertes left an hour later, but not before inviting Atretes

The Seed

to one of the banquets before the games. He said the proconsul of Rome was eager to pay his respects. Atretes sensed the undercurrent of warning. One didn't slight a high official of Rome without consequences. Still, he declined.

Sertes became more direct. "One should be very careful about insulting the wrong Roman."

"I've learned many things during my captivity, Sertes. Even Caesar himself is afraid of the mob. And as you well know, the mob still loves me."

"You are also wise enough to know that the mob is like a fickle woman. Stay away from her long enough and she'll forget. Besides, what the mob wants most is to see you fight again."

Atretes said nothing, but Sertes saw that the words had struck a raw nerve. Good. As he went down the steps with Atretes at his side, he saw a young woman with a baby, walking in the sunshine of the barren courtyard before the villa. At first, he thought it was Julia Valerian and was surprised. His spies had reported the relationship ended some months ago. They'd also informed him that Julia Valerian had been carrying a child rumored to be fathered by Atretes. He had ordered his spies to watch the house until the birth. They reported the child had been cast upon the rocks to die. A pity. Had the child been Atretes' and lived, it might have proven very useful.

Pausing, Sertes stroked his chin and watched the young woman with open interest. She was small and very nicely curved. She glanced their way. His smile broadened. She turned away again and disappeared around the corner of the building. "You always did have an eye for beauty." He cast Atretes an amused glance. "Who is she?"

"A household servant."

Sertes sensed Atretes' annoyed withdrawal and wondered about it. He glanced in the direction the woman had gone, curious. "And the child? Is it yours?"

"The child is hers."

Sertes said no more, but a seed of speculation had been planted in his fertile mind.

*

Rizpah turned and saw Atretes striding toward her. She knew he was angry. Everything about him exuded his foul mood. Shifting

Caleb in her arms, she sighed, wondering what she had done to displease him now.

"You're not to leave the villa unless I order you to do so!"

"You wish to make your son a prisoner, my lord?" she said, striving for calm.

"I wish to protect him!"

"As do I, Atretes. I'm within the walls."

"You will stay in the *villa*!"

"What possible harm can come to Caleb out here? You have guards—"

"Woman, you will do as I say!"

Her hackles rose at his imperious tone. The man was impossible! She had never taken well to being commanded to obedience. Shimei had always dealt with her in a more gentle fashion than this thick-headed German. "If you are reasonable, I will obey. In this case, you aren't."

His eyes narrowed dangerously. "Press me, and I'll throw you right out that gate."

She looked straight back at him. "No, you will not."

Hot color flooded his face. "What makes you so sure?"

"Because you're as concerned for Caleb's good health as I. I don't know why you're so incensed, Atretes. You watched me walk Caleb around the yard yesterday and the day before and had no objections. Today you look like a melon ready to burst."

Atretes struggled to hold his temper. She was right, which only maddened him further. He *had* watched her yesterday and the day before, and he'd found pleasure in doing so, possibly for the same reasons Sertes had just enjoyed watching her. She was beautiful and full of feminine grace. He seethed now. She knew, for the sake of his son, he couldn't throw her out the gate. His hands sorely itched to throttle her. He had seen the look of speculation in Sertes' eyes before he left.

Rizpah saw the conflicting emotions in his face, anger overriding everything else. She should have handled things differently. She should have sealed her lips and gone into the villa and chosen a better time to state her opinions. She sat Caleb on her hip. "What's happened that you think it necessary to keep Caleb in the confines of the villa?"

Atretes watched his son grasp the front of her tunic, pulling it slightly. "It's enough that I command you."

"Must we go through this again?" she said with strained

patience. "Has it something to do with the friend that was visiting with you?"

"He is no friend! His name is Sertes, and he's editor of the Ephesian games."

"Oh," she said. "He came to talk you into fighting again, didn't he?"

"Yes."

She frowned. "Did he succeed?"

"No."

She sensed there was something very serious behind his anger and not just the pique of a man's pride. "You must tell me where the danger lies. I seem to have blundered and don't know how."

He saw no other way to convince the stubborn woman but to tell her the truth. "If Sertes could find a way to force me to fight again, he would do it. He asked who you were. I said you were a servant. He asked about *him*." He nodded curtly to his son.

Her heart began to race as she sensed the danger. "And?"

"I said the child was yours."

She let out her breath, her mouth curving ruefully. "That must have choked you."

"You think the situation amusing?" he said through his teeth.

Rizpah sighed. In another moment, he wouldn't be able to think clearly through the red haze of his rising temper. "No," she said calmly. "I don't think it's amusing. I think it's very serious and I'll do as you say."

Her capitulation took him off guard. Speechless with frustration, Atretes watched her walk away. She went around the side of the villa. Still hungry for a good fight, he went after her. She was entering the back door of the villa when he caught up with her. Hearing him, she glanced back. "Would you like to play with your son for a while?"

He stopped just inside the doorway. *"Play?"* he said, taken aback.

"Yes, *play*."

"I haven't time."

"All you have is time," she said and entered the bath chamber.

"What did you say to me?"

She turned to face him. "I said, all you have is time. You'd enjoy playing with Caleb more than running around in the hills, jumping over rocks, or spending hours in your gymnasium lifting weights and terrorizing your guards."

A hot flush came over his face.

"Here," she said. Before he could think of a retort burning enough, she handed him the baby.

His rage evaporated in a wave of alarm. "Where are you going?"

"I need to find some clean linen. Caleb's soaking through those wraps." Hiding her amused smile, she walked away.

Atretes grimaced. He could feel the dampness seeping through his fresh tunic. When his son began nuzzling his chest, Atretes held him away. "He's hungry!" he shouted after her.

Rizpah stopped beneath the archway. "Be at ease, Atretes. He's not *that* hungry." She laughed, and the musical sound floated around him in the marble-tiled chamber. "Besides, I doubt he'll draw much blood. Not until he has teeth."

Alone with his son, Atretes paced nervously. Caleb squirmed and looked ready to cry, so Atretes held him close again, cold sweat breaking out on the back of his neck. He found it ironic that he had faced death hundreds of times and never been reduced to the sweating fear he felt now holding a baby—*his* baby.

Caleb's tiny pudgy fingers grasped the ivory chip hanging from a gold chain around Atretes' neck and stuffed a corner of it into his mouth.

Scowling, Atretes tugged the gold chain and ivory chip, which declared his freedom, from his son's mouth. He tucked it quickly out of reach inside his tunic, muttering under his breath about women who deserted their babies. His son's lip quivered.

"Don't start crying," he said gruffly.

Caleb's mouth opened wide.

"By the gods, not again," Atretes groaned. He winced at the howling wail that came forth. How was it possible for such a small child to make so much noise? "Very well. Eat it!" he said, pulling the chain out from beneath his tunic again and dangling it temptingly before his son. Still whimpering, Caleb grasped the chip and gummed it.

Atretes carried his son over to a massage table and placed him on it.

"*Rizpah!*"

Her name echoed off the marble, muraled walls around him. Startled, Caleb lost hold of the chip again and screamed. Gritting his teeth and holding his breath, Atretes unwound the soiled wraps and tossed them in a heap near the wall. "You need a bath, boy. You stink." He picked him up and carried him into the pool. Caleb stopped screaming as he felt the warm water of the *tepidarium* swirl up around him. Gurgling happily, he grabbed the chip again and pounded it against his father's chest, splashing water into Atretes' face.

Supporting the babe under the arms, Atretes held him away and dipped him up and down in the water. Caleb squealed with delight, fists hitting the water. Atretes' mouth softened and tipped up on one side. He studied Caleb as he splashed. The babe had Julia's dark eyes and hair. Frowning, he wondered how much more of her was in him.

Rizpah stood in the archway, linens draped over her arm. "You called, my lord?" she said sweetly. She came to the edge of the pool and watched him wash Caleb. She laughed. "He's a baby, Atretes, not a soiled garment."

"He needed a bath," Atretes said.

Rizpah felt on fire with embarrassment when Atretes walked up the steps out of the pool, for the wet linen tunic molded Atretes' body. Though he seemed not the least concerned at how much was revealed, she was unnerved. She looked quickly away and studied the muraled walls, scarcely realizing what the pictures depicted.

Caleb didn't like the cool air as much as the warm water and began fussing again. "Take him," Atretes said, holding him out to her.

Tossing the linens onto her shoulder, she did as he asked, relieved to be distracted. She kissed Caleb's wet cheek. "Did you have a nice bath?" she said, laughing at his chuckle. She bounced him gently as she headed for the massage table.

Atretes stood watching her. He had noted her discomfort when he came out of the pool as well as the way her gaze was quickly averted from his body. He recalled her embarrassment the day she fed the baby, too. The woman seemed to be an odd combination of contradictions: fiery and rebellious, unafraid to challenge him, and yet thrown into painful embarrassment by the sight of a man's form. He frowned as he watched her.

Her voice was soft and sweet. She laughed and leaned down, letting Caleb grab her thumbs. Kissing his chest, she blew air into his belly button. The baby gave out that funny chuckle again. Mouth curving, Atretes walked over to watch his son kicking and waving his arms happily. Rizpah ignored his presence and talked to the baby the whole time she swaddled him in linen, but as she lifted Caleb, she glanced up at him. Her expression held awareness.

His pulse jumped and, with it, his mistrust. He'd seen beautiful dark eyes like hers before.

Rizpah was disturbed by the intensity of his look, for it touched her in some instinctive elemental realm. When his gaze moved downward over her, she felt a rush of warmth. She drew back a step, holding Caleb against her like a shield. "You will please excuse me, my lord," she said, eager to take Caleb and escape those predatory eyes.

"No, I will not."

She blinked. "My lord?"

"Take him into the triclinium."

"Why?"

"Do I need a reason?"

She hesitated, uncertain as to his motives, distressed by the emotions stirring within her.

"Do I?" he said again, eyes narrowing.

"No, my lord."

"Then do what you're told."

Why must he use that tone with her? "Caleb is ready to be fed and put down to rest," she said, trying to keep calm.

"He can do both in the triclinium."

Seeing he had no intention of relenting, she carried Caleb out of the baths. The inner corridor was thankfully cool. She entered the lavishly furnished triclinium and sat down on a couch. Caleb fell asleep as he nursed. She wrapped her shawl around him and placed some cushions around him. Her hands shook as she folded them tightly in her lap and waited.

Lagos entered. "Lady Rizpah!" he said in surprise. Since being admitted to the household, she had taken her meals in the servants quarters. What was she doing in the master's dining room?

"Atretes ordered me here," Rizpah said, seeing the question in his eyes.

"Oh."

Her nerves tightened as though the Spirit within her warned of the battle to come. "Why do you say it in that tone, Lagos?"

"No reason."

"He wants to spend more time with his son."

Lagos could not imagine Atretes bouncing a baby on his

knee, but said, "Of course," to set her mind at ease. He had seen Atretes standing on the balcony overlooking the yard when Rizpah was taking the baby out for air. Silus and Gallus had also noticed and remarked on it. They made bets as to how long it would be before Rizpah warmed Atretes' bed.

Rizpah watched him tidy the pillows. "Say something, Lagos."

"What would you have me say?"

"You know him better than I."

"I know him hardly at all, but what I do know is that he's unpredictable and dangerous. And he has only one use for women."

"You talk as though he's an animal."

"Not far from it," Lagos said grimly.

"He's a man, Lagos. Like you. Like any other."

Lagos gave a nervous laugh. "Not like me, and not like any man I've ever known. He's a barbarian gladiator, and believe me, Lady Rizpah, that's as close to an animal as you can get."

They both heard Atretes' footsteps. Rizpah put her hand protectively on Caleb; Lagos went to the archway and greeted his master. "Would you like your meal served, my lord?"

Atretes looked across the room at her. "Are you hungry?" he said dryly.

"Not very." In truth, she wasn't hungry at all. Lagos' words had destroyed what little appetite she'd had.

"Bring wine," Atretes said, dismissing Lagos.

Feeling his gaze on her, Rizpah took up Caleb and held him close, comforted by the warmth of his small body.

Atretes looked at the way she held his son cradled tenderly on her thighs. "It's occurred to me that I know very little about you," he said, reclining on the couch opposite her and studying her face.

Even when he relaxed, Rizpah sensed the alertness about him.

"What happened to your husband?"

Surprised and dismayed by the question, she said, "He died."

"I know he died," Atretes said with a cold laugh. "You wouldn't be a widow had he not. What I want to know is *how* he died."

She looked down at Caleb's precious face, stilling the pain rising inside her. Why must he ask about such things? "My husband was struck down by a chariot," she said softly.

"Did you see it happen?"

"No. He was on his way to work. Friends brought him home."

"He didn't die right away?"

"He died a few days later." The memory of those days was still deeply etched into her heart.

Atretes looked at her pale profile and was silent a moment. Clearly these memories were painful to her. Or was it pretense? Lagos brought in a pitcher of wine. "Leave," Atretes said tersely. Lagos set the tray down quickly and departed. Atretes continued staring at Rizpah. He sensed he had probed open wounds. "Did you ever find out who was driving the chariot?"

"I knew on the day it happened. The man was a Roman official."

"I wager he didn't even stop."

"No, he didn't."

Atretes' mouth curved slightly. "It seems we share a common hatred of Romans."

His observation caused swift remorse. "I don't hate anyone."

"Don't you?"

She paled, wondering. Hadn't she overcome her feelings about what had happened? Was she still harboring anger against the man who carelessly cost the life of a man for whom she cared deeply. *Lord, if it be so, cleanse me of it. Search me and change my heart, Father.* "It's not the Lord's will that I hate anyone."

"The Lord?"

"Jesus, the Christ, the Son of the Living God."

"Hadassah's god."

"Yes."

"We will not talk of him," he said, dismissing past, present, and future on the subject as he rose from the couch. He poured wine into a silver goblet. A second goblet was on the tray, but he offered her nothing.

"It's the one thing I would wish to talk about with you," she said quietly.

He slammed the pitcher down so hard she jumped. Caleb awakened and started to cry.

"Pacify him!"

She lifted Caleb to her shoulder and rubbed his back. He cried harder.

"Make him stop crying!"

She rose, distressed. "May I have your permission to leave the room?"

"No!"

"He'll go back to sleep if I nurse him."

"Then do so!"

"I can't! Not with you staring at me!"

He glared at her from across the couches. "You bared your breast for him in the kitchen four nights ago."

Heat flooded her face. "The circumstances were different," she said tightly. Besides, she had been covered, her back to him.

"How so? He was screaming then and he's screaming now!"

"Stop shouting!" She was immediately ashamed of her outburst. The wretched man brought out the worst in her! Apology sticking in her throat, she paced on one side of the room. She was so angry she was sure her milk was curdling into lumps of cheese. Caleb screamed louder.

Atretes paced on the other side of the room, his face rigid as he glared at her. "By the gods, woman. Sit down and give him what he wants!"

Shaking with frustration, Rizpah plunked down. Presenting her back to Atretes, she set about tending the baby. The shawl was wrapped around Caleb and she needed it to drape over herself for modesty. Her hands shook as she removed it.

She let out her breath as Caleb began nursing and the room fell silent. She heard the scrape of metal against metal and knew Atretes was pouring himself more wine. Did he intend to get drunk? He was intimidating enough when sober. She didn't even want to think what he would be like reeling from too much wine.

An image of her own father rose like a demon, gripping her mind with anger and fear. Remembered violence. She shuddered and pressed it away.

Judge not lest ye be judged. Forgive and be forgiven. Ask and it shall be given. Her control slipping, she grasped hold again, clinging. *Lord, walk with me through the valley. Talk with me. Open my ears and heart that I may hear.*

"What are you muttering?" Atretes growled.

"I'm praying for help," she snapped, heart still pounding fast and hard. She was surprised Caleb didn't notice her tension.

"Is he asleep yet?" Atretes said quietly from behind her.

"Almost." Caleb's eyelids looked weighted. His mouth relaxed and then began to work again. Finally, he relaxed completely.

"Thank the gods," Atretes said with a sigh and reclined. He watched Rizpah's back as she readjusted her clothing. Sitting sideways on the couch, she began wrapping his son in her shawl again. "What happened to your own child?" Her hands went still, and he saw the soft color ebb from her cheeks. It was a long moment before she answered him.

"She took fever and died in her third month," she said tremulously. She lightly brushed Caleb's cheek. Turning on the couch, she looked at Atretes, her eyes awash with tears. "Why do you ask me these questions?"

"I'd like to know a little more about the woman who nurses my son."

Her dark eyes flashed. "How much did you know about the woman you bought, other than she was German?"

"Perhaps my interest in you has changed."

His cold, cynical smile had a dismaying effect upon her. Her body responded to the look in his eyes, for having been married, she was not unfamiliar with a man's needs, and what Lagos had just told her about Atretes' inclination toward women was distressing. Certain things had to be made plain now. "You may play with Caleb anytime you wish, my lord, but do not think you can play with me."

His brow lifted. "Why not?"

"Because it would strain an already tenuous relationship when I said no to you."

Atretes laughed at her.

"I'm sincere, my lord."

"It would *seem* so," he said dryly. "But then sincerity is a trait rarely found among women. I've only known three who possessed it: my mother, my wife, Ania, and Hadassah." He gave a bleak laugh. "And all three of them are dead."

Rizpah felt a wave of compassion for him.

Atretes saw her dark brown eyes soften and fill with warmth. His heart responded even as his mind rebelled. "You may go," he said, jerking his head in rude dismissal.

Rizpah scooped Caleb into her arms and rose, eager to depart. She felt his gaze follow her. She paused beneath the archway and looked back at him. For all his fierceness and hardness of heart, she sensed he was a man in terrible pain.

"I give you a solemn vow, Atretes. I will never lie."

"Never?" he said mockingly.

She looked straight into his beautiful, empty blue eyes. "Never. No matter the cost. Even if it costs my life," she said softly, then left him alone.

5

Sertes stood on the balcony overlooking the practice arena. Below him, two gladiators sparred, one with sword and shield, the other with trident and net. Disgusted with their unexciting display, he grasped the iron railing. "Use the coals on them!" he shouted down at the *lanista*.

Shaking his head, he stepped back. "If this is the best we have to offer, no wonder the people are bored!" He turned to the man standing beside him. "What did you find out about the woman living in Atretes' villa?"

"Her name is Rizpah, my lord. She's a widow. Her husband was a silversmith who was run down by Ceius Attalus Plautilla."

"Nephew of the proconsul?"

"The same. He's given to excessive drinking and—"

"Never mind," Sertes said, gesturing impatiently. "I know all about him already. What more did you learn about her?"

"She's a Christian, my lord."

"Ah," Sertes said, smiling broadly. "That will be useful." He rubbed his chin, thinking just how useful it could be, especially if Atretes was in love with her. "And the baby?"

"There's conflicting information about the child, my lord. One source said the woman had a baby girl that died within a few months, while another argued she had a son who lived."

"Perhaps the child is Atretes'."

"I don't think so. No one has ever seen this woman with Atretes, my lord. But it is strange. When I asked about her at the insula where she lived, I was told she took the baby one morning and left. A man came the next day and collected her things. She hasn't been seen in the city since."

"Keep looking. I have a feeling there's more to this than we yet know."

*

Atretes pushed the door of Rizpah's chamber open and peered in. Moonlight streamed down from a small high window, casting a soft glow of light over the room. The baby's bed was empty. Rizpah was lying asleep on a floor mat, curled on her side, his son nestled against her, warm and protected.

Entering silently, Atretes crouched and stared for a long moment at them. Then he looked around the small room. Against the east wall was a single trunk in which were Rizpah's few possessions. On it was a small clay lamp, unlit. Other than those few things and the baby's bed, the room was bare.

The small barren chamber reminded Atretes of his cell in the ludus: stone, cold, empty.

His gaze drifted again to Rizpah, moving up from her bare feet over the slender curves of her body. Her hair had come free and flowed black over her shoulder. He reached out and took a handful of it, rubbing it between his fingers. It was thick and silky. When she stirred, he snatched his hand away.

Opening her eyes, Rizpah saw a shadowy shape crouched in front of her. Breath catching in her throat, she scooped Caleb up and scooted quickly back against the wall, heart pounding.

"Don't scream," Atretes commanded.

Her breath came out shakily. "What's happened? Why are you here in the middle of the night?"

He heard the tremor in her voice and knew he had frightened her. "Nothing's happened," he said gruffly, raking a hand back through his hair. He gave a hoarse laugh and lifted his head. Nightmares had awakened him again.

Rizpah saw his face in the moonlight. "Something *is* wrong."

He looked at her again. "Why the name Caleb?"

The question was unexpected. "My husband told me about him."

"Did your husband trade in men?"

She heard the dark anger in his tone. "No," she said, wondering why he would make such an assumption.

"Caleb fought in Rome," he said. "How would your husband know anything of him unless he traded in gladiators?"

She thought she understood. "There are many Calebs in the world, Atretes. The Caleb after whom I named your son lived hundreds of years ago. He came out of Egypt with Moses. When the people reached the Promised Land, twelve men were sent into Canaan to spy out the land. When they came back, Caleb told Moses and the people the land God had given them was good and they should take possession of it, but the others were afraid.

They said the Canaanites were too strong and they wouldn't conquer them. Moses took their advice rather than listen to Caleb. Because of that, all the people of that generation wandered in the wilderness. And when the end of the forty years came, only Caleb the son of Jephunneh and Joshua the son of Nun were allowed to enter the Promised Land. Only they followed the Lord wholeheartedly. Even Moses, the lawgiver, never set foot in the Promised Land." She stretched out her legs and placed the baby on her thighs. "Caleb is a name for a man of strong faith and courage."

"Caleb is a Jewish name, and my son is *German*."

She lifted her head. "Half German."

Atretes stood so abruptly, her heart jumped. He loomed over her for a moment and then took a step away, leaning back against the wall to the right of the window opening. Standing where he was, his face was hidden in the shadows while the soft moonlight shone in on her.

"He should have a German name," he said. Expecting an argument, he waited.

"What name would you wish to give him, my lord?"

He hadn't thought about it until then. "Hermun," he said with decision. "After my father. He was a great warrior-chieftain of the Chatti and died honorably in battle against Rome."

"Caleb Hermun," she said, testing the name.

"Hermun."

She started to protest and then lowered her head. A contentious woman was worse than a leaking roof. And the child *was* his. She lifted her head again. "Hermun . . . Caleb?" she said tentatively, offering a compromise. "A warrior of strong faith and courage."

Atretes said nothing, nor did he move from the shadows.

Rizpah felt uncomfortable beneath his stare. What was he thinking? "Who was the Caleb of whom you spoke?"

"A gladiator from Judea. One of Titus' prizes." His tone was bitter.

"Is he still alive?"

"No. We fought. I won."

His voice was flat and bleak, and she felt sudden pity for him. "You knew him well?"

"A gladiator hasn't the luxury of knowing anyone well."

"But had you friends, you would have wanted to count him among them."

"Why do you say that?" he said coldly.

"Your bitterness and the fact that you still remember him."

He gave a harsh laugh. "I remember them all!" He put his head back against the cold stone wall and closed his eyes. He couldn't forget them. He saw their faces every night. He could see their eyes as their life's blood drained into the sand. No amount of drink could exorcise them.

"I'm sorry," she said softly.

Disbelieving, he looked down at her. The sheen of tears in her eyes angered him, for tears had been used against him before. Pushing away from the wall, he crouched down before her again and glared. "Why should *you* be sorry?" he sneered.

She was not intimidated. "Your life has been difficult."

"I've survived."

"At great cost."

He gave a cold laugh and stood again, restless. "Better had I died. Yes? Then you would have the child all to yourself."

"Had you died, Caleb might never have been born. And he is a gift from God, worth any sorrow."

Atretes looked out the window at the bare compound and thick walls beyond. He felt as though he was back in the ludus. He wanted to scream and break down the walls.

Rizpah felt his wrath as though it was a dark being in the room with her. She recognized its malignant presence and the terrible danger of it. What could she possibly say to soothe him? She had no words. She couldn't even imagine what his life had been like, nor was she sure she wanted to know. Her own had been difficult enough. She hadn't the strength of faith to help him carry his burdens as well.

He turned. "We didn't finish our conversation this afternoon."

She saw Atretes wanted a fight, and it would appear she was the only available opponent with whom he could wage a battle.

We are mismatched, Lord. He can annihilate my heart.

"How long were you married?"

"Why do you ask me such a question?"

"It's enough that I do!" he snapped, then drawled caustically, "You said you wouldn't lie."

"Nor will I."

"Then answer."

She gave him a pained smile. "Will you leave when I do?"

He wasn't amused. "I will leave when I please."

She let out her breath slowly, fighting the inclination to war with him as he wanted. "I was married for three years." Caleb made a soft sound and she lifted him.

Atretes watched how she drew her shawl around her and his son so that they were wrapped together. "Were you faithful?"

She lifted her head and looked at him. "*Yes*, I was faithful."

He sensed she was hiding something and hunkered down in front of her again, his eyes narrowed on her pale, moonlit face. "In our tribe, an unfaithful wife is stripped and whipped before the villagers. Then she's killed."

The hidden things of Rizpah's own heart roused anger. "What of the man?"

"What do you mean, what of the man?"

"Adultery involves *two* people, doesn't it?"

"Woman entices."

She gave a soft laugh. "And man succumbs like a brainless ox?"

His hands tightened into fists as he thought of how easily he had fallen prey to Julia's charms.

She laid Caleb down on her thighs again. "Man and woman are equal in the eyes of God," she said, trying to keep her voice level.

He gave a cutting laugh. "Equal!"

"Shhh." She put a finger to her lips. "You'll wake him." That should strike terror in this gladiator's heart. She removed her shawl and covered the baby with it.

"Since when is a woman equal to a man?" he said between clenched teeth.

"Since the beginning when the Lord created both. And according to Mosaic law. The man and woman involved in adultery were *both* executed to prevent sin from spreading like a disease through the nation of Israel. Justice was to be dispensed equally."

"I'm not a Jew!"

"Would that you were, my lord." Even as she uttered the words, she regretted them. The silence that fell in the room was hot. *Forgive me, Father. Make me mute! I listen to him and remember my life before Shimei, before you. And I want to fight back, even when I know I can't win.*

"Did your husband permit you to talk like this?"

Shimei. Precious Shimei. Tender memories rescued her from darker ones. She smiled. "Shimei often threatened to beat me."

"As well he should have."

She lifted her chin. "His threats were empty and meant in jest. Much of what I know of Mosaic law, he taught me."

"Ah," he said with heavy sarcasm. "And what did he teach you?"

"That the heart of the law is mercy, but what God gave, man corrupted. Despite that, God prevails. God sent us his Son, Jesus, to be the sacrifice of atonement for all mankind, men *and* women. He was crucified, buried and raised from the dead, thus fulfilling hundreds of years of prophesies concerning the Messiah. God sent his only begotten Son into the world that whoever believes in him should not perish, but have eternal life."

Atretes' eyes glittered. "No god cares what happens to us."

"The price paid for our redemption shows how much God does love us. Whatever you believe or don't believe, Atretes, there's only one truth and that truth is in Christ."

"I believe in vengeance."

She felt saddened at the unrelenting quality of his voice. "And judgment. Judge, and you shall be judged with the same measure of mercy you mete out."

He gave a hard laugh.

"God is not partial," she said. "You can't bribe him or overpower him. He doesn't think as man thinks. If you stand on the law, *any* law—Ephesian, Roman, or German—you bear the judgment already for disobedience. And the sentence is always the same. Death."

He stood and glared down at her. "It wasn't by my choice that I became what I am!"

"But by your choice you continue in it." She watched him move away into the shadows again. Everything about him revealed his bitter rage and frustration. Did he think his anguish and sense of hopelessness were no less obvious? She knew more about what he felt than he could ever guess.

O Lord, why was it his child you gave to me? Why did you send me here to this man so that I remember the things done to me? Shimei interceded and brought me to you, and you healed me. Now, I see Atretes and feel the old wounds reopened. Hold me fast, Father. Don't let me slip; don't let me fall. Don't let me think as I used to think or live as I used to live.

"Life *is* cruel, Atretes, but you have a choice. Choose forgiveness and be free."

"Forgiveness!" The word came out of the dark shadows like a curse. "There are some things in this world that can never be forgiven."

Her eyes burned with tears. "I once felt the same way, but it turns back on you and eats you alive. When Christ saved me, everything changed. The world didn't look the same."

"The world doesn't change."

"No. The world didn't. *I* did."

He said nothing for a moment and then spoke heavily, "You know nothing of pain, woman."

"I know all I ever want to know." She wished she could see his face and look into his eyes as she spoke to him. "We're all walking wounded, Atretes. Some wounds are physical and obvious. Other wounds are secret and hidden so deep that no one but God sees them."

"What wounds do you bear?" he said sardonically.

She didn't answer. She would not open herself to his mockery or disdain.

Atretes frowned. He could see her face in the moonlight, and it wasn't defiance that held her silent. "What wounds?" he said more gently, wanting to know.

"*Private* wounds," she said doggedly.

Her stubbornness infuriated him. "There's nothing private between us. You're here because I suffer your presence for the sake of the boy. Now tell me of what you speak."

She shook her head. "Perhaps one day I will, Atretes, but not because you command me to do so. It'll be when we can *both* trust one another and not until then."

"That day will never come."

"Then we will never speak of it."

Atretes stepped from the shadows. Rizpah felt instinctive fear of him. She knew this was the look countless men had seen just before they died. She went cold inside, waiting for the blow.

Atretes looked into her dark eyes. She said nothing. She just sat, waiting. As others had waited.

Tightening his fist, he remembered the young Chatti gladiator, standing before him with his arms outstretched, waiting for the final thrust through the heart. He remembered so many more. . . .

And still, Rizpah sat, afraid, but making no protest or appeal.

The calm resignation on her face stirred him—and suddenly an image filled his mind: Caleb on his knees, head tipped back slightly, exposing his neck as the mob screamed, *"Jugula!"*

The Jewish gladiator's words echoed in Atretes' mind once again: "Free me, my friend." As Caleb had placed his hands on Atretes' thighs and tipped his head back, the German had been overwhelmed by his friend's courage . . . and by the strange peace that had seemed to settle over Caleb as he prepared for death. Atretes had given his friend his wish. He had set him free. And as he did so, he had been filled with a deep hunger for whatever it was that made a man so strong, so courageous.

What gave you such peace, my friend? he wondered now as he had wondered many times before. And he was met with the same silence. The same emptiness deep within.

Atretes took a step closer to Rizpah, seeing how she shivered in response to his nearness. "Caleb is a strong name, a warrior's name," he said, his voice low with an emotion she did not understand. "Keep it."

With that he picked up the blanket that lay by the mat, dropped it beside her, and went out.

*

Rizpah obeyed Atretes and stayed within the walls of the villa. She offered to help the servants, but they said the master wouldn't like it. It seemed she was relegated to some position between slave and free, a nebulous, undefined place within the household. Atretes avoided her and the others had resolved to be safe and do the same.

She found herself wandering around the huge villa in much the same way Atretes wandered about at night. When Caleb wasn't sleeping or nursing, she'd find a place in the sunlight and place him on her shawl. Smiling, she would watch him kick, play, and make noises.

One afternoon, she entered a room on the second floor. It appealed to her, for sunlight streamed in from its balcony. It was empty of furnishings except for a big brass urn with a palm in it. She put Caleb on her shawl in a beam of sunlight. He rocked back and forth on his stomach, kicking his strong chubby legs. She sat down to watch him.

"You're a little frog," she laughed.

He gave a gurgling squeal and kicked faster. She saw what interested him and took hold of the edges of the blanket, pulling it across the smooth marble surface. "You always want what you can't reach," she said, patting his bottom.

Caleb stretched out his hand toward the shiny curve of the large brass urn. His legs kicked again, toes catching in the shawl and pushing him an inch closer. His tiny fingers brushed the brass; he kicked harder, rocking and reaching. Her smile softening, Rizpah took hold of her shawl again and turned it so that Caleb was alongside the big urn. He turned his head, staring curiously at the other baby in the brass.

"That's you, Caleb."

He left fingerprints on the shiny golden surface.

Loneliness engulfed her unexpectedly as she watched him reaching out to his own reflection. Were they always to be alone like this, cut off from the rest of the household? She stood and went out onto the balcony, looking down into the barren yard. Two guards passed the time near a gate, talking and laughing together. Other servants were tending the vegetable garden inside the walls.

"Lord," Rizpah whispered, "you know how much I love Caleb. I thank you with all my heart for him. Don't think I'm ungrateful, Father, but I miss Shimei and John and all the rest. I know I didn't talk to them very much when I had the opportunity, but I miss being among them. I miss standing beside the river and singing and hearing your Word."

The road that led back to Ephesus was just beyond the gate. As it dipped down and turned west, there was an old terebinth tree. She could see men and women beneath it, some sleeping, some talking, others looking toward the villa. Were they weary travelers resting in the shade? Or were they the amoratae Atretes so despised, waiting for a glimpse of their idol?

The hills, green from a recent rain, were a more welcome sight. What pleasure it would be to walk up there, to sit on a hillside and let Caleb feel the grass between his toes.

She glanced back at him and saw he had fallen asleep beside the urn. Smiling, she went and knelt beside him. She gazed down at him for a long time, thinking how beautiful and perfect he was. She touched his palm. He grasped hold of her finger, his mouth working as though he nursed even in his dreams.

"What a miracle you are," she said and lifted him tenderly. She laid him softly against her shoulder and lightly kissed his cheek. Closing her eyes, she breathed in deeply the scent of him. Sweet innocence. New beginnings.

"What are you doing in here?"

The hard deep voice startled her. Glancing back, she rose, facing Atretes in the doorway. "I'm sorry. I didn't know I wasn't allowed in this chamber."

Atretes entered the room and looked at her shawl still lying on the floor beside the shiny urn. "Do as you like."

She retrieved her shawl and shook it, draping it over her other shoulder, out of the way of Caleb. She smiled at him in appeal. "What I would like is to take Caleb for a walk in the hills."

"No," he said, angry that he was struck again by her beauty.

"Under guard?"

"*No.*" He came toward her and stopped a few feet away. His eyes narrowed. "And you will not stand out on the balcony where you can be seen again either."

She glanced toward the balcony with a frown. "Where were you that you could see me?"

Atretes stepped by her and went out into the sunlight. "You can be sure Sertes' spy saw you."

"Spy? Where?"

He leaned against the balcony wall and nodded toward the road. "He's sitting under that tree down there."

"They look like travelers."

"I recognized him from the ludus."

"Oh." She let out her breath softly. "Perhaps he'll assume I'm a servant cleaning the upstairs chambers."

"Standing idle and gazing out into the hills?"

She blushed. "Are you sure *he's* the one spying on me?"

Atretes pushed away from the wall and walked back inside. "Yes, I have you watched. I know exactly where you are and what you're doing every minute of the day." He stopped in front of her. "And night."

She forced a smile, her heart drumming. "I'm thankful to know Caleb is so well guarded."

A muscle jerked in Atretes' cheek. His gaze flickered over her. He stepped past her again. She felt as though she was being circled by a hungry lion.

"This was once my room," he said without inflection.

"Pilia told me."

He came around the other side of her, his eyes hard. "Did Pilia tell you anything else?"

"She said you don't like to come in here." She glanced around, admiring the marble walls and muraled floor. "It's a lovely room, full of sunlight."

"The largest and best in the house," he said, his tone acrid.

Troubled, she glanced up at him. Questions flooded her mind, but she held her silence.

He cast a cursory glance around the empty room, his face hard. "A bedchamber fit for a queen."

"I apologize for intruding where I shouldn't have. I won't come in here again." Excusing herself, she left the chamber, breathing a sigh of relief when she was in the outer corridor and out from under that cold, blue stare.

Rizpah spent the rest of the afternoon in the atrium. She held Caleb on the edge of the pond and let him kick his feet in the water. When he became hungry, she adjourned to an alcove and nursed him.

When Caleb was replete, she went to the kitchen and asked for something to eat. The cook put bread, fruit, and thin slices of meat on a platter. He carried it, along with a small pitcher of wine, into a room with a long table where the slaves ate. Setting the meal down, he left her. Sitting at the bench, Rizpah gave thanks to God and ate alone. The silence was oppressive.

Pilia came in with baskets of bread. Rizpah smiled and greeted her, but the girl plunked a basket down and walked quickly away from the table. Her eyes were red and puffy from crying, and when she glanced back at Rizpah, her expression was one of unveiled resentment. Frowning in confusion, Rizpah watched her set the remaining baskets of bread on the table and leave.

Sighing, Rizpah rose. When she went out into the corridor, she saw the girl coming back with a tray of fruit. Pilia marched past her, pointedly ignoring her. Annoyed, Rizpah followed her into the small hall. "What's wrong, Pilia?"

"Nothing."

"You appear very upset about something."

"*Upset?*" She banged the tray down. "What right have I to be upset?" She marched out of the room again.

Rizpah shifted Caleb and waited. Pilia entered again with a stack of wooden plates. Rizpah watched her slam them one by one into place along the opposite side of the table. "Have I offended you in some way?"

Pilia stopped at the end of the table, clutching the remaining wooden plates against her. Her angry eyes filled with tears. "It would seem I'm no longer to be called to Atretes' bed."

Rizpah hadn't known of their relationship and was dismayed by the pang she felt upon hearing of it. "What has that to do with me?"

"Don't pretend you don't know," Pilia said and began laying out the rest of the plates.

"I *don't* know," she said uneasily.

Finishing her task, Pilia swept out of the room again.

Troubled, Rizpah lifted Caleb, secured him to her with her shawl, and went to her room. When she opened the door, she found the room bare. The blood drained from her face. She went in search of Lagos and found him in the *bibliotheca*, the large library, going over household accounts.

"Where are my things?"

"The master ordered them moved to the bedchamber on the second floor."

She thought of Pilia and her face went hot. "Why?"

"He didn't say."

"Where is he?"

He glanced up in clear warning. "If I were you, I wouldn't—"

"*Where is he?*"

"In the gymnasium, but—"

She swung around and left.

When she entered the gymnasium, she found Atretes, stripped down to a loincloth, his arms draped across a beam on his shoulders as he did knee bends. His eyes were fixed on her as though he had heard her coming along the outer corridor and had been expecting her.

Drawing a calming breath, she walked over to him. He didn't pause from his exercises, though his powerful body streamed sweat. "Please have my things moved back downstairs."

"You said the room was *lovely*."

"It is, but that doesn't mean I want to live in it."

He shrugged off the beam. It banged loudly on the marble floor, the sound echoing around the walls. Startled from his sleep, Caleb made a soft mewling cry. Rizpah drew the shawl more securely around him as the beam bounced noisily and rolled against the wall. She rubbed Caleb's back to comfort him.

"I prefer to be downstairs where I was," she said with more calm than she felt.

"I don't care what you prefer." Atretes took a towel and wiped the sweat from his face. "You'll be upstairs in the room next to mine."

Her stomach tightened in alarm. "If I'm in such close proximity to you, the servants will assume—"

Atretes tossed the towel angrily onto the floor. "I don't care what anyone assumes!"

"I care! It's *my* reputation that's being bandied about."

"As it has been from the first day you arrived."

"For reasons other than the situation you're creating!"

"Do you think anyone really cares what goes on between us?"

She almost blurted out that Pilia obviously did, but stopped herself. She didn't want to get the girl in additional difficulty. She wanted to get herself out of it. "It is not proper."

"But it *is* convenient," he said with a decided gleam in his eyes.

Her face went hot. "Anytime you wish to see your son, you've only to snap your fingers and I'll bring him to you," she said, pretending to misunderstand.

Smiling faintly, he approached her. He put his hand over hers on his son's back. She withdrew hers, heart thudding. He rubbed Caleb's back slowly, staring into her eyes. She felt the baby relax against her. Atretes lifted his hand and put it lightly around her throat, forcing her chin up with his thumb. "And if it's you I want, have I also only to snap my fingers and you'll come to me as well?"

She stepped back and swallowed convulsively, her heart racing. She could still feel the heat where he had touched her. "No!" she said firmly.

His mouth curved. "You think not?" He had felt the pulse hammering in her throat. It matched his own. A few nights with her and the fire in him would burn itself out. "It would be easy to convince you otherwise."

She stiffened, ashamed of her own response to him. "I'm not one of your amoratae, my lord."

He walked back and picked up another towel. "I'm not looking for someone to *love* me," he said. Grinning wryly, he rubbed the perspiration from his chest.

"I asked you not to play with me, Atretes, and this is the sort of playing I meant."

"You said the other day I *needed* to play."

"With your son. Not with me."

"I think you'd be more fun."

She would take care of moving her things herself. Turning, she started for the doorway with that intention.

Atretes caught her arm and yanked her around to face him again. "Don't turn your back on me."

Caleb awakened and started to cry.

Atretes gritted his teeth. "I didn't call you in here," he said. "I didn't summon you."

"My apologies. If you let go of me, I'll leave."

His fingers tightened painfully. "Now that you're here, you'll leave when I dismiss you." His blue eyes were ablaze. "You're moved into Julia's room whether you like it or not." Seeing her wince, he released her.

"I *don't* like it," she said succinctly, holding Caleb instinctively closer while stepping back from his father.

"You'll stay where I put you. Willingly or not, *your* choice. But stay, you will!" His smile turned contemptuous. "And you needn't look at me like that. I've never raped a woman in my life and I don't intend to start now." His gaze moved down over her disdainfully. "If you're as *chaste* as you claim, you won't have a problem, will you?"

She clenched her teeth.

He walked back to the beam and hefted it onto to his shoulders. Turning, he saw she was still standing in the middle of the room, her eyes fixed on the distant wall. He sensed her discomfort and the reason for it.

"May I go *now*, my lord?" she said tautly.

"Not yet." He began his exercises again, leaving her to stand for several minutes in silence.

She stood rigid, waiting. He took pleasure looking at her and even greater pleasure in her vexation. Let her grind her teeth as she made him do. He let the moment stretch to two, three, four. Then he dropped the beam.

"You may go. But remember this: The next time you wish to speak to me, send Lagos first to ask my permission!"

6

Gallus sent word that Sertes had been sighted coming up the road from Ephesus. Atretes swore under his breath, in no mood to deal with him. He almost told Gallus to refuse him entrance to the villa and then thought better of it. Though he cared nothing about giving offense to Roman officials, he knew instinctively that Sertes was one to handle with great caution.

"Admit him and bring him to the triclinium," he said, and Gallus departed. "Lagos, bring wine and have the cook prepare food for us."

"Yes, my lord," Lagos said. "Is there anything else?"

Atretes frowned, his mind working quickly. He remembered all too clearly the interest Sertes had shown toward Rizpah and the baby during his last visit. "Tell the widow to remain in her chambers. Make sure of it. Lock the door!"

"Yes, my lord." Lagos hurried off to do his bidding.

"And have Pilia serve us!" Atretes shouted after him. The girl was pretty, perhaps pretty enough to divert Sertes from speculating about Rizpah. He would make sure of it.

Sertes clasped Atretes' hand in greeting, smiling broadly at the warm welcome, shrewdly aware there was some hidden reason for it. "You are looking well, my friend," he said, gripping Atretes' upper arm.

"Sit. Enjoy some wine," Atretes said, gesturing casually toward one of the comfortable cushioned couches while he reclined on one himself.

"After your last greeting, I expected to be turned away at the gate," Sertes said, accepting the invitation.

"I thought of it, but you'd only persist."

"You know me too well." He smiled. "As I know you, Atretes. After months of seclusion, you must be mad for distraction. Otherwise, you wouldn't be so amenable."

Atretes turned a cynical gaze on him. "Perhaps, but I'm not mad enough to return to the arena."

"A pity," Sertes sighed, "but I live in hope." He watched a pretty slave girl enter the room with wine. She served Atretes first. Sertes observed how Atretes' gaze moved down over the girl's lush curves in an intimate, almost fond, perusal. What was this? he wondered in annoyance. The girl's skin took on a rosy hue. She seemed flustered when Atretes smiled at her. "Don't forget my guest," he said softly, running his hand down over her hip and patting her bottom lightly.

"I'm sorry, my lord," she stammered and turned to Sertes.

When she departed, Sertes raised his brow. "A new acquisition?"

"I bought her for Julia." He grinned roguishly. "She serves me instead."

Sertes laughed, hiding his displeasure as he sipped his wine. "And what of the pretty widow I saw the last time?"

"Pilia is a better fit," Atretes said and tried to remember if he'd told Sertes Rizpah was a widow. If he hadn't, it boded an ill wind that Sertes knew anything about her.

How much more did he know?

Sertes assessed Atretes' expression. "So you've tired of the other already?"

"Her expectations were greater than my intentions."

"She is very beautiful."

"Her tongue has the sting of a scorpion."

"Sell her to me."

Atretes' blood went hot. "And waste her on a man who likes fair-skinned women from Britannia?" he said sardonically.

Sertes had seen a flash of fire before Atretes had hidden it. He smiled to himself. Pilia had been a pretty ploy and nothing more. Whatever relationship there had been between Atretes and Rizpah remained. "I can think of a dozen gladiators who would enjoy her company," he said with a shrug, playing out his game while keeping surreptitious watch on Atretes' reaction.

"What do you say?" Sertes said, a catlike smile playing on his lips. "Put a price on her."

The fire within him turned to ice. "Let me think about it," Atretes said, as though taking Sertes' offer into consideration. He poured himself more wine. Leaning back, he grinned. "Of course, you'd have to take her squalling brat as well." He watched Sertes' eyes carefully and saw them flicker.

Atretes' mention of the baby startled Sertes. If the child was Atretes', surely he wouldn't be so eager to dispose of it? "I forgot she had a baby."

"Oh, indeed, she has a baby. You saw it on your last visit. She keeps it wrapped in her shawl and tied to her breast. It's become like a growth on her."

"I take it the child is the cause for your disaffection," Sertes said.

"You might say that," Atretes said dryly.

Pilia entered the triclinium with a tray of delicacies. Her eyes were aglow as she offered her master the tray first. Atretes knew what she was thinking. Were all women such fools? He took a roll of rich pork and dipped it in some honey sauce, forcing himself to eat despite his lack of appetite. Sertes seemed amused.

"Speaking of women," Sertes said, helping himself to a handful of dates, "people are saying the great Atretes, never defeated by a man in the arena, has been brought low by a daughter of Rome." There was no mistaking Atretes' flash of temper now. Good. Atretes' pride had always been his greatest weakness.

"Who started the rumors, Sertes? You?"

"And come here to tell you about them? I'm not a fool, Atretes, nor am I eager for an early grave. Perhaps the Lady Julia has spoken of you . . . in less than glowing terms?"

"For all I care, the witch can shout whatever she wishes on any street corner in Ephesus!"

"As long as you are left alone to lick your wounds on this mountaintop?"

Atretes looked at him. "Lick my wounds?" he said softly.

Sertes felt the hair on the back of his neck rise at the look in those blue eyes, but sought to prick the gladiator's pride still further. "Whatever the truth may be, Atretes, that's how it appears."

"Even to you?"

Sertes hesitated deliberately. Atretes' face hardened. The German took up offense as quickly as he had once taken up a sword. "I must admit, I did wonder. Or have you forgotten, I was the one who arranged the purchase of this villa?"

Atretes hadn't forgotten, nor the reason why he had wanted it. For Julia Valerian.

"Think no more of the rumors," Sertes said, fully aware that, as desired, he had planted the seed that would cause a tangle of thoughts to grow in Atretes' mind. He had a warrior's heart and wouldn't like the idea of anyone thinking a woman had defeated him. "Rufus Pumponius Praxus sends his regards."

"Who in Hades is Praxus?" Atretes growled.

"Nephew of the prefect of Rome. He's holding a feast in honor of Titus' birthday. You're invited."

"Neatly timed, Sertes," Atretes said and leaned back against the cushions. "I suppose you see this as an opportunity for me to put an end to the talk about me." Atretes told him what the nephew to the prefect could do with his invitation.

"Praxus is not a man to insult. He could put you back in chains."

"I *earned* my freedom."

"Then don't throw it to the winds by offending a man with the ear of the emperor and his brother, Domitian."

At the mention of Domitian, a muscle jerked in Atretes' jaw.

"Praxus is sickened by these Christians who sing when they die," Sertes went on. "He'd like nothing better than to hunt them all down and exterminate them."

"What have I to do with Christians?" Atretes said, knowing full well why Sertes was dropping this information. "The only one I knew was Hadassah, and she's dead."

"Then I suggest you keep your distance from any others with whom you might come in contact."

Atretes thought of Rizpah in the upstairs chamber. If Sertes knew she was a widow, he very likely knew she was a Christian as well.

Sertes saw his warning had sunk in. "Praxus respects you for your courage. You fight with the heart of a lion and he wants to honor you. Let him." His mouth curved faintly. "Your less than delicate refusal will be taken as an insult."

"Then tell him the lion is still licking the wounds Rome inflicted on him."

Annoyed, Sertes rubbed the date still in his hand. "If Praxus even suspected you were encouraging the spread of this cult, he'd have you back in chains with the snap of his fingers."

Atretes looked at him coldly. "And who says I am?"

Sertes popped the date into his mouth and ate it. Washing it down with wine, he stood. "I can see I've overstayed my welcome."

"When has that ever kept you away?"

Sertes smiled and shook his head. "One day your pride will destroy you, Atretes."

"Pride is what has kept me alive." He rose. Draining his goblet, he set it down with a hard thump. "But perhaps you're right. I've been on this mountain too long." He walked with Sertes through the atrium and into the *antechamber.* "Say nothing to Praxus for now. I'll think over his invitation and send you my answer."

Sertes savored his victory in secret. "Don't take too long. The feast is in seven days." A servant opened the front door as they approached. Sertes clasped Atretes' arm. "You vanquished every foe in the arena, Atretes. It's time now to know the enemy outside it!"

"I'll heed your advice," he said with an enigmatic smile. His eyes grew cold as he watched Sertes walk across the yard, say a few words to Gallus, and go out the gate.

*

Rizpah heard something crash against a wall. Startled, she stopped pacing and listened. From the moment the guard had come and told her Sertes had arrived and she was to remain in her bedchamber, she'd closed the door and begun praying.

Atretes shouted something indiscernible. She winced, wondering grimly what had transpired downstairs that had put him in such a foul temper. Not that he was ever in a good one, she thought, with grim amusement.

Someone rapped twice on the door. Taking a deep breath, she crossed the room and unbolted it. Silus stood outside. "Atretes wants to talk with you."

"Now?" Whatever had occurred downstairs, it appeared she would get the brunt of it.

"He said to leave the baby."

"In whose care? Yours?"

Silus withdrew a step. "He didn't say."

She went back for Caleb. When the baby was settled warm and secure in the wrap of her shawl, she followed Silus out of the large chamber and down the upper corridor. Atretes' chamber door stood open. She stopped at the threshold. Atretes turned. He saw the baby and swore in German. "I said to leave him!"

"There was no one to tend him, my lord," she said, not entering the room.

"Where's the wet nurse?"

"Hilde works in the kitchen now."

"Not tonight. Get her!" Atretes said, jerking his head at Silus. The sound of the guard's hobnailed sandals echoed in the upper corridor. Atretes paced, muttering in German. The furs from his bed had been tossed on the floor. He kicked one out of his way.

Hilde arrived breathless and red faced. Rizpah untied the shawl and laid Caleb in her arms. "He'll sleep if you put him back in his bed," Rizpah said and laid a gentle hand on the woman's arm. "Don't leave him alone."

"I won't, my lady." She cast a nervous glance in Atretes' direction and left. Silus stood to one side, allowing her to pass.

"Walk the perimeter," Atretes snarled at him. "I'd like a word with *Lady* Rizpah in private." Silus left her standing alone in the doorway. "Come in and shut the door behind you," Atretes said in a tone that left no room for argument.

Rizpah obeyed, heart beating fast. Atretes' agitation could mean only one thing. "Sertes knows about Caleb, doesn't he?"

"No, but Sertes knows who you are." He gave a dark laugh. "In fact, he probably knows more about you than I do!"

Rizpah let out her breath in relief. "There's not much to know. And of what possible interest could a common woman like me be to a man like Sertes?"

"He intends to use you as leverage to get me fighting again." He noted her look of confusion with growing irritation. His mouth curved cynically. "He thinks you're my mistress."

Color poured into her cheeks. "I hope you corrected his misconception, my lord."

"I told him you had the tongue of a scorpion, which you do. I told him I was tired of you, which I am. He made a generous offer to buy you. I'm considering."

She blanched. "You're *what*?" she said faintly.

"I knew you were a curse on me the moment I laid eyes on you!" German oaths poured forth.

"You can't sell what you don't own!" She was trembling violently inside. Had the man gone completely mad?

"You're a *Christian*," he said in accusation.

"You knew of my faith before I came here."

"It would seem having you in my house makes me suspect to a man who has the power to revoke my freedom."

She closed her eyes. "Oh." She let out her breath slowly and looked at him, troubled. She was not going to suggest she leave, for she couldn't, not without Caleb.

"I'd like to throw you out."

Biting her lip, she clasped her hands in front of her. *Not one word,* she told herself. *Lord, keep me quiet.*

"Unfortunately, if I threw you out, Sertes' spies would go back and report it. They'd also report that the baby remained here with me. He'd want to know why and he'd figure it out in a bow-snap."

"O Lord God, protect us," she murmured, quickly grasping how easily an innocent child could be used by a man as callous as Sertes.

Atretes swore again. "And so, because of *you,* I've got to go pay homage to some bloody Roman aristocrat or end up back in the arena!" His voice rose to a shout, and he kicked over a table and shattered an elegant clay lamp.

Rizpah winced, but remained standing where she was. *Father, show me a way. Give me words. What do we do?* Her mind suddenly whirled with an appalling, frightening idea. She didn't even want to speak of it, but it was the only solution that came to her. "You said you wanted to return to Germania."

He swung around, glaring at her. "I'd have done that months ago except for two things!"

"Your son," Rizpah said, supplying one with complete understanding. Caleb was only four months old, and travel would be hazardous as well as difficult. "What other reason have you?"

Atretes uttered a short, foul curse and turned his back on her. Thrusting both hands back through his long blonde hair, he went out onto the balcony. Rizpah frowned. Whatever the other reason, it was clear he didn't want to tell her. He came back inside, his resentment etched in his handsome features.

"It took months to get me to Capua," he ground out. "Then I was transported to Rome. Sertes made a deal with Vespasian and brought me here. By ship. The journey took *weeks.*" He laughed almost hysterically. "I'd go back to Germania right now if I knew *how to find it*!"

She saw how much his admission cost him and answered quickly. "We'll find out exactly where it is and how to get there."

Atretes tilted his head, eyes glittering. *"We?"*

"You said you wouldn't leave your son behind."

"I won't."

"Where Caleb goes, *I* go."

He gave a sharp laugh. "You'd leave Ephesus and all it has to offer," he said dryly, unconvinced.

"I would rather stay here, yes," she said frankly. "All I've ever heard about Germania doesn't commend it." She saw Atretes' eyes harden as he took offense. "Caleb's safety is more important than whatever fears I may have about leaving all I know. If Sertes is all you think he is, and I don't doubt you, he won't think twice about using an innocent baby in whatever way he can to get at you, would he?"

"No."

"Then the only way to make sure Caleb is safe is to get him as far away from Sertes as possible."

His continued scrutiny made her increasingly uncomfortable. What was he thinking? "The journey will cost a great deal of money," she said.

He laughed grimly. "A fortune, no doubt, and most of what I earned was poured into this villa." He looked around the room as though seeing it for the first time. "Now I understand why Sertes was so willing to arrange the purchase of this place," he said darkly. "These walls close me in every bit as tightly as the ludus ever did."

"You can sell it."

"Not without him knowing about it, and I doubt I could manage it before Rufus Pumponius Praxus holds his little feast!" He swore in frustration.

"God can accomplish the impossible."

He gave her a mocking look. "What makes you think your god is going to help *me*?"

"What convinces you he won't?" She didn't wait for his response. "I'll go and speak with John. He'll help us."

"You won't leave this villa!"

"I must if we're going to gather the information we need. There are people from every walk of life in the body of Christ. I know of one merchant who has traveled all over the Empire. If anyone can tell us how to find Germania, he can. Perhaps he could provide us with maps to show us the way." Atretes looked ready to argue, so she plunged ahead.

"Another thing to consider: My leaving could throw doubt on Sertes' speculations about me and about Caleb. If I leave, *with* Caleb, might not Sertes assume I don't mean as much to you as he thought? And you would hardly send me away with a child of yours."

Atretes frowned, thinking her idea had merit. Yet some niggling doubt remained. "Sertes might have you brought to the ludus for questioning."

She glanced toward the balcony, troubled by his suggestion. "Is he out there under the terebinth, watching the house?"

"Sertes left. His spies remain."

She put a trembling hand to her throat, slightly relieved. "Unless he left instructions to bring me to the ludus, I doubt they would act upon their own initiative. They'll watch and report and await his instructions. By the time they get them, I'll be back in Ephesus."

"And within easy reach," he said, annoyed. "At least one of them will follow you."

"I've been followed before, Atretes. I know how to hide." She knew immediately it was the wrong thing to say.

Atretes' eyes narrowed in suspicion. "So," he said with dangerous softness, "if you're so good at hiding, how will I find you?" Sneering, he laughed. "You almost had me convinced. I'm not a fool. You think I'll just hand my son over to you and watch you walk away?"

"Atretes, I give you my word—"

"Your word doesn't mean dung to me!" He turned away, rubbing the back of his neck in agitation.

She let out her breath, struggling with frustration. He wasn't going to trust her just because she assured him he could. Trust had to be earned, and there was no time. "Perhaps there's another way," she said flatly.

"There'd better be."

"What if you went to this feast and appeared to enjoy yourself." He turned sharply.

Her exasperation grew. "Or you could go grudgingly, glower at everyone the way you're glowering at me, and insult this Roman official to his face! That would salve your pride, wouldn't it? And accomplish everything Sertes has planned for you!"

A muscle jerked in his jaw.

She came toward him, desperate in her appeal. "Atretes, *please*," she said. "Set aside your anger for the sake of your son. *Think* before you do anything."

Atretes gave a cynical laugh. "Perhaps I'll tell Sertes I tire of being out here on this mountain and want to live in Ephesus where all the excitement is," he said sarcastically. "That would please him." He felt like one of the lions being prodded into the arena. No way back. No escape. Somehow, some way, Sertes would get what he wanted—and he wouldn't care what he did or who he used to accomplish it!

"Let me go to John," Rizpah said softly. "He'll help us." Atretes said nothing. She came closer and put her hand lightly on his arm. His muscles tensed. She took her hand away. "Please. I'll learn what I can and send word. I promise, on my life!"

"It would appear I have little choice," he said grimly.

"I should go as soon as possible," she said, turning toward the door. "I'll take enough to make it appear you've cast me out."

Atretes caught hold of her. Whipping her around with one hand, he grasped her neck with the other. "Know this, woman. If I hear nothing from you in two days' time, I'll come looking for you. Don't try to run away with the boy, because if you do, I swear by all the gods in the universe, I'll use *any* means, even Sertes, to find you again! And when I do," he said, his hand tightening slowly, "you'll wish you'd never been born!" He let go of her as though merely touching her angered him.

Rizpah put a hand to her throat, her breath coming shakily. Tears of reaction filled her eyes. "I know you don't trust me now, but perhaps when we've come through this together, you'll know you can."

Frowning, he watched her walk to the door. "*Two* days," he repeated.

She went out, closing the door behind her. Heart beating fast, she hurried along the corridor to the bedchamber.

"Is everything all right, my lady?" Hilde said when she entered. "You're so pale."

"Nothing is all right," Rizpah said truthfully. "I must leave." She took up her shawl and wrapped Caleb into it, tying it securely around her shoulders.

"He's casting you out? Where will you go?"

"I have friends in the city. I'll go to them." She looked at the small trunk of possessions and shook her head. "I have Caleb. That's all that matters."

"He'll never let you leave with his son!"

"Caleb is *my* son, and Atretes will make no effort to keep me from taking what belongs to me," she said. She could still feel where his fingers had pressed in on her throat.

As she went out the door, her heart jumped at the sight of Atretes in the corridor. *O Lord, God of mercy, don't let him change his mind!* He looked uncertain and oddly vulnerable.

"Remember what I said," he muttered as she passed by him.

She paused and looked back at him, her eyes swimming in tears. "Remember what I said as well." She went down the stairs quickly. She crossed the barren yard to the gate where Gallus stood at his duty station.

"Where do you think you're going?" he said, stepping into her path.

"Let her pass," Atretes commanded, coming down the front steps and striding across the yard toward them. "I told her to get out."

Gallus gave her a pitying look and opened the gate.

Atretes held out a pouch to Rizpah. "Take it," he commanded. She obeyed, grimacing as she did so. The leather was dripping wet and slimy. It was the same pouch she'd flung at him the first day they met. Apparently it had remained in the fountain pool until today; it was heavy with gold coins.

"Consider it payment for services rendered."

She saw his intent. Nodding, she turned away and went out the gate. She hurried down the road, bundling Caleb closer to protect him from the cold wind blowing in from the east, where winter was coming.

As she passed by the terebinth tree, she saw several men sitting and talking in the shadows. They appeared to have no interest in her. Reaching the bend in the road, she glanced back surreptitiously.

One was following.

7

Despite all her attempts to lose the man following her, Rizpah sensed he was still somewhere close by when she reached John's house. Exhausted, she knocked at the door. Cleopas opened it and gave an exclamation of delighted welcome.

"John was called out earlier, but he should return soon," he said, bringing her inside. "Sit. You look tired."

"I am," she said, sinking down gratefully on a couch near a brazier. The warmth was welcome after the long walk in the cold wind. "I've come from Atretes."

"There's trouble?"

"Great trouble," she said, loosening the shawl and lowering Caleb and the pouch of gold coins to the couch beside her. She shivered.

Cleopas moved the brazier closer to her. "Caleb looks well," he said, smiling down at him. "And much heavier than the last time I saw him."

"He's twice what he was when John placed him in my arms," she said thankfully, though she had felt every ounce of him and the additional weight of the gold coins during the long walk into the city. Smiling, she let Caleb grasp her fingers and try to pull himself up.

Cleopas put his hand on her shoulder. "I'll bring you some wine and something to eat."

She thanked him and returned her attention to the baby. "Now, beloved, you're no longer bound. Wiggle all you want," she said, tickling his stomach. Gurgling happily, he kicked his legs. He grasped his foot and stuck it in his mouth, gumming his toes while grinning up at her. She patted his bottom and rose.

Going to the window, she peered out cautiously. The man who had followed her was standing in the night shadows beside a building just down the street, watching the house. She drew back, a hand against her heart.

Trembling, she went back and sat down beside Caleb again.

Cleopas returned. "Can I do anything to help?"

"I may be bringing trouble to John," she said as he set the

The Seed

tray down on the table before her. "A man followed me. I tried to lose him on the way, but he's like a barnacle on the hull of a ship. You can see him. He's wearing black robes and he's standing just down the street. Perhaps I should leave now before—"

"And go where?"

"I don't know, but the man behind the trouble is powerful and connected to the arenas." Fear rose inside her at the thought of repercussions to John and other friends if they stood in Sertes' way. "I didn't think . . ."

Cleopas poured wine into a small copper-lined clay cup and handed it to her. "It's very late. Drink. Eat."

His calm assurance set her mind at ease. He was unafraid. God was in command, not Sertes. Not even the emperor of the whole Roman Empire had the power of the Lord. She smiled up at Cleopas. "I've missed you and John and all the others."

"As we've missed you."

The sound of the front door opening startled her. Wine spilled over her hand, and she set the cup down. So much for her calmness! Cleopas put his hand out in a comforting gesture and rose. "It's John or one of the brethren," he said and went out to the antechamber. She heard voices and recognized that of the apostle.

"Thank God," she said, rising and going to him as he entered the room. She threw her arms around him, tears burning her eyes. He held her tenderly, as a father might. When she finally withdrew, John took her hands and gave her a holy kiss. He was dismayed by her tears.

She gave him a watery smile. "It's so good to see you, John."

"And you," he said.

Caleb gave a squeal from the couch and Rizpah jumped. John gave her a comforting touch and stepped past her. Laughing, he picked up the baby. "Look who comes to see us, Cleopas!" he said, grinning into Caleb's face. Caleb kicked his legs like a little frog, delighted to be the center of attention again. John held him close and ran a finger under Caleb's chin, gaining another chuckle.

Rizpah relaxed slightly watching the apostle with her son. Contrary to Atretes' manner, John was perfectly at ease with a baby. She came back and sat on the couch, smiling as she watched. The apostle sat and laid the boy in his lap, Caleb's feet against his stomach. John took his ankles and pumped his legs playfully. Gurgling, Caleb waved his hands happily.

"What is more beautiful than the innocence of a child?" John said, smiling down at Caleb. "I remember how children flocked around Jesus as we traveled through townships." He shook his head. "At first, we'd try to shoo them away, thinking of them as no more than a swarm of pesky flies," he said with a soft laugh, "and Jesus would gather them to him and bless them one by one. He told us unless we become like children, we will not enter the kingdom of heaven."

Rizpah smiled tenderly. "Humble and helpless."

"And completely open to the love and truth of God," John added, smiling. He glanced up at Cleopas and the servant came and took Caleb, then went to sit on another couch near Rizpah and laid the baby on his lap. He dangled a knotted cord and Caleb tried to capture it.

"It's fear for Caleb that brought me to you," Rizpah said. "A man named Sertes is going to great lengths to force Atretes to fight again. If he should find out Caleb is Atretes' son, Sertes wouldn't hesitate to use even a baby to gain what he wants. I'd hide him if I could, but Atretes would never allow me to take him away on a permanent basis."

"How can we help you?"

"Atretes needs help in leaving Ephesus. But now that I've come, I'm not sure you should become involved. Sertes is very powerful."

"More powerful than God?"

Rizpah let out her breath softly and closed her eyes. "No," she said softly. She looked at him again, somewhat embarrassed at her lack of faith. "I'm weak, John. Over the past weeks, away from your teaching and my brothers and sisters, I've slipped repeatedly. Living with Atretes is . . . difficult." How could she explain to a man like John how Atretes affected her? "He trusts no one. Me, least of all."

"Yet he allowed you to come to me."

"Because he saw no other way to gain the information and help he needs to leave Ionia. I don't mean to criticize him, John. It's just that he's led such a hard, violent life. He's so full of hatred I can feel the heat of it. Because he was betrayed by one woman, he assumes every other is untrustworthy."

"He allowed you to bring Caleb with you."

She rose, agitated. "Had Atretes breasts to feed Caleb, he would've yanked him from my arms and thrown me out the gate the first day!"

Cleopas rose. "I believe this little one needs to be bathed."

Rizpah glanced at him, embarrassed by her outburst. "I don't have any fresh linen with me," she said in apology.

He smiled. "We have some cloth that will do."

Rizpah knew he was giving her the opportunity to speak with John alone. "Thank you, Cleopas," she said softly. Nodding, he left the room with Caleb.

She looked at John. "I'm sorry," she said. "I always speak before I think better of it." So many thoughts rushed through her head.

"You're not alone in having a tongue of fire, Rizpah." His mouth tipped. "Jesus called me and James *Boanerges*. Sons of Thunder."

She laughed. "You? Well, perhaps there's hope for me after all."

"You've given your life to Christ, and rest assured, he will mold and make you into the vessel best designed to his purposes."

"Yes, but I wish I knew what that purpose was."

"You do know. God's will isn't hidden away like the myths and philosophies and knowledge of the world. Jesus told us openly and daily what his will for us is. Love one another. *Love one another.*"

"But how? You can't even imagine the kind of man Atretes is."

"Love the Lord your God with all your heart and with all your soul and with all your might. In God we live and move and have our being. In God, we *can* love one another."

She nodded. It would take God to overcome her trepidation where Atretes was concerned. It would take God to protect her from the forces she felt moving around him.

"Jesus also told us to go and make disciples of all the nations," John said, "baptizing them in the name of the Father and the Son and the Holy Spirit, teaching them to observe all that he commanded us."

"Oh, John," she said and closed her eyes. *And so I must go to Germania, Lord? I must make Atretes a disciple? How?*

"Cast your burdens on the Lord. He will sustain you."

"It's ludicrous to think *I* could ever bring Atretes to a saving faith in Christ."

"Christ will bring Atretes to saving faith, if it's his will to do so. Not you. Your call is to show Atretes God's love, just as Shimei showed you."

Her eyes filled. Shimei. Blessed Shimei. "I understand," she said softly.

He knew she did. "Pray with me," he said and held out his hands to her. She came to him, and they knelt together.

The fear and tension began to ebb from her as she listened to John's strong yet gentle voice. Surely the apostle's prayers would be heeded more than hers. He was faithful and full of confidence in the Lord, while her own mind and heart were divided by turmoil. He had walked with Jesus.

I am weak, Lord. Forgive me. Please protect Caleb and raise him up to be zealous for you. I beseech you, Father, redeem Atretes. Bring him out of the darkness and into the light. Use me as you will.

John gave thanks for the food that had been set before them and helped her rise. A sense of serenity filled her; a peace she hadn't felt since the day John had come to her and told her that Atretes wanted his son back.

"Now," John said, smiling, "tell me what has transpired between you and Atretes." He took a small loaf and broke it, giving her half.

She poured out every encounter with the ex-gladiator, from the first moment she had met him until the last conversation in the upper room of his villa. "He must leave Ephesus," Rizpah said. "If he remains here, Sertes will find some way to make him fight again. The man has spies watching the villa every minute. He's even sent men to ask questions about *me* in the city. If Sertes finds out that Caleb is Atretes' son, I can't even begin to imagine how he might use that information against Atretes . . . and what danger it would present to Caleb." She took the pouch of gold Atretes had given her and handed it to John. "Atretes sent this. He wants to return to Germania. How far will it take us?"

John opened the pouch and spilled the gold coins into his hand. "About halfway to Rome," he said and poured them back in. He set the pouch on the table between them.

"I must get word back to Atretes that we'll need more money.

I gave my word I would be in contact with him within two days. One is already gone."

John watched her move restlessly and prayed for her silently. She peered out the window again and then drew back, her face pale. "Sertes' spy is still outside," she said. "He followed me from the villa. I tried to lose him, but . . ." A dozen consequences rose to torment her. "I never intended to bring trouble to your doorstep, John."

"Sit and eat, Rizpah. You will need your strength for what's ahead."

"All of his money is invested in his estate," Rizpah said, sitting down again.

"The Lord will provide what's needed."

"I hope the Lord will also provide maps. Atretes doesn't know how to find his way to Germania, and all I know is it's somewhere far north of Rome." She blinked back tears. "I've heard it's an uncivilized, barbaric place. If Atretes is an example of the people there . . ." Shaking her head, she held the bread clenched on her lap. "I can't believe I suggested he return. What was I thinking? Even the thought of Germania fills me with an unspeakable dread."

"The earth and all that's on it is by God's creation," John said and smiled. "Even Germania."

"I know, but it's so far from *you* and Cleopas and all the others whom I love. And I'd be alone with Atretes, dependent upon his good will." She gave a bleak laugh. "We can't be in the same room together without some kind of argument arising between us."

"Has he done you physical harm?"

"No, though he can be intimidating at times." She looked away, remembering Atretes exercising in the gymnasium.

"Are you attracted to him?"

She blushed. Lowering her head, she said nothing for a long moment. "Yes, I am," she finally admitted, embarrassed. "What's worse, he knows it."

"The Lord has put you together with Atretes for a purpose, Rizpah."

She raised one brow. "To tempt me?"

"God cannot be tempted, nor does he tempt anyone. Our own lusts entice us and carry us away."

"I haven't been carried away yet. Nor do I intend to be."

She tore off a piece of bread and dipped it into the wine. She ate the morsel, gaining time to think. Her emotions were too confused to put into the right words. She looked at John, so calm in countenence and spirit. "It isn't just Atretes' physical beauty that draws me, John. It's something deeper, something held tight inside him. He's hard and fierce and violent, but he's in terrible pain. He told me one night he remembers every man he ever killed." Tears burned her eyes. "I look at him and . . ." She shook her head. "The desire to comfort him could open the way to . . . other desires."

"Then you must guard yourself. God is faithful, Rizpah. Set your mind upon pleasing him. He won't allow you to be tempted beyond what you are able to withstand and he will provide the way of escape also, that you may be able to endure it."

"I will try to be strong."

"Don't trust in your own strength. None of us is strong in him or herself. It's the Lord who upholds us."

She rose again, restless. "I wish I could come back to Ephesus and live in the insula. Life was easier and far less complicated." Better had she never met Atretes at all, for even now, away from him, she couldn't stop thinking about him.

"There are days when I struggle, too," John said.

She turned, surprised. "You? But you're an apostle."

"I'm human, just like you are."

"There's no one else left like you, John. You're the last apostle. All the others have gone to be with the Lord."

"Yes," he said, "and sometimes I ask the Lord why I'm still here on this earth. As much as I love you and the others, oh, how I long for the day when I'll be face-to-face with Jesus again."

Rizpah heard the longing in his voice and ached for him. She saw the gray in his hair and beard, the lines of age around his eyes. She came and knelt before him. Taking his hands, she kissed them. "I'm selfish," she said in a choked whisper, "for I hope you'll be with us a while longer." She raised her head, her eyes swimming in tears. "When you've passed on, John, there'll be no one left who walked with Jesus, who touched him and heard his voice. You're the last living witness of the Christ."

"No, beloved," he said. "That's why God gave us the Holy Spirit, that each one of us who accepts him as Savior and Lord may become a living witness to his love." He took his hands from hers and cupped her face. "As you must be a living witness to Atretes."

She closed her eyes. "I'm a poor witness."

"God takes the poor, foolish things of this world to bring glory to his name. Jesus wasn't born in the exalted halls of kings, but in a stable." He put his hand on her shoulder. "We are all one in Christ, beloved. You know who the enemy is. Satan is a powerful adversary who knows you almost as intimately as does the Lord. He attacks through the mind and flesh, trying to separate you from Christ."

"That doesn't fill me with confidence. Who am I to fight Satan?"

He smiled tenderly. "You don't. The Lord is with you and goes before you in battle. You only have to stand firm in your faith. Remember Paul's letter to us. God has provided us with armor—the girding of truth, the breastplate of righteousness, the sandals of the gospel of peace, the shield of faith, the helmet of salvation, and the sword of the Spirit which is the word of God."

"I remember."

"Each piece is another name for our Lord. Christ *is* our armor. He encloses us in his protection. Remember the things you've been taught. Renew your mind in Christ."

"I know in my mind and still I struggle." She rose, moving away again. "You know how difficult my own life was before I met Shimei and he brought me to you. What you don't realize is Shimei had to constantly turn me back onto the path. He was so strong in his faith. Even when he was dying, he didn't question God." Her eyes burned with tears. "I'm not like him. I'm not like you. I lived so long in the streets and fought so hard for survival, it's ingrained in me to go on doing the same thing."

"Christ has made you a new creation."

She laughed sadly. "Then perhaps salvation didn't take because I'm the same stubborn, stiff-necked girl without a home who was stealing food in the marketplace, hiding from the gangs, and sleeping in doorways. Atretes reminds me of those days. He makes me want to fight back." She turned away. "I thought I'd changed, John, and then I find myself with a man like him and the old me is resurrected. I'm not worthy to be called a Christian."

He came to her and put his hands on her shoulders, turning her to face him. "None of us is worthy, Rizpah. It's by God's grace we're saved and given an inheritance in heaven, and not through any righteousness of our own. You *are* a Christian. Your belief in Jesus makes you so."

She gave him a bleak smile. "Would that I were a better one."

His eyes warmed. "A commonly held goal." He took her hand in both of his. "I'm confident that he who began a good work in you will perfect it."

Cleopas entered the room again, a fussing Caleb in his arms. "He wants his mother," he said, looking harried.

Laughing, she took the baby and kissed him. "He's hungry, and there's not much you can do about that." Cleopas showed her into a small alcove where she could be alone to nurse her son. As she did so, she thought of all the things John had said to her and felt peaceful. God knew what he was doing.

Forgive my doubting heart, Lord. Put a right spirit within me. Let me see Atretes through your eyes and not through the eyes of my old self. And if it be your will for us to go to Germania, well, I don't like it, Lord, but I'll go.

Nourished and bundled in soft, warm linen, Caleb slept contentedly as she rejoined John and Cleopas in the triclinium.

"Cleopas tells me I had visitors earlier this evening, before you arrived," John told her. "It would seem Atretes isn't the only one wanting to leave Ephesus."

8

Atretes stood on his balcony looking down the road toward the terebinth tree. He hadn't slept much the night before for thinking about Rizpah and his son. As soon as she had left, he had come here and watched her walk along the dusty road toward the city. One of the men sitting in the shadows of the terebinth tree had watched, risen, and followed.

"I've been followed before, Atretes. I know how to hide."

Those words filled him with unease and raised questions within him. Who had followed her and why? From what or whom had she been hiding?

He had almost gone after her then, but thought better of it. Now he wondered if he had made a mistake after all. What if she didn't come back? Could he find her? Or would her Christian friends secret her out of Ephesus?

One day had passed. He worked out ways in his mind to enter the city and look for her. He would start by finding and questioning the apostle.

"I know how to hide."

He ground his teeth in frustration, wishing he hadn't trusted her. She had his son and he didn't know where to find her. She had said she was going to the apostle, but that didn't mean that was where she had gone.

"I'll send word. I promise, on my life."

And like a fool, he had let her go. He had let her walk out of the villa with his son. *His* son.

Hadn't he trusted Julia all the while his gut instinct had told him what she was the day he had met her in the Artemision. He had gone to her anyway, allowing lust to burn away reason. He had handed her his heart on a platter, and she'd carved it up and devoured it.

And now this cursed woman comes into his life with her beautiful brown eyes and luscious curves, and what does he do? He hands over his son to her. He places his freedom in her hands. He hands over to her the means to destroy him.

Cursing, he turned away from the balcony railing. Struggling to gain control of his riotous emotions, he reentered his bedchamber. He went to the marble table against the wall and sloshed wine into a silver goblet. Draining it, he poured more.

When the pitcher was empty, he held the goblet. Mouth twisting, he stared morosely at the figures of wood nymphs being pursued by satyrs. Julia would have liked it. It would've appealed to her sense of carnal adventure.

"I'll do anything for you, Atretes. Anything."

Clenching his teeth, he squeezed until the goblet was misshapen. "Then you can die, witch. *Die* for me," he said through his teeth and dropped the twisted goblet on the tray.

Stretching out on his bed, he stared at the ceiling. It pressed down on him. He felt the walls closing in. The voices came again, voices of the men he had killed. Groaning, he rose. Dragging several furs off the bed, he went out of the room. Lagos appeared at the foot of the stairs, ever ready to be at his command. Atretes went past him without a word, striding along the inner corridor. There was no sound but the echo of his own footsteps. He went through the baths to the back of the villa. It was cold outside, a wind blowing in from the north. He strode across the yard to the heavy door in the back wall.

"All's well, my lord," Silus said. Ignoring him, Atretes flipped up the bar, yanked open the heavy door and went out.

Lagos followed, disturbed. "Did the master say how long he was going to be gone?"

"No, and I didn't ask."

"Perhaps someone should follow."

"If you're suggesting that someone be me, forget it. Did you see the look on his face? The gate will stay open. He'll come back when he's ready."

Gallus approached from the darkness. "Atretes left again?"

"He's probably heading for that cave again," Silus said.

Gallus went outside the gate. Lagos saw him signal someone and then come back inside.

Troubled, Lagos said nothing.

*

Atretes breathed easier with the night-shadowed hills around him. When he reached the knoll beyond and above the villa, he squatted on his heels and drew the furs around him. Here, beneath the expanse of the starry heavens, he felt closer to freedom. No walls to close him in. No one watching him. He could smell the earth and it smelled good. Not as good as the forests of Germania, but far better than the confines of a ludus or even a luxurious villa.

Releasing his breath slowly, Atretes lowered his head to his knees. The wine was beginning to take effect. He felt a flush of warmth and light-headedness, but knew he hadn't drunk enough to accomplish what he wanted. Oblivion. He wished he had thought to bring another wineskin with him so he could get so drunk he'd forget everything, even who he was.

He'd give everything he owned for one night of dreamless sleep and a sense of well-being in the morning. He gave a bleak laugh that sounded hollow in the darkness. Everything he had wouldn't be enough to undo the past, to give life back to those he had killed, to wipe away the grim memories and his own foul guilt. He was twenty-eight years old. He had been eight when his father had begun training him for combat. It seemed since that time combat consumed his thoughts, his actions, his very being. His talent lay in taking life. Swiftly. Brutally. Without remorse.

His mouth curved bitterly. *Without remorse?*

He had felt no remorse when killing warriors from other tribes who had dared enter Chatti boundaries. He had felt no remorse when killing Romans who had invaded his homeland. He had felt triumph when he had killed Tharacus, the first lanista at the ludus in Capua where he had been brought in chains.

But the others? He could still see their faces. He couldn't forget Caleb, the Jew, kneeling before him, head tilted back. Nor could he obliterate the face of the Chatti clansman he had killed during his last battle in Rome. The boy's words still reverberated in his mind. *"You look Roman, you smell Roman . . . you are Roman!"* What had it felt like to be a child running free in the woods? He couldn't remember. He tried to remember what his young wife, Ania, had looked like and couldn't. She had been dead more than ten years now, a faint memory of a life that no longer existed, if it ever really had. Perhaps he had dreamed those happier times, a trick of his imagination.

He closed his eyes tightly and felt the darkness close in around him.

"Out of the depths I have cried to you, O Lord; Lord, hear my voice!"

The words came back unbidden, fleeting, springing from his anguish. Where had he heard them before? Who had said them?

Soft light filled him as he remembered Hadassah standing in the opening of a cave. He wished she was here with him, that he could talk with her, but she was dead by now. Another casualty of Rome.

"Though he slay me, yet will I trust in him," she had said of her god the last time he saw her. She had been in the dungeon beneath the arena, awaiting her own death. *"God is merciful."*

He looked up at the night sky and other words came back to him in a soft whisper.

"The heavens tell of the glory of God, and their expanse declares the work of his hands."

He buried his head in his hands again, trying to press the words away. Hadassah was another of his burdens, another whose life had slipped through his hands. If her god had such power, if he were really the "one true God" as she and Rizpah claimed, why had he allowed Hadassah to die? No god worth following would allow such a faithful follower to be destroyed! But the fact that Hadassah's god had let her down didn't bother Atretes so much as the fact that *he* had let her down as well. Hadassah had saved his son, and he had let her die. Had he stayed he couldn't have saved her, he knew that—but he could have stood beside her and died with her. That would have been honorable. That would have been right.

Instead, he had chosen to live in order to find his son.

And then he had let him go again.

Atretes closed his eyes and lay back against the cold ground. "One more day, Rizpah, and then I'm coming after you," he said into the stillness. "One more day, and you die."

9

John sent Cleopas and another young man to bring those who had come earlier, seeking advice about leaving the city. Within a few hours, the apostle's house was crowded with men, women, and children. Of those who arrived with their families, Rizpah knew only Parmenas, the beltmaker.

Parmenas arrived with his wife, Eunice, and their three children, Antonia, Capeo, and Philomen. The beltmaker owned his own shop in which he displayed the *cingula* for which he was best known. These elaborate belts made for members of the Roman army served as badges of office. The apron of decorated leather strips protected the soldier's groin in battle and, when the soldiers marched, made such a horrific sound as to spread terror through most adversaries.

John introduced others as they arrived. Timon, who bore the marks of a savage beating, was a fresco painter who had run into difficulty when he had been summoned by a priest of the Artemision and been commanded to paint a fresco honoring Artemis.

"I refused. When he demanded a reason, I told him my conscience forbade me creating anything honoring a pagan goddess. He was less than pleased with my answer."

His wife, Porcia, held their children close, looking distressed and fearful. "Some men came into our home last night and destroyed everything."

"They made my mother cry," one of the boys said, his dark eyes on fire. "I'd like to make them cry."

"Hush, Peter," Porcia said. "The Lord would have us forgive our enemies."

The boy looked mutinous, as did his younger brother Barnabas, while little Mary and Benjamin clung to their mother's sides.

Prochorus was a baker, and with him were his wife, Rhoda, and his sister Camella with her daughter Lysia. The man looked harassed, less by persecution for his faith than by the two women who stood on either side of him. Neither looked at the other. Lysia was the only member of the family who looked serene.

Four young men arrived, having heard from others that a band of Christians were leaving Ephesus. Bartimaeus, Niger, Tibullus, and Agabus, all not yet twenty, had already received the blessings of their families to go out into the world and spread the gospel. "There are voices enough here," Niger said. "But what of Gaul or Britannia?"

"We want to spread the good news to those who haven't heard it yet," Agabus said.

The last man to arrive was Mnason. Rizpah was immediately impressed by his manner of speech.

Eunice leaned close. "He's a well-known *hypocrite*," she said in a whisper and smiled. Rizpah noted the way her eyes shone as she spoke. Apparently the woman was quite pleased at the prospect of being in the company of a renowned actor. "He's called frequently to perform readings before the proconsul and other Roman officials. Isn't he handsome?"

"Yes, he is," Rizpah agreed, though she thought him somewhat affected. Mnason was a man of obvious dignity and polish, his voice proclaiming careful training and deliberation. He drew attention and was comfortable with it, almost expecting it. "Mnason recited one of King David's psalms to guests of the city clerk who'd gathered for a feast the night before the Plebeian Games," Eunice said softly, lifting little Antonia onto her lap.

"Which song did he recite?"

"Psalm two. 'Worship God with reverence, and rejoice with trembling. Do homage to the son.' At first, the guests thought Mnason was giving honor to their newly deified emperor, Vespasian, and his son Titus, now our illustrious caesar. Others suspected otherwise. Someone demanded an explanation, but Mnason said his courage failed him at that point. He told them the writer had been inspired of God, but that he did not know which god and the meaning was for each man and woman present to discern for themselves. 'If you have ears to hear, you will hear,' he said. Most of the guests thought it a riddle then and made a game of guessing. There were some who were not amused."

Porcia joined them. "I don't think Mnason should go with us. He'll draw attention to us."

Rizpah thought Mnason would draw far less attention than

Atretes. The German would overshadow Mnason in an instant. Atretes wouldn't even have to open his mouth or utter a word. His physical beauty was enough to command attention and his fierce charisma fascinated.

"The only ship taking on passengers is one from Alexandria," Cleopas said. "It's scheduled to leave in two days, weather permitting."

"What's its destination?" John said.

"Rome."

"Rome!" Prochorus said in dismay.

"Have you ever heard Mnason recite?" Eunice asked Rizpah.

"No, I haven't," she said, wishing the woman would pay more attention to her two sons, Capeo and Philomen, who were arguing over a toy, and leave her alone to hear what the men were saying.

"The Lord blessed him with a remarkable voice and memory," Eunice said, oblivious to her sons' squabblings, her eyes fixed in admiration on Mnason. "When he became a Christian, he was hungry to learn as much Scripture as he could, and he did. He can recite over a hundred psalms and he knows Paul's letter to our church in its entirety. When he's reciting, I feel as though I'm hearing God's voice."

"I've heard the persecution is worse there," Parmenas was saying.

"Are we going to Rome, Mama?" Antonia said, confused and frightened by the heightened emotions of the adults in the room. Eunice kissed her cheek. "Wherever we go, the Lord will go with us," she said, smoothing the child's hair back.

"How can we go to Rome?" Porcia said, her face pale and strained. "Who will protect us?"

"The Lord will protect us," Mnason said, having overheard her remark.

"As he's protected us here?" Porcia said, her eyes filling with tears. "As he protected Stachys and Amplias? As he protected Junia and Persis? As he protected Hadassah?" she pressed, listing fellow Christians who had been sentenced to death in the arena.

"Hush, Porcia," Timon said, embarrassed by her outburst.

She wouldn't be hushed. "You've been beaten, Timon. Everything we've worked for has been destroyed. Our lives have been threatened, our children tormented. And now we're to go to

Rome where they make Christians into torches to light the arena for their games? I'd rather go into the wilderness and starve."

Little Mary began to cry. "I don't want to starve."

"You're upsetting the children, Porcia."

She drew the two little ones close. "What of our children, Timon? Mary and Benjamin are too young to even understand what it means to believe in Jesus as Lord. What happens if—"

"Enough!" Timon commanded, and she fell silent, her mouth working as she fought her tears.

Rizpah put her hand over Porcia's and squeezed. She understood the woman's fears very well, for Caleb was her own primary concern. Hadn't she come here to John in an effort to find a way of protecting Caleb from being used by Sertes? She wanted Caleb to grow up strong in the Lord and not in captivity as a pawn used against his father. If Atretes or Sertes took him from her, he would never have the opportunity to know the Lord.

O God, show us a way to bring our children out of this. What would it be like to live in a place where one could worship freely without fear? What would it be like to see buildings rise to the glory of God rather than to some empty pagan idol? Rome tolerated every religion conceived by man and denied the very living God who had created her and the world in which her inhabitants lived. Rizpah closed her eyes.

Almighty Father, you created the heavens above and around us. All other religions are man's attempt to reach God. The Way is God's attempt to reach man, giving up his throne and becoming incarnate. Every religion man created brought him into bondage while Christ stood arms outstretched in love, already having set men free.

O Father, why are we so blind? In Christ Jesus, we are free. We need not fear anything. Even a slave can have wings like an eagle and soar into the heavens. Even a slave can open his heart and God will dwell within him. Why can't we accept the gift without question and be convinced that no walls, no chains, not even death itself can hold captive the mind, heart, and soul that belongs to Christ?

It took hearing Porcia's fears to make her see her own failings where she herself too often erred.

You are my sustenance, Jesus, my life. Forgive my forgetfulness.

She felt joy bursting within her, a swelling bright and warm that made her want to cry out in exultation.

"Even fear can be used to God's good purpose," John was saying, his gentle eyes on Porcia. "I was afraid of death the night they took Jesus from the Garden of Gethsemane. I despaired when I watched him die. Even after I knew Jesus had arisen, I knew fear. When my brother James was cut down by the sword on Herod's order, I was afraid. Jesus had given his mother into my keeping, and I and the brethren needed to get her out of Jerusalem to safety. I brought her here to Ephesus, where she remained until she went to be with the Lord."

He smiled sadly. "We've all known fear, Porcia, and still do at vulnerable moments in our lives. But fear is not of God. God is love. There is no fear in love, but perfect love casts out fear. Jesus Christ is our refuge and our fortress against any and all enemies. Trust in him."

Rizpah could feel Porcia relaxing beside her. John's words of assurance were a mere reflection of the assurance of Christ within him. It was impossible not to believe in the presence of the apostle. But what about later?

Timon came and stood behind his wife, one hand on her shoulder, as they all listened to the apostle speak. Porcia put her hand over Timon's and looked up at him.

"Persecution drove us from Jerusalem," John said, "but Christ used it to good purpose. Wherever we go, be it Ephesus, Corinth, Rome, or even as far as the frontiers of Germania," he said, smiling at Rizpah, "the Lord himself goes with us. He is our provision as we carry the gospel to his children."

Germania, she thought. Surely, it could not be the barbaric place she had heard it was.

As the men talked over plans to leave Ephesus and Ionia, Rizpah gave in to exhaustion. Curled on her side, Caleb held close, she slept. Some time later, Caleb awakened her, hungry. As she rose, she noted that someone had covered her with a blanket and left the brazier burning. The others were gone. As she nursed Caleb, she went to the window and looked out. The man was no longer standing beside the building down the street.

Cleopas entered. "You're awake."

"He's gone," she said, turning from the window.

"Someone replaced him several hours ago. The new man is in the *fanum* across the street. Sit. You'll need to eat before you leave. You haven't much time before you must return to Atretes, and I've much to tell you before you go. I'll awaken Lysia. She's agreed to exchange clothing with you. She's going to leave with a bundle Caleb's size. Hopefully, the man outside will follow her." He left and returned a few minutes later with a tray of food and a pitcher of watered wine. While she ate, he explained the details of what had transpired the night before while she slept.

"The final arrangements are being made as we speak. All you need to do is take the information to Atretes and be at the ship by midnight tomorrow."

"Do any of those accompanying us know how to reach Atretes' homeland?"

"No, but John has gone to speak with a man who was in Germania ten years ago. His name is Theophilus and he mentioned wanting to carry the gospel to the frontier. If he chooses to go with you and Atretes now, he can guide you. If not, he'll be able to draw out a map and give instructions of how best to reach his destination."

"I don't think I've met him."

Cleopas smiled. "You would remember him if you had."

10

Atretes walked through the open, unguarded gate late the following afternoon. He entered the back of the villa and strode through the baths and gymnasium to the inner corridor. Lagos was sitting in the kitchen, eating a modest meal while talking to the cook when their master entered. Both were startled to see him. "My lord!" Lagos said, bumping the table as he rose.

Picking up a loaf of unleavened bread, Atretes tore off half and sat down to eat. Within a few minutes, the cook had placed a plate of fruit, sliced meat, and boiled eggs in front of him. Atretes glanced at Lagos as he peeled an egg. "Did Rizpah return?"

Lagos frowned slightly. "No, my lord. I thought you sent her away."

"I did."

"Do you wish me to send for her, my lord?"

"Would you know where to send?" he said dryly.

"Wherever you instruct, my lord."

Atretes barked a dark laugh and ate the egg. The woman be cursed. He knew where the apostle lived. He would start with him. When he found her, she would wish she had never been born.

In silence, he finished the rest of the food that had been placed before him. Scorning the elegant silver goblet, he drank the wine from the pitcher. Emptying it, he slammed it down, making both slaves jump. Glowering at them contemptuously, he wiped his mouth with the back of his hand as he rose. "Send Silus to my room," he said and left.

By the time the guard arrived, Atretes had changed into a fresh tunic and was tying the leather strips of his heavy belt. "We're going into the city," he said, picking up a dagger and shoving it into its sheath.

"I'll send for more guards, my lord."

"No. Just you. More guards will draw attention." He pushed the knife into the belt and donned a long flowing Arabic robe. "The woman Rizpah took something I want back."

"Rizpah, my lord? She was here a short while ago."

Atretes' head came up sharply. "Here?"

"At the gate, not more than an hour ago." The color was seeping from his face. "She said she wanted to speak with you, but I sent her away."

"Without telling me?"

Silus stood rigid, whitefaced. "You cast her out, my lord. Your orders were very clear."

Atretes said one short, exceedingly foul word. "Where is she now? *Speak, you fool!*"

Silus swallowed. "She left, my lord."

"Which direction did she go?"

"I don't know, my lord," he stammered. "She turned away and I closed the gate."

Atretes grabbed him by the throat, his heart pounding a battle beat. "Then I suggest you go and find her, *fast*," he said through his teeth and shoved him back.

Silus left quickly, the sound of his cingulum jangling loudly as he ran down the corridor to the stairs. Atretes strode out on the balcony and scanned the road. Rizpah was nowhere to be seen. Swearing, he turned and came back inside. Impatience burned through him, he threw off the robe and shouted out a string of German curses.

The house was still and utterly silent. Undoubtedly, the servants had already run for their usual hiding places.

Atretes strode out onto the balcony again. The gate stood open. Silus was running down the road toward the city. Atretes clenched his teeth in frustration.

"Atretes," came a hushed voice behind him. He swung around and saw Rizpah standing just inside his doorway, a finger to her lips. She closed the door quietly as he came inside.

Annoyed at the way his heart jumped at the sight of her, he was terse. "You're late!"

She gave a soft laugh of surprise as he strode toward her. "I wasn't exactly greeted at the gate. I had to sneak in."

Atretes resented the rush of strong emotions he felt. She was flushed, her eyes bright. Worse, she seemed perfectly at peace, while the last two days of his life had been filled with torment. "Silus said he turned you away. How'd you manage to get in?"

He sounded as though he wished she hadn't come back. "Someone left the back gate door open." She unwrapped the shawl sling as she crossed the room. "You?"

"An oversight." He hadn't thought about it when he had come in from the hills this morning.

She smiled up at him as she placed Caleb on his big bed. "If it hadn't been left open, I'd have climbed the wall." His son gave a gurgling laugh and kicked his legs, obviously happy to be loosed.

"I was about to come looking for you," Atretes said, putting his hand on her hip and nudging her aside so he could pick up his son.

Rizpah noted the dagger tucked into his belt. "Were you planning to slit my throat when you found us?"

"I was considering it," he said and grinned into Caleb's face as the babe tried to grab his hair. He nuzzled the child's warm neck, relieved to have his son back in his possession.

"You can trust me, Atretes."

"Maybe," he said without looking at her. "You kept your word. This time." He put Caleb back on the bed again. Drawing the sheathed dagger from his belt, he dropped it beside his son. Caleb rolled onto his side and reached for it.

"What are you doing?" Rizpah gasped, moving quickly to take it away.

Atretes grasped her wrist. "Leave it."

"I will not!" She tried to jerk free.

He was amazed at how fragile her bones felt and was careful not to hurt her. "He's not strong enough to pull the dagger free."

"It's what it represents," she said and tried to reach for the weapon with her other hand. Atretes yanked her back. She glanced up at him and went still. His blue eyes stared into hers. She couldn't fathom what he was thinking, nor was she sure she wanted to know. His gaze drifted, causing worse upheaval within her.

"He's the son of a warrior," he said, looking at the curve of her mouth, "and will be a warrior himself one day."

"He needn't start training at seven months."

His mouth curved wryly as he ran his thumb lightly across the smooth, soft skin of her wrist. He allowed her to jerk free. She turned from him abruptly, took the dagger from Caleb and set it firmly on the table beside the bed. Caleb, stripped of the new and intriguing toy, rolled onto his back and cried petulantly. Rizpah quickly took a wooden rattle from a fold in her belt and shook it over him. The sound distracted him briefly, but when she put the toy in his hand, he shook it once and sent it sailing past her head.

Atretes smirked. "He's *my* son."

"He certainly is," Rizpah said dryly, watching Caleb's face turn red as he wailed louder.

Atretes' mouth tightened. He took the sheathed dagger from the table and held it in front of her face. "It's looped," he said. "Do you see?" He flicked the leather strap with his index finger and tossed the dagger onto the bed beside Caleb. When she started to reach for it again, he caught her arm and spun her around. "Leave him be. He can't hurt himself with it. Now, tell me what you've learned over the last two days."

She let out her breath sharply, but made no further effort to take the weapon from her son. Atretes would only give it back to him. "We can sail for Rome tomorrow morning at dawn. All we have to do is make it to the ship."

"Good," he said, a surge of excitement spilling through his blood. He was going home! "I take it the money I gave you was enough."

"Enough to take us part way, but you needn't worry. John and the others have seen to the rest of the expense."

He frowned, a muscle tightening in his jaw. "The others? What others?" His eyes darkened. "How many people did you tell about these plans?"

"There are twenty—"

"*Twenty!*"

". . . going along with us." She raised her hands at the look on his face. "Before you explode and lose all reason, *listen*." She told him of the others' plights as quickly as she could. When she finished counting off the various members of the party, all except one best left unmentioned until unavoidable, Atretes uttered one word in Greek that made her cringe and then blush.

"And I'm to guard this little band of yours," he said, glaring at her.

"I didn't say that. We will be in their company."

"I'd rather go alone."

"If that's your wish, I bid you God's speed. Caleb and I will remain here."

His eyes caught fire.

O Lord, I've done it again! She shut her eyes briefly and then looked up at him. "Atretes, would you discard the welfare of others as your welfare was so easily discarded by Rome? Would you allow them to be used as you were used? Their need to leave

Ephesus is great," she said. "If they remain, they'll end up in the arena."

A muscle jerked in his jaw, but he said nothing.

"Rome is becoming less and less tolerant toward the Way," she said. "Officials on all levels misunderstand our faith. Most believe we preach rebellion against the Empire."

"Rebellion?" Atretes' interest quickened.

"Rome holds up its emperor as a god, but there is only one God, Christ Jesus our Lord, who died for us and rose again. Jesus himself told us to yield unto Caesar what belongs to Caesar. We pay taxes. We obey the laws. We give respect where respect is due and honor where honor is due. But we yield our lives and works to the glory of the Lord. Because of this, Satan has moved them to destroy us."

Only one thing Rizpah said made any sense to Atretes. "Rebellion," he said again, tasting the word and finding it sweet as revenge. "So, if this faith spreads throughout the Empire, it could bring Rome to its knees."

"Not in the way you mean."

"It could weaken her."

"No, but it could take the sword from her hand."

Atretes laughed softly, the sound chilling. "Take the sword from Rome and death follows."

Rizpah had never seen his eyes more alive or on fire. "Not death, Atretes. Transformation."

"We'll travel with them," he said in decision. "Anything Rome fears, I'll protect."

She started to speak, but a knock came on the door.

Atretes strode over. "Who knocks?" he demanded, his head near the door.

"Gallus, my lord. Silus hasn't found the woman yet."

"She's here with me."

Caleb gurgled happily as he gummed the leather sheath.

"He'll be much relieved, my lord. Did she bring your son back?"

Rizpah tensed at the question. "Atretes, don't . . ."

He opened the door and Gallus saw her. "She brought him. Go back to your post for now. We'll need you later tonight."

"She will return to the city, my lord?"

"I'll be going with her." Closing the door, Atretes turned to her. He frowned slightly. "What troubles you?"

103

She shook her head. "Perhaps I'm becoming like you. Distrustful. I wouldn't have told anyone in this household that Caleb was here or that we were leaving tonight. Least of all Gallus."

His eyes narrowed. "I bought him out of the ludus. He owes me his life."

She bit her lip, saying nothing. She had suspected there were spies within the household. She knew Gallus was one. Once, while standing on the balcony of the room next door, she had seen him speak to a man through the small window opening in the gate. A moment later, that man had walked away, joining another beneath the shade of the terebinth tree. They had spoken briefly, and then one man had headed down the road for Ephesus. Atretes himself had told her later the men at the tree were Sertes' spies. She had wondered then if Sertes had spies other than Gallus within the household, watching and reporting everything Atretes said and did.

Now, looking at Atretes' cold face, she wished she hadn't said anything about her suspicions. She was afraid of what he might do about them.

"We can leave without saying anything more," she said. "He doesn't know our destination."

Atretes stepped past her. Crossing the room, he moved into the shadows near the balcony and looked out.

Caleb fussed, and Rizpah sat down on the bed to distract him. She nibbled playfully at his toes, his laugh making her laugh. He lost hold of the sheathed dagger, and she talked to him as she carefully slipped it out of reach and sight. What a loathsome toy to hand a child.

Atretes still stood near the balcony, looking out, saying nothing. She was disturbed by his cold concentration. Why had she spoken?

Atretes muttered a curse and turned.

"What is it?" she said.

"You were right," he said, striding across the room.

Her heart jumped in alarm. *What cost my careless words, Father?* "Wait!" She rose and ran to the door, standing in front of it to bar his way. "Where are you going? What are you going to do?"

"What needs doing," he said and yanked her roughly aside.

"Atretes, please . . ."

"Feed the babe and get him ready to travel."

"Atretes, *don't*...."

The door clicked shut behind him.

When Rizpah tried to open it, Atretes pulled it shut again and locked it. "Be silent," he commanded when she called his name again.

※

Atretes went down the steps quickly and strode through the atrium. He took the corridor that led to the gymnasium instead of the one leading to the front door. He would deal with Gallus later. Right now, he had to prevent word from getting to Sertes.

He took a framea from the wall as he passed through the gymnasium. He strode into the baths, passed between the pools, and went outside to the back gate. When he was beyond the wall, he ran along it, around to the south side, away from the road, where Gallus and Silus wouldn't take notice of him.

He caught up quickly to the man Gallus had spoken to by the gate. He was alone on the road and walking fast, carrying his information to Sertes. Atretes recognized him from the ludus.

"Gaius!" he called, and the man turned sharply. When he saw Atretes, he froze one split second before he started to run. His hesitation proved fatal, for the framea hit him in midstep and sent him crashing forward into the dust.

Grabbing the dead man by the arm, Atretes dragged him off the road and left his body behind some brush.

Retrieving the framea from the body, Atretes looked up at the sun and judged the time left before sunset. Another two hours. Now that Gallus' message to Sertes had been circumvented, they could wait for dusk.

※

When he opened the door and entered his bedchamber again, Atretes saw Rizpah standing in the shadows near the balcony, looking out. She turned sharply, her face ashen and blotched from weeping.

"Oh, thank God," Rizpah said, relief washing over her at the sight of him. Gallus was still standing at the gate. "I was so afraid you were going to kill him. I prayed you wouldn't bring sin upon yourself because of my . . ." Atretes just stood there, staring at her, his face without emotion, his eyes lifeless. Her relief evaporated. "Where did you go?" she said tremulously. "What's happened?"

He turned from her. "We'll leave when the sun goes down." He took the sheathed dagger from the bed and shoved it into his belt. He turned to her again, his eyes like blue glass, cold and lifeless. "Don't try to warn Gallus. Remember that Caleb's life is in the balance."

Filled with tension, Rizpah fed Caleb, washed him and rewrapped him for the journey into the city. Atretes said nothing over the next two hours. She had never known a man to be so silent and still. What was he thinking?

"Stay here," he commanded and went out into the corridor, shutting the door behind him. She heard him shout for Lagos, and then a moment later, he issued a series of impatient commands. He wanted a sumptuous meal prepared immediately. He wanted Pilia bathed and perfumed. "Tell her she's to dance for me."

Rizpah thought he had gone mad.

"How much gold coin is in the villa?"

Lagos told him.

"Bring it to me. I want to count it for myself."

"Yes, my lord," Lagos said, accustomed to Atretes strange, dark moods. He departed and returned within a few minutes.

"The back gate was left open this morning," Rizpah heard Atretes say. "Tell Silus to stand guard there until I tell him otherwise." Every servant in the household was given something to do. "The gold first. Go!" Atretes said, and Rizpah could hear Lagos' sandals slapping hastily along the marble-tiled hallway.

Atretes opened the door and strode across the room to take up a plain cloak. Donning it, he then tied the pouch of gold coins inside the heavy leather and brass-studded belt. She realized then what he had done. He had sent the servants on errands that would keep them away from the upper corridor and the atrium. Shaking, Rizpah scooped up Caleb and tied him carefully into her shawl.

"Come," he said and she followed.

Atretes preceded her watchfully down the steps. No one noticed their departure until they left the house and crossed the barren courtyard.

Gallus came out of the shadows and stood waiting for them.

Her heart pounded heavily as she looked up at Atretes' cold face. "Atretes—"

"Shut up," he snapped in a ruthless whisper. "One word out of you and by all the gods, I'll . . ." He left the threat hanging unfinished in the darkening air.

Gallus moved from his post by the front gate. "Shall I summon Silus and the others, my lord?"

"No. You'll do." Atretes stepped past him and pushed the gate open himself. He jerked his head for Gallus to go ahead. Rizpah glanced up, and he caught hold of her arm, squeezing painfully. "When I order you on ahead, you go."

"Atretes, for the love of God . . ."

He gave her a hard shove out the gate.

They walked down the road past the terebinth tree. No one was there. They continued on, rounding the bend in the road out of sight of the villa. "Stop here," Atretes commanded Gallus. "Go on ahead, Rizpah."

"Atretes."

"*Go!*"

Gallus looked uneasy. "Shall I accompany her, my lord?"

"No." Atretes grabbed her arm, yanked her around to face the road, and shoved her hard. Atretes watched her walk away. She paused once and glanced back. She knew what he was going to do. Better that she didn't see the deed done. He swore at her. "*Do as I commanded you!*" Bowing her head, she clutched Caleb to her bosom and hurried her steps.

"I thought you were going with her, my lord."

Atretes waited until she rounded the curve before turning to answer. "Is that what you told Gaius?"

Gallus' eyes changed. "My lord, I swear I—"

Atretes hit him in the throat, crushing his windpipe. "Gaius is dead." Gallus sank to his knees, choking and gasping. Atretes yanked the guard's helmet off and gripped his hair. Drawing Gallus' head back, he glared into the man's terrified eyes. "Join your friend in Hades." He drove the heel of his hand into Gallus' nose, snapping the cartilage and sending it like a spear into his brain. Gallus fell back, convulsed once in the throes of death, then went limp.

Atretes glanced up and saw Rizpah standing frozen in the curve of the road. As he stepped over Gallus' body, she turned from him and ran.

11

Atretes caught up with Rizpah easily. When he took hold of her arm, she cried out and tried to escape him. "O God!" she cried out. "God! God!"

He jerked her around and caught hold of her flaying hands. "I told you to go on ahead."

"You murdered him. You—"

Atretes clamped his hand over her mouth. She struggled wildly, waking Caleb in his securely knotted pouch against her breasts. Horses were coming, and Atretes had no time for gentleness. He hit her. As she sagged, he caught her up in his arms and strode quickly into the shadows well off the road. She was stunned only briefly and within moments began struggling again. "Shut up unless you want to get us all killed," he hissed in her ear. She made no sound after that and Caleb quieted with her—but Atretes could feel her trembling.

A company of Roman soldiers rode by. Atretes swore under his breath as he watched. He had forgotten Romans patrolled the road. They would come upon Gallus' body within minutes.

"We must go *now*," he said, pulling Rizpah up. She was shaking violently, but didn't resist him. He kept hold of her arm, half supporting, half shackling her to his side as he strode along the road. He wanted to put as much distance between himself and the soldiers as possible.

Rizpah stumbled, and he realized the pace he set was too difficult for her. Two of her steps barely matched one of his.

Gritting his teeth, he slowed enough to let her catch her breath.

"They're coming back," she gasped, the sound of horses coming from behind them.

"If they stop, say nothing. I'll do the talking."

"Please. Don't kill any . . ."

His fingers dug into her arm. "What would you have had me do? Let him warn Sertes of my leaving Ephesus? What do you think would've happened then? I killed two men tonight. How many more do you think I'd have to kill to be free again?" She lifted her head and he saw the bright sheen of tears. "Keep your head down so they don't see your face."

He started walking again, forcing himself to a more leisurely pace this time. His heart beat harder and faster as he heard horses coming up behind him. He touched the hilt of his dagger and was satisfied it was handy, then turned slightly, showing the proper amount of respect and curiosity.

When they came closer, Atretes moved to the side of the road and waited. Only two. The others were nowhere in sight.

"Atretes, please don't. . . ." He looked at her, and her mouth went dry.

"It's late to be on the road," one of the soldiers said as he came toward them.

Atretes looked up at him. "We've been walking since morning. We hoped to make it before dark, but . . ."

Caleb began to cry softly.

The soldier's horse sidestepped and pranced nervously. "Traveling with a baby tends to slow one down," the soldier said. "Any trouble along your way?"

"We've not been troubled, but there was a man lying dead in the road about a mile back."

"Yes, we know."

"The sight upset my wife."

"Did you see anyone suspicious?" the soldier said, coming closer, studying him.

"I didn't linger long enough to look around. My apologies, but my one thought is to get my wife and son to safety."

"We'll see you to the city gates."

Atretes hesitated only for an instant. "I'm sure my wife will appreciate the reinforcement," he said in a tone that gave nothing of his feelings away. He looked at her and the cold humor in his expression shocked her.

The two soldiers rode on either side of them. Rizpah wondered if the one riding closest to her could see how she was shaking. Atretes slid his hand down and took hers. The strength of his grasp was clear warning to keep silent. The soldier beside Atretes asked where they had come from, and Atretes named a village some distance from Ephesus. "We've come to pay homage to the goddess, Artemis."

The city gates loomed ahead. "You'll be safe enough from here," the soldier said.

"Our thanks to you," Atretes said with a deep bow, the mockery lost upon the guards. The soldiers swung their horses around and started east again. "Roman scum," Atretes said and spit on the ground.

Swinging around, he led Rizpah through the darkened alleyways of the city. She didn't question him, too burdened with her own tormented thoughts. There was a quicker way to the harbor, but she wasn't in a hurry to board a ship with Atretes. Was it really God's will that she be with this man?

When they finally reached the docks, she was physically exhausted. "Which ship?" Atretes said, speaking the first words that had been uttered between them in hours.

"One with Poseidon on the prow."

They walked along the docks looking for it amidst the confusion of men loading and unloading ships.

"There," Atretes said, pointing it out to her. It was much like the vessel that had brought him to Ephesus.

"There's John," Rizpah said, feeling relief so acute she wanted to run to the apostle. Atretes caught hold of her arm and stopped her from doing so.

"Say nothing of what happened. Put it from your mind."

"Put it from my mind? How?"

"I told you to go on. Do you remember? I didn't mean for you to watch."

"Not seeing would have made it all right?" She tried to escape his grasp, but his fingers tightened. "Let go of me."

"Not until you swear to me."

"I swear no oath to anyone." She turned her face away, the image of Gallus lying in the road permanently etched in her mind. "I wish I hadn't looked back." She looked up at him again, angry and grieving. "I wish I hadn't seen what you're capable of doing to another human being."

"You've only seen part of it," he said through his teeth.

She felt cold. One minute, Gallus had been standing alive in the road. The next, he was lying dead in the dust. There had been no great struggle. No shouting. No cursing. No accusations or defenses. "I've never witnessed anything so blood-chilling in my life, even when I was living in the streets. You haven't an ounce of mercy in you!"

"No mercy?" Something flickered in his eyes and then they went dead again. "I could've broken every bone in his body and then dispatched him to Hades where he belongs. As it was, I killed him in the quickest way I knew how." Two short, swift punches. "He hardly felt anything."

"And now he's lost."

"Lost? He was found out. Woman, he deserved to die."

"*Lost* for all eternity."

"Like a thousand others. Like you and Caleb and me if *he'd* lived."

"Not like *him*," she said. "You don't even know what I'm talking about. You don't even know what you've done!"

His face was cold with disgust. "You cry for him?"

"He was unsaved and now he's dead. Yes, I cry for him. You murdered him without offering him the least chance."

"Chance to do what? Betray me again? I didn't murder him. I *executed* him. Had I let him live, I'd have forfeited my freedom and life as well as that of my own son. Should I have let him live? May his bones rot!"

"We could've left without him knowing."

"He'd already passed information to Gaius. How far do you think we'd have gotten if Sertes had gotten that information? Where do you think Caleb would be right now?"

The blood drained from her face as she realized where he had gone early in the evening and what he had done. Not one but *two* men were dead because she had spoken. "God, forgive me," she said, covering her face. "O God, forgive me. I should've told you nothing."

Angry, Atretes caught her wrists and pulled her hands down. "Forgive you for what? For protecting my son from captivity? For protecting *me*?"

"For giving you an excuse to kill again!"

"Lower your voice," he said in a harsh whisper, glaring at a man who glanced at them. Atretes drew her behind some crates. "You warned me of something I was too stupid to see for myself. You kept all of us out of the arena."

"And that makes everything all right?" she said in a voice choked with tears. "Two men are dead because of me. Better that I had kept my suspicions to myself."

"Where do you suppose the boy would be right now if you'd kept silent?"

"Where he is now, without blood on his father's hands!"

Atretes swore in frustration. "Woman, you're a fool. You

know nothing about anything. All three of us would be in the ludus."

"We're both free...."

"Do you think Sertes cares about your rights or mine? He has friends in high position, friends with more political power than your apostle and all his followers put together. One word in the right ear, and your freedom would end like that," he said and snapped his fingers in her face. "You know what happens to the women working in the ludus? They're passed around to whatever gladiator deserved a reward. Maybe I would've gotten my turn with you, too. Eventually."

She tried to pull free.

"That shocks you, doesn't it?" Atretes said, jerking her back again. "Didn't you know that's what a gladiator gets when he's performed for his master?" His mouth twisted into a sardonic smile. "A woman to couple with while the guards watch through the bars. Not a very pleasant prospect for a woman of your sensibilities, is it? But then, don't think for a minute Sertes would care."

She wanted desperately to block out his words and the frightening possibilities they created in her mind. "Even if all you say is true, it doesn't make what you did right."

His face paled in anger. "I killed two men tonight. For good cause and without regret. How many more would I have had to kill to get my son back if I'd gone to the arena? And if *I* was killed, what use might Sertes find for a child then? Caleb could have ended up in one of those booths under the arena stands, or do I have to explain them to you as well?"

"No," she said faintly, unable to bear hearing more.

"Then save your pity for those who deserve it." He let go of her in contempt.

"God would have shown us a way, Atretes. I know he would have."

"Why would your god show me anything?"

"Because he loves you, just as he loved Gallus and the other you killed tonight."

He grasped her chin. "Tell me, woman. Does your heart bleed as much when you think of the man who betrayed your Christ?"

His words cut her, spreading an infection of doubt. "I share the blame for what you did."

He let go of her abruptly. "Then be absolved," he said sardonically. "Gaius' and Gallus' blood is on my head, not yours. As is the blood of better men I killed before them." He turned her toward the quay again.

As they wove their way along the quay amid the activity of men loading and unloading ships, Rizpah sensed Atretes wanted to hold back rather than hurry. She glanced at him and saw his gaze fixed upon the apostle.

My God, she prayed in distress, *what do I say to this man to make him understand? Father, bring him up out of the pit or I know he'll pull me down into it with him.*

"Say nothing," Atretes said heavily.

"Nothing is done in secret."

"As you wish," he said bitterly. "Tell him and see if it matters."

Rizpah glanced up at him and thought he looked oddly vulnerable. "I was speaking of the Lord, Atretes, not John."

John came to meet them. He took her hands and kissed her cheek. "The others have boarded ahead of you. They have bedding for you as well as supplies for the journey. Did you encounter trouble?"

"No," Atretes lied.

John gave them each passage papers.

Rizpah clutched the document that proclaimed passage had been purchased and struggled against tears. She had never been away from Ephesus and now she was journeying to Rome and then on to Germania. With a murderer.

John touched her cheek. She closed her eyes, pressing her own hand over his. She wouldn't see him again, and the prospects of the future looked dark and fearsome right now.

"The Lord will be with you wherever you go, beloved," John said gently.

"Give me the boy," Atretes said, holding out his hands.

Rizpah wanted to hold Caleb closer, but relinquished the sleeping baby to set Atretes' mind at rest.

Babe in arms, Atretes looked at the apostle. "My thanks," he said gruffly. "I never expected to receive help from you."

John smiled. "The Lord uses unexpected ways and means to rescue his people."

"But then I'm not one of his people, am I?" His gaze flickered to Rizpah, then he stepped onto the gangplank and left them standing on the dock.

"I think he's hoping I'll stay here," Rizpah said. "Perhaps I should."

"He took Caleb to make sure you didn't."

Rizpah looked up at the apostle, all her fear and misgivings showing. "Oh, John, I don't know if this venture is God's will or Atretes'. I've never known a man with a darker soul." It was on her tongue to blurt out what Atretes had done, but she kept silent. It wasn't her right to reveal another's secret. *"Their blood is on my head . . . as is the blood of better men I killed before them."* His angry words had been filled with anguish.

Her heart cried out a desperate, silent prayer, for she realized she ached more for him than for the two men he had killed. Was she already sinking into a mire? Would her growing attraction to Atretes be the undoing of her faith in Christ?

"Stand firm, beloved," John said gently. "We ourselves were once deceived. We were no different than he is now. We lived in disobedience, hateful and hating. Stand firm in the truth. Christ has redeemed us from every lawless deed and purified us for his good purpose."

"But Atretes . . ."

"Is anything too difficult for God?"

"No," she said because she knew it was the expected answer.

"Let the light of Christ so shine in you that Atretes will see your good works and glorify Christ Jesus. In all things show yourself to be a pattern for him. To the pure, Rizpah, all things are pure. As you are pure in Christ. Speak of these things to him. Speak of the things that will edify and light his way out of darkness."

"I will try."

"Don't try. Do it." He smiled, full of confidence. "Love him as Christ loved you, beloved. Bear Atretes' burdens. The Lord will finish the good work he's begun in you." Seeing her tears, he cupped her face. "Know the presence of the Holy Spirit is in you at all times. Yield to him. God will show you the way." He kissed her forehead. "And I will pray for you."

She smiled tremulously. "I shall need and be thankful for every prayer you utter." She embraced him, clinging to him briefly before she let go. Embarrassed by her weak faith, she took his hand and kissed it before she turned away.

As she went up the gangplank, she saw Atretes above her. How long had he been standing there, waiting? Holding Caleb in the crook of one arm, he held his hand out to her. Hesitantly, she took it. His fingers closed firmly around hers as he gave her support down the steps onto the deck of the ship. His expression was veiled, his mouth hard.

"I didn't say anything," she said. "What happened is between you and me and God." Surprised, she felt his grip relax as though her words had relieved his troubled thoughts. The muscles in his face eased as well, making him look less wary and distant.

"Do you want to take him back?" Atretes said, shifting so she could retrieve the baby from his arms if she chose to do so.

She recognized the peace offering and offered her own. "He looks content in his father's arms."

Atretes looked into her eyes then. It was a full look that made her pulse jump and her face fill with heat. Disturbed by it, she looked away.

John was on the dock below. She drew comfort from his presence, for he had always offered safety and godly wisdom. Now, he was leaving, milling his way through the workers toward the streets of Ephesus. Watching John disappear among the crowd, she felt utterly alone and frightened.

"If I can learn to trust you, maybe you could learn to trust me," Atretes said wryly.

One of the ship's officers approached and demanded their passage papers.

"Rizpah!" Porcia said, coming to her in relief. "I was so afraid you wouldn't come in time. The ship is due to sail in a few hours."

Rizpah embraced the woman briefly before introducing Atretes. Smiling, Porcia looked up at him. "We are pleased to count you among our members," she said, but her words and smile died. Atretes looked down at her without expression, his blue eyes unblinking. Rizpah could feel Porcia's rising misgivings.

"There are only fifty-seven passengers on the ship, so we'll have plenty of space," Porcia said as others approached, greeting them. Everyone was clearly interested in Atretes, but he responded not at all. He stood, his son in his arms, silent, grim, and forbidding. He looked around once, as though eager to escape, whether from the ship or the people, Rizpah wasn't sure.

"We didn't have time to bring anything," Rizpah said.

"John and Cleopas gave us bedding and supplies for you," Parmenas said.

"Are there many other passengers besides us?"

"About twenty-five to thirty. A few Illyrians and the rest Macedonians," Mnason said. "The ship's loaded with expensive cargo destined for Corinth. You can smell the spices from Sheba. The crates the stevedores are loading now are full of purple fabric from Kilmad and the finest embroidered linens from Aram."

"There are rugs from Canneh as well," Timon said.

Mnason laughed. "Do you suppose the captain would allow us to unroll a few?"

"Has everyone in our party arrived?" Rizpah said.

"We're short one member," Prochorus said.

"Theophilus," Porcia said, her brow furrowed as she glanced toward the stairs. "What do you suppose is delaying him?"

"Be at ease, Porcia," Timon said, soothing his wife.

"The ship won't wait for him."

"John said he'd come and he'll come, though I suppose, if he doesn't make it, he'll be safer than any of the rest of us here in Ephesus. The city clerk is a personal friend."

Atretes' eyes narrowed. "Who is this Theophilus of whom you speak?"

Rizpah put her hand lightly on his arm. "He's the man who's agreed to show us the way to Germania," Rizpah said.

His gaze swept the others and he jerked his chin at her. "We should find a place for ourselves."

"You can join us, Atretes," Tibullus said, his youthful face warm and friendly. "The crew showed us a place where we can set up a tent to protect us from the winds."

"I remain with Rizpah and my son."

Rizpah's face flooded with heat. The others stood around them, silent, shocked. Had he no thought of what the others might misconstrue about their relationship? What was he thinking? Or perhaps he knew exactly what he was about. "I'll be with the women, Atretes."

His mouth tipped sardonically. "A wife's place is beside her husband."

Her face flamed. "I'm not your wife."

"No, you're not, but I assume these women are traveling with *their* husbands and I highly doubt they'd appreciate your intrusive company."

An embarrassed silence followed as everyone seemed unable to think of anything to say. Too angry to speak herself, she wondered if he meant to make matters worse for her.

Camella pressed forward between Prochorus and Timon. "I heard what you said, Atretes, and you're quite right. Rizpah, I'm traveling with my brother and his wife, and I'm sure they would appreciate it very much if *my* intrusive company was removed from their midst." She smiled at Rizpah. "I'd be delighted if you joined me and my daughter Lysia. Come. I'll show you where we've put our things."

"Thank you," Rizpah breathed in relief, eager to depart.

"Bartimaeus and the others aren't far away," Rhoda said, and Camella's eyes flickered slightly. Rizpah sensed Rhoda's remark was made less to reassure Atretes than to suggest impropriety on the part of her sister-in-law.

"If you'd prefer we remain with you, we'll do so," Camella said, ignoring Rhoda and speaking directly to her brother.

The poor man looked harassed. "Do as suits you best, Camella."

"By all means, do as suits *you* best," Rhoda said under her breath and turned away.

Caleb began to fuss. "Take him," Atretes said, dumping him in her arms.

Rizpah followed Camella. Crew members paused to grin at them.

"Atretes isn't a Christian, is he?" Camella said, ignoring a sailor who made a comment to her as she passed.

"No, he's not," Rizpah said bleakly.

"Not that we're behaving as Christians ought," Camella said. She smiled apologetically. "Do you suppose it was the tension between Rhoda and me that made him so eager to leave?"

"I don't think so." She doubted Atretes cared. "It's been a difficult night." She shuddered in memory of it. She glanced back and saw Atretes had separated himself from the others. Was he thinking over what he had done tonight? Did he feel guilt or remorse? He had said he didn't, but there had been anguish in the angry words he had spoken to her on the dark road to Ephesus.

O Jesus, please, let him feel the repentance that leads to salvation. Search me, Lord, and cleanse me. Let me be a tool in your hands and not a slave to my weaknesses.

Caleb squirmed in her arms and let out a wail of discontent. "Let me get my things," Camella said, pausing to take bedding and supplies from a pile stacked against the inner wall of the deck. "There is room over there, near the mast and those barrels." She glanced at the babe in Rizpah's arms. "He sounds hungry. You feed him while I go and find the blankets John left for you. Atretes can take care of himself."

She had been gone only moments when Atretes appeared. She knew by his expression something was terribly wrong. "We've got to get off this ship."

"Why?" she said.

"Feed him later," Atretes said, looking back. "A Roman centurion just came aboard with six soldiers."

"Oh, Lord."

"*Move*, woman."

"If I stop nursing him, he'll scream, and that'll only draw attention to us," she said quickly. "Sit down beside me."

He stiffened and she heard the sound of hobnailed sandals approaching. Atretes turned slowly and he looked ready to do battle. She grabbed the hem of his tunic as she saw the soldiers. The leader was speaking with Parmenas and the others.

"Do nothing," she said, rising quickly. Caleb cried when she stopped feeding him. Her heart was hammering wildly. "Please. *Wait*."

"We've been betrayed," Atretes said as the centurion turned and looked straight at him. Rizpah had never seen such a look of fear and rage in Atretes' face. "They won't take me alive this time."

"Atretes, don't!" she said, reaching out to stop him.

He shoved her out of his way, heedless of the fact that she held a baby in her arms. She lost her balance and fell heavily against the mast. Caleb screamed. Clutching him protectively, she found her feet again, "No!"

The centurion dodged Atretes' fist, turned sharply, and made a hard sweep with one leg. Atretes jumped back. His foot tangled in a coil of rope and he went crashing down onto the deck. Before he hit, the Roman soldier had his *gladius* out and pointed at Atretes' throat.

"Don't kill him!" Rizpah said in anguish. "Please!"

The Roman centurion stood motionless, poised and ready. He

was as tall and as strongly built as Atretes. "I didn't come to kill him," he said gruffly.

Atretes felt the tip of the blade lift from his skin. The centurion stepped back and sheathed his gladius in a smooth, liquid movement that bespoke many years of experience. "My apologies, Atretes. A reflex action." He held out his hand to assist him to his feet.

Ignoring it, Atretes rose on his own.

"Stand at ease," the centurion said. He removed his helmet and tucked it under his arm. He was a distinguished looking man with hair graying at the temples and a face deeply tanned and lined. "My name is Theophilus," he said to Rizpah and Atretes. Then his eyes met Atretes' angry glare, and a faint smile curved his mouth. "I've come to show you the way home."

THE SOIL

"Other seed fell on good soil. . . ."

12

A hand squeezed Atretes' shoulder, rousing him from sleep. Above him, the square sail billowed, driving the ship before the wind.

"Will you join us for worship this morning, brother?"

Atretes opened one bleary eye and swore at young Bartimaeus, who stood over him. "I'm not your brother, boy. And if you wake me again, I swear I'll break every bone in your hand."

Bartimaeus withdrew.

Atretes pulled the heavy blanket over his head, blotting out the starlight and cold wind.

"Is he coming this time?" Tibullus asked.

"No."

"We won't give up on him," Agabus said. "Men more stubborn than Atretes have come to know the Lord."

"He said he'd break my hand the next time I woke him up. I think he really would."

"Then we'll get a pole and prod him at a safe distance," Tibullus said with an amused laugh. Pushing back the blanket, Atretes sat up. One look at his face and the three young men crossed the deck to where the others were waiting. Muttering curses under his breath, Atretes relaxed back, relieved for the moment of their irritating presence. They had stayed up most of the night talking about their dream of carrying the "good news to a dying world." What good news? And what dying world? Not much of what they said made any sense. But then, why should it? Their religion made no sense. Their god made no sense. Any deity with power would avenge the murder of his son, not forgive and adopt those who had done it.

Women spoke nearby. Caleb began crying. Flipping the blanket off, Atretes sat up again, but the crying stopped. He could tell by her position, that Rizpah was nursing his son. The babe was content against the warmth of her breast, his hunger answered. Atretes lay back, stilling his own frustration.

The woman's attitude toward him disturbed him. He couldn't stop thinking about her and wanting to explain why he had killed Gallus and Sertes' spy. He wanted her to understand. As it was, she seemed to keep her distance.

He had been furious upon meeting Theophilus and thought Rizpah had known the man was a centurion beforehand. She had insisted she had known only that he was Roman. Grudgingly, he believed her, but it hadn't improved matters between them. She far preferred the company of her religious friends than him.

He had sought her out yesterday and found her sitting in a sheltered corner, Caleb at her breast. She had been speaking softly to the babe as he nursed. She was so beautiful and serene, his heart squeezed tight. He stood unnoticed, above her and behind a barrel, watching his son suckle. The sudden longing that had swept over him had been so intense and acute he had hurt physically. He had thought all his emotions, save anger, had died long ago. Like a limb without the circulation of blood, he had been deadened. But now the blood flowed back, bringing numb emotions back to life—and with life, came excruciating pain.

Sensing his presence, she had glanced up. One look into her eyes and he had known he would never be able to say enough to make her think he had acted correctly in killing Gallus and the other. She had covered herself quickly, draping the shawl across her and Caleb as though forming some kind of protective barrier against him. Somehow, that act in itself hurt and angered him more than anything else she might have said or done. In her eyes, he was a murderer.

Perhaps he was. Perhaps that was all that was left of him. But whose fault was it? His or Rome's?

Ever since setting foot on this wretched ship, he had been cut off from her. She was always in the company of the others, more often the women. When she was by herself, circumstances were such that he knew not to seek her out. He resented the influence the others had over her. It was his son she tended, not her own or one of theirs. Didn't that give him some rights where she was concerned?

That bloody Roman centurion seemed to have no difficulty in speaking alone with her. Atretes had seen them standing on the prow of the ship, the wind whipping Rizpah's hair. She talked to the centurion easily. And often. He had seen them laughing together once and wondered if he was the subject of their humor.

Every member of the group looked to the Roman for leadership, even Mnason who had seemed only too willing for the

The Soil

attention of such an exalted position. But the Roman had quickly taken up John's standard. He rose before dawn to honor his god in praise and prayer. One by one, the others joined him until the predawn gathering had turned into a celebration!

Right now they were at it again. Atretes gritted his teeth beneath the blanket, listening. Theophilus was teaching them how to please their crucified Messiah.

"Do not be conformed to this world, but be transformed by the renewing of your mind."

"Amen," the others said in unified agreement, grating Atretes' already raw nerves.

"Exercise your gifts as the Lord directs. Let love be without hypocrisy. Abhor what is evil and cling to what is good."

"Amen."

"Be devoted to one another in brotherly love, giving preference to one another in honor. Be fervent in the Spirit, serving the Lord with joy."

"Amen."

"Persevere in tribulation, devoting yourself to prayer and contributing to the needs of the saints. Bless those who persecute you and curse you."

Atretes jaw stiffened, pricked at being reminded of the curses he had called down on Theophilus' head at their first meeting, curses he laid down every time he saw the man. He'd see Theophilus in Hades before he ever let him put a foot on Chatti land and had told him so!

"Rejoice with those who rejoice. Weep with those who weep. Be of the same mind toward one another. Do not be haughty in mind, but associate with the lowly. Do not be wise in your own eyes."

These words from a *Roman*? Atretes wanted to rise up and laugh at the irony of it.

"Never pay back evil for evil, but respect what's right in the sight of all men."

And what was right by Roman standards was to strip all men of their freedom! Hadn't they stripped him of his? What was *right*?

"Be at peace."

Pax Romana! he thought bitterly. *Ha! Be at peace with Rome? Not while I have breath in my body!*

"Be at peace with all men."

Never.

"Never take your own revenge, but leave room for the wrath of God."

I'll call upon all the forces of the Black Forest to avenge myself upon you, Roman!

"Do not be overcome by evil, but overcome evil with good."

"Amen."

"Remember, beloved, that God demonstrates his own love toward us in that while we were yet sinners, Christ died for us."

Not for me, he didn't.

"For God so loved the world, that he gave his only begotten son, that whoever believes in him should not perish, but have eternal life. For God did not send the Son into the world to judge the world, but that the world should be saved through him."

"Amen," the voices rang out joyously.

"Therefore, beloved, love one another."

"Amen."

"Love one another."

"Amen!"

"Love one another as Christ loved you."

"Amen!"

"Hear, O children of God. And know."

"The Lord is our God, the Lord is one," they said together. "And I shall love the Lord my God with all my heart and with all my soul and with all my might."

"Praise be to God!"

"Glory to God in the highest!"

"Who reigns now and forevermore!"

They began to sing, their voices blending beautifully:

> *"He who was revealed in the flesh, was vindicated in the Spirit, beheld by angels, proclaimed among the nations, believed on in the world, taken up in glory, destined to return, to him be the glory now and forever more. Amen. Amen."*

A hush fell over the lower deck as the gathering of Christians knelt in a circle and began to pass around the bread and wine. Atretes had observed the ritual once and asked Rizpah about it. She had told him they were eating the flesh and drinking the blood of their Christ.

"And you call me the barbarian?" he had said in disgust.
"You don't understand."
"Nor do I want to."
"If only . . . ," she started to say and then fell silent. He had wondered at the look of infinite sorrow in her eyes before she turned away and rejoined the others.

As she was with the others now, joining them in their gruesome rite.

Had she left Caleb in the small bed she had made for him? Had she set her duties to his son aside, forsaking him for this god of hers? He threw off the blanket and rose. If she had, he'd drag her away from that gathering of flesh eaters and give her something to pray about.

Stepping around several barrels, he saw those gathered on their knees. His son was nestled in Rizpah's arms. Beside her, a head taller, was Theophilus. Black hatred filled Atretes as he watched the Roman tear off a piece of bread and feed it to her. He followed that act by holding the cup of Christ's blood to her lips so she could drink. Then he drank himself and passed the cup to Parmenas.

Anyone watching would think Rizpah and the baby belonged to the Roman!

Atretes' heart pounded hard, hot blood surging through his veins. He clenched his teeth. Theophilus raised his head slightly and looked across the deck at him. Atretes glared at him. *I'll drink blood, and it will be yours,* he vowed.

The offensive meal completed, they began their time of prayer. They spoke softly, bringing up needs and mentioning names. They prayed for John. They prayed for Cleopas. Black Hades! They were praying for *him*. Making a fist, Atretes sent up his own prayer to Tiwaz, the sky god of Germania. *Give me the life of Theophilus! Put it in my hands that I might crush it and send him to oblivion!*

The heat rose so hot in him, he knew if he didn't move to the other end of the deck where the Illyrians and Macedonians were still sleeping, he was going to kill Theophilus without thought of the consequences.

Rizpah glanced up at him as he passed them, her expression troubled.

He stood on the windward side of the ship, the cold breeze whipping his hair and numbing his face. The ship dipped with the rolling seas and a frothy wave burst high over the prow. The sun was coming up.

The ship's captain shouted an order and sailors scrambled over the deck, readjusting ropes and securing two cargo crates that had inexplicably come loose. Another salty wave shot over the prow and Atretes spread his feet, bracing himself. Better the roar of the sea and stinging cold than the quiet voices and communal warmth of a group of religious fanatics.

Gripping the side of the ship, Atretes saw land in the distance. "What is it?" he shouted above the storm to a sailor nearby.

"Delos!"

The clouds opened and rain pounded the deck and him. Cold and soaking wet, Atretes remained where he was, stubborn, cursing life itself.

Rizpah appeared. Caleb wasn't with her. He turned to her, angry. "Where's my son?"

"In the shelter where it's warmer."

"Alone?"

"No."

His blood went hot. "Who's with him? The centurion?"

She blinked, surprised. "Camella is watching him."

"Camella. The mother who never had a husband."

She turned away. Atretes caught her arm. He felt her stiffen at his touch. "Stop avoiding me."

"It's not my intention to avoid you, Atretes."

"I can feel your resistance."

She forced herself to relax. "Why did you leave your shelter?"

"You think I should stay and listen? You think I should get on my knees with the rest of you? You think I'll follow that bloody Roman of yours!"

Her dark eyes flashed up at him. "He's not *my* Roman, Atretes, and it's the Lord we follow, not Theophilus."

"He feeds you like a pet."

"My hands and arms were full with your son. Had you been beside me, I would have taken the bread from your hand!"

His heart beat fast. He looked into her dark brown eyes and saw something that warmed his insides. When his gaze dropped to her mouth, she lowered her head. His temper rose again. "Why do you always avoid me?" he said roughly.

"I don't."

"You do. You've cut me off from my own son."

She looked up at him again, her cheeks pale from the cold. "It's you who avoid us."

"I care nothing about them," he said, jerking his chin in a sharp dismissal of the rest.

"Nor about me," she said. "I even wonder sometimes how deeply you care for your own son. Do you love him? Or is it simply a matter of having what you think belongs to you?"

"You both belong to me."

"Careful where you tread, my lord. You're paying me a denarius a day. Remember?"

He was pleased to have made her angry and grinned down at her to show her so. "You look more yourself this morning. On fire." She turned from him, and he yanked her back. Catching hold of both her shoulders, he lowered his head close to hers. "Take up your sword, Rizpah. Cross it with mine and see what it gets you. Do it. I'm sorely in need of a fight."

She said nothing, but he saw it was a struggle. Clearly, it wasn't fear that kept her silent, for he saw no evidence of it in her steady gaze. He loosened his hands, wondering if he had hurt her. It hadn't been his intent.

"I wish you would join us and hear the good news," she said with exasperating calm.

He cupped the back of her head and pulled her close, his lips against her ear. "I'll embrace you, my beauty, but I'll never embrace your god or your religion." Breathing in her scent, he let her go, satisfied to see he had rattled her.

Rizpah retreated to the tent she shared with Camella and Lysia.

From where he stood with the others, Theophilus glanced at her as she ducked inside the tent and then looked at Atretes thoughtfully.

Safely inside the shelter, Rizpah picked up Caleb. He was in a mood to play, and she needed distraction from the feelings Atretes roused in her. Her heart was still racing.

"Are you all right?" Camella said, looking at her curiously.

"Of course. Why do you ask?"

"You're shaking."

"It's cold this morning."

"You don't look cold. You look . . . alive."

Rizpah could feel the heat filling her cheeks and hoped dim light from the sunrise would conceal her embarrassment. She *felt* alive. She was trembling, her heart still pounding from the encounter with Atretes.

O God, I don't want to feel this way again, not about him!

"Lysia, why don't you go and see if Rhoda needs any help this morning?" Camella said.

"Yes, Mother."

Glancing at Rizpah, Camella picked up her blanket. "Did you speak with Atretes?" she said as she folded it.

"Is it that obvious?"

Camella set the blanket down and sat on it. "Not so the others would notice. Unless they were watching."

"Are they?"

Camella grimaced. "Rhoda is. So is Theophilus, though for different reasons. Besides," she said with faint amusement, "wherever Atretes is, everyone knows he's there."

"Who could ignore him when he's in a temper and marching past us?"

"I wasn't speaking of moments like that."

"His beauty, you mean."

"I've never seen a more handsome man, but even his beauty would pale if he didn't possess some undefinable quality as well." She took her shawl and drew it around her shoulders. "Had Theophilus not come aboard, Atretes might easily have become our leader."

"God forbid."

"Apparently, he did," Camella said with a smile and then explained. "A man like Atretes will never walk unnoticed. He'll either lead men to God or he'll lead them away."

Rizpah turned Caleb onto his stomach and watched him try to crawl. "Atretes rejects Christ."

"For now."

Rizpah looked at her. "If you can lead him to Christ, please do so. With my blessing."

Camella's smile disappeared. "I don't think so. I wouldn't dare get so close." She gave Rizpah a self-deprecating smile. "I know myself. I succumb too easily to fleshly passions. Lysia is evidence of that, though I'd rather give up my life than not have had her. And most of the others have their own struggles, too. I know you've noticed the way Eunice looks at Mnason, how she always seems to end up near him, oblivious to how it looks to anyone. Even Parmenas." She shook her head sadly.

"No, we have too much already to face. I think Atretes is going to be up to you."

Peter and Barnabas ran in front of their shelter, playing a lively game of some sort, as they usually did each day. "Can't catch me! Can't catch me!" Peter shouted. Barnabas, following, caught his foot in the rope that held their shelter secure and almost brought it down.

"Boys!" Camella said in irritation.

Sometimes their youthful zest was extremely annoying, as it was now, when their ruckus frightened Caleb and started him crying again. Rizpah picked him up and comforted him. Something fell over not far away, and she wondered what destruction the boys had caused this time. Yesterday, when the weather was clear, they had annoyed the sailors with their racing back and forth and getting in the way. When Timon had finally interceded and told them to play something else, Peter had worked at the knots holding several crates.

"Atretes reminds me in some ways of Lysia's father," Camella said when the boys had run back toward the others. "Handsome, commanding, virile. Am I embarrassing you? I won't speak of him, if you'd rather I didn't."

Rizpah wasn't sure if she meant Lysia's father or Atretes. "Somewhat," she admitted ruefully. "Though not for the reasons you might think. I'm no stronger than you, Camella."

Camella recognized the acceptance offered, as well as the confession. "Good." She put her hand over Rizpah's. "We'll keep one another accountable and ward off temptation when it comes."

Rizpah laughed. Caleb had scooted as far as he could go. She picked him up and set him back down near her, so he could try again.

"He'll be crawling before you reach Rome," Camella said, watching him.

"And walking by the time we reach Germania."

"You're not eager to be going, are you?"

"Would you be?"

"Very. More than anything else, I long for a new beginning."

"You can begin anew wherever you are, Camella."

"Not when you have someone reminding you of your past every step of the way or expecting you to fall prey to the same failings."

Something struck their tent, startling them both. A ball of material rolled in front of Caleb. "Those boys, again," Camella said, picking it up as Peter appeared around the corner.

"That's our ball," he said, out of breath.

"Yes, we know. Please play elsewhere," she said tossing it to him.

He darted away, out of sight but not out of hearing.

*

The weather changed for the better. Peter and Barnabas were running along the deck, weaving around people and sometimes bumping into them in their exuberance. Capeo and Philomen joined them for one round on the deck before their father, Parmenas, stopped their wild play and settled them at more peaceful games. For a little while, the children settled down, and then Peter and Barnabas began to shout and laugh and race about again, annoying every member of the crew as well as passengers too polite to do anything. Timon and Porcia made no effort to curb their offspring's activity, even when Peter knocked Antonia down.

"For heaven's sake, Porcia!" Eunice said, obviously frustrated at having the conversation she'd been having with Mnason interrupted. She bent to pick up her daughter.

"He didn't mean to do it," Porcia said in quick defense, sending Peter off again while Eunice wiped her young daughter's tears away. "Besides, you have little room to judge! Your attention has hardly been focused on your family!"

A dull red filled Eunice's face and she glanced uncomfortably toward Mnason, then fell silent.

Atretes came to stand beside Rizpah. Camella looked up at him and then glanced at her. "I think Lysia and I will take a walk around the deck," she said, taking her daughter's hand.

"You needn't leave."

"Yes, leave," Atretes said coldly.

Sorry she had said anything, Rizpah turned to look out at the sea, mortified by his rudeness. She could feel Atretes watching her and wondered what he was thinking. "Did you want to talk to me about something?" she said when the silence began to wear on her nerves. He didn't answer. "Would you like to hold Caleb?"

"Are you so desperate to distract me?"

"Yes!"

Grinning, Atretes took him. "In all things honest, aren't you?"

"I said I would be."

His mouth flattened into a hard line. "Even with yourself?" She refused to rise to his baiting. She watched her son, troubled that she had handed him over to a man who could take men's lives without the least remorse. Sometimes she struggled with it, wanting to withhold Caleb from his father. This was the first time since the dreadful night they had left the villa that Atretes had held him, other than when he had carried Caleb onboard the ship. Why had she handed him over so eagerly? Just to distract Atretes' interest in her? She half expected, half hoped, Caleb would put up a fuss. He didn't. Instead, he grabbed the ivory chip around his father's neck and chewed on it. He looked at the interesting object and then pounded it on his father's chest. "Da . . . da . . . da . . ."

Atretes' expression changed markedly. Forgetting her, he began to talk to his son. All the world-worn hardness left his face, and Rizpah glimpsed the man he might have been had circumstances been far different. He spoke softly, German words she couldn't understand. But the tone was easily understood.

Atretes lifted Caleb above his head and jiggled him, drawing a delighted sound from the little boy. Rizpah stood by, watching, pierced.

Someone ran into her from behind, and she uttered a sharp gasp of pain and fell forward against Atretes. Atretes lowered Caleb quickly, holding him secure in one arm as he steadied her with the other. Barnabas tried to dart around the side of her, but Peter was too fast.

"Caught you!" Peter shouted triumphantly, giving his younger brother a hard shove.

"Not fair! Not fair!" Barnabas complained and the two boys began arguing loudly.

Atretes thrust Caleb into Rizpah's arms. Making a sweep of his foot, he sent both boys crashing to the deck. "Ouch!" Barnabas cried out. Bending down, Atretes caught each one by an ankle and lifted them high and right over the side of the ship.

"No!" Rizpah cried out in fright, sure he meant to drop them.

Barnabas screamed in terror, arms swinging wildly for some hold and finding none.

"It's time you two learned a lesson!" Atretes said and shook them hard enough to make their teeth rattle. When he stopped, Barnabas screamed louder, but Peter dangled, shocked into uncharacteristic silence, eyes huge.

Hearing the commotion, everyone turned, Porcia and Timon last of all. When Porcia saw Atretes holding her sons by the ankles and dangling them overboard, she screamed and ran toward them, frantic to reach them before they met a watery death. "Someone stop him!"

"Atretes, please don't," Rizpah said, hardly able to breathe.

"No one would miss two worthless, yapping little curs!"

Barnabas went on screaming while Peter hung upside down, limp and, for all appearances, determined to die with more dignity than his younger brother.

"Timon!" Porcia wept. "Do something!" She looked around wildly for her husband, who was hurrying after her, his face ashen.

Atretes gave Barnabas a hard shake again. *"Be silent!"* Barnabas stopped screaming as though someone had grabbed him by the throat and squeezed off his air.

Everyone stared. No one dared move, not even Porcia who had reached the side of the ship where Atretes held the boys and stood weeping and wringing her hands. "Don't drop them," she wept. "Please don't drop them. They're only babies. Whatever they did, they didn't mean to do."

"Shut up, woman. You are a fool."

He lowered the boys as though ready to drop them and everyone caught their breath. "You're going to listen, aren't you?"

"Yes!"

"You will not run or shout or fight anywhere on this ship. If you do, I'll feed you to the fish. Do you hear me?"

Hair hanging, eyes huge, they nodded quickly.

"Repeat what I just told you."

They did.

"I want your word on it."

Barnabas jabbered it out, while Peter answered solemnly.

Atretes let them dangle a moment longer, and then swung them high and dumped them on the deck at their mother's feet. Porcia gathered her sons quickly to her.

Two of the soldiers laughed and several members of the ship's crew cheered. One passenger called out that Atretes should've dropped them while he had the chance.

"As for you two," Atretes said to Porcia and Timon, "tend your children, or the next time I will heave them overboard, and you right after them!"

Porcia drew them up quickly and away from Atretes. "Don't go near that man again. Stay as far away from him as you can. He's a barbarian and he'll kill you." Her words were loud and clear enough for many to hear.

A muscle jerked in Atretes cheek. He looked around in cold challenge at those staring at him.

Barnabas cried and clung to his mother's skirts, but Rizpah noticed Peter hung back, gazing up at Atretes with rapt adulation. She glanced up at Atretes and saw he noticed the boy as well. He smiled faintly and jerked his chin for the boy to go.

Timon cupped the nape of his son's neck and shoved him along the deck behind his mother and brother. "Listen to your mother."

Turning away from those still looking at him, Atretes put his hands on the ship's rail. She had never seen him look more grim. She moved to stand close beside him and he looked down at her in surprise. His expression darkened. "What're you smiling about?"

"You," she said, the floodgates of her heart opening.

His eyes narrowed, distrustful of the warm glow in her brown eyes, even more wary of the hunger he felt for her acceptance. "They deserved it."

"You wouldn't have dropped them."

"No?" He almost reminded her that only a few nights before he had killed two men in cold blood.

"No."

"So you think you understand me?"

"No. I don't understand you at all," she said frankly. "But I know enough about you to make a new beginning."

She put Caleb back in his arms.

13

The ship reached Corinth without incident. Theophilus and the soldiers removed the trunk being sent to the emperor while the slaves, who had manned the oars from Ephesus to Corinth, unloaded rugs, aromatic spices, and amphorae of wine, and loaded them into wagons for the journey over the isthmus. *Sburarii* unloaded the sand ballast for the Corinth arena. It would be replaced on the other side of the hill with grain destined for Rome.

Once stripped, the ship would be dragged from the water. It would take days to haul the *corbita* the few miles to the Savonic Gulf where it would be launched in order to continue the voyage to Italy. Nero had begun work on a canal through the faulted limestone of the isthmus, but the work had stopped upon his death, making the arduous overland trek still necessary.

The slaves strained at the ropes of a ship nearby. Sweat glistened on their brown bodies as they labored to pull the ship up a amp. Weeks of travel south and west into the Mediterranean would be saved by taking the ship overland. September had come and gone and the sea was notoriously dangerous by November. Crossing the windswept plateau might be bothersome and difficult, but it was safer than challenging the elements.

Atretes was little interested in the details of unloading and moving ships. He had been restless, confined on board one. Now he was tense from the level of activity on the docks and nearby city streets. Corinth was too much like Ephesus. Marbled temples rose grandly, piercingly white in the sunlight. Wandering auctioneers and town criers advertised goods and rewards for lost slaves. Wholesalers jammed the ports, and ships captains traded spices for honey, drugs, and perfumes to take to Rome.

While everyone gathered their belongings, Bartimaeus, Niger, Tibullus, and Agabus told the others they had letters from John to deliver to members of the Corinthian church. Mnason left in their company.

"Atretes is waiting for you," Camella said as they walked together.

Rizpah raised her head and saw him far ahead. His manner toward her had changed subtly, giving her cause for caution. She knew she would be faced with her own temptations. Would she be wise in her choices, heeding the quiet voice of God? Or would she be like Eunice, hankering after sin?

The wind rippled Atretes' clothing and tossed his blonde hair. He stood for a long moment, looking at her. Turning away, he went on. Even at this distance, she could sense his annoyance. Did he expect her to run and catch up to him? She was saddened that he was so determined to remain aloof from the others, yet thankful as well. She did not think he had overheard the grim news about the church in Corinth, or witnessed Eunice's struggles. She hoped not, anyway. He would judge the Christian woman faithless. Eunice was a weak and foolish woman who toyed with sin without even realizing it.

Atretes paused again.

"I think you'd better go," Camella said.

"I can't keep his pace."

Camella gave her a droll smile. "You'd better reach an understanding now, before you're on your way to Germania."

Rizpah shifted Caleb in her arms. "I can't allow myself to worry about tomorrow, Camella. Today's trouble is more than enough."

Camella laughed. "Well, it appears there are some who crave his company," she said as they both watched Peter run up the hill.

The boy captured Atretes' grim attention. He was talking rapidly. Atretes listened briefly and then turned and started walking again, ignoring him.

Porcia looked frantic. "Peter! Stay away from him." Her son gave her a quick wave of acknowledgment and ran to catch up with Atretes again. "Do something, Timon!"

"I'll get him," Barnabas said and raced up the hill after his older brother. When he caught up, he fell into step with Peter, dogging Atretes' footsteps.

"I think they'll be all right," Timon said and returned to his conversation with Prochorus. Porcia caught Benjamin's hand in a firm clasp when he started after Peter and Barnabas. "Lysia, would you please carry Mary for me?"

"Yes, ma'am," Lysia said, eager to please.

Camella chuckled. "Well, at least the children aren't afraid of him."

Rizpah watched the two boys trotting alongside Atretes. They behaved like excited puppies. He didn't slow down to accommodate them, but kept on, shoulders set, head high. After a while, the boys slowed, unable to keep up. Barnabas came back to Porcia and Timon, but Peter continued on, following Atretes. Shoulders set. Head high.

"Peter!" Timon called finally and signaled for him to come back. The boy's countenance fell, but he obeyed. Soon Atretes was out of sight.

Theophilus returned from the garrison where he and the other soldiers were staying for the night. He had made lodging arrangements for the others and showed them the way to an inn overlooking the port and gulf. The establishment catered to travelers waiting for ships to be pulled over the isthmus.

"Rest here," Theophilus told them. "The food is plentiful and good. The proprietor's name is Arrius. He's not a believer, but he's sympathetic. I'll send word when the ship is launched and the captain's ready to board passengers."

As the others entered the gate, Rizpah remained behind.

"Atretes is down at the port," Theophilus said.

"You spoke with him?" she said hopefully.

"No. Had we been somewhere away from others, I would've tried, but he's itching for a fight. It wouldn't be to his best interests to allow it to happen within sight of a garrison. He'd find himself back in a ludus. Or worse, he'd be crucified."

She was disturbed by his words. "You wouldn't fight him, would you, Theophilus?"

"It may come to that."

"But he'd kill you."

"If God allows."

"He's been trained to fight."

His mouth turned up ruefully. "So have I." He started to walk away and then turned back. "Right now, you have more influence over Atretes than anyone. Use it."

Influence? She wanted to laugh at the implausible idea that she could change Atretes' thinking. She entered the inn. She nursed Caleb, changed his soiled wraps and let him play on a blanket while she washed his swaddling clothes and hung them to dry in the small partitioned area allotted to her, Camella, and Lysia.

Lysia sat down on the blanket and played with Caleb. Smiling, Camella watched her daughter.

The young men returned from their errand late in the afternoon. Agabus reported Mnason's chance encounter with an old friend whereby he had decided to remain in Corinth.

"He has a troupe of players, and one of the leading hypocrites died of a stomach ailment a few days ago. He worked with Mnason in Antioch and was very pleased to find him in Corinth," Tibullus said.

"Mnason played the same part in Ephesus not more than a month ago and still remembers the lines," Niger said.

"Which he began to recite right there before the baths." Tibullus grinned. "Everyone who heard him was impressed."

"He's decided to stay here rather than go on to Rome," Agabus added, "and asked us to extend his love to all of you. He'll pray for us."

"Perhaps we should think about staying in Corinth," Eunice said.

Her remark drew a sharp glance from her husband, Parmenas. "We're going on to Rome."

"But we might encounter worse persecution there than we did in Ephesus. The church meets openly here."

"Because they've watered down the gospel to make it palatable for the populace," Niger said grimly. "We attended a service yesterday and were appalled at what they're preaching."

"Two Nicolaitans were professing their philosophies," Agabus said.

"With the approval of the elders," Tibullus added.

"There were notices posted of classes offered," Niger went on. "One is being taught by a self-proclaimed prophetess who's teaching the freedom of Christ means we can enjoy pleasures of *any* choosing."

"Did you correct them?" Timon said.

Tibullus gave a bleak laugh. "We spoke with several deacons. Two agreed with us, but half a dozen others were openly hostile. They said we were meddling."

"One said I have a very narrow, plebeian view of Christ's love," Niger said. "He said Christ told us to be at peace with all men, and therefore that means we can't condemn anyone's practices. Some of these Christians have turned the freedom of Christ into license to do all manner of evil."

"Those who have ears will hear what the Spirit says," Timon said.

"Those I met were deaf," Niger said.

"You only met with them for a day. You shouldn't judge," Eunice said in quick defense.

"I never meant to imply we were," he said, dismayed.

Tibullus looked grim. "Sometimes one day is enough to discern truth from lie, Eunice. The Holy Spirit tells us. The gospel being preached in that church doesn't resemble the gospel according to Jesus Christ. And I'll tell you, one day in that church was enough to understand why they're meeting openly without persecution: There's no difference between them and the world."

"We've had our difficulties in Ephesus," Prochorus said.

"True, but we had John to hold up the standard of Christ and correct us."

"Don't the Corinthians read the letters Paul sent them?" Prochorus said.

"Not anymore," Tibullus said.

"One of the two elders we spoke with who agreed with us said that the last time they read one of Paul's letter to the congregation, there was a general feeling of discomfort."

"They recognized their own sin and didn't like being reminded," Niger said. "Many of them protested."

"Better the discomfort that leads to repentance and restoration than temporal comfort and eternal damnation," Timon said.

"Unfortunately, they appear to have chosen the latter."

"What if the church in Rome is the same as the one here?" Porcia said, distressed.

Timon put his arm around her. "We'll know when we get there."

"And if it is?"

"We hold to the truth of the gospel. We have copies of Paul's letter to Ephesus and John's letters."

"The church in Corinth isn't dead yet," Tibullus said. "There are still two elders who are retaining the pure gospel. I think John was writing to them about false teachers."

"What can so few do when struggling against so many?"

"Don't forget who is on their side," Tibullus said, grinning at her. "Christ has overcome the world. The world will never overcome him."

"But what about Mnason?" Eunice said. "We should warn him and encourage him to accompany us."

Parmenas' face darkened. "You think too much about Mnason."

"He's our brother."

"And our *brother* has *decided* to stay in Corinth. We're going to let him."

A taut silence fell over the group, and then they discussed other things. Eunice stood tight-lipped. Capeo, Philomen, and Antonia gathered close around her. She glanced back toward the gate once. As she did so, Parmenas called his children to him. They obeyed quickly, leaving their mother standing alone, outside the group. She hugged her arms around herself, looking bereft and confused.

"I think she's about to meet her judgment," Camella said with dismay.

"I pray not," Rizpah said. She had seen Eunice's infatuation for Mnason grow. Mnason had noticed as well. It was to his credit that he had removed himself from the path of temptation. But would Eunice choose to leave well enough alone? And would her husband forgive her in either case?

Rizpah prayed silently for them.

Lysia giggled as Caleb sneezed. Rizpah smiled, fond of the young girl. "Would you watch Caleb for me for a while?"

"Oh, can I?" Lysia said, delighted. Camella nodded, reassuring Rizpah that she would be near.

As she crossed the courtyard to the main gate, Peter ran to catch up with her. "Are you going to talk to Atretes?"

"I'm going to try."

"Can I go with you?"

"I'm not sure your mother would agree, Peter."

"Mama!" he shouted across the courtyard of the inn. "Can I go with Rizpah?" Busy tending Benjamin and little Mary, Porcia was too distracted to be bothered and waved approval. "See?" Peter beamed up at her.

"I'm not even sure where Atretes is, Peter. I have to look for him at the port."

"I'll help you find him." He started out the gate ahead of her. Resigned, Rizpah put her shawl over her hair and followed. The street was crowded with people traveling to and from the port. Goods were being carted both ways.

"There he is!" Peter said and darted off.

Rizpah saw Atretes sitting in a fanum, staring straight at her, his face as cold as the marble that surrounded him.

Atretes curbed his annoyance as he saw Peter running to him. He wasn't in the mood for his chatter. "We were looking for you, Atretes," the boy said, entering the fanum.

"Were you?" He gave the boy a cursory glance and fixed his attention on Rizpah again as she walked toward him. She was perfectly formed, slender, yet fulsome. Her black hair was modestly covered, but wayward strands escaped to frame her lovely face. Men noticed her, though she appeared oblivious to their admiring glances.

She stopped just outside the fanum, her dark, luminous eyes meeting his. "There's a place for you at the inn," she said.

He allowed his gaze to drift. "Is there?" He wondered if she was aware of the effect she had on him.

When she didn't answer, Peter looked up at her. "Why's your face all red?"

Atretes laughed and ruffled his hair. "Go back to your mother and father, boy."

"But . . ."

"*Go.*" It was a command this time.

"I'll get lost," Peter said, still resisting.

"Follow the road back up the hill. Unless you're a baby who needs a woman to hold your hand."

Peter obeyed. "There's a booth near ours," he said, walking backward. "You can sleep there."

"Was that necessary?" Rizpah said when the boy was out of hearing.

"You'd rather I didn't send him away?" he said, pretending to be obtuse. His eyes gleamed. "I'll call him back if you feel safer with him around."

"You deliberately embarrassed me," she said, curbing her annoyance with him.

His smile turned sardonic. "Is it what I said or what's in your own mind that embarrassed you?" A faint frown flickered across her face, and he tilted his head slightly, his smile challenging. He half expected her to go back to the inn and the safety of her friends. Instead, she stayed, though clearly nervous about doing so. Something was on her mind.

"We need to talk."

"If you want to talk, come inside and sit." He noted she

entered the fanum as though entering a lion's cage. She sat down on the marble bench opposite him and folded her hands primly in her lap.

"We need to reach some kind of understanding before we go any further."

Atretes' mouth curved slowly. "We haven't gone anywhere yet."

"Please consider my words seriously, Atretes."

"Oh, I am serious, deadly serious," he said coolly, unwilling to question why his emotions were roiling. He knew the kind of understanding he wanted, but doubted she would be agreeable. The truth have it, he would be disappointed in her if she was.

"What will be our relationship when we reach Germania?"

"What will it be?" He lifted a brow.

She clasped her hands more tensely. If only his face were not so shuttered and his tone so mocking. "I'm not exactly a servant, but I'm not . . ." She grimaced, searching for words.

"A wife, either," he said for her. She was beautifully formed, more beautiful, he imagined, than Julia had been.

Her color heightened. Even Shimei had never looked at her with such raw hunger. Her body responded to what she saw in Atretes' eyes, and heat spread. With it came realization. "I've given you the wrong impression," she said and rose.

"Where are you going?"

"Back to the inn," she said, eager to escape. Before she could, he caught hold of her wrist.

"Why?"

Her breath was constricted. "Let go, Atretes. This isn't a good time or place for us to talk about anything."

"Because you haven't got a baby in your arms?" He rose. "Do you feel vulnerable without your human shield?"

"Caleb isn't a shield, but at least when I'm holding him, you see me as a mother and not as . . . as . . ."

"A woman?" He ran his thumb along the smooth, silky skin of her wrist and wondered how the rest of her would feel. His own pulse was hammering, rousing his defensive anger. "You asked me a question. How about this answer? By the time we reach Germania, my son won't need a wet nurse."

"He'll still need a mother."

"A *foster* mother of his own kin." The bones of her wrist felt as fragile as a bird's, but far less fragile than what he saw in her dark eyes. He had hurt her deeply with his cutting words. Worse, he had frightened her. He let go of her.

Rizpah sat down on the bench again because her legs wouldn't hold her. She fought back tears.

Atretes silently cursed himself. He wanted to say he was sorry, but the words choked him. Why had he lashed out at her? To avenge himself for what others had done to him? Or for what he had felt when he saw her walking down the street toward him?

She looked up at him, her brown eyes swimming. "I have left home and country behind, Atretes. Have I done so that you might take Caleb from me when we reach yours?"

In truth, Atretes could imagine no other woman caring for his son but her. "No," he said. "I won't take him from you. I swear on my sword."

She reached out impulsively and took his hand between both of hers. "I believe you without your oath."

Leaning back against a marble pillar, he looked down at her, eyes cold, everything else hot. When she released his hand, he was disappointed—and grateful. She made him feel vulnerable, and he didn't like it.

She rose again, disturbed by his enigmatic stare. "Come back to the inn with me, Atretes. You belong with us."

"I think not."

"Theophilus is with his men at the garrison," she said, thinking that might be the reason he hesitated. "Please." She held her hand out to him. "Don't stay out in the cold when you're welcome by the fire."

When he took her hand, she smiled at him and turned to step outside of the fanum. His grip tightened, keeping her inside. "Not yet."

She looked up at him in question and then her eyes went wide, instinctively warned even before he pulled her into his arms. She stiffened and opened her mouth to protest. Cupping the back of her head with one hand, he covered her mouth with his own, kissing her with all his pent-up passion. He pulled her body closer and felt her hands pressing for freedom. He felt as well her warmth and the wild beat of her heart against his own.

Satisfied that she was no less affected than he, he released her. "Do you still want me to come back with you?"

Rizpah stepped back, trembling and trying to get her breath.

"The arrangements are the same as they were on the ship," she said, clutching the front of her tunic and wishing she could quiet the clamor of her heart.

"What about being welcome by the fire?" He lightly brushed her burning cheek.

She slapped his hand away. "If you can't behave properly, perhaps it would be better if you stayed here!" Swinging around, she left him alone in the fanum.

Laughing, Atretes caught up with her. "I was behaving properly," he said, falling into step beside her. She'd never be able to outrun him. "For a *barbarian*. Or would you prefer I handled you like a *berserker*? I've been called that, too."

"Don't handle me at all."

"Why? Because you liked it too much?"

She stopped and faced him, looking more distressed now than angry. "Because it doesn't mean anything to you."

"And it does to you?"

Face aflame, she left him standing in the road. He caught up again, but made no further comment. She felt his amused glance and thought she had never met a more insensitive human being.

Peter was at the inn gate, Barnabas with him. They ran to meet them and fell in alongside Atretes, affording Rizpah escape. Atretes followed her into the courtyard, muttering a curse as Tibullus and Niger came to greet him. He had thought he was rid of them. "We'll be sleeping over there, Atretes," Agabus said, joining them.

Atretes looked over the younger man's head to see where Rizpah went. She joined Camella and her daughter on the opposite side of the courtyard. Removing her shawl, she knelt on the straw and picked Caleb up. He kicked his chubby legs in the air in his excitement at seeing her. She glanced in his direction, and he could almost see the relief in her face. Relief that she was away from him. Out of reach. Her shield back in place.

Not for long, Rizpah. I got over your walls once. Next time, I'm going to rip them down around your ears.

"Why's he grinning at you like that?" Camella said softly, looking from Atretes to Rizpah, who was clearly flustered.

"To be obnoxious."

"Did you two quarrel?"

"Not exactly." She glanced back and watched him walk away

with Tibullus and the others to the sleeping space reserved for them. Peter was running ahead of them, undoubtedly wanting to make certain there was space for him.

Atretes glanced back at her again, and she could feel her body going hot with embarrassment. Why had he behaved in such a manner? Worse, why had she made a fool of herself? Had she had any hint of what he intended in the fanum, she would have stayed out of it.

"Mind if I join you ladies?" Prochorus said, and Camella greeted him affectionately. He joined them and passed the time with his sister, his fondness for his niece apparent as he watched her play with Caleb. Rhoda joined them after a while, but the conversation became stilted with her presence. Rizpah saw that the woman's affection for Lysia was genuine and reciprocated, but she treated Camella with pained politeness, while Camella, clearly resentful, retreated into silence.

*

From across the courtyard, Atretes watched Rizpah. Around him, the young men were working on memorizing Scripture. Tibullus had a copy of Mark's Gospel and Paul's letter to the Ephesians. All four were committing the latter to memory.

"'Finally, brethren, be strong in the Lord and in the power of his might. Put on the whole armor of God, that you may be able to stand against the wiles of the devil,'" Tibullus read. The others repeated the passage.

"Again, Niger," Tibullus said. "You forgot 'in the power of his might.'" Tibullus reread the passage and Niger quoted it back to him.

Passage by passage, they worked together, carving it into their minds word by word. "'Gird your loins with truth . . . put on the breastplate of righteousness . . . shod your feet with the preparation of the gospel of peace . . . taking up the shield of faith . . . take up the helmet of salvation and the sword of the Spirit, which is the word of God.'"

Atretes wished he had stayed overnight in the fanum.

Tibullus began to speak again, and Atretes interrupted. "Do you really think any of that will save your lives?"

Tibullus was too surprised to answer.

"What good is truth against the sword of Rome?" Atretes said darkly. "What good are words of peace against an empire bent on shedding blood? Tell me that!"

They each looked at one another, hoping another would take up the challenge.

"A shield of faith!" Atretes mocked them. He stood, unable to sit and listen to them anymore. "A helmet of salvation! A sword can cut through both and leave you *dead*."

Niger drew back from his anger.

"The body, yes, Atretes, but not the soul," Agabus said, and Atretes fixed his anger on him.

"Therein lies the rub, doesn't it?" he sneered. "I have no soul." Nor had he anything in common with these men, sons of merchants and craftsmen. He had been trained as a warrior from the time he was a boy. Ten years had hardened him even more. Would any one of these *boys* know what it felt like to face death?

"You have a soul, Atretes," Bartimaeus said.

"And it cries out for God." Another voice joined to the first.

Atretes looked at Tibullus. "If I have a soul, it cries out for vengeance."

"Revenge will bring you death," he replied, gaining courage from the other two.

"Maybe, but in the process, *satisfaction*."

"We've good news for you, Atretes," Niger said. "The Savior has come."

"'Savior,'" Atretes said in disgust and cast a cold look around the circle. "Are you saved?"

"Yes," Bartimaeus said. "And you can be, too."

"I've heard about your Jesus and his *good news*. A slave girl told me while she waited to face the lions. And now I hear about it from all of you. Day in. Day out. You never shut up about it. You speak of life, but death hovers over you like a buzzard."

"Death has no hold over us," Agabus said.

"No?" Atretes' voice was cold and challenging, his gaze filled with disdain. "Then why are all of you running from it?"

*

Rizpah heard Atretes' voice raised in anger. Glancing across the common, she saw him standing over the four younger men. They all rose, Bartimaeus stepping forward from the rest. His stance was one of appeal, not challenge. Atretes grabbed him by the front of his tunic and spoke right into his face. The younger man put his hands up in a gesture of surrender, and Atretes shoved him back contemptuously. He said something, spit on the ground, and walked away.

When Peter and Barnabas followed after him, Porcia called out to them. Barnabas stopped and protested, but Peter ignored her. She called again, more sharply this time, and the younger boy obeyed. When Atretes squatted down near the fire, Peter hunkered down beside him. Atretes said something and glowered at him. Peter said something, and Atretes jerked his head. Peter rose dejectedly and walked away. Porcia met him halfway. Glancing nervously at Atretes, she put her arm around her son's shoulders and hurried him into their booth. Atretes watched them and then turned his head away.

Rizpah's heart ached. She scarcely listened to the stilted conversation going on between Prochorus, Camella, and Rhoda, for she wondered what had set Atretes against the younger men. Night was upon them, and he sat down near the fire, staring into the flames, his face a hardened bronze. He looked so alone, cut off from everyone.

On impulse, she picked up Caleb from the blanket and rose. "Excuse me," she said and stepped past the others.

"You aren't going to go out there to him, are you?" Rhoda said. "Not in his present mood."

"Why shouldn't she?" Camella said.

Rhoda cast her an annoyed glance. "Because she might make matters worse," she said in a hushed voice. "And a man like him is unpredictable."

"You're as afraid of him as Porcia is," Camella said.

"Why shouldn't we be afraid of him? Remember what he was."

"That's it, isn't it? You can't let anyone forget their past and start over."

"I don't think he wants to start over. He just wants to go home."

Lysia drew back into the corner of the booth, her forehead against her raised knees.

Rhoda glared at Camella. "Besides, I wasn't talking about you."

"Weren't you?"

"I don't need to explain myself to you."

"No, you don't. You're plain as day. You're always aiming barbs at me."

"Camella," Prochorus said softly, but his sister wasn't listening.

"Every chance you get, you—"

"I do not. It's your own guilty conscience that makes you take offense at everything I say!"

"My brother and I were having a pleasant conversation before you joined us. Why don't you leave?"

"That's enough!" Prochorus said, aggrieved.

Quick tears filled Camella's eyes. "I'm sick of being criticized and condemned by her!"

"You're sick of *me*? Do you hear what she says? Do you see how she treats me?" Rhoda said, standing up. "Now do you believe me about her?" Eyes full of angry tears, she looked at her husband for reinforcement. He sat silent, looking sick. "Are you coming, Prochorus?"

"No."

Rhoda's face paled. "No?" Her eyes filled with tears.

"I'll be along in a few minutes," he said, but it was too late.

"I'm your wife, but you always take her side."

"I'm not taking anyone's side."

"No? Well, fine. Stay. I don't care. My feelings don't matter anyway, do they?" Tears ran down her cheeks. She looked at Camella. "We took you into our home, and you've done nothing but try to tear us apart." Her mouth worked. "Well, you've finally won, haven't you, Camella? I hope you're satisfied." Bursting into tears, she turned away.

Prochorus watched his wife run back to their booth. He looked at Camella and then put his head back against the clay brick wall. "Jesus," he said softly and closed his eyes.

"I'm sorry," Camella said weakly.

"You're always sorry." He rose slowly, looking old and worn. "It doesn't help much, does it?"

"Maybe I should just stay here in Corinth."

"Talking foolishness doesn't help matters, Cam."

"Who's being foolish? *You* for thinking this would ever work! I should've stayed in Ephesus."

"And how would you have lived?"

"I don't know. I would've found a way."

"You're my responsibility."

"Is that all I am to you? A responsibility? I'm your *sister*."

"And Rhoda is my *wife*," he said harshly. "What neither of you can get through your heads is I love you both. I wish to God you could love one another. Isn't that what we're supposed to do?"

"I've tried, Prochorus. I have."

"How did you try tonight, Cam? You started it."

Camella looked as though he had struck her. Rizpah bit her lip, embarrassed to be witnessing such an argument, yet unable to escape it.

"You've always given in to your emotions. It's what got you into trouble in the first place, isn't it?"

"Are you going to start throwing my past in my face, now, too?"

"I don't have to, do I? You're the one who can't forget. You wallow in it." He noticed Rizpah. "I'm sorry," he said, clearly ashamed. "I'm sorry," he said again and left.

Camella looked up at her. "You think I'm in the wrong, too, don't you?" she said, mouth jerking. "Go ahead. Blame me. Everyone does." As Rizpah left the booth, Camella finally noticed her daughter huddled and crying silently in the back corner. "Oh, Lysia," she said, her face crumpling.

Rizpah grieved for all of them.

What's happening to us, Lord? We were all so close in Ephesus. Is it the strain of the journey? Or did we hide our sins so well, we only thought we knew one another? If we go on like this, we'll be useless to you.

She came up behind Atretes. He was so still, she didn't think he had heard her approach until he spoke.

"So you have your shield in place."

Pushing out from Rizpah, Caleb turned and put his arms out to Atretes. "He wants to play with you," she said, smiling.

Atretes rose and took him. Brushing past her, he strode away. Rizpah followed him to a vacant booth near the back corner of the courtyard. It was isolated from the others. The torch burned outside. Rizpah hesitated, wondering what the others might say if she went in with him.

Atretes reclined in the fresh straw and sat Caleb beside him. Caleb immediately flopped over and tried to eat a handful of dried grass.

The Soil

"No, no," she said and stepped over quickly. Kneeling, she sat him up and plucked pieces from his mouth. "No, Caleb," she said firmly when he tried to eat more. Removing her shawl, she spread it and set him on it. Uttering a sharp squeal, Caleb flapped his arms like a bird wanting to take flight and dove forward again.

Atretes chuckled. "It's nice to know my son won't lie back and let a woman tell him what to do."

"I don't want him grazing," Rizpah said in annoyance and sat down close to Caleb, watching over him lest he stuff straw into his mouth again. He arched his back and rocked on his stomach, making funny noises. Tucking his legs under, he pushed himself up with his hands. "He'll be crawling soon," she said.

Atretes studied her. She had put up walls since their encounter in the fanum. "If I were a civilized man, I suppose I'd apologize for . . ."

"It's forgotten, Atretes."

His mouth tipped. "I can see how forgotten it is," he said, admiring the color filling her cheeks.

His sultry look unnerved her. Rather than retreat, she spoke what was on her mind. "Why were you angry with Agabus and the others?"

A muscle jerked in his jaw. He leaned back against the partition wall. "They're fools."

Though he looked physically relaxed, she felt his coiled tension and the anger building in him. It was a constant presence, just beneath the surface. The lightest stirring wind was enough to roll in the highest tide. He turned his head and looked at her, his blue eyes as beautiful as they were frightening. "For all their grandiose claims, they have about as much faith in your god as I have," he said. "None!"

She was deeply troubled by his observation. "They're struggling against the bonds of this life, like all the rest of us."

"They don't believe what they preach, and I'm sick of listening to them talk endlessly about this god of yours. They talk about death having no hold over them." He gave a dark laugh. "All I had to do was touch one of them to show the hold it has."

"Agabus dropped his hands because he didn't want to fight with you."

"He dropped his hands because he was afraid I'd kill him. I wanted him to know his faith isn't a shield against anything."

"Faith is all we have."

"If that's so, what kept me alive? I have no faith."

"You live by faith just as we do, Atretes."

"I don't believe in the old gods anymore, nor will I ever hold to yours!"

She refused to be intimidated by his wrath. "We all live by faith in this world, faith in *something*. Your faith lies in yourself. Don't you see? You think because you survived ten years in the arena you can go on surviving in the same way, with brute strength and a sword. Agabus and the others have chosen to believe in a power greater than themselves. Even when our faith is weak, God *is* our strength."

He gave a dry laugh and looked out at the courtyard where others gathered in warmer camaraderie. He was free, and yet he still felt as though he had his back against a wall. Rizpah looked at his stony face and was saddened.

Why can't I reach him, Father? Why does he refuse to listen?

"Atretes, someday, everything you've learned will be of no use to you."

His expression was sardonic. "And you think the words they commit to memory will keep them alive?"

"God's words will always prove true and right, no matter who questions them."

Atretes saw in her what he had seen in Hadassah the night she spoke with him in the lower-level dungeons. She had far more fire than the slave girl, more passion, but they shared a common peace. Despite circumstance. It was the kind of peace he hungered for and knew he could never have. "At least you *believe* what you say."

"So do they, Atretes, but they're young and untried."

"They'll be tried," he said heavily, "tried and then crucified."

She was silent for a long moment, his words preying heavily on her heart. "Perhaps you're right. They might die like so many others have. But you don't understand the fullness of it, Atretes, or the rightness of it. Whatever comes, they will not be lost."

His eyes narrowed. "And you think I am."

She looked him straight in the eyes. "Yes."

Her bluntness always surprised him. He smiled in wry amusement, but his eyes were cold. "Geographically."

Tangled in the shawl, Caleb cried loudly. Rizpah picked him up and sat him on her lap. She unwound the shawl from around him. When his legs were free, he kicked, wanting to be put down again. Spreading the shawl, she kissed Caleb's neck and put him back on his stomach. He pushed himself up and gave a gurgling laugh. Smiling faintly, Atretes watched his son.

"We're so much like Caleb," she said. "You and I and all the rest of the world. We want to walk upright. We want to run. But we become entangled by our own will. We allow sin to bind us as strongly as any shawl around our son. And don't we do the same thing he does? Cry out for help, each in our own way? Struggle and fail, in and of ourselves?"

His face was so still and enigmatic, she wondered if he could ever understand what she wanted him so desperately to know. "God lifts us up out of the mire, Atretes. No matter how many times we stumble and fall because of our own foolishness and stubborn will, Jesus is there holding out his hand to us. If we take hold, he removes the sin from our lives and sets us down again on solid rock. He is the rock. And gradually, through his tender mercies, he also transforms us into his likeness and brings us into the throne room of God."

His expression revealed nothing. Nor did he say anything. Ignoring her, he watched Caleb play for a long time. He didn't even look at her. She was filled with such frustration that she wanted to jump on him and pound the words through his thick skull.

He lay back in the straw and put one arm behind his head. "Take him and go."

Letting out a soft sigh, she rose and did as he commanded.

*

Far into the night, Atretes lay staring at the beams above him. He had known his silence frustrated her, and frustrating her had given him some satisfaction. Yet her words continued to plague him. And he knew why.

A year ago, a dream had tormented him night after night in the hill caves outside Ephesus. He had been sinking into a bog, about to drown in it, when a man dressed in glowing white appeared. "*Atretes,*" he said and held out his hands to rescue him.

Both palms had been bleeding.

14

Theophilus came to the inn late that night and called everyone together. When Atretes remained in his booth, he made no comment.

"There's a ship leaving for Rome the day after tomorrow," he announced to the gathering. "It's an Alexandrian freighter, fourth dock from the north end of the harbor. Stevedores are loading her now. I've arranged passage for all of us." He tossed a pouch of gold coins to Bartimaeus. "Dispense the money so that all can purchase provisions for the journey."

As the others talked among themselves, Theophilus took Rizpah aside. "Walk with me to the gate." He glanced across the compound to where Atretes sat with his back against the post. The ex-gladiator watched the proceedings with cold intensity.

Tucking his fingers into his belt, Theophilus took out several gold coins. "Since Atretes is too bullheaded to take money from me, I'll give it to you."

Rizpah put her hand over his. "I appreciate your concern, Theophilus, but Atretes brought gold with him."

He hesitated, perusing her face lest it be pride that held her back. It wasn't, and he nodded. "Enough to get him to Rome anyway," he said. "He must have left a vast fortune behind."

"None of it counted against his desire to return home."

Theophilus' mouth turned up in a mirthless smile. "Of all the races I've faced in battle over my twenty-five years, I found the Germans the fiercest and the most determined to regain their freedom. They are an unrelenting people. The Jews are much the same, but Titus has almost succeeded in exterminating them. Those few who survived the holocaust in Judea have been scattered across the Empire."

"The hunger for freedom is innate in all men."

"With godly purpose. The trumpet of Christ blares, and by his grace, I heard. Pray to God that Atretes will also."

"I do pray. Constantly."

"No doubt," he said and touched her cheek.

"Will it cost a great deal to make the journey to Germania?"

"More than he has on him. We'll learn if he's wise enough to accept help."

Rizpah saw him out the gate. As she turned, she came up against Atretes.

"You had a lot to say to one another," he said, his eyes almost black.

"Theophilus is a friend." She was alarmed at the wrath she saw in his eyes.

"Your friend, perhaps. Not mine."

"He could be yours, Atretes."

"What did he give you?"

"He offered us money to buy provisions for the journey to Rome." She saw his face harden. "I knew you wouldn't want me to take it, so I didn't."

"I'll purchase supplies tomorrow morning."

"He said you haven't enough to make the journey to Germania."

"I'll get what we need when we need it."

Rizpah was dismayed at his tone. She had no intention of asking how he intended to do that.

"The next time you speak with him, tell him if he touches you again, I'll kill him." With those words, he strode out the gate, heading in the opposite direction of Theophilus.

Rizpah heard him pound on the locked gate long after dark. The proprietor let him in and she rose slightly, watching him cross the compound to his booth. He walked unsteadily and fell into the hay. She lay back, heart pounding in disquiet.

The next morning, as she knelt with the others in prayer, he rose and left the inn. Others noticed as well.

"Would you like to go with us to the marketplace?" Porcia said.

She declined, forcing a smile and confidence she was far from feeling. Had Atretes gone out to drink again? She prayed not. If he returned without having taken care of his responsibilities, then she would decide what was best to do.

She played with Caleb until he fell asleep and then lay down beside him in a beam of sunlight. The warmth felt good. She traced Caleb's features lovingly, marveling at his perfection. Curling herself around him, she fell asleep with an inexplicable assurance that all would be well if she left Atretes and herself in God's hands.

✶

When Atretes returned, he found Rizpah asleep in the straw, his son snuggled against her. He stood for a long time just looking at her. It was a luxury he seldom was afforded. He wanted her in ways beyond the physical, ways he couldn't even understand, and that fact filled him with unease. His weakness for dark-haired, dark-eyed beauties made him wary of this woman; he had the heavy premonition that she could cut his heart into smaller pieces than Julia ever had.

Annoyed, he put his burdens down. The thud and rustle of hay awakened Rizpah. Her brown eyes were cloudy as she sat up and brushed away curling strands of dark hair with the back of her hand. "You're back," she said and smiled.

His blood warmed even as his defenses rose. "Take a look and make sure we have all we need," he said tersely.

Rizpah wondered how one man could remain angry so long over a trifle. She wanted to say something about Theophilus, but knew it would do no good. Atretes would choose to think what he wanted and protestations from her would only serve to make matters worse.

Atretes crouched down and watched as she opened a sack and sifted her fingers into a mixture of dried lentils, corn, beans, and barley. He had purchased dried fruit and some dried meat as well. She picked another pouch. "Salt," he said. "That amphora contains olive oil. The other, honey." He lifted the full skins from his shoulders and set them down more carefully than he had the others. "Wine. Watered, so it'll last at least a week."

She lifted her head and looked at him, her expression full of light. She was so lovely, his heart jumped. "You've done well," she said and her simple statement of praise broke through the barriers he had painstakingly erected around his heart. Yet as the tender emotions swelled, so too did his inner cry of alarm.

Retreating into his fortress of anger, he glared down at her. "And that surprises you," he said with biting sarcasm. "Do not doubt this, woman. I will get my son to Germania by my own resources and without help!"

Stunned and hurt, Rizpah watched him walk away and wondered what on earth she had done wrong now.

15

They boarded the Alexandrian freighter during the predawn hours. There were more passengers this time, one hundred fifty-nine in all, and deck space was precious. Several wealthy passengers had sent servants ahead, and they had set elaborate shelters and prepared beds for their masters, leaving little room for others who had wives and children.

Small sturdy crafts powered by half a dozen oarsmen attached lines and towed the ship from dockside into the deeper waters of the Gulf of Corinth. For two hours they sat becalmed, and then the wind came up. The sails flapped and filled, and the ship sailed down the wide passage toward Actium and the Mediterranean.

Camella was quiet and pensive as she watched her daughter talking with Rhoda.

"They're very fond of one another," Rizpah said, observing them as well.

"Rhoda's never done anything to hurt Lysia. It's only me she tries to hurt."

"As you do her."

Camella glanced at her sharply, feeling the gentle reprimand. "She succeeds."

"So do you. You're both very capable in that regard. It's painful to hear, even more painful to watch."

Camella grimaced and drew her blanket around herself. She leaned back, staring up at the sail. "I don't know why we say the things we do," she said wearily. "I don't even remember when it started. Sometimes just the way she looks at me makes me want to slap her face." She looked at Rizpah. "I made a mistake. I know it. I don't have to be reminded of it all the time. She's always watching me and waiting for me to do something wrong."

"The same way you watch and wait for her to find fault."

"That's not fair!"

"It's true," Rizpah said gently. "One of you has to stop."

Camella looked away again. "If I knew how, I would."

"You've heard the Word of God as clearly as I have, Cam. Pray for her."

"Easier said than done," she said, so full of resentment there was room for nothing else.

"Empty yourself. Obedience to God is seldom a matter of ease, but it always brings blessing." She picked Caleb up from his nap and went for a walk on the deck. It was cold. She far preferred the small tent shelter, but Camella needed time alone to think.

"Join us, Rizpah," Rhoda said as she came near. Rizpah saw how her gaze flickered to the small shelter where her sister-in-law sat.

"I need some exercise," Rizpah said, sensitive to Camella's feelings. She didn't want Cam or Rhoda thinking she was taking sides.

Agabus and Tibullus stood near the bow, talking to several passengers. Parmenas and Eunice were with Theophilus while their three children sat on the deck nearby playing a game of pick-up sticks. Niger and Bartimaeus were standing near the mast, talking together. Several soldiers sat gambling near the door to the hold. Timon and Porcia were struggling to work together and reerect their small tent shelter, which had collapsed. Mary, Benjamin, and Barnabas were nearby, playing in a coil of ropes.

Rizpah found Atretes leaning against the bulwark of the shipowner's cabin, his arms crossed. He stared out at the southern hills, appearing not to hear a word Peter was saying to him. She debated joining them, then decided against it.

Others walked the deck. A swarthy Macedonian passed by her, and she was filled with disquiet at the way he assessed her.

Though the wind held steady, it was slow going down the Gulf of Corinth. The sun rose and fell several times before they sailed past Patrae and Araxos on the coast of Greece. Sailing out of the gulf, they headed west, passing by the southern tip of Cephalonia. Beyond lay the Ionian Sea.

One day rolled tediously into another until a ship was sighted. "It's a two-banked *hemiolia*!" an officer shouted to the captain, causing general alarm to all those who were aware that such a ship was favored by pirates. "It's heading straight for us!"

The ship, sometimes referred to as a one-and-a-halfer, was

powered by rowers as well as under sail. It sped through the waters, while their own Alexandrian ship moved sluggishly, burdened by cargo and indifferent winds.

"It's Illyrian, Captain, and coming fast!"

Passengers began to panic. Theophilus shouted for order and commanded the women and children get below.

"There's no room!"

"*Make* room!"

"I was told the Roman fleet patrolled these waters!" one of the wealthy passengers shouted. "Where is it? Why aren't they protecting us?"

"There's a squadron out of Brundisium, but they can't be everywhere at once. Now, *move*!"

Atretes watched the passengers scrambling for possessions while others ran for the portal to the ladder below. Theophilus was shouting orders. Men were cursing. Women and children were screaming. Two slaves carrying a small but obviously heavy trunk were pushing their way through the throng at the command of their master.

"Set up the catapults!" Theophilus was shouting, watching how the oars of the hemiolia rose and fell with speed and precision driving the ship through the water.

Atretes swore and looked around the deck for Rizpah.

"Peter! Where's Peter?!" Porcia cried out as Timon pushed her and the three other children toward the portal to the cargo decks.

Atretes looked down at the boy by his side. "Go with your father!" he said.

"I want to stay with you!"

Atretes gave the boy a hard shove in the direction of Timon and ran toward Rizpah, who was standing outside her tent shelter, staring in terror at the oncoming ship. She gasped in pain as he grasped her arm and yanked her toward the door of the owner's cabin. The hemiolia was so close, Atretes could see armed men on the main deck. "Get in there and bar the door!" he said in a voice low with fury.

Atretes knew his dagger was no match for the battle that was coming and looked for a better weapon.

"Atretes!" Theophilus shouted and tossed him a spear.

A volley of arrows zinged over the narrowing span of water between the ships, one just missing his head. Others found their marks in the passengers still trying to get below. Screams of pain and panic rent the air. The captain shouted orders.

The line of oars on one side of the hemiolia went up sharply and retracted. The ship swung hard around.

Atretes' heart constricted at what he saw.

"They're outfitted with ravens, centurion!" a soldier shouted.

Theophilus had already seen the movable boarding bridges being rotated about the stump-mast set in the prow of the hemiolia. Beneath the outer ends of two he could see the sharp spike. If dropped aboard the Alexandrian freighter, the spike would penetrate and hold them fast. "Fire!" he commanded and the catapults were released, sending jars of oil across. They shattered on the deck at the same time the soldiers released a volley of flaming darts.

The hemiolia swung round and came hard against the Alexandrian. The blow rocked Atretes on his feet and sent screaming passengers down the ladderway. The ravens dropped, and Illyrians charged across, screaming war cries.

Rather than throw the spear, Atretes used it as a pugil stick. Giving his own war cry, he brought the end hard against the side of one Illyrian's head and then came around to slice the throat of another. Dodging a sword, he rammed his shoulder into his attacker, knocking him backward into several others.

The crash of blade against blade echoed across the deck, as well as the screams of dying men. Leaping to the higher deck, Atretes felt a sharp sting along his right shoulder as an arrow shot by him. Enraged, he threw his spear, skewering a bowman and pinning him against a barrel.

He knew it was a mistake as soon as it left his hands, for he stood in the open, virtually defenseless. Someone knocked him back as three Illyrians came up the steps.

Theophilus struck the first man's shoulder, then kicked the fallen sword to Atretes as he blocked a sword blow from the second attacker. He kicked the man down the stairway, knocking two others back.

Atretes took up the sword and almost used it on the man who had just saved his life. Gritting his teeth, he stood, feet planted as Theophilus turned. Seeing his fighting stance, the centurion smiled grimly. "Galls, doesn't it?" He lowered his sword.

Knocking him aside, Atretes jumped down onto the main deck

and entered the worst of the fray, venting his rage on anyone who dared come close.

*

Rizpah could hear the battle through the door of the owner's cabin. Two hard thuds sounded against the door. Someone shouted and there was another thud, harder this time. The bar cracked. Opening a trunk, Rizpah threw out half the owner's clothing. She put Caleb inside and closed the lid.

The door burst open as she turned. In the doorway was the Macedonian passenger. He entered with a gladius in his hand. "The prize I want," he said, his dark eyes gleaming. "She'll bring a good price." He stood aside as two others entered the small quarters. "Take her." The command given, he left.

She stood still as though cowed with terror until they came close. Then she used everything she had learned in the streets of Ephesus to keep them from laying hands on her. She struck, kicked, bit and scratched, screaming as she did so.

*

Atretes saw the Macedonian enter the cabin, but he was too deep in the fray on the main deck to do anything. He slashed the abdomen of one attacker and kicked another back. Ramming his shoulder into a third, he tried to drive his way through the melee. He saw two Illyrians enter the cabin as the Macedonian left, guiding others to the booty below.

Atretes hacked his way forward as he saw the two pirates dragging Rizpah from the cabin. She was fighting them every inch of the way. One struck her with his fist, and Atretes gave a bellow of rage. He reached them before the Illyrian had time to lift her to his shoulder. Seeing Atretes, both withdrew from her, but not in time to save their lives.

"*Roman galleys!*"

Many of the pirates managed to release their booty and retreat across two of the ravens, but grabbing up a spear, Atretes leaped to the third ramp, preventing the others from escaping.

"Atretes!" Theophilus shouted. "Let them go!"

Bellowing his war cry, Atretes struck blows to the right and left. Pain burst in his right shoulder and he fell forward. Losing balance, he fell headlong in the water. He hit hard and sank into the cold water of the Ionian Sea. Arrows rained down around him, barely missing their mark. Unable to move his left shoulder, he kicked his way up. As he burst the surface, he saw the raven above him being raised. The oars of the hemiolia made a loud bang as they came out, and as they swung down, one struck him on the head.

*

Theophilus saw what happened from the deck of the Alexandrian. Stripping off his helmet and breastplate, he shouted an order and dove in. Quick, strong strokes brought him to Atretes as he sank, and grabbing the German's long hair, he dragged him to the surface and caught hold of the rope that was dropped. Atretes was unconscious, blood streaming from a gash in his forehead. Struggling to keep himself afloat and Atretes from sinking, Theophilus tied the rope securely. "Haul him up!"

"Watch the line!" A second rope was dropped to him and he grasped hold. Planting his feet against the side of the ship, he walked up as his men pulled from above.

Atretes lay facedown on the deck, the arrow protruding from his left shoulder. "Hold him down in case he comes round," Theophilus said, going down on one knee and grasping the shaft. He pulled the arrow out with one firm yank. Atretes groaned and raised his head slightly, then relaxed again.

"The wound needs to be cauterized," he said and sent one of his men to see if a brazier was burning and, if not, to have one lit.

*

A searing pain ripped across Atretes' left shoulder, snapping him out the the darkness that surrounded him. He tried to rise and escape the burning, but a strong hand pushed him down again. "We've seared your shoulder wound to stop the bleeding and prevent infection."

Recognizing Theophilus' voice, Atretes struggled to rise. "Get your hands off me!" He regained his feet and swayed slightly from loss of blood. A soldier took hold of his arm to steady him, and Atretes knocked him aside. "Touch me, Roman, and I'll kill you." The soldier put his hands out in acquiescence and shrugged at Theophilus before turning away.

Atretes turned and looked across the deck. "Where's Rizpah?"

"She's all right," Theophilus said. "She's in the cabin with your son."

A resounding crack suddenly echoed across the waters as a Roman galley rammed the hemiolia, snapping oars and splintering a wide hole into the side of the pirate ship. Turning to watch, Atretes shouted German curses down on the Illyrians' heads as the screams of slaves tied to their oars could be heard across the water. The sea poured into the hull as Roman ravens dropped aboard the hemiolia and soldiers went to put the pirates to the sword.

Theophilus stood silent, staring grimly at the scene. Another Roman galley was closing in on the leeward side of the hemiolia, ready to give assistance to their comrades should it be needed. It wasn't.

Turning away, the centurion faced the carnage on the deck around him. Closing his eyes, he knelt and bowed his head. "God, to you be the glory for our deliverance," he said, his deep voice breaking in grief at the cost of carrying out his responsibilities as a soldier. What price the greed of men?

Atretes stepped over the fallen as he headed for the owner's cabin. When he entered, Rizpah was inside, sitting on the berth, comforting Caleb. When she glanced up, he saw the swelling bruise on her jaw where the Illyrian had struck her. His blood went hot again, his heart pumping hard and fast.

"Atretes," she said softly, her face showing her relief and concern. Blood seeped from an open wound in his forehead. She quickly rose, replacing Caleb in the trunk before coming to him. "You're bleeding. Sit down."

Turbulent emotions poured through him making war with one another. He laughed grimly and caught hold of her. "I've been wounded before."

"Sit down!"

Surprised, he did as she commanded. Bemused, he watched her rush about the small cabin, raking through garments. Finding one that suited her, she ripped it down the middle. "I wonder what the owner will have to say about you tearing up such a fine tunic."

"I don't care what he says." She opened the owner's amphora of wine and sloshed it onto another expensive garment.

He smiled wryly. "Stop crying, Rizpah. I'll live."

"Another word and I'll wrap this around your throat instead of your head!"

He winced as she dabbed the blood from his forehead with the wine-soaked cloth. Her whole body was trembling violently. So was his, as it always had in the aftermath of battle. His blood still hummed. He had forgotten what it felt like to feel *alive*.

Rizpah's closeness roused other instincts long-conditioned by careful training under the system of punishment and reward. He grasped her hips and drew her firmly against him. "Whenever I did well in the arena, I always knew there'd be a beautiful woman waiting in my cell when I was returned to the ludus."

"Let go of me, Atretes."

"I don't want to let go of you. I want to—*ouch*!" He released her abruptly when she slapped the wine-soaked bandage on his wound. He swore vilely in German, barely containing himself from striking her.

"Just because they treated you like an animal doesn't mean you've become one."

Grimacing, he glared at her. "I should've let the Illyrians have you!"

Face white, she finished tying the bandage in place despite his protests. She rested her hands lightly on his shoulders and smiled sadly. "I'm glad you didn't."

Setting her aside, Atretes rose. As he bent over the trunk to lift his son out, Rizpah saw the other wound. "Your shoulder!"

"Don't even think about it! I'll find a gentler hand than yours to tend to it." Ignoring her, he placed Caleb on the bunk. Stripping off the baby's garments, he ran his hands over his son's body. "He appears unharmed."

"He was well-hidden in the trunk. They didn't touch him."

Atretes bent down, resting his forearms on either side of his son, and he rubbed his face against him, breathing in the scent of life and innocence. As he drew back, he saw he had unwittingly smeared Caleb with blood. The sight of it opened long-hidden, but momentarily forgotten wounds. "Wash him," he said hoarsely and left the cabin.

Rizpah did as Atretes commanded. Then, hearing the cries of the wounded outside the door, she tied Caleb into her shawl-sling. Her help was needed on the main deck. She couldn't remain cocooned in the owner's cabin and leave the others to aid the injured. She stepped outside the cabin door, wholly unprepared for the horrifying scene before her.

Wounded and dying lay tangled among the already dead while able-bodied crew members and passengers lifted bodies and dumped them overboard without care or ceremony. Not far away, the Roman galley was withdrawing from its conquered foe. The Illyrian ship was sinking, flames licking up the mast to the broad sail. Men jumped over the side and were left to drown.

A woman's piercing cry of grief brought Rizpah sharply around. Rhoda was on her knees, holding Prochorus in her arms. She rocked his lifeless body back and forth, her face etched in anguish. Camella stood helplessly by, holding Lysia and weeping.

A man lying near the doorway was crying softly for his mother. Weeping, Rizpah knelt beside him and took his hand. He held on so tightly she thought he would crush her bones. The gaping wound in his abdomen was mortal, and the few words of comfort she was able to say before his hand loosened upon hers fell upon unhearing ears.

*

Atretes picked his way over the dead, looking into their still faces. He found Agabus among them. Kneeling down, he stared at the young man in death. He lay with his eyes wide open as though gazing up at the sky. His face was tranquil; unlike many of the others, there was no sign of struggle, of pain or fear. If not for the mortal wound in his chest, one might have thought he was alive.

Perplexed, Atretes studied him. He remembered only one other face that had looked so at peace after meeting a violent death—Caleb, the Jew he had killed in the arena.

Stirred in a way he did not understand, Atretes murmured, "Perhaps there is something in what you said." He reached out a gentle hand to close the young man's eyes. He lifted the young Christian and carried him to the starboard side, away from the hasty and heedless discarding of dead Illyrians. "Your Christ have you," he said with respect and let Agabus' body drop with a quiet splash into the sea. The young man's body floated briefly, arms flung wide, rising and falling gently on the waves, and then it sank slowly into the blue depths.

"A good thing the centurion saved you from drowning, or you'd be food for the fish with the rest," a sailor said, grunting as he carried another body to the side.

Atretes faced him sharply. "What did you say?"

"When you fell from the raven," he said with another grunt as he released his burden into the sea, "an oar struck you. He stripped off his armor and dove in after you."

Turning, Atretes saw Theophilus standing amid the slain. Helmet beneath his arm, the centurion appeared to be praying.

It sat ill with Atretes that he owed his life to that accursed Roman. Not once, but *twice*! Had the centurion not kicked him a weapon, he would have been cut down well before the battle reached its height. Now he knew he would never have regained consciousness in the water. Resentment filled him, yet reason prevailed.

Had he died, what would have become of his son and the woman? Thank whatever gods there were, it wasn't his fate to survive ten years in the arena only to die at the hands of Illyrian pirates while on board an Alexandrian ship carrying precious cargo to Rome! What cruel irony that would have proved to be. His death would come, but when it did, he intended it to have meaning and purpose. There was great honor in dying in battle, but let it be in a battle against Rome! Had he been killed today, he would have died *defending* a merchant ship in the service of the emperor. By the fates, what a grotesque joke. It hadn't even occurred to him until now.

As though sensing his stare, Theophilus looked his way. Their gazes met and held. Atretes clenched his teeth, pride stiffening his neck. The centurion had saved his life, and honor-bound, Atretes knew he had to acknowledge the fact and give him his due. Theophilus stood motionless, enigmatic, undoubtedly awaiting the opportunity to gloat. Swallowing his pride, Atretes gave him a slow nod.

Theophilus' mouth curved, but his smile held neither mockery nor triumph, only a grievous understanding.

16

The Alexandrian freighter sailed under the guard of the two Roman galleys until they reached the straits at the boot of Italy. The escort then headed east as the Alexandrian proceeded past Sicily into the Tyrrhenian Sea.

Sailing north, Atretes noticed the devastation along the shoreline. "Mount Vesuvius erupted a year ago," one of the crew told him. "Covered the cities of Heraclea and Pompeii. You can't even tell they existed. The Jews believe it's their god's judgment on Titus for what he did to Jerusalem."

Atretes was beginning to like this god.

The farther up the coast they sailed, the more ships were sighted. Under oar and sail, they came from every part of the Empire, carrying cargo to the gluttonous markets of the Eternal City.

Atretes stood near the prow, dreading his return to Rome. Dark memories tormented him. He slept little, plagued by a premonition that he would be captured and forced to fight for the Roman mob again.

"What's that you're holding, Atretes?" Peter said, sitting on a barrel nearby.

He opened his clenched fist and stared at the ivory chip in his palm. "My proof of freedom," he said grimly. His only proof.

"What if someone stole it from you? Would that mean you weren't free anymore?"

"I don't know, boy."

"What would you do if they tried to put you back into a ludus?"

"I wouldn't give up without a fight."

*

Rizpah saw little of Atretes, choosing to remain inside the small shelter and keep Rhoda company. She was worried about her. Rhoda hadn't spoken a word since her husband's body was delivered into the sea. She sat silent and pale, grieving. Camella, mourning the loss of her brother as well, remained outside the shelter until nightfall, avoiding her sister-in-law's company for as long as possible. Poor Lysia, torn between love for her mother and her aunt, went back and forth between the two.

Camella finally entered the shelter and sat down. She gave a cursory glance at Rhoda and then smiled at Rizpah. "One of the ship's officers just told me if the winds hold, we'll be in Ostia by the Ides of March. That's the day after tomorrow."

"I'm a little frightened at the thought of Rome," Rizpah said. Caleb was asleep at her breast. She laid him down and covered him with a soft blanket. His mouth worked as though he was still nursing.

"He's beautiful," Rhoda said softly, surprising both women. She began to weep, tears coursing down her white cheeks. Leaning forward, she put her finger into Caleb's palm. His fingers closed instinctively around hers. "I've always wanted a child. For as long as I can remember, that was the greatest desire of my heart. Prochorus said the Lord would bless us with one in his good time. I prayed unceasingly for a baby. Now I'll never have one."

She raised her head and looked across at Camella, who stiffened and drew back slightly, expecting attack. Instead, Rhoda spoke softly.

"When you came to live with us, it was as though God mocked me. From the time I was a child, I've believed in the Lord and served him. I never strayed—" Her voice broke and she looked at Caleb again.

"The way I did, you mean," Camella said in brittle tones. "Isn't that what you want to say?"

"Cam," Rizpah said, aggrieved.

"No. It's true. Let's have it all out in the open now. She lost a husband. Maybe she's forgotten I lost my brother!" She glared at Rhoda, tears flooding her eyes. "What are you going to say now, Rhoda? That his death is my fault?"

"No," Rhoda said brokenly.

"No?" Camella said. "You've been sitting there for days, not saying a single word to me, just thinking and thinking of ways to blame me. Go ahead. Blame me." She drew her shawl tightly around herself and turned her face away.

"I have been thinking. I've harbored ill will against you and slandered you. I've wronged you and I've been able to think of

The Soil

nothing else!" She blinked back tears, staring down at her tightly clasped hands.

Camella looked at her with distrust.

"I wasn't angry with you as much as I've been angry with God. I thought he had abandoned me." She raised her head again, stricken. "God gave you what I wanted most: a child! You came to us with a beautiful baby in your arms, and I cried out in my heart. Why did God bless you and not me? I thought I was deserving. But I wasn't. I wasn't deserving at all."

She shook her head, filled with remorse. "All the while I thought I was serving God, I wasn't." Weaving her fingers together, she strove to go on. "When Prochorus died, I realized I'd even put my desire for a child ahead of him. I've done nothing but think about the past. I've done everything for the wrong reasons. All the good works people credit to me are nothing because I did them expecting God to repay me. I thought if I worked hard enough, God would have to give me what I wanted. The truth is I've never served the Lord at all. I was always serving myself." Cheeks wet, she looked at Camella. "I've been unkind to you so many times, Cam. Please forgive me."

Camella sat for a long moment, saying nothing. "I forgive you," she said bleakly. She got up quickly and left the shelter.

Rizpah left Caleb with Rhoda and went out to her friend. Camella sat alone near the prow, weeping. Rizpah sat down with her. "What is it?" she said softly.

"I've always wanted her to beg for my forgiveness. I've prayed for this moment, just so she'd know what I've felt. And now I feel so ashamed."

Camella wiped the tears from her cheeks and stared up at the sail. "Rhoda and I are a lot alike. She wanted a child. I wanted a husband who would love me the way my brother loved her."

"And now you have one another."

"Maybe. If we can learn to bear one another's burdens instead of adding to them."

"Now is a good time to start," Rizpah said softly. Camella studied her friend's face for a moment, then nodded. They returned to the shelter. Lysia took Caleb and played with him as her mother sat down nearby Rhoda.

"Rhoda," she said softly, hesitant. "I want to speak with you about the past."

"You don't have to tell me anything."

"Please, Rhoda. Just this once, let me talk about it, and then I'll never mention it again." She waited until Rhoda nodded before going on. "When Callistus left me, I was so hurt. You can't imagine how much I loved him and how foolish I was over him. I knew when I left my family and went to him that what I was doing was wrong, but I didn't care. All I could think about was being with him. And then he turned out to be everything my family and friends told me he was. I had nowhere to go, no one to take care of me. I even thought about drowning Lysia and committing suicide."

Rhoda closed her eyes, shaking softly with silent weeping.

Camella lowered her head. "You didn't know how bad it was, Rhoda. Prochorus knew, but he didn't offer any help. I finally swallowed my pride and asked him for it, and he said he'd speak to you first before he decided." She didn't say anything for a moment. She looked away, tears running down her cheeks, swallowing convulsively.

"I knew I'd created my own problems, but all I could think about was my own brother cared more for your feelings than he did for my life." She let out her breath shakily. "I was jealous of you. I came into your home full of hurt feelings and resentment. I took offense at everything you said and I did everything I could to come between you and my brother. I've made everyone miserable for the past several years, and now you ask for *my* forgiveness when it's your forgiveness I need."

Rhoda leaned forward, stretching out her hands. Camella grasped them. Pride cast aside, she cried openly. "He loved you. You know he did. And he adored Lysia as much as I do. You say you'll never have a child, Rhoda, but Lysia is your daughter as much as mine. She loves you. I love you, too."

They talked far into the night, about Prochorus, about their concerns of what they would do when they reached Rome. Rizpah lay down with Caleb to her breast and listened. As joy over the reconciliation swept over her, she looked out through the tent opening and saw Atretes.

He was standing at the railing, his blonde hair whipped about his face by the wind. He looked so grim, so unrelenting. What would her future and Caleb's be when they reached the dark forests of Germania?

17

The Alexandrian freighter entered the imperial harbor of Ostia on the Ides of March. The port at the mouth of the Tiber built by Ancus Marcius seven hundred years before had grown into a commercial and storage center for Rome's grain supplies as well as a port of refitting and repair for vessels going to Portus. Galleys from the Roman fleet were in noticeable numbers alongside a royal barge decorated for an elaborate celebration.

Theophilus called the Christians together as the ship was being towed into the harbor.

"I won't be able to meet with you again until I deliver the gifts to the emperor and am dismissed of my duties. When you disembark, follow the main road out of Ostia. It will take you to the gates of Rome. Look for the Temple of Mars. Nearby is a marketplace. When you find the vendors of fruits and vegetables, ask for a man named Tropas. He has a booth among them. He's one of us and can be trusted. He'll direct you to safe housing."

Rizpah went to Atretes to relay Theophilus' instructions, but he dismissed them. "We go on our own," he said, picking up the blanket rolls and last of the food supplies.

"Is that wise?" Rizpah said, afraid to leave the others. She saw the warning glint of anger in his blue eyes. Packs already tied to his back, Atretes took Caleb from her and headed for the line of passengers disembarking.

Struggling with misgivings, she hurried after him. "Let me hold him, Atretes."

"I'll give him back to you when we're off this ship."

Helpless to stop him, she looked back at the others. All were occupied with gathering their belongings, and he wouldn't listen to them anyway. Peter ran to Atretes before he could disembark.

"Where are you going? Aren't you going to stay with us?"

"No," Atretes said, casting the boy an impatient look.

"Theophilus told us where to go."

"Go back to your mother."

"But—"

"*Go!*"

Blinking back tears, Peter backed away.

Rizpah watched the boy and turned to Atretes. "Why were you so cruel to him? He loves you."

"Be silent!" He stepped onto the plank walkway and started down. She had no choice but to follow. When they reached the dock, she had to walk quickly to keep up with him. He was in a hurry to be away. His demeanor was such that people moved out of his way as he strode down the quay toward some large warehouses. Several soldiers who stood by a man with a manifest noticed him. One in particular stared long and hard and then said something to one of the others.

"You there!" one of them called out, and Rizpah's heart jumped and began pounding heavily.

Atretes swore under his breath and tilted his head in arrogant question as two soldiers approached him while others along the way stopped to stare in curiosity.

"What's your name?" one soldier demanded, while the other said, "Atretes! I tell you, Ancus. I swear it's him." He stared at Atretes almost in awe. "I saw you fight Celerus. I'll never forget it. It was the most magnificent fight I've ever witnessed."

"Glad you enjoyed it," Atretes said without inflection.

"Then you *are* Atretes," Ancus said with a snort of disbelief, looking over his common garb and the turban he had wound on his head to cover his blond hair.

"Yes," Atretes said, and Rizpah glanced up, surprised he revealed his identity. She could see a pulse throbbing in his neck. Cold alarm spread through her.

"Your son?" Ancus said and reached out to brush Caleb's cheek. Atretes shifted his body. He moved only a fraction of an inch, but as the babe was taken out of the soldier's reach, the message was as loud as a trumpet calling forth a battle. Ancus' eyes narrowed. A cold silence fell. Rizpah could hear her own heartbeat in her ears. She prayed frantically, beseeching God for help.

"Ulpius, since you're the expert on gladiators, you can tell me. Wasn't Atretes sold and sent to Ephesus?"

"Three years ago," Ulpius said. "Not that the mob has forgotten him. They were so much in love with him, vendors still sell statues outside the—"

"Then he's still a slave," Ancus interrupted smugly.

"I earned my freedom," Atretes said and drew the gold chain

and ivory pendant from beneath his tunic and cloak. He held it out, his expression dark and mocking.

"A pity," Ancus said, "but then, things can change, given the right circumstances."

Atretes handed Caleb to Rizpah without looking at her.

Ancus put his hand on the hilt of his sword. Ulpius stepped forward, his hand extended between them. "Don't be a fool."

"Is there a problem here?" came a hard voice.

Ulpius turned. "Centurion!" he said, startled and clearly relieved. He hit his breastplate in formal salute. Ancus immediately saluted as well.

"I asked you a question, soldier," Theophilus said to Ancus, the full dignity and authority of his rank evident in his command.

Ancus' face reddened. "This man is a slave of the imperial ludus."

"He is a slave no longer, soldier, or didn't you notice the pendant he wears?" Theophilus looked at Atretes and inclined his head respectfully. "I didn't have the opportunity to bid you farewell and offer my thanks for your assistance aboard the ship. I do so now. The emperor will be pleased to hear of your part in thwarting the Illyrian pirates."

A muscle jerked in Atretes' jaw and his lips whitened.

Theophilus looked at Ancus. "We were attacked and outnumbered. Without this man's assistance, the Illyrians would've taken the ship and the gifts I bring Titus."

"Centurion, this man is *Atretes*."

Theophilus' expression darkened. "Is that why you detain him? To fawn over him like a couple of amoratae? Go back to your duties. Now!" As soon as they were out of hearing, he looked at Atretes. "It's unfortunate you're so readily recognizable."

"I don't intend to be in Rome any longer than necessary."

"It'd be safer if you stayed out of the city entirely. I'll make arrangements for you to stay on the outskirts of Ostia and meet you when I've completed my commission to the emperor."

"I make my own arrangements."

"Stop being a stiff-necked fool and use some common sense!"

"Have I your permission to depart, my *lord*? Or do you intend to detain me as well?"

Theophilus' eyes ignited. "You're free to go where you wish, all the way to Hades if it pleases you." He stepped back and inclined his head. "But take care lest you drag your son and Rizpah down with you."

Atretes' body was rigid, hot blood flooding his veins. He stood his ground, gritting his teeth. "I know someone in Rome who will help us."

"An ex-gladiator?" Theophilus said, struggling against his own temper and impatience with this stubborn, thick-skulled German.

"Gladiators are more to be trusted than Romans."

"As Gallus was trustworthy," Rizpah said and received a black look from him.

"Go and put yourself in the care of your ex-gladiator," Theophilus said, angry. "Hopefully you won't find yourself back in the ludus. I warn you now, it won't be easy for me to get you out of there."

"I can take care of myself."

"In the arena, I would agree."

"Anywhere."

"He's only trying to help us," Rizpah said.

"I don't need his help, woman, nor have I asked for it."

"Why won't you listen to him? He knows Rome. He knows the emperor. He knows—"

Atretes snatched Caleb from her arms and strode off. Frightened and filled with frustration, she stared after him and then turned to beseech Theophilus. "What am I going to do?"

"Go with him. I'll find you." He gave a soft laugh without humor. "He'll make it easy."

Rizpah caught up with Atretes. Caleb was screaming in his arms. "You're frightening him." He thrust the baby into her arms without slowing his pace. She did her best to calm Caleb as she hurried alongside Atretes. It took three of her steps to match one of his strides and she was quickly out of breath.

"I can't keep up with you!" she gasped, and he slowed his pace slightly, a hand clamped on her arm to keep her with him. "Do you know where you're going?" she said, feeling less secure as the distance between her and Theophilus widened.

Atretes' jaw stiffened.

"Theophilus knows his way—"

Atretes stopped and turned on her, his face livid. "Shut up! Do not mention his name to me again! Do you understand? I suffered his presence aboard ship because I had no choice. Now, I do!"

They walked for hours, falling in among the throng of travelers heading for Rome. They kept well to the side and out of the way of the numerous vehicles that sped in both directions. Four-wheeled, four-horsed *raeda* passed by bearing families. A two-wheeled, two-horsed *cisium* raced down the road, urged by a wealthy young aristocrat oblivious to the risk of others. There were ox wagons carrying goods, and litters carrying officials, merchants, and wealthy sightseers who were heading for Rome carrying messages, merchandise, or grand hopes of fulfilling their dreams. Hundreds walked; Atretes and Rizpah, Caleb in her arms, were among them.

They paused briefly by one of the milestones that was placed every thousand paces, recording the nearest towns and the name of the emperor during whose reign the roadwork had been completed. Road repairs were also noted on the milestone with each succeeding emperor named during whose reign the work had been done. Atretes could read none of it, and Rizpah only part, having been taught by her husband, Shimei.

Atretes opened the pouch tied to his belt and gave Rizpah a handful of dried grain to eat. He tossed some of the rich mixture into his mouth. Unlooping the wineskin, he dropped it into her lap. "It's almost empty," she said, after taking a sparing drink and holding it up to him.

"We'll get more," he said, looping it back on his shoulder. "Nurse the child on the way."

They entered the city as the sun was setting. Outside the gates, merchants grumbled as they were forced to wait until the following morning before entering the city. No wheeled vehicles were allowed into Rome after sunset.

"How far?" Rizpah said, exhausted.

"Far," Atretes said grimly. He could see the emperor's palace in the distance and knew they had hours yet to walk before coming to an area of Rome with which he was familiar. Once they found the ludus, he was certain he could find the way to Pugnax's inn. If not, he would find someone to take a message to Bato, the lanista of the Ludus Magnus. It was too far to go tonight. He could make it, but Rizpah was exhausted.

He saw a park not far ahead. "We'll sleep there for the night."

Rizpah noticed a gathering of rough-looking people loitering nearby, but made no protest. If they were attacked, it would be on Atretes' head.

It was getting cold, and dark clouds gathered overhead. Atretes led Rizpah along a cobbled footpath between a copse of trees. Just on the other side was a vine-tangled fanum. She stopped and stared at it with misgivings.

"Thinking of the last time you and I shared one of these?" Atretes said mockingly.

"I'll sleep over there," she said, pointing to row of thick bushes.

"I don't think so."

"I don't care what you think! I'm tired and hungry and I'm not going to argue with you!"

He heard the catch in her voice and knew she was close to tears. "It's going to be cold, Rizpah."

"Don't offer to keep me warm!" Yanking the blanket from the pack on his shoulder, she left him on the path and headed for the shrubs.

Clenching his teeth, he went into the fanum and made a bed for himself. He could hear Caleb crying, the sound pitiful in the growing darkness. The clouds moved across the moon, shrouding the small fanum garden in darkness. His son's crying frayed his conscience. A rumble of thunder rippled around him and rain poured down, pounding against the marble arch above him.

Atretes arose and went out to find Rizpah; his son's crying made that easy. Stooping down before a heavy shrub, he looked at her huddled beneath the wet blanket. "Go away," she said, and he could tell she was crying with the baby.

"Woman, I'm not the only one who's stiff-necked and stubborn." The cold rain was pouring down on his head and running down the back of his neck beneath the heavy woolen blanket around him. "Think of the babe."

Teeth chattering, she rose and followed him back to the fanum. Shaking the moisture off her own woolen blanket, she lay down on the marble tiles. He sat on the bench and said nothing. Her body was shivering. He could hear her speaking softly to the baby. When Caleb cried harder, she shifted, rearranging her clothing so that she could nurse him.

Leaning back against a marble column, Atretes watched her body slowly relax in exhaustion. When he was sure she was sleeping, he lay down behind her and drew his own blanket over her and the baby. Her body was cold. He tucked her body firmly into the curve of his own so that his warmth could seep into her. She fitted him perfectly. The scent of her flesh aroused him, and he forced his thoughts to other things designed to chill his ardor. Gallus, for one.

Rizpah's reminder had served its purpose. He had only met Pugnax once, and for business purposes. Bato had accompanied him. If not for the lanista's presence, Atretes knew he might not have survived that night. The inn had been a mean little place compared to other establishments where he had been taken since then. Pugnax hadn't much to show for his years in the arena. Atretes' mouth curved bitterly. How much did he himself have to show for ten years of fighting for his life? Everything he had earned had been spent on that grand villa and its elaborate furnishings back in Ephesus. And for what? Julia. Beautiful, shallow, corrupt Julia.

Rizpah moved closer in her sleep, and Atretes sucked in his breath. Raising his head, he looked over her at his son. Even in her sleep, she snuggled the babe close, protecting and loving him. He brushed the stray tendrils of dark hair from her cheek and found her skin smooth and soft. He laid his head down again and closed his eyes, willing himself to sleep.

When he did, he dreamed he was chained in a small, dark cell without a door or window. There was no iron grate above him through which the guards could spy on him, only walls pressing in on him, the darkness growing. He opened his mouth to scream, but no sound came. He couldn't breathe and struggled.

"Atretes," someone said softly and he felt a gentle hand on his face. "It's all right. Shhh."

He drifted again, on calmer seas.

When he awakened, he saw Rizpah asleep beneath the marble bench. Annoyed, he prodded her. "It's dawn."

Atretes spent the last of his money on food on their way into the heart of the Empire. When he asked directions to the arena, Rizpah spoke for the first time all morning.

"Why are we going there?" He had been so determined to avoid it in Ephesus. Why was he seeking the place out in Rome?

"The Ludus Magnus is close by. I know a man there who can help me." Just beyond the bustling construction of the colossal Flavian amphitheater was the ludus where he had spent the darkest years of his life.

"We can't go there, Atretes."

"There's no other place we can go. You were right about Gallus," he said grimly, "but there's one man I can trust, and he's at the ludus."

"How can you trust anyone in that place?"

"Bato saved my life more than once."

"A gladiator is worth more alive than dead."

He took her by the arm and jerked her around, almost propelling her in the direction he intended to go. "We're wasting time." He looked at the thick walls as he came round to the heavy iron gate. Four guards were on duty, making sure that no amoratae gained admittance. Only paying customers were allowed in to view the gladiatorial practices or participate in them. He had first seen Julia standing on the spectators' balcony. She had come with her promiscuous friend to view him in practice.

"Let's go away from this place while we can," Rizpah said.

His fingers tightened, silencing her. "Is Bato still lanista?" he said to one of the guards.

"None other," the man said, glancing from Atretes to Rizpah. He smiled slightly, his gaze moving down over her in open admiration.

"Cover your face," Atretes commanded her impatiently and stepped in front of her as she did so. "Tell Bato there's a German at the gate who would speak with him," he said coldly.

"Should he be impressed?" the guard said.

Another measured him, curious. "He looks familiar."

"Send the message," Atretes said.

The guard to whom he spoke gave a piercing whistle. Startled, Caleb began to cry in Rizpah's arms. A messenger came on the run. "Inform Bato a barbarian wishes to have an audience with him," the guard said.

Atretes waited until he saw Bato step out onto the balcony over the practice arena and look toward the gate before he removed his turban. The guards stared at his long blonde hair. "By the gods," one said under his breath. "I know who this man is."

Bato went back inside. The servant who had been sent with the message came running. "Admit him and escort him to Bato immediately."

When the gate swung open, Rizpah held back. Atretes put his arm around her shoulders and drew her in alongside him. The

The Soil

gates closed behind them. His hand dropped to the small of her back, pressing her forward.

They crossed the courtyard and entered the building. Two guards escorted them down a long corridor and up marble steps to the second story. They walked along a portico overlooking a barren yard where twenty men, clad in little more than breechcloths, were going through a series of martial exercises. The trainer shouted sharp commands and walked back and forth along the front line, watching their performance. Against one wall, Rizpah saw a man tied to a post, his back showing the bloody stripes of a recent flogging.

Atretes took her arm and drew her along. "Say nothing."

The two guards stopped outside an open doorway, and Atretes entered. He let go of her as soon as he passed the threshold. A black man stood in the middle of the room. He was as tall and as powerfully built as Atretes. Though he gave Rizpah nothing more than a cursory glance, she felt the impact of acute intelligence and grave dignity.

Without a word, Atretes drew the gold chain from his tunic and let the ivory chip drop against his chest. The African looked at it and smiled. "That answers my first question," he said in heavily accented Greek. A mere lift of his head and the two guards departed. Rizpah could still hear the voice of the trainer in the compound. A whip cracked as a command was repeated.

"Would you care for some wine?"

"And food," Atretes said.

Bato nodded once to a servant and the man departed to do his bidding. Bato studied Atretes briefly and then looked at Rizpah again, studying her this time. She was very beautiful and clearly distressed to be in the ludus. A baby was wrapped in a shawl tied around her shoulders, and she put her arms around him and drew him closer as Bato studied her. A whip cracked again, and this time a man gave a cry of pain. Wincing, she glanced toward the door, her face paling.

Atretes closed the door and gave her a light push into the center of the room. "Sit over there," he told her in a tone that allowed no argument. She did as he commanded.

Bato poured wine. "What brings you back to Rome, Atretes?"

"I need money, lodgings, and a map to show me the way back to Germania."

"Is that all?"

Ignoring the lanista's sarcasm, Atretes took the proffered goblet.

Bato poured another and carried it to the woman. She had beautiful dark eyes like Julia Valerian, but it wasn't her. "Sertes sent a representative about six months ago," he said, looking at the child. The babe had her coloring. "I was informed you'd earned your freedom in an elimination match and now owned a villa grander than the proconsul." She took the goblet from his hand and looked up at him. His mouth tipped slightly. He could see quite plainly that she didn't trust him.

"I did," Atretes said. He said nothing about Rizpah, though Bato was looking her over with open interest and unveiled question. The less he knew about her, the better. Women were of little value in this place.

"What happened?" Bato said, turning to him and leaving his perusal of the woman and child.

"I left Ephesus in a hurry."

"Did you murder Sertes?"

Atretes gave a brittle laugh and drained the goblet of wine. "Had I time and opportunity, it would've been my pleasure."

Rizpah looked at him and saw he meant it.

"So why did you leave in such a hurry?"

"He'd found a way to force me back into the arena." His gaze flickered pointedly to the woman and child.

"And you think it'll be different here?"

Her heart began beating wildly.

"Meaning?" Atretes said coldly, setting the goblet on the table.

"Meaning you haven't been gone long enough for certain people to forget you. Domitian, for one. Or have you forgotten the emperor's brother?"

"I earned my freedom."

"Freedom is easily revoked. You deliberately humiliated one of his closest friends during an exercise match."

"That was a long time ago, and Domitian took his revenge when he matched me with one of my own tribesmen."

"Small revenge by his standards, Atretes. Domitian won't consider the score settled until you're dead. It's your good fortune that you haven't been gone long enough for the mob to forget you as well."

"Surely you aren't suggesting Atretes fight again."

The Soil

Bato was surprised she had spoken. She had seemed a beautiful but meek little thing when she entered the room. Now, he wondered. There was fire in her eyes. "He may have no choice."

She left the couch and stood in front of Atretes. "Let's leave this place, *now*. Please."

Atretes might have been deaf for all the attention he paid her.

"If Domitian finds out you're here, you may not get out alive again," Bato said frankly.

"Do you plan to tell him?" Atretes said, eyes narrowing.

"No, but he has friends among the guards. One was at the gate when you arrived." He looked pointedly at the woman. "This is the last place you should've brought her and the child."

Atretes' eyes darkened. "If Pugnax is trustworthy, I'll take lodgings there."

"So be it. Your presence at the inn will guarantee him additional business. Make sure he pays you well. Do you remember how to get there?"

"No. It was in the middle of the night when you took me. Remember?"

Bato laughed. "I remember that night very well." The servant entered. As the platter was put on the table, Bato dismissed him with a wave of his hand. "Eat while I give you instructions," he told Atretes and Rizpah.

Rizpah had no appetite. She listened carefully to Bato's instructions while studying the lanista. Could he be trusted? Or was he another of Gallus' bent, pretending to be a friend while plotting ways to use Atretes?

Atretes ate a hearty portion of meat, bread, and fruit and downed two more goblets of wine before his hunger was satisfied.

"We'll go through the tunnels," Bato said. "The guards won't see you leave and will assume you're still here."

He led them down the portico overlooking the training grounds. The gladiators were going through exercises with wooden swords. Atretes didn't pause or even turn his head. Now that she had seen a glimpse of the brutal life of the ludus, Rizpah ached for him.

They went down steps to the baths and then down another corridor. Bato took a burning torch from a wall mounting as he opened a heavy door. "Through here."

Rizpah imagined the men who had gone down this long,

darkened corridor knowing they would face death at the other end. Bato and Atretes said nothing as they walked ahead of her. Their silence was respectful and full of the grim history that lay between them. A door stood open at the far end, giving entry into more corridors that led to holding cells beneath the arena itself. They followed the granite steps up into a large room with benches against the stone walls. Rizpah saw the arena through the iron gate.

Atretes paused and looked out at the wide expanse of freshly raked sand and the tiers of marble rows where thousands of spectators sat during the ludi. There were moments, as now, when the excited fury of the mob still rang in his ears like a strong heartbeat quickening his blood.

How many times had he stood in this room, armor polished, sword sharpened, greave in place, waiting to step out into the glaring sunlight and face death and the impassioned throng crying out his name over and over? He had hated it, hated them. At times, he had even hated himself.

Why, then, did he miss it?

Turning, he saw Bato standing near another doorway. "You begin to understand," the lanista said solemnly.

"They took more than my freedom. They took my soul."

Compassion filled Rizpah at the bleakness in his voice. She went to him. He looked down at her with haunted eyes, and she took his hand. "You have a soul, Atretes," she said. "Before God, you have a soul. He gave it to you."

Bato offered no advice or comfort; Atretes was a man to accept neither and resent both. Yet as the woman took Atretes' hand and placed it on the sleeping child, Bato saw a softening, not when Atretes touched the babe, but when he looked at the woman. He had a feeling this one would prove herself far better than Julia Valerian.

"This way," Bato said and led the way down another corridor that opened into a large room inside an iron gate that looked out into the arena.

"What is this place?" Rizpah said in a hushed voice, for it oppressed her spirit.

"The dead are brought through those gates," Atretes said.

"This is the best way out," Bato said and showed them along the corridor where the bodies were carried to waiting wagons that removed them for burial outside the walls of the city.

Rizpah let go of Atretes' hand. She could hardly breathe, staring down the long, dark corridor. Atretes put his arm around her shoulders and drew her into the onerous hallway along with him. Her heart beat heavily as they followed the lanista.

Bato set the torch into a mounting at the end of the stone corridor. He took several coins from his belt and held them out to Rizpah. "You'll find your appetite when you leave this place." She took them and thanked him for his kindness.

"May her god protect you," he said to Atretes as he opened the heavy door. Beyond it was a Roman street and sunlight.

18

Pugnax had increased in girth as well as wealth over the three years since Atretes had last seen him. His cropped hair was graying at the temples and the lines in his face had deepened. Atretes took in the grander surroundings, well aware that the largess had come from the mural painted on the front of the inn depicting himself in combat. He couldn't read the sign, but had a good idea what it said.

"So you earned your freedom," Pugnax said, noting the ivory chip hanging from the gold chain around Atretes' neck. He admired Rizpah, if not the babe in her arms, adding with a grin, "And have more to show for it than I."

Atretes didn't like the way Pugnax stared at Rizpah. "I need to earn enough money to make the journey back to Germania."

Pugnax gave a hard laugh. "You carry a vain hope, Atretes. You can't go back. You're no more German anymore than I'm a Gaul."

"Speak for yourself."

"You think I'm wrong? Like it or not, you aren't the man the Romans captured ten years ago. Rome has changed you."

"That may be so, but I'm still Chatti."

"Whatever you were, your people will know the difference now, even if you don't." He gave a slight wave of his hand. "But then, what does it matter? The Chatti are long dead."

"*I'm* alive. Others will be also."

"Scattered and disorganized." Pugnax felt the silence in the common room and glanced around, noting how his patrons stared at Atretes and whispered among themselves.

Atretes noticed as well, though he liked it less than Pugnax. "How much will you pay me to stay here?"

Pugnax laughed. "You've no subtlety at all, have you?"

"There were games enough in the arena."

"Philo, Atretes and I will have the best wine," he announced loudly enough to be heard by anyone in the room. A shiver of alarm raced through Rizpah as she felt the ripple of excitement spread. "It *is* him," someone whispered as they passed by.

"By the fates, I'd give half of what I own to see him fight again," said another.

Well satisfied with the stir he had caused, Pugnax gestured grandly. "Come, my friend. Sit and have some wine. We'll talk of old times."

Men stared at Atretes and then looked at Rizpah as he took hold of her arm, drawing her alongside him as he followed Pugnax to a table clearly reserved for more affluent patrons. Reclining on the proffered couch of honor, Atretes gestured for her to join him. She sat, Caleb on her lap, his head leaning comfortably against her breasts as he slept. She was uncomfortable being the focus of so much attention.

"They haven't forgotten you," Pugnax said with a hint of envy.

"A fact that will bring you benefit. Think how many will come and buy your wine when they know I'm here," Atretes said dryly.

"They will bring gifts to lay at the feet of their idol."

Atretes' eyes narrowed. "Do you mock me, Pugnax?"

"No more than I mock myself. The light of glory doesn't shine long on any man. Make the most of it while you can."

"All I want is enough gold to get me home."

Pugnax's mouth curved. "One match in the games scheduled for next week and you'd have that. You could name your price, and Titus would pay it."

Rizpah glanced at Atretes, concerned that he might consider fighting again. His expression was veiled.

Atretes smiled without warmth. "I prefer that you pay it," he replied. "My terms are simple: an equal share of your profits for as long as I remain in this inn." When Pugnax started to protest, he added, "If you prefer, I'll go down the street and make the same offer to your competitor."

"No need to do that. I agree to your terms."

"One hundred denarii . . ."

"*One hundred!*"

". . . in advance, and arrange for guards, enough of them to prevent a repeat of my last visit here. I don't want my clothes torn off by a mob of women." He ignored Rizpah's raised eyebrow. "And see that the woman and her child have comfortable, secure lodgings," he added, jerking his head toward Rizpah almost as though an afterthought.

Pugnax took the opportunity to look her over again. "On the

premises, or would you prefer her elsewhere?" Pugnax cast him a knowing smile. "You may wish to entertain admirers."

Atretes understood his meaning and was unaccountably annoyed by it. "I want her close at hand, but not so close she's in my bed." Color filled Rizpah's cheeks, and she cast him an annoyed glance. "Unless I want her there," he added.

"Consider it done," Pugnax said and rose to make the arrangements.

Atretes looked at Rizpah, his mouth tipping in amusement. "You look disturbed, my lady. Was it something I said?"

"You know very well what you said and what you were implying to your friend."

"He's not my friend, and I thought it best to let him know you belong to me."

"The fact of my coming here with you said enough."

"It needed stating."

She could feel people staring at them and felt intensely uncomfortable. "Are you sure we'll be safe here?" His mouth tightened as she looked around. "I never realized how well known you would be here."

He turned his head slowly. His hard, challenging stare made most patrons look away. "There are certain advantages to being recognized," he said coolly, all trace of his earlier amusement gone.

"What advantages? Bato warned us about Domitian. You're placing your life in the hands of Pugnax, who will no doubt hire criers to go about the city announcing your presence here."

"I don't intend to stay long."

"You may be in Rome forever if the brother of the emperor wants you in chains."

His eyes blazed. "Woman, why must you always try my patience?" He sat up and leaned toward her.

Impossible man! "Why must you grow angry at everything that's said to you? You're deliberately putting yourself in danger here, and you've put Caleb in danger with you. Don't expect me to be happy about it."

A muscle jerked in his cheek. "I don't care if you're happy or not. The fact is I need money to get us where we're going. This is the cleanest and fastest way I could think to get it."

"Cleanest way?"

"No doubt you prefer me in the arena."

She would rather he had trusted Theophilus, but knew saying so would only exacerbate his darkening mood. She had already learned Atretes couldn't do anything the easy way, especially if it meant swallowing his monumental pride. "No, I don't want you in the arena. I want you safe and at peace with yourself and God."

"And you think that would've been the case if I'd handed myself over to that bloody centurion of yours."

"Theophilus saved your life twice. He said—"

Atretes made a harsh sound. "The arena would be the quickest way." He raked his hands through his hair. "I'd either have the gold to return home or I'd be dead. Either way, I win."

Appalled at his words, she stared at him. "You can't mean it."

"I mean it. Oh, I mean it."

"If it was my wayward tongue that put such a thought in your head, forgive me. Atretes, please," she said, laying her hand against his cheek, "you have too much to live for to allow yourself to think in this way."

Her touch sent a rush of sensation through his body, rousing an intense physical desire as well as a deeper longing he didn't want to analyze. He looked straight into her eyes. Hers went wide and she took her hand from him. "Why must you always misunderstand me?" she said and looked away.

He turned her face back and smiled sardonically. "Maybe I do have something to live for, but I doubt the reasons I can think of right now have any similarities to yours." He liked the rosy color that poured into her cheeks, the warmth of her skin when he brushed it with his fingertips.

She drew back from his touch. "People are watching us," she said, embarrassed.

"Good. They'll know to stay away from you."

Pugnax showed them upstairs and opened the door into a spacious bedchamber. Rizpah didn't move from the corridor until Atretes took her arm and pulled her into the room.

"Through here, my lady," Pugnax said. He showed Rizpah into a small connecting room meant to accommodate a manservant or lady's maid and left her there.

"Close enough?" she heard him say to Atretes. "Or would you prefer more privacy and her in a chamber not connected to your own?"

"She will be safe where she is."

"And if you want other women?"

Atretes said something low and dismissed him.

Pugnax did exactly as she feared. *"Atretes has returned to Rome,"* a crier called below their window. *"You can see him at the inn of Pugnax, gladiator of the great Circus Maximus!"* Within hours, people began to arrive. Pugnax charged a fee for entry into his inn, the price increasing as did the numbers.

Although Atretes agreed to spend several hours in the banquet room so that guests could see him, he made no attempt to entertain anyone with stories of his exploits in the arena. In fact, he made no effort to talk to anyone who approached him. Women were enticed by his reticence; men resented it.

Rizpah remained in the upstairs room, eager to avoid curious eyes and embarrassing speculations. Atretes would return to the room tense, restless, and it worsened with each day that passed.

Caleb fussed incessantly. She was afraid he was sick until she felt the two small nubs sink into her breast and realized what was the matter. She rubbed his sore gums. Still he cried in frustration, and she put him down on a blanket, watching as he crawled off of it and headed across the room toward the carved legs of a couch. When he began to chew on one, she picked him up and put him back on the blanket again. He screamed in outrage.

Sure the sound carried right through the walls, Rizpah snatched up one of the fancy cushions and dangled it above him. "Caleb," she said and swished his nose with a tassel. He stopped crying and reached up to grasp hold. She sat down and watched him chew on the captured cushion. He was not distracted for long.

She was exhausted when Atretes entered the room. He threw a pouch of coins onto the bed and stared at her for a moment in silence. "I've been invited to a banquet," he finally said cryptically.

She was sure it wasn't the first or only kind of invitation he had received over the past few days. She had dared go downstairs only once, curious to see his many amoratae and how they behaved toward him. It had only taken a few minutes to see the temptations he faced. Women surrounded him; beautiful, bold women who wanted him.

"Are you going?"

He turned his head and looked at her. Did she want him to leave? Was his company so distasteful? "Lady Perenna is not without a certain charm," he said cynically, testing her reaction.

She fought down the sudden desire to jump up, slap his face, and scream at him the way Caleb had been screaming all afternoon. Instead, she rose from the floor and picked Caleb up with as much dignity as she could. "Do whatever pleases you, my lord, with Lady Perenna or anyone else who might wish to kiss your feet." She carried the baby into the small servant's quarters.

Caleb started to cry again. She tried to hold him close and comfort him, but he screamed louder, pushing at her. "Oh, Caleb," she whispered brokenly, fighting back tears.

"Why don't you nurse him?" Atretes said, standing in the doorway, smiling faintly.

"While you stand watching? I think not."

His jaw stiffened. "There's more to view downstairs."

"Then *go* downstairs."

"Give him suck, woman, or he'll scream the walls down around our heads."

Her eyes pricked with angry tears. "It won't do any good. He's not hungry."

He frowned, straightening. He stepped into the small enclosure and knelt down before her. "Why didn't you tell me something was wrong with him?"

"Nothing's wrong. He's teething. He hurts, and I can't do anything to soothe—"

"Give him to me."

"I thought you were going to a banquet this evening."

He looked at her, brows raised slightly.

Heat flooded her cheeks, and she was immediately ashamed. She sounded like a nagging wife and she was nothing to him. He took Caleb from her, and she lowered her eyes, mortified. As Atretes straightened, she could feel him staring at her, willing her to look up at him. She closed her eyes and fought her roiling emotions. If he didn't leave soon, she would completely humiliate herself by dissolving into tears.

He left her small servants quarters, and she took a ragged breath, relieved that he had said nothing to mock her.

She knew what was wrong. O Lord, she knew, but prayed Atretes didn't. She was in love with the wretched man and jealous over the lovely, wealthy women who fawned over and petted him. She had loved Shimei, but it had been a sweet love, full of tenderness as he led her closer to the Lord. She had never felt the fierce, frightening, heart-pounding passions Atretes roused in her. Surely such feelings were not of God. They made her feel vulnerable. The man touched her, and she trembled. He looked at her, and her insides melted. She put her clenched fists against her burning eyes.

Atretes stretched out on the bed, waiting for Rizpah to come back into the room, willing her to do so. He put his fretting son on his chest and let him chew on the ivory chip. When Caleb began to quiet, he took the chip away, knowing his crying would bring Rizpah quicker than any command he might give her. The woman didn't have a submissive bone in her body. Just as he thought, a moment later she appeared around the corner. As she did so, he gave the chip back to Caleb to calm him again. She started to turn away.

"Count the money and tell me how much there is," he said, annoyed. He watched her walk to the foot of the bed, pick up the pouch and pour the gold coins into her hand. She told him how much there was.

"This is more than you had with you when we left Ephesus."

"Not enough to get us to Germania."

She poured the coins back into the pouch.

Her expression was telling. "You have something to say?" he asked, his voice challenging.

She raised her head, her beautiful dark eyes meeting his. "Would you listen?" she said quietly.

"If your words have any merit."

"You have enough now, Atretes," she said, not rising to his provocation. "The Lord has provided you with the means to return home."

"There are other things to consider," he said coolly.

"What things?" A muscle tightened in his jaw but he didn't answer. She moved to the table near the head of the bed and put the pouch on it. "Sometimes I find myself wondering if you're so conditioned to fighting for your life that you only feel comfortable when your life is at risk."

"Don't talk like a fool."

"Is it foolish? The longer we remain, the greater the risk becomes. And you know it." She leaned down to take Caleb. "I think money is the least of the reasons we are here," she said, straightening.

His eyes flashed. "Then why do you think we're here?"

She hesitated and then told him the truth. "There's a part of you that wants to fight again."

19

Bato came the following night. He spread out a map on the table. Atretes held the clay lamp over it. "Here's Rome," Bato told him, tapping his finger on the scroll. "All of this is Germania," he said, sweeping it up and across a broad portion of the map. "I hope you know exactly where you're going."

Atretes set the lamp down and held the scroll open, staring at it bleakly.

What Rizpah had said had plagued him for the past two days. She was right, and it disturbed him no small bit. The battle aboard the Alexandrian had brought back the heated rush he had always felt in the arena. He hadn't realized how much he missed it or how good it had sometimes felt. He felt it here, in this inn, facing the crowds and waiting.

But waiting for what? To be locked in a cell again and brought out only for training, viewing, and fighting in the arena?

He shook the thoughts from his head. He was faced with even worse questions at the moment. He looked at the map on the table and was overwhelmed with a terrible realization: It had been ten years since he had been brought in chains by wagon across the mountains and down the boot of Italy past Rome to Capua. It had taken months to make the journey, long, arduous months of travel, attempted escapes, and savage beatings. He had given no thought to memorizing landmarks or townships. Instead, hatred had fed upon him and given him reason to live, all the while blinding him to what he needed to remember in order to return to his homeland.

Studying the scroll, he realized the vast territory it represented. How many rivers and mountains lay between him and home?

Rizpah stood looking at him, Caleb in her arms. The question he was asking himself shone in her eyes. Could he find his way back to his people?

"Are you still going?" Bato said, fully aware of the monumental task ahead if Atretes should choose to do so.

"Yes."

"You could name your price in the arena," he said and earned a hard look from Atretes. "As you will it, my friend, but I suggest you leave soon. Domitian knows you're here. He sent for me yesterday and told me to make you an offer."

"Save it."

Bato wished him well and left.

"We'll leave at first light," Atretes said and saw relief flood Rizpah's face.

"Thank God," she murmured.

"Pugnax owes me for the last two days. It will be enough for our purposes." He left the room to collect it.

A hum of excitement filled the banquet room as he entered. People greeted him, some staring at him in awe while others spoke to him with an unearned familiarity as he passed. Atretes spotted Pugnax across the elaborately decorated chamber. He was speaking to a man dressed in a fine white toga trimmed richly in red and gold.

"A word with you, Pugnax," Atretes said, jerking his head.

Pugnax's guest turned to face him, and Atretes recognized him immediately. He had changed little in the four years since he had seen him and Atretes was in no doubt of why he had come.

"Ephorbus Timalchio Callistus," Pugnax said with the respect due a man of power and position. Atretes ignored his look of warning as well as the proffered wine goblet.

"Atretes," Callistus said with a catlike smile. He lifted a goblet in mock salute. "We met once before, though I doubt you remember my face."

Indeed, he remembered. The son of a senator had come to the ludus for the fashionable exercise of sparring with a gladiator. Bato had tried to warn Callistus away from Atretes, but the supercilious little aristocrat insisted. With no choice, Bato spelled out the rules to Atretes. He followed them to a point and then cast them to the wind. He had toyed with the arrogant young man, intending to kill him in the end. It would have given him great satisfaction to cut down the Roman aristocrat who thought he was better than a German slave. Had Bato not stayed his hand, Callistus wouldn't be standing here with only a scar on his cheek and another hidden beneath his expensive embroidered toga. He'd be entombed along the Appian Way.

Atretes smiled coldly. "Do you still go to the ludus to spar with gladiators?"

Callistus' eyes narrowed at the challenge. "Indeed. I've thirteen kills to my credit since my match with you."

A war cry echoed in Atretes' head. "Match?" he said, contemptuous. "Is that what you call it?" He sneered. "I imagine your opponents were given the same command I was. Don't draw the boy's blood."

Callistus' expression changed. His eyes flickered to those around him, feeling the hush and then the whispers as Atretes' words were spread around the room.

Atretes smiled as he watched the scar he had put on Callistus' face whiten.

"Perhaps you've forgotten the results of your last insult," Callistus said quietly.

"Results?" Atretes said sardonically. "I know what you hoped to see. Me, crucified. I was told Vespasian felt that was a sorry waste of money already spent on my conditioning and training. So he sent me into the arena a few months earlier than scheduled. As you can see, I survived. And earned my freedom."

"Only a fool would speak to *me* in such a manner."

"Or a man who knows who and what you are," Atretes said with disdain.

Pugnax grasped his arm in warning. "Enough," he said under his breath.

"You're asking to die," Callistus said, shaking with rage.

Atretes looked straight into his eyes and laughed contemptuously. "Do you really think *you* could kill me?" He stepped forward and saw fear pour into Callistus' eyes. "Do you think you'd come out alive in a match against me? You know what I think? I think you're still the same spoiled *boy* who tucked tail and ran to Domitian."

Several spectators drew in their breath at his words, moving back to whisper among themselves.

Red-faced, Callistus turned away. Halfway across the room, he turned back, face mottled with rage. "Enjoy your freedom while you can, barbarian! It's about to end!"

Atretes took a step forward, but Pugnax blocked his way. He tried to shove past him, but the ex-gladiator had the help of two bodyguards. "Running to Domitian again, you coward?" Atretes shouted.

"Have you gone mad?" Pugnax said, grappling with him.

"You want a fight, Callistus? I'll give you one. Anytime. Anywhere!"

"Shut up!"

Atretes broke his hold and pushed one of the guards out of his way, but Callistus was already gone. People drew back from Atretes as though he had gone mad. What man in his right mind would insult and challenge a man with the ear of Domitian, Emperor Titus' own brother?

Atretes stood in the middle of the room and felt the force of their stares. He looked around, his gaze passing from face to face and saw what they wanted, what they hoped, had been accomplished. And he knew if he stayed, it would happen.

*

Rizpah jumped when the door burst open, banging loudly against the wall as Atretes stormed in. Caleb yelped in fright and started to cry. She picked him up from the floor where she had been playing with him and rose.

"What's happened?" she said softly and received no answer.

Atretes paced like a caged animal, pausing only long enough to pick up a wine goblet and send it crashing against a wall as he muttered blackly in German.

Pugnax entered and tossed a pouch of gold coins onto the table. "Take it and get out of here while you can."

Atretes swept the pouch onto the floor. "*I'm* not tucking tail and running from that little—"

"Then you'll be back in the ludus by tomorrow night! Just in time to get a good night's sleep before the games begin!"

Atretes spat out a harsh word and kicked the table over. Rizpah drew back sharply.

"You knew what you were doing!" Pugnax said in accusation. "Did it salve your bloody pride? Will it when they have you in chains? By the gods, you may have me in chains as well!"

"Remind Callistus you kept me from breaking his neck!"

"What about her?" Pugnax said, nodding to Rizpah, who stood on the far side of the room trying to calm a screaming Caleb.

Atretes stopped and turned, his expression dangerous. "What about her?"

"Have you forgotten how things work? Domitian and

Callistus will make her part of whatever they've planned for you. And it won't be pretty."

Atretes looked at her ashen face and remembered some of the things he had seen done to women in the arena, things too foul and depraved to even contemplate happening to a stranger, let alone *her*. He would rather forfeit his own life than see Rizpah harmed in any way, and the realization shook him.

"Let me take her," Pugnax said.

Atretes turned on him. "Get out!"

"Her fate will be on your head."

As Pugnax left, Rizpah came close to him and put her hand on his arm. "My fate is in the hands of the Lord, Atretes. Not in yours, not even in my own."

Atretes looked down at her. If only he could believe in something as strongly as she believed in her Christ! What was it about this Christ that made his followers so sure of him? Atretes shook his head. Faith in anything of this world had been beaten from him long ago. "Take the gold and go to your friends. They'll keep you safe."

"My place is with you. God set me at your side."

Atretes caught hold of her arm, his fingers biting painfully into her flesh. "Don't argue, woman! Do what I tell you!" He gave her a shove toward her small chamber just as someone rapped hard on the door. "A centurion and four soldiers just came in," one of the bodyguards said through the closed door.

"*Move,*" Atretes snarled at her, but she stood her ground, no fear in her eyes.

"If it's the Lord's will we go to Germania, he will deliver us."

He turned at the familiar sound of hobnail sandals and the jangle of brass-studded belts. Soldiers were in the corridor outside.

"Get back in there," he said, shoving her toward the doorway to her small chamber. "And keep the babe quiet."

"I'm not leaving you."

"Do as I say!"

She stood firm.

There was a stubbornness in her he knew could never be broken. "You'll be in my way." Before he could make her do his will, the door burst open, and two legionnaires took positions just inside on either side as a third, in the full crimson and polished brass regalia of a Roman centurion, appeared.

"*You!*" Atretes said, his rage full-flower.

"I'm taking you under guard, Atretes," Theophilus said in an uncompromising tone. "Give me your sword."

Atretes drew it. "Where do you want it?"

Theophilus snapped his fingers, and two soldiers moved so that Atretes had to turn his head back and forth to watch them. Two more entered the room just behind Theophilus. "I'll make myself clear. We're taking you under guard, whether you like it or not."

"Don't do this, Theophilus," Rizpah said, heart sinking at the sight of a loosened whip in the hand of one soldier and manacles and chains in the other.

"I have to," Theophilus said grimly. "He's left me with no choice."

"What'd I tell you about trusting a *Roman*?" Atretes said. He spit on the floor at Theophilus' feet and took a fighting stance.

"Move back, Rizpah," Theophilus said.

"This isn't right," she said weakly, stepping forward so that she was almost between them.

"Make it easy, Atretes, or Rizpah might get hurt."

"Don't do this," she said. "Please."

"*Don't beg!*" Atretes said, furious to hear her pleading for him. Grasping her arm, he propelled her to one side. As he did so, his attention shifted just enough for the opening Theophilus needed.

"*Now!*" The two soldiers in the room moved fast as two others entered.

"No!" Rizpah cried out.

Atretes felt the sting of the whip as it snaked around his sword arm. Conditioning overcame instinct, and he retained hold of his weapon. He turned the blade and cut the bond, but not in time to avoid Theophilus' fist.

Atretes fell back from the stunning blow and felt the sting of another whip snaking around his ankles. Chains looped his wrist, staying his sword arm from making an accurate swing at Theophilus' head. Theophilus hit him again, harder this time. Jolted back, Atretes felt his feet yanked from under him. He hit the floor hard. When he tried to rise, someone kicked him back and a heavy foot came down on his sword hand, but he held on.

Uttering a cry of rage, Atretes fought against the four soldiers who held him down until the hilt of Theophilus' gladius cracked into the side of his head. He felt a sharp explosion of pain and then enveloping blackness as Rizpah cried out.

Theophilus sheathed his sword and looked across the room to where she stood, the screaming baby held close in her arms, tears running down her pale cheeks. She tried to go to Atretes, but one of the centurion's men blocked her way. She looked at Theophilus then in hurt accusation and disbelief.

He smiled grimly. "He's got a hard head, Rizpah." His men put shackles on Atretes. "He'll live."

20

Atretes awakened on the wooden planks of a bouncing wagon, sunlight on his face. "Thank God," he heard Rizpah murmur and felt her hand, cool and soft against his forehead. Disoriented, he realized his head was in her lap. When he tried to sit up, heavy fettering chains around his wrists and ankles prevented him from doing so.

"Don't try to move. You'll only hurt yourself more."

He uttered a black oath in German and tried to rise again, yanking hard at his bonds. Pain exploded in his head, and her face doubled above him. A wave of nausea dissolved his strength, and groaning, he lay back.

"Rest," she said, gently smoothing the cold sweat from his forehead. "Try to relax."

Rest? He clenched his teeth, fighting down the nausea. Relax? He remembered Theophilus and his soldiers taking him down and knew every foot this wagon traveled brought him closer to death and her with it. She didn't understand what was ahead or she wouldn't sit so calmly stroking his forehead.

He should have left the banquet room the moment he recognized Callistus instead of giving in to his cursed pride and rage. Hadn't the lanista in Capua told him his temper would be the death of him? Hadn't Bato repeated the same warning at the Great School? Anger had given him an edge in the arena; it had given him strength and kept him alive. Not once had he thought what his anger might do to the innocent.

Each bounce of the heavy wagon sent stabs of pain through his skull. He needed to find a way for them to escape. Instead, grim images filled his mind. He felt fear for the first time in years, a fear that gnawed on his insides. He didn't want to contemplate what Domitian and Callistus might do to Rizpah and his son, yet ugly recollections filled his mind. Better if he took her life now than let her suffer the torture and degradation of the arena.

And what of his son? If he wasn't killed, he would be made into a slave.

Better he died now, too.

He closed his eyes tightly. "Where's the baby?"

"Caleb's with us. He's asleep in a basket."

He tested his bonds again, gritting his teeth against the pain.

"Don't move, Atretes."

"I have to get free!" He jerked hard and tried to sit up again. Blackness closed in like a tightening tunnel, bringing with it nausea. He fought both.

"You can't." She put her arm across his chest. "Lie back. Please."

The blackness receded slowly. He knew he couldn't run and he couldn't fight, but he still could manage to do what had to be done. And he had to do it now, before they arrived at their destination and she was taken from him.

"There's a part of you that wants to fight." Hot tears burned his eyes and his throat closed. That part of him had made him wait just long enough to get her and Caleb killed. He swallowed hard and drew in his breath, fighting against the wave of nausea as he raised his head. "Can you loose me?"

"No. I've tried several times, but the chains are attached to rings in the side of the wagon. Theophilus secured them before we left the inn."

"Didn't anyone try to stop him from taking me?"

Rizpah bit her lip, remembering the throng of people and the shouting. She had feared a riot when Atretes was carried downstairs and out to the wagon, but Theophilus had announced that the great Atretes would fight again. No one had interfered after that. "No," she said.

He understood all too well. The mob had what it wanted. "Help me sit up."

"Why?"

"Don't question me, just do it," he said through clenched teeth.

"Why must you be so stubborn?" Rizpah said as she put her arms around him and helped him rise. His strong fingers bit into her shoulder, the weight of the chains linked between his wrists thumping hard against her. She winced. When he was sitting up, he grasped hold of the side of the wagon and pressed her back. Her heart jumped as his hand moved sluggishly up to encircle her throat.

"He's taking us back to the ludus," he said, his deep voice

thick with emotion. His vision blurred and he fought the pain. He had to stay conscious. There was little time. "You don't know what's waiting for you there. I can't let them. . . ." Breaking her neck would be quicker and less painful than strangling her. He moved his hand slightly, feeling her pulse. "Rizpah," he said heavily, "I . . ."

Do it, he told himself, *just do it and have it done.*

Looking into his blue eyes, she saw his anguish and realized what he intended. Rather than be afraid, a deep compassion filled her. She touched his face tenderly. He closed his eyes as though her touch hurt. "He's not taking us to the ludus, Atretes. I thought so, too, at first, but I know we can't be going there."

"Where else would he take us?" His thumb brushed the pulse in her throat. Warmth. Life. Why did he have to be the one to take it?

"We passed through the city gates."

"The gates?"

"We're no longer in Rome. We're outside the city walls."

His hand loosened. "We can't be. The ludus—" The wagon gave a hard bounce and pain exploded in his head. Groaning, he grasped the side of the wagon more tightly, trying to hold himself up as the blackness closed in around him again.

She gave him what support she could. She had never seen his face so white and was afraid for him. "Theophilus isn't taking you back to the ludus, Atretes."

"Where else would he take me?"

"I don't know." She laid her hand against his cheek. "You must lie back."

His vision became a long dark tunnel. "Capua," he said with a groan, leaning back. He was too heavy for her, dragging her with him. His head banged against the floor of the wagon, and he groaned. "He's taking me back to Capua." He remembered the hole, the tiny cell in which the guards had locked him. There hadn't even been room to sit up or stretch out his legs. He had been shut into darkness for days until he thought he'd go mad. "Better to be dead."

She raised him slightly and laid his head upon her lap again. "We're not heading south. We're heading east."

East?

Where was Theophilus taking them?

Rizpah dabbed the beads of perspiration from Atretes'

forehead and wished she could remove the pain as easily. "Be at peace, Atretes. We're in God's hands."

He uttered a hoarse laugh and winced. "You think your god will get us out of this?"

"God has plans for our welfare. He will give us a future and a hope."

"Hope," he said bitterly. "What hope is there in this wagon?"

"All things work together for good to those who believe."

"I don't believe in anything."

"I *do*, and whether you do or not, we've both been called to his purpose."

The woman's tenacious faith defied all logic. "I'm in chains again, you and the babe with me. There's only one purpose in that."

She ran her fingers slowly across his brow and smiled down at him. "God has seen me through worse situations than this."

He opened his eyes and looked up at her. Was she talking about the night they had left the Ephesian villa? Was she referring to the battle on the Alexandrian ship? "God's gotten you out of nothing. *I* got you out." He closed his eyes against the piercing glare and wondered how she could be at peace in these circumstances. What could possibly sustain her so? "And I'll get us out of this, too. Somehow."

"You haven't gotten us out of anything. You're always running *to* trouble, not away from it."

He glared up at her, affronted. "You think your god is the one protecting you?"

"I know he is."

He gave a hoarse laugh. "Who saved you from Sertes? Who saved you from the Macedonian?"

"Who saved you from death countless times? Is it by accident or design that you're alive now?"

"I saved myself." A frown crossed his forehead briefly as he remembered Theophilus blocking a sword thrust. His efforts then were negated by his actions now.

"Has there never been anyone who has stood between you and death?"

"When it served their purposes." How much would the Roman get when he was delivered to Domitian?

"God will rescue us again."

"Don't put your hope in a god you can't see and who let his son be crucified. What good was he to Hadassah?"

"It's because of God's Son that I do have hope. All my hope rests in him." Her fingers lightly combed the hair back from his forehead and temples. "Even my hope for you."

His head ached too much to argue with her or even think more deeply on what she said.

Atretes heard horses galloping toward them from behind. The sound of their beating hooves on the heavy stones of the Roman road reverberated in his aching skull. He knew they were Roman soldiers by the jangling of their brass-studded belts.

"No one is following," a man said.

"That way," he heard Theophilus command, and the wagon gave a hard bounce as it left the road. Atretes let out a groan, spots of color bursting behind his closed eyes. He wanted the darkness, the oblivion in which there was no pain, no torturous thoughts of what lay ahead. Neither came.

They traveled a long time over softer ground. He knew they were well off the main road.

Theophilus spoke occasionally, but the words were indistinct. When they stopped, the Roman came close. "Keep watch while I get him out of the wagon."

Atretes heard the chains released and felt them pulled through the rings on his ankles.

"We're at the *hypogeum* of Gaudentius Servera Novatian. His great-granddaughter, the Lady Alphina, is a Christian," Theophilus said, tossing the chains and removing the manacles. "Sorry I hit you so hard, my friend." He took Atretes by the arm and pulled him up easily. "I had no time to explain." He looped Atretes' arm around his shoulder. "Not that you would've listened."

Atretes muttered something under his breath, and Theophilus grinned as he bore the burden of the German's weight against his side. "Instead of cursing me in German, you could say thanks in Greek."

"We thought you were taking him back to the ludus," Rizpah said, ashamed for having doubted him.

"So did everyone else at the inn," Theophilus said, helping Atretes down the ramp that had been lowered from the back of the wagon. "That's why there wasn't a riot. All of Rome would like to see this stubborn fool back in the arena."

She took up the basket in which Caleb slept. Two men came running from what appeared to be a mausoleum. Theophilus gave Atretes over to their care and returned to his men. "Apuleius, my friend. I thank you." He clasped arms with him. "Give Domitian no opportunity to question you. Do not return to the praetorian." He took a small scroll from inside his chest armor. "Take this and ride to Tarentum. Give it to Justus Minor, no one else." Theophilus slapped his shoulder. "Now, go."

The soldier said something under his breath and handed him a pouch before he mounted his horse. He stretched out his hand in salute. "May God protect you, my lord." The others followed suit.

"And you, my friends. God be with you."

Apuleius swung his horse around and galloped across the field toward the main road, the others falling in behind him.

Rizpah set Caleb down in his basket and went to Theophilus. Tears blurring her eyes, she went down on her knees and put her hands on his feet. "Forgive me," she said, weeping. "I shouldn't have doubted you."

He caught firm hold of her and raised her to her feet. Tilting her chin, he smiled. "You're forgiven, Rizpah." He brushed her cheek lightly and then said more briskly. "Think no more of it. Had your distress not been genuine, everything might have gone differently at the inn. Your doubt served good purpose."

Caleb roused. Theophilus stepped past her and took him from his basket. Caleb cried louder. "It would appear only his mother will do," he said with a laugh and handed the baby to her. "I'll carry the basket." Caleb snuggled against her, peering at Theophilus from the safety of her arms. He let out a squeal and leaned toward Theophilus, who chucked him playfully under the chin.

"It was fortunate you found us when you did," she said as they walked together.

"I knew within hours where to find you. I told you Atretes would make it easy." He shook his head. "He has more courage than sense."

"What sort of trouble will this bring upon your head, Theophilus? You're still in service to the emperor."

"Not as of two days ago. My required twenty years of service were completed five years ago. Now I have asked permission to retire, and Titus granted it. I have in my possession a proclamation with his seal giving me the right to claim a portion of land in any frontier province of my choosing. He suggested several where there are *civitates* started and run by retired soldiers; Gaul for one, and Britannia." He gave her a lopsided grin. "He made no mention of Germania, nor did I." They reached the narrow stone doorway to the catacombs.

Theophilus went ahead of her down the steep stairway cut into the soft Latium tufa, his hand beneath her arm to give her support. "Don't be alarmed by the appearance of the place," he said. "Your customs are somewhat different in Ionia. These tunnels have been here for several generations. Gunderius Severas Novatian was the first of many to be entombed here. His great-grandson, Tiberias, heard the apostle Paul speak before Caesar and was redeemed by Christ that day. Before he died of a fever, he told his sister to use this place as a sanctuary for those who had need of it."

The stairway ended and followed a short, narrow earthen passageway to an underground chamber, called a *cubicula*, that constituted the nucleus of the family vault. It was illuminated by a pitlike opening in the ceiling that had served for removal of earth during the excavation.

The room was cool, a large natural spring filling a tiled *refrigeria* used for funeral libations. The walls of the cubicula were plastered and frescoed with flowers, birds, and animals.

Two *arcosolia* were before her. These cells for the dead had been hollowed out of the tufa, plastered, and sealed with horizontal slabs for lids over the graves surmounted by two arches. In the lunette of one was a fresco of Hercules bringing the heroic Alcestis back from Hades to her husband, Admetus, for whom she had sacrificed her life. The legendary scene symbolized conjugal love. In the other lunette was a fresco of Hercules killing the Hydra.

Another cubicula opened off to Rizpah's right. In it was a single arcosolium. The lunette bore the fresco of an *orant*, a draped man or woman with arms outstretched in prayer. The closure bore the name Tiberias.

"This way," Theophilus said, his deep voice echoing softly in the stillness.

Rizpah followed him through a doorway to her left. She drew in her breath softly as she saw the tunnel stretch ahead. The catacomb smelled of damp earth, sweet spices, and incense. Rectangular niches called *loculi* had been dug into the tufa walls and sealed with a brick or marble slab door. She knew each loculus contained a body. Small terra-cotta lamps filled with scented oil were placed above many of the tombs, filling the somber gallery with flickering light and the cloying aroma of perfume that mingled with the smell of decay.

Drawing Caleb closer, she walked along the passageway, looking at the doors of the tombs beside and above her on either side. Each bore a name: Pamphilus, Constantia, Pretextatus, Honorius, Commodilla, Marcellinus, Maius. She saw an anchor cut into one slab, a peacock symbolizing eternal life on another, two fish and a loaf of bread on a third.

Theophilus turned a corner, and she followed him by another arcosolium with the vivid colors of a fresco depicting the Good Shepherd with the lost lamb over his shoulders.

"Are all these departed ones Christians?" she said, her voice sounding strange to her own ears.

"Eighty-seven of them are, most in the newer tombs near the bottom where we are. The ones higher up are the older tombs and hold members of the Novatian family. Friends of the family were also allowed to bury their dead here. There are also several generations of slaves accounted for among the loculi."

She heard voices ahead of her. Theophilus led her up another earth and stone stairway into a passageway that widened into another large cubicula. Light came in from above. Atretes sat on a woven pallet against the wall, his face ashen.

Several men were in the room, hovering around Atretes and speaking all at once, but it was the small, elderly woman Rizpah noticed immediately. Her gray hair was curled, braided, and pinned into a coiffure of elegance and dignity. She was attired in a simple blue linen *palla* of very fine quality, but wore few jewels. She handed one of the men a silver goblet of wine, which was offered to Atretes. The lady turned, her lined face lovely and serene.

"Theophilus," she said, clearly holding him in great affection. She held out her hands to him, smiling.

"We are indebted to you, Lady Alphina," he said, taking her hands. Bowing with fond respect, he kissed both.

"You are not indebted to me, but to God," she said. "Our prayers have been answered, have they not?" Her eyes shone with joy as she patted his cheek as though he were a boy and not a weathered soldier.

He laughed. "Indeed, my lady."

"And this lovely girl is the Lady Rizpah," she said, holding out her hand. "Welcome, my dear."

"Thank you, my lady," Rizpah said, drawn to her warmth.

"Please call me Alphina. We are all one in Christ Jesus." She glanced pointedly at Atretes. "I must admit I was curious to see the great Atretes."

"He's looked better," Theophilus said dryly.

"He's exactly as Rufus described: built like Mars with the face of Apollo," she said. "Rufus is my son," she explained to Rizpah. "He went to the inn two nights, but couldn't get near enough to speak with Atretes. He said the amoratae were as thick as corrupt politicians in our senate. We had hoped to bring you here several days ago."

"Atretes wouldn't have come," Rizpah said.

"We needed more gold," Atretes said from where he sat and then looked at her. "We should have enough now. Where is it?"

Rizpah could feel the blood draining from her face and then filling it again, burning hot. "Oh, my lord . . ."

"You forgot it?" he said in consternation. The pain in his head almost blinded him as he swore.

"Apuleius made certain all your possessions were brought," Theophilus said. He untied a heavy leather pouch and tossed it at Atretes' feet. "Including your gold." His mouth curled ruefully. "Rizpah had you on her mind."

Atretes looked from the pouch of gold coins to Theophilus. Troubled, he leaned his head back against the cool, plastered wall.

"I must return and make preparations for this evening," Lady Alphina said. "Domitian is holding a banquet to celebrate some momentous event." She noticed Atretes' sharp, suspicious glance at her and smiled. "He will have to invent a new reason to celebrate now that you've escaped. Rufus said he heard it rumored he was going to have you brought and shown at the feast."

"Are you sure it's wise to go to the palace?" Theophilus said.

"It would be unwise not to go. Besides, I'm concerned for Domitian's young niece, Domitilla. She has a heart for the Lord and I want to use whatever opportunity God gives to speak with her."

She put her hand on Rizpah's arm. "You needn't stay here, Rizpah. If you wish, you may follow that passageway to the *cryptoporticus*. It's quite lovely and right beneath the villa. Caleb would delight in the pretty tiles on the floor, and you'd both be quite safe there."

"She stays with me," Atretes said.

Lady Alphina glanced at him. "My servants are all trustworthy."

Atretes looked back at her coldly. "She stays."

Lady Alphina's expression softened with understanding and pity. "As you wish, Atretes. I suppose it must be difficult for you to trust any Roman, even those who only wish you well."

"Especially if you've a head harder than granite," Theophilus said. He lifted his hand. "I will see you to your villa, my lady."

He walked with Alphina down the long lamplit earthen passageway and entered the cryptoporticus. It was a peaceful place, beautiful with its marble arches, colorful murals, frescoes, and small fountain pool. Beams of sunlight entered from carefully constructed openings in the vault ceiling. It was an underground hideaway from the pressure of daily life, a place of solace that had become a sanctuary for those who shared faith in Christ.

"Perhaps Atretes will join us here tomorrow morning and hear the reading of the apostle Paul's words."

"I'd need the manacles and chains and four men to carry him."

Lady Alphina turned and looked at him. "Despite what you say, Theophilus, I sense how much you admire him."

"How can I not admire a man who's survived ten years in the arena?" He shook his head. "But I don't know how to reach him. He looks at me and doesn't see a man. He sees Rome."

"And is it any wonder?" Lady Alphina said gently, letting her gaze travel pointedly over him. "The Roman army destroyed his people and took him captive. He's been under guard ever since. Even during his brief time as a freeman, I imagine he's been guarded by soldiers. Perhaps it is exactly as you say. He only sees the outward man." She smiled. "God sees the heart, Theophilus, and he's placed you in the company of this man to good purpose. Let the Lord guide you."

She smiled and touched his arm affectionately, then walked away. Theophilus stood for a long time in the peaceful chamber. He removed his helmet and ran his hand over the shiny metal.

Brushing his fingers over the cropped red plumes on the top, he let out his breath heavily and looked up.

Theophilus had trained to be a soldier from childhood, determined to follow in his father's footsteps. As soon as he was old enough, he had joined the army. He had served under Claudius before his corrupt and capricious nephew, Nero, had been named emperor. Following that disastrous reign came an even worse one. Rome exploded into civil war as the succession of ambitious but ineffectual politicians fought to rule the empire. Galba, Otho, Vitellius—all strove for power, and each was murdered by his successor. Theophilus had escaped the worst of the bloody happenings in the Imperial City, for at that time he was immersed in the Germanic revolt, fighting against the rebel Civilis and the united tribes, including Atretes' people, the Chatti.

When Vespasian had taken the reins of power, he had rejoiced to have an able military commander in power. Rome needed stability. Over the ten years of Vespasian's reign, he had served in the Praetorian Guard, been posted to Alexandria, and been sent to command troops in Ephesus.

God had called him as a soldier, and he had served the Lord faithfully while continuing to carry out his duties. Not once had he ever been faced with a choice between God and the emperor and he knew it had often been solely due to divine intervention. Certain questions had never once been asked.

Now God had given him another commission: Take Atretes back to Germania. During his first meeting with John, the apostle had said only a few words when he had felt compelled to do this. Even knowing what he might face in Germania among the Chatti, he was certain he was following God's lead. Protect this man and see him home. God had a plan for Atretes, and he was part of that plan whether he liked it or not.

The army had been his life, but God had set him upon another path now. His choice was simple: obey or not, his will at work or God's. His mouth curved ruefully. God had had his hand in Theophilus' life from the beginning, for his years in the Roman army had prepared him for this moment. The army had taught him to obey authority, to discipline himself in the face of hardship, to be loyal to his commanders, to overcome fear when faced with death.

Take off the old and put on the new.

It was not easy. He had loved his life in the army, the discipline, the routine, the respect. He had poured twenty-five years of his life into his career and what he wore proclaimed his accomplishments.

Take off the old. Put on the new.

He set the polished helmet on a marble bench. Removing the red cape, he folded it with care and laid it down. Removing the pendant of his rank, he clenched it for a long moment. Tossing it on the bed of crimson, he left the cryptoporticus.

"As you will, Father," he said.

Turning away, he headed back down the narrow passageway to the hypogeum where Rizpah and Atretes waited.

21

The disturbing atmosphere of the hypogeum made Atretes increasingly uneasy. He knew those around him saw the place as a refuge where they could freely worship and discuss their god, but to him it was nothing more than an underground cemetery and foreshadowing of Hades.

Death no longer merely approached; it surrounded him.

When Rufus brought food and placed it before him, he couldn't bring himself to eat the meal, no matter how succulent, because the table on which Rufus set it was a sarcophagus. Civilized people burned their dead! The bloody Romans wrapped them up like presents and tucked them away in niches or great stone casings for posterity. Those who were rich enough to have cubicula even came to sup with their deceased relations and friends. And Germans were called barbaric! Even more disgusting to him was the habit of these people, Rizpah included, to dine on bread and wine and refer to it as the body and blood of their Christ.

"I have to get out of here," he said to Rizpah.

"Theophilus said it's not safe yet."

"The games started two days ago!"

"Domitian has soldiers looking for you everywhere. Several came to the villa. You know Domitian would like nothing more than to show you to—"

He stood abruptly and a wave of dizziness made him sway.

"Atretes," she said in alarm and rose quickly to slip her arm around his waist and give him support.

He shoved her away. "I can stand on my own." He bent down carefully and picked up his bedding and small pack of belongings, including the gold, and headed unsteadily toward a doorway, expecting her to follow.

"That way will take you deeper into the catacombs," she said calmly, picking Caleb up and sitting him on her hip. "This way will take us to the cryptoporticus."

"I don't want to go to the cryptoporticus! I want to get *out of here*!" She disappeared through a narrow doorway.

"Rizpah!" His harsh voice reverberated in the cubicula, assaulting his nerves even more. He uttered a single sharp word in German.

If she went that way to get to the cryptoporticus, then it made sense to him to go through the opposite doorway to escape the hypogeum entirely. He entered a long corridor, loculi on both sides of him. He tried not to touch the walls, all too aware of what was decaying within them.

The passageway went for some distance and then turned. When it branched in three directions, he took the one to the left. It ended at a stairway that led down instead of up, and he knew he wasn't going where he wanted. He swore aloud, and the sound of his voice was strange to his own ears in the dank tunnel. The place made his skin crawl.

Turning back, he retraced his steps and took the passageway to the right. He came to another turn and the corridor forked into three more passageways. Few lamps flickered here and the darkness felt heavier, the air colder. His heart began to pound. Cold sweat broke out on his body. He was lost in a labyrinth of catacombs, trapped among the dead. He fought against panic and retraced his steps again. He couldn't remember from which passageway he had come.

Silence closed in around him. All he could hear was his own breathing, shallow and tense, and the pounding of his heart bringing on an agonizing headache. He could feel the eyes of the dead watching him, smell the decay of flesh and soft, dry earth and age. Groaning, he looked around, frantic.

"Atretes," came a low, deep voice.

He swung around in a defensive stance, ready to fight whatever came at him. A man stood at the corner of another passageway. "This way," he said, and though his face was shadowed and his voice different in the narrow earthen passageway, Atretes knew it was Theophilus. For the first time since he had met the Roman, he was glad to see him.

Theophilus led him to the cryptoporticus where Rizpah was waiting. "You found him," she said in relief, rising as Atretes followed him into the large chamber. "I'm sorry, Atretes. I thought you were behind me."

Without a word, he dumped his bedding and pack of belongings and went to the fountain pool. He cupped water into his face, once, twice, three times. Shaking the water off, he straightened and released his breath slowly. "I'd rather take my chances in the arena than stay in this place."

"A company of soldiers came here yesterday," Theophilus said. "They're still patrolling the area. If you want to turn yourself over to them, go ahead."

Angered by his casual tone, Atretes took the challenge. "Show me the way out."

"Go back through there, keep following the passageways to your right. When you come to a stairway . . ."

Atretes muttered a curse and slapped his hand across the water. "How much longer am I going to have to stay in this place?"

Theophilus could understand Atretes' frustration. He felt it himself. Days of inactivity didn't sit well with him, either. It was one thing to visit the catacombs and worship with other Christians. It was something else to *live* in them. "That depends on Domitian's determination."

"You know him better than I do," Atretes sneered. "How determined is he?"

"I'd say we'd better make ourselves comfortable."

Atretes uttered another foul German word and sat down on the edge of the fountain. He rubbed his head; it was still a bit sore where Theophilus had hit him with the hilt of his gladius. He looked across the room at the Roman. Theophilus raised his brow slightly.

Caleb crawled between Atretes' spread feet and grabbed one of the straps around his muscular calf. Atretes put his hands down between his knees and took his son's hands. With a delighted squeal, Caleb struggled and worked until he pulled himself up and was standing.

"He'll be walking soon," Rizpah said.

"I know," Atretes said grimly. "In a graveyard." He picked his son up and sat him on his knee, holding him there and studying him. He had Julia's eyes and hair. Caleb flapped his arms and made happy garbly sounds.

Rizpah laughed. "He's trying to talk to you."

How could she laugh in this place? How could she sit and look serene, talking to Theophilus and the others as if they were sitting in a villa or in a banquet room instead of an underground cemetery? Surroundings didn't matter to her anymore than they mattered to the baby. Wherever she was, she would be the same. He wanted his son to learn to walk on new grass, not on the dark earth of a passageway walled in by death.

Rizpah saw the troubled look on Atretes face and came to sit beside him on the edge of the fountain. "We won't be here forever."

Forever. Like death. He had never allowed the fear of death to plague him. It would weaken him, shift his concentration, give an opponent an opening. Now he could think of nothing else. And it was because they were in this place!

He thrust Caleb into her arms as he rose. "We've been here long enough." Caleb's cry filled the cryptoporticus.

"Where else can we go and be safe?" Rizpah said, holding the child close and patting his back. She kissed him and murmured comforting words to him.

Watching her pour all her affection upon his son made him angry. "Anywhere would be better than this!"

"Even a dungeon?" Theophilus said to draw his anger elsewhere. Atretes was itching for a fight, and Rizpah wouldn't give him what he wanted. "Or perhaps you'd feel more at home in a cell, one about five feet wide and eight feet long." He earned a dark look, but nothing more.

When Caleb stopped crying, Rizpah set him down on a mural of a dolphin. Distracted by the colors, shapes, and textures of the tiles, he cooed in delight again and began to crawl around until he came to a spot of light. Sitting up, he tried to grasp hold of the beam of sunshine, which came down from a small opening in the painted dome ceiling.

Atretes watched him bleakly. "He should be up with the living, not down here with the dead."

"He will be, Atretes," Theophilus said.

"Send Rizpah up from this Hades, or are she and my son prisoners, too?"

"We'll stay with you where we belong," Rizpah said firmly.

"None of you are prisoners," Theophilus said, noting how Atretes ignored her. The only time he ever looked at Rizpah was when she was looking elsewhere, and then his perusal was intense and revealing to anyone who chanced to see it. "As to moving to a different place, ask Lady Alphina when you see her this evening."

Atretes looked around the large chamber with its arches and

frescoes. "This is better than that other place you've put me. I'll stay here."

Theophilus laughed. "Lady Alphina offered you the use of this chamber the first day you arrived."

"She offered it to Rizpah and the babe."

"The invitation included you. She'll be pleased you've decided to be in here. She was surprised you preferred the cubicula. It depresses her." Amused by Atretes' look of consternation, he stretched out on a marble bench, put his arm behind his head, and crossed his ankles in comfort. "I much prefer this place myself."

Atretes' eyes narrowed. "What do you find so amusing?"

"The way God works." Theophilus gave a soft laugh and closed his eyes. The Lord had plunked this stubborn, mule-headed gladiator right down in the middle of his sanctuary.

*

Rufus and Lady Alphina joined them that evening, two servants following with trays of food and wine. Lady Alphina was delighted they had decided to stay in the cryptoporticus. "It's so much nicer here," she said. "More air."

Rufus grinned as Atretes took an apple from the tray and bit into it. "I'm pleased to see your appetite's returned. We were beginning to worry."

"Should any soldiers come to search the villa, one of the servants will come to warn you," Lady Alphina said.

"Some of the soldiers are being called back. There's a fire in the city," Rufus said, as one servant poured wine. Theophilus took two goblets, handing one to Atretes. "It started in one of the poorer insulae south of the Tiber, and I'm afraid it's spreading fast."

"You can see the smoke from the balconies," Lady Alphina said grievously. "It reminds me of the Great Fire during Nero's reign."

"Titus has sent more legionnaires to help the firefighters, but it's burning out of control," Rufus went on. "The problem is some insulae are so old, they explode. Hundreds of people are dead, and even more are without shelter."

Atretes relished Rufus' report. Rome was burning! What more could he ask, other than the demise of Callistus and Domitian?

"Disease will follow," Theophilus said grimly. "I've seen it happen before."

Rizpah saw how Atretes was taking the news and was disturbed by his callousness. "Don't be pleased by this, Atretes. Innocent people are losing their homes and their lives."

"Innocent?" Atretes said derisively. The others looked at him. "Were they all *innocent* when they filled the seats around the arena and screamed for blood? My blood or anyone else's. Let them burn. Let the whole rotten city burn!" He gave a hoarse laugh and raised his goblet in salute. He didn't care if he offended or hurt anyone present. They were Romans, after all. "I'd like the pleasure of watching."

"Then how are you any different?" she said, appalled by his lack of pity.

His eyes went hot. "I'm different."

"You've suffered. Can you feel no pity for those who are suffering now?"

"Why should I? They're getting what they deserve." He drained the goblet and glanced around at the others, daring anyone to challenge him.

"The Jews agree with you, Atretes," Rufus said. "They think God has cursed Titus because of what he did to Jerusalem. First Vesuvius erupts and kills thousands, and now this fire."

"I like your god more and more," Atretes said and tore a leg off the cooked pheasant.

Rizpah looked at him in sorrowful disbelief.

Theophilus filled the embarrassed silence. "Perhaps this will give us the opportunity we need to leave Latium."

Several more people arrived, most of them poor folk who lived outside the gates of the city. Some were involved in the transport services on the Appian Way while others worked in markets that catered to the hundreds of travelers who came to Rome every day. Someone began to sing, and the gathering of people began to take their places for the reading of the apostle Paul's letter to the Romans.

Despite numerous warm invitations to join them, Atretes took a pitcher of wine and a goblet and retreated to the furthest recesses of the chamber. He was somewhat surprised to see it wasn't Theophilus who led the worship. It was the slave who had served wine. He was younger, without the breadth of a soldier, a humble looking man, his voice gentle but somehow powerful.

"'Therefore you are without excuse, every man of you who passes judgment, for in that you judge another, you condemn yourself; for you who judge practice the same things. And we know that the judgment of God rightly falls upon those who practice such things. And do you suppose this, O man, when you pass judgment upon those who practice such things and do the same yourself, that you will escape the judgment of God?'"

Atretes felt an inexplicable shiver of fear run through him at the words being read. It was as though whoever had written them had looked into his very heart. The words ran together, and then something would burst upon his mind, pouring hot coals upon him.

"'There is no partiality with God. . . . God will judge the secrets of men. . . .'"

The pitcher of wine was empty, and he craved more, wanting to drown the niggling fear eating at him.

"'. . . their throat is an open grave. . . .'"

The letter had been written to the Romans! Why then did it cut him and leave him bleeding? He pressed his palms against his ears to shut out the man's voice.

Theophilus saw and gave thanks to God. *He hears you, Father. Plant your word upon his heart and bring forth a new child of God.*

Rizpah wept silently and unnoticed beside the Roman, not over hope for Atretes, but in despair of her own sin. Had she not judged Atretes when he stood in judgment of others? She had asked him how he was different. Was she not the same?

O, Father, I want to be like you, *and this is what I am! Forgive me. Please, Abba, forgive me. Cleanse my wicked heart and make me your instrument of love and peace.*

*

When all had gone and night had fallen, Atretes lay restless upon his pallet, the words he had heard still plaguing him. Men had tried to kill him with sword and spear. He had been chained, beaten, branded, and threatened with castration. Through all that, fear had not touched him as it had upon the reading of a single letter by a man he didn't even know.

Why? What power did this scroll have to torment his mind

with the heaviness of what lay ahead of him? Death. Why should he be afraid now when he had never been before? All men die.

"'. . . be buried with him through the baptism into death. . . .'"

His goal had been to survive. Now there was a resounding echo, *Live! Arise and live!* Arise from what?

When he finally slept, the old dream returned, the dream that had afflicted him in the hill caves outside of Ephesus.

He was walking through a blackness so heavy he could feel it pressing against his body. All he could see were his hands. He kept on walking, not feeling anything. And then he saw the Artemision. The beauty of it drew him, but as he came close he saw the carvings were alive, writhing and uncoiling upon the marble structure. Stone faces stared down at him as he entered the inner court. When he reached the center, he saw the grotesque goddess. The walls around her began to crumble. He ran to escape, huge blocks falling and just missing him. The temple was coming down around him in fire and dust. He could feel the heat and hear the screams of those inside. He wanted to scream, too, but had no air as he ran between the great columns. He was knocked from his feet as the temple fell. The earth trembled.

Everything was black again, a cold devoid of light and color and sound. He rose and stumbled on, his heart beating faster and faster as he searched for something to which he couldn't put a name.

Before him was a sculptor. The piece of stone on which he worked was the form of a man. As Atretes came closer, he saw the form take shape. It was a statuette of him, like the ones the vendors sold outside the arena. He could hear the roar of the mob like a hungry beast overtaking him, but he couldn't move.

The sculptor drew back the hammer.

"No," Atretes groaned, knowing what he was going to do. "No!" he cried out. He wanted to rush at him and stop him, but some force held him where he was as the sculptor brought the hammer down with a mighty blow and shattered the stone image.

Atretes fell to the ground. He lay there for a long time in the darkness and when he finally got up, he couldn't move his legs. Cold pressure surrounded him, and he felt himself sinking.

Around him was the forest of his homeland. He was standing in the bog, his people around him, watching, but doing nothing to help. He saw his father, his wife, friends, all long dead, staring at him with vacant eyes. "Help me," he said, feeling the weight pulling at his legs. The cold pressure of the morass sucked him down chest deep.

"*Help me!*"

And then a man was there before him. "Take my hand, Atretes."

Atretes frowned, unable to see his face clearly. He was dressed in white and unlike any man he had ever seen before. "I can't reach you," he said, afraid to try.

"Take my hand, and I'll raise you from the pit." And then he was close, so close that Atretes felt the man's warm breath as he held his hands out to him.

The palms were bleeding.

Atretes came awake abruptly, breathing hard. Someone touched him and he uttered a hoarse cry and sat up.

"Shhh. It's all right, Atretes," Rizpah said in a hushed voice. "You were having another nightmare."

His heart drummed; sweat streamed from his body. Shuddering, he shook his head as though to dispel the feeling of the dream.

Rizpah took the blanket from her own shoulders and draped it around him. "Were you dreaming about the arena?"

"No." He felt the stillness of the cryptoporticus around him. One small flame flickered from a small clay lamp across the chamber. Theophilus wasn't on his pallet. He remembered the Roman had left with Lady Alphina and Rufus as soon as the gathering dispersed.

Rizpah noticed his glance. "Theophilus hasn't returned yet. He wanted to see for himself what's happening in the city. He told me he'd be back by dawn."

"I want to get out of this place."

"So do I," she said softly.

"You don't understand. I've *got* to get out."

She brushed his hair back from his face. "It'll be all right." She rubbed his back. "Try to think about something else. You need to sleep."

She spoke to him like a child! She *touched* him like a child! When his arm encircled her waist, she gasped. "What're you doing?"

"You want to comfort me? Comfort me as a man!" He caught

her chin and kissed her angrily, holding her captive despite her struggles.

When at last he let her go, she gave a soft, gasping sob. "What am I to you, Atretes? Another face in the screaming mob? I wasn't there! I swear to you before the Lord, I was *never* there." Her voice broke. Turning her head away, she started to cry.

Shame washed over him. He drew back. Pushing at him frantically, she sat up and tried to leave. He caught hold of her arm. He could see her face in the faint light of the lamp and cursed himself for being a brutish fool.

"Wait," he said softly.

"Let go of me." She was shaking violently.

"Not yet." He touched her hair, and she jerked away from him. She tried to break his hold and, when she couldn't, turned her face away and wept. Her sobs tore at his heart. "Don't," he said raggedly.

"I love you. God help me, I *love* you, and you would do this!"

Her startling words filled him with a sense of relief and remorse. He knelt behind her and pulled her back into his arms, locking her there when he felt her body stiffen in resistance.

"I won't hurt you. I swear on my sword." He rested his head in the curve of her shoulder. "Let me hold you." Her body shook with weeping. She made hardly any sound, which only made it worse. She didn't trust him now, and why should she?

"I'm different," he had said, but how different was he when he took out his wrath upon her? And why? Because she touched him with the tenderness she showed his son rather than the passion he craved?

"When you treated me like a child, I saw red," he said against her hair, trying to find an explanation to wipe away the inexcusable. He shut his eyes tightly. "I was mad. I wasn't thinking."

"You're always mad. You never think. Let me go," she pleaded tearfully.

"Not until I make you understand—"

"Understand what? That I'm nothing to you, that you see me as no different from the women given to you in the ludus?" She fought again, gasping soft broken sobs when he held her so easily.

"You're beginning to mean *too much* to me," he said hoarsely. He felt her go still in his arms. "I've loved three women in my life. My mother, my wife, Ania, and Julia Valerian. All three are gone. My wife died in childbirth and took my child with her. My mother was killed by Romans, and Julia Valerian . . ." He closed his eyes tightly. "I'm not going to feel that kind of pain again." He released her.

She turned and looked at him, her soulful dark eyes full of tears. "And so you'll close your heart to anything that's good."

"I'm not going to love like that again."

She didn't tell him of her own losses. Family, husband, child. What was the use? "You'd rather I gave myself to you like a harlot, wouldn't you? You'd rather have dross than gold."

"I didn't say that."

"You didn't have to say it. You show me every time you look at me, every time you *touch* me!" Grief and anger mingled in her pale face. "You judge me for *her* actions and take your vengeance."

"I should've known you wouldn't understand. How can a woman understand a man?"

"I understand you refuse to let yourself love your own son fully because he *might* die or be taken captive, or grow up and disappoint you like his mother did. Does a *man* embrace such foolishness?"

A muscle jerked in his face, his eyes narrowing in anger. "Careful."

"Of what? Your wrath? You've done your worst to me already. You're brave with a sword or spear in your hand, Atretes. You have no peer in the arena. But in the things of life that really matter, you're a *coward*!"

She rose quickly and returned to the other side of the chamber. Flinging herself down on her pallet beside Caleb's basket, she curled on her side, and covered her body and head with the blanket.

Atretes lay back again on his own bed, but he couldn't sleep for the soft sound of her weeping.

22

When Theophilus returned, Atretes lay in the dim light watching him. The Roman crossed the chamber quietly and stood over Rizpah. Caleb had awakened, and she had nursed him. When she had finished, she had kept him with her. Theophilus bent down and rearranged the blanket to cover her.

Atretes stood slowly, an uncomfortable heat tightening in his chest as he watched the tender gesture. Theophilus glanced toward him and straightened, not appearing surprised to see him awake. He smiled easily as he walked toward him, his smile dimming as he read his expression. "What's wrong?"

"When can I get out of here?"

"We leave today," Theophilus said in a hushed voice. "The city is in chaos. Soldiers have been recalled to fight the fire and control the panic. It'll be easy for us to become a part of the mass of sojourners leaving the city right now."

Atretes forgot his anger. "What about horses?"

"We'll buy them farther north. They'll be less expensive. Besides, if we're in too much of a hurry we'll draw the attention of the soldiers patrolling the road."

"We'll need supplies."

"Rufus has already arranged it. We'll carry enough provisions for a week and stay to the main roads where it'll be least likely for Domitian's soldiers to look for you."

"What about Domitian?"

"His wrath is assuaged for the moment."

Something in his tone warned Atretes that all wasn't well. "What did you find out that you're not telling me, Roman?"

Theophilus looked at him grimly. "Pugnax is dead."

"Dead? How?"

"He was sent to the arena on charges of harboring an enemy of the emperor."

Atretes swore under his breath and moved away. He rubbed the back of his neck. "Well, Pugnax got what he wanted, a chance for more days of glory."

"I'm afraid not."

Atretes turned and looked at him.

"Domitian fed him to a pack of wild dogs."

"Dogs?" he said, sickened. There was no worse shame than for a man to be fed to wild animals. It was a death of humiliation. He looked at Theophilus and frowned. "There's more, isn't there?"

"Domitian ordered the lanista at the Great School questioned."

"Bato," Atretes said dully. His heart sank.

"Domitian imprisoned and tortured him. When that didn't avail him the information he sought, he pitted the lanista against another African. Bato wounded him, and the crowd gave the *pollice verso*. Your friend turned the dagger on himself instead."

A heaviness gripped Atretes. His spirit sank into black despair. Groaning, he turned away, not wanting the Roman to see his feelings. Two more deaths could be accounted to him.

Theophilus knew he was stricken. "Domitian will answer for what he's done," he said quietly, putting his hand on Atretes' shoulder.

Atretes shook his hand off. "Answer to whom? His brother, the emperor?" he sneered, his pale blue eyes glittering with angry tears. "To Rome, who craves human sacrifice for its altars of *entertainment*?"

"To God," Rizpah said, standing on the other side of the cryptoporticus, Caleb in her arms.

"My apologies, Rizpah," Theophilus said. "I didn't want to awaken you."

"It'll be dawn soon," she said, looking up at the openings in the vaulted ceiling. "I'll make myself and Caleb ready."

Theophilus looked from her to Atretes, sensing tension between them.

"What are you looking at?"

Theophilus gave him a level look. "Gather whatever you intend to take. We'll leave within the hour," he said and went to do likewise.

※

As the sun came up, Theophilus, Atretes, and Rizpah, Caleb bundled and tied on her back, melted into the throng leaving Rome. The sky was smoke gray, and the air smelled heavily of soot and ash. They walked to the side of the road among the peasant sojourners while wealthier citizenry in their chariots took possession of the road, making haste for the safety of their country estates.

Rizpah shifted Caleb's weight. Though she had settled him with ease at dawn, each milestone they passed seemed to add pounds to his small frame. When he began to wriggle and cry from the lengthy confinement, she untied the shawl and removed it, riding him more easily on her hip. After another mile, he was petulant; she, exhausted.

Theophilus noticed her weariness. "We'll rest by that stream."

Atretes said nothing, keeping the same distance between them that he had set at dawn. Theophilus glanced at him as he dumped his pack. Whatever had happened between them the night before still preyed as heavily on Atretes' mind as on hers. They made a study of not looking at one another.

Rizpah winced as she set Caleb down. She sat beside him near the stream. With a squeal of delight, the babe took off crawling straight for the burbling water. "Oh, Caleb," she said, exhausted and vexed. She longed to sit down and soak her aching feet in the cool water, but knew Caleb couldn't be caged any longer.

"Sit down and rest," Atretes said in a tone of equal frustration. She paid him no heed and rose. Muttering something in German, Atretes planted a hard hand on her shoulder and pushed her down again. "I said *sit*!" Scooping Caleb up off the grass, he strode down the bank, the infant dangling under his arm like a sack of meal.

Face flushed, Rizpah rose, annoyance and alarm momentarily overcoming her weariness. "Don't carry him like that, Atretes. He's a child, not a sack of grain."

Theophilus suppressed a smile as he watched Caleb's legs bob. "Let him go. Caleb will come to no harm in the arms of his father."

She glared after Atretes, fighting back tears. "I wish I shared your confidence," she said dismally. She bit her lip and looked away.

Theophilus leaned back on his pack. "Go ahead and cry for him, Rizpah. It'll give you some ease."

"I wouldn't be crying for him. I'd be crying for myself." She swallowed the painful lump in her throat. "He's the most frustrating, bullheaded, thick-skinned . . ." Struggling with her tumultuous emotions, she sat down and lowered her head to hide her face from Theophilus' scrutiny.

"What happened last night?"

She blushed vividly. "Nothing that should have surprised me," she said grimly.

Theophilus was left to wonder. He had ideas of his own, but hoped they were incorrect. He had seen how Atretes looked at her. He smiled to himself. If he were a few years younger, or she a few older, Atretes wouldn't have a clear field where she was concerned. "He's a little rough around the edges, but give him time." He received a hot look that surprised him and gave him a hint of what happened. His outrage was swift. "Did he—"

"No," she said quickly and looked away, embarrassed. "He changed his mind."

That's something, Theophilus thought. A man's decency could be destroyed after a couple of years in a ludus. Atretes had spent over ten years in them.

"He's been chained, beaten, branded, and trained like a prize animal, Rizpah," he said, feeling compelled to explain the barbarian. "He won't become civilized overnight."

"I didn't do any of those things to him."

"No, but you're more of a threat to him than anything else he's faced so far. His emotions are on fire."

"I didn't fan them."

"Your proximity is enough to do that, or haven't you noticed?"

"The only emotion Atretes possesses in any great quantity and quality is *anger*!" she said, her dark eyes glittering.

"He's had to hone it to survive. Can you blame him?"

"I can blame him for what he does to me," she said, hurt that Theophilus of all people should defend him.

"And how far will it get you toward what you want?" He saw his question made her uncomfortable. It would appear Atretes' emotions weren't the only ones on fire. "Aren't you hiding behind your own anger right now because he hurt you? Love him the way you've been called to love him. If you can't, how in God's name is he going to know the difference between what he's had and what you and I offer?"

What was she offering? "It's not that easy."

He smiled gently. "Is it ever easy?"

"You don't understand," she said weakly and looked down

at her clasped hands. How could he when even she didn't fully understand herself.

He laughed softly. "I'd bet my salt he said the same thing to you last night." He lay back on his gear. "'Frustrating, bullheaded, thick-skinned. . . .'" he said, repeating her own words as he made himself comfortable. He gave a wide yawn and closed his eyes. "You two are a matched pair."

Piqued, she sat silent. As Theophilus dozed in the sunshine, she thought deeply, praying that the Lord would cleanse her of her ill feelings and renew a right spirit within her.

"Keep my mind set on you, Father. Atretes is hardheaded, insensitive, boorish, impossible," she whispered, so as not to awaken Theophilus.

Forgive as you have been forgiven.

"Lord, I didn't deserve such treatment. I meant to comfort, not entice him. And he thought to use me like a harlot."

Forgive . . .

"Father, remove my attraction to him. I pray you will dissolve my feelings where he's concerned. They're distracting and disturbing, and it's hard enough walking this road without feeling pulled by my weak flesh. I don't want to go to Germania. Couldn't you change his mind? Maybe a small village in Northern Italy? Germania is so far away and if his people are anything like him . . ."

I desire compassion and not sacrifice.

The remembered Scripture made no sense to her in the face of her tumultuous feelings, but she knew whatever she thought or felt, God called her to obedience. Jesus said *forgive*, and she would forgive whether she felt like it or not.

Continuing to pray, she rose and walked along the high bank. "I don't want to forgive him, Lord. I need your heart if I'm to do so. My own is shrivelled beneath of the heat of Atretes' anger and my own. I want to slap his face and scream at him. If I were a man and had his strength—"

Beloved, be still.

Pausing, Rizpah bowed her head, ashamed, her heart aching.

"If it's your will for me to forgive him, Lord, then please change my heart, because it's black right now, so black I can't see my way up out of the hole Atretes threw me in last night. Help me do your will. Show me another side of him."

She heard Caleb's squeal and headed along the bank again.

She saw them below through a screen of leafy branches. Atretes sat on the sandy bank, his legs spread wide, Caleb sitting between, facing him. Caleb clung fast to his large hands, pulling himself up into a standing position and taking a wobbly step toward him. His chubby legs buckled, and he sat down hard. When he started to cry, Atretes picked him up, nuzzled his neck, and kissed him.

Her chest tightened, and her anger melted away. The same barbarian who had assaulted her last night rocked his son with a tenderness that bespoke his love louder than any shouted proclamation. When Caleb was calm again, Atretes set him down on the sand once more and ran his hand gently over the dark baby-fine hair. Caleb flapped his arms happily.

Rizpah watched them through her tears. *I asked, Lord, and you've answered.*

Steeling herself, she went down the embankment. Her misgivings remained as to what Atretes' manner might be, for last night was still a raw wound, leaving her cautious. A small cascade of rocks loosened beneath her sandaled feet. She saw Atretes stiffen and glance back. His expression tightened, then he turned back to Caleb, ignoring her. The tot gave a delighted squeal, flapping his arms. "Mama . . . mama . . . mama . . ."

She sat down on a rock and drew her shawl around her shoulders. The air was cool, or was it just her frame of mind? She watched her son grasp Atretes' fingers and pull himself up again. He gave a squeal and tipped, almost pitching over. Atretes shifted his leg, supporting him. Caleb's tiny fingers dug into the tanned skin of Atretes' muscular thigh.

Disturbed by the German's physical beauty, Rizpah lowered her gaze to her hands. Gathering her courage, she spoke before she let pride get in her way. "However much you want to protect your heart, it's already too late, isn't it, Atretes?" Feeling his cold silence, she looked at him, wondering if she had driven the thorn in deeper. She hadn't meant to.

O Lord, give me words. Not my words that wound, but yours that heal.

She rose and came closer, but not so near she couldn't retreat should Atretes decide to act the barbarian again. She wanted no misunderstandings as to her reasons for coming to him.

As though sensing her thoughts, Atretes cast her an impatient glance. "If you came to take him, *take him.*"

"You can't make anything easy, can you?" She fired back, then fell silent, struggling within herself. She wanted to hit him and cry over him at the same time. By what right was *he* angry with her? He was the one who had caused the breach between them with his reprehensible behavior.

"He's had to hone his anger to survive. . . ."

She was dismayed, remembering Theophilus' words. She wanted to understand Atretes, to make him see how different life would be with the Lord. But how did you reach a man like him who had been chained, beaten, used, and betrayed? Could he be reached when he was so set against love?

O God, help me.

"We're all like children, Atretes. We want to stand and walk all on our own. And just like Caleb, we have to cling to something in the effort to pull ourselves up out of the dirt." She looked at him. Was he even listening? Did anything she say matter to him? "Sometimes we cling to the wrong things and go crashing down."

She gave a soft, broken laugh. Closing her eyes, she lowered her head and sighed. "I was as hopeless as you. In many ways, I still am. I can't take a single step without the Lord holding me up. Every time I let go, even for an instant, I fall flat on my face again. Like last night."

Raising her head, she opened her eyes and found him staring at her. Her mouth went dry and her heart began to race wildly. What had she said to make him look at her like that? What was he thinking? Afraid of the possibilities, she plunged ahead despite the hard intensity of his stare, eager to finish and be gone from him.

"I'm sorry I said hurtful words to you last night." His eyes narrowed and she wondered if he believed her. "I'm sorry," she said again, from her heart. "I wish I could promise it won't happen again. I can't." A hundred excuses for why she had said what she had flew unbidden into her mind, but she choked off every one of them for a single abiding purpose: to make amends and build a bridge between herself and the cold, silent man sitting before her. "Please, Atretes, don't hold on to anger. It will end up destroying you."

When he said nothing, she felt desolate. "That's all I wanted to say." She started to turn away.

Atretes stood.

Startled, she caught her breath and stepped back from him. It was an instinctive action, one of self-preservation, and it told him more clearly than any words ever could where he stood with her. Should he be surprised or hurt now by her distrust in the wake of his behavior last night?

Caleb started to crawl toward the stream. Atretes took one step and caught his son up under his arm again.

"You shouldn't hold him like that."

He ignored her motherly concern and cut to the issue between them. "You don't have to be afraid of me. I won't repeat what I did last night."

"I didn't think you would."

"Didn't you?" he said dryly, noting the pulse throbbing in her throat.

"You startled me. That's all."

He just looked at her, wanting her all over again. When he had heard her approach, he'd expected words of retaliation, insults, even mockery. He had been prepared for those things, equipped with his own weapons. If she had railed at him, his guilt could have been salved. Instead, *she* apologized . . . and stripped him of his armor. He searched for words and couldn't find any sufficient.

She waited a moment for him to speak. Searching his face, her own softened, her dark eyes filling with compassion and tenderness. "I forgive you, Atretes. I won't speak of it again." She turned away again and stepped up the bank. He saw the raw skin around her ankles where the leather straps of her worn sandals had rubbed over the long hours of walking. Not once had she complained. He wanted to wash her feet and rub salve in and then wrap them. He wanted to hold and comfort her.

"Rizpah." His voice came out rough and hard, not the way he had intended. He waited until she looked at him. "If you hadn't spoken as you did last night, I would not have let you go, and to Hades with your feelings," he said with painful honesty.

"I know," she said with equal frankness. "I know other means of protecting myself, but I didn't want to hurt you."

He laughed. It was such an outrageous statement. She smiled back, her dark eyes guileless and warm. His laughter died. It struck him again how deep his feelings for her went.

"I can't promise it won't happen again." His mouth curved bitterly. "It comes of being what I am."

The Soil

"It comes of what you've *allowed* Rome to make you."

His mouth tightened. He shifted Caleb in his arms and came closer. "I haven't touched another woman since you came to my villa. It wasn't for lack of opportunity."

She blushed, wondering if he knew what he was revealing to her. His physical strength and beauty had always intimidated her, but never so much as this confession did, for it was as close as he would get to admitting he held her in any esteem whatsoever. Her response to him was appallingly strong.

Lord, don't let this man be my undoing. You know all my weaknesses. Lord, put stumbling blocks between Atretes and me; otherwise I don't know if I'll be able to stand firm.

Atretes studied her face intently and saw a great deal he knew she didn't intend him to see. He walked toward her slowly, feeling her tension increasing with each step. She moved a foot up to higher ground. He understood; she wanted distance between them. He looked into her eyes and saw something else. She didn't want distance because she loathed him, but because he could breach her walls.

"Take him back with you." He held Caleb up to her. She had to come down two steps to take him. As she did, she looked at him again. Atretes watched the pupils of her brown eyes widen until he felt drawn inside her. Need swept over him. He smiled bleakly. "You'd better keep your little shield close."

23

Theophilus was ready to go when they returned. Atretes shouldered his gear, and they walked another six miles, making camp beside another small stream. Rizpah went down to a small pool and soaked her aching feet while she bathed Caleb. The water was cold, but the child loved it, splashing and babbling in pure pleasure. She laughed when he slapped the water. "Enough," she said and plucked him out.

She carried him up the bank, where he squirmed, wanting to be free. She lowered him, supporting him under his arms so that he could walk. The soft blades of new grass tickled his toes, and he kept lifting his feet off the ground. Laughing, she put him down and let him crawl, remaining close to be sure he didn't try to put anything in his mouth. It seemed he wanted to taste everything in the world around him.

Theophilus watched Rizpah following Caleb. Her laugh carried and made him smile. "She's a good mother."

Atretes sat silent and morose, his back against the oak tree. He watched her for a long moment, then rested his head back, looking north, his expression grim. Theophilus suspected Atretes was just beginning to realize the monumental task he had set for a woman carrying a child on her back, a child bound to get bigger and even more active and demanding along the way.

The sun set, and Theophilus built a fire. He and Rizpah shared devotions of Scriptures and songs. Uncomfortable, Atretes rose and left them, seeking the solitude of a distant copse of trees. He returned later and watched Rizpah feed Caleb a portion of her own grain gruel. When the babe was replete, he wanted to play. Intrigued by the flickering fire, he crawled toward it.

"No, no," Rizpah said gently. Over and over, he tried to go to it, and she would get up and retrieve him. Caleb cried in frustration, and she looked sorely ready to join him.

Annoyed, Atretes rose and came round the fire. "Give him to me."

"He'll settle soon."

He reached down and scooped the child up, then returned

to his space on the opposite side of the fire. Kneeling, he released him.

"He's too close to the fire, Atretes."

"He'll learn to stay away from it."

She rose as Caleb crawled straight for the flames.

"Sit down!"

"He'll burn himself!"

"He has to learn boundaries." Atretes made no move to stop him. "No, Caleb," he said firmly. Leaning forward, he lightly smacked the small hand reaching for the bright embers on a stick. Startled, Caleb drew back and hesitated. Fascination won over obedience. He reached out again. *"No."* Atretes smacked his hand harder. Caleb's lip quivered, but after a brief hesitation, temptation won.

Rizpah rose quickly, but it was already too late. Caleb's expression of wonder changed to one of surprised pain. Theophilus caught her wrist and held her where she was when Atretes plucked his son off the ground.

"How could you?" she cried.

"A few blisters won't kill him," Atretes said. "And he'll learn obedience." He tucked his son in the crook of his arm. "Next time, you know better, *ja*?"

"Let me have him back before more harm comes to him."

Atretes ignored her and spoke softly in German as he examined his son's scorched fingers. He sucked on them, and Caleb's crying eased. When the tot stopped crying completely, Atretes examined his fingers again.

"No serious damage."

Rizpah glared at him speechlessly, her eyes awash with tears. Caleb plucked at his father's lip, delighted to be the center of his attention.

Atretes uttered a playful growl and snapped at the tiny intrusive fingers, drawing a squeak of laughter. He nibbled his son's fingers and sucked gently on the sore ones a moment longer before setting him down again.

Caleb looked at the fire.

"Oh, Lord," Rizpah said. Theophilus' hand tightened, keeping her where she was. "Atretes, don't let him—"

"He's a *boy* and not to be coddled!"

"He's a *baby*!"

Still fascinated, Caleb rocked back and forth, thinking.

Atretes leaned back and watched.

"He's as willful as you," Rizpah said. "If you let him hurt himself again, so help me, I'll—"

Caleb started to crawl toward the pretty flickering lights. "No!" Atretes said firmly. Caleb plopped back on his bottom and flapped his arms, jabbering loudly as he made his frustration known. Theophilus laughed, releasing Rizpah.

Rizpah let out her breath softly, but kept watching Caleb lest he change his mind and head again for disaster. He headed for the packs and sat playing with the leather straps.

"He's willful," Atretes said, grinning smugly, "not stupid."

She wasn't amused or mollified. "Well, thank God he wasn't on a cliff."

A muscle jerked in Atretes' jaw. His blue eyes turned hard and mocking. "You think you take better care of my son than I do? A painful lesson is hard learned, but never forgotten." He stared straight into her eyes. "Pain teaches a man not to make the same mistake twice."

She knew he had just deliberately smashed the bridge that had been built between them this afternoon. And it was her own fault. *Lord, when will I learn to hold my tongue?* She looked bleakly back at him and felt the boundaries he had drawn around himself. After all these months together, he still equated her with Rome and Julia Valerian. He would enjoy having her as his mistress, but heaven forbid he let her close enough to be a companion and friend.

O Abba, Abba . . .

Turning her head away, she hoped he wouldn't know how easily he could cut through her own barriers. She had almost regained control when Theophilus put his hand over hers. The tender gesture broke down all defenses. "Excuse me," she said in a choked whisper and rose.

Atretes came to his feet as she walked away into the darkness.

"Sit down, Atretes."

"Stay out of this."

"You got your victory. Enjoy it if you must, but let her withdraw with honor."

"Mind your own business, Roman."

"So be it, but if you're going to chase her down, take Caleb with you." He settled back comfortably on his blanket. "I'm going to sleep."

Frustrated, Atretes clenched his fists and stayed where he was. Rizpah went down the bank and disappeared from sight. He wanted to go after her, but knew if he did, he would say or do something more to regret. He had seen the effect his words had upon her.

Stooping down, he picked up a thick branch, broke it in half, and tossed it onto the fire, causing a burst of sparks to fly heavenward.

"We'll try for Civita Castellana tomorrow and then head west for the Tyrrhenian Sea," Theophilus said without opening his eyes.

*

Rizpah sat down on the bank of the stream, her knees drawn up against her chest.

"O Lord, I need you," she whispered brokenly. "Am I going to contend against this man for the rest of my life? I miss Shimei. I miss the safety I felt being with him. Why couldn't I have gone on that way?"

She rested her chin on her knees, thinking she should go back and watch over Caleb. But Atretes had proven himself more than capable of that. Moonlight cast shimmering reflections, like sparkling jewels, on the dark moving stream. She let out her breath slowly, drawing on her faith.

"You are the God of creation, who gave us Jesus. How can I sit here and say you don't understand? Who but you can understand, Lord?"

She stood and held her hands out palms up, looking to the heavens.

"Father, I thank you for the blessings you have bestowed upon me. You brought me out of the darkness in which I was living and placed Shimei in my life. He was such a pure, sweet man. He never made the mistakes I did. He deserved someone better than I. Some people are born obedient to your will, Lord, and Shimei was such a man."

Her voice was thick with tears. "Help me remember you made me as I am for your own purposes. I don't have to know what they are. I don't know why I had to lose Shimei or why Rachel had to die. I don't know anything other than you sustained me, Lord. Out of my sorrow, you gave me Caleb and joy."

She lowered her hands.

And now there was Atretes.

She shook her head faintly, closing her eyes and lifting her face to the cool night. "It's so peaceful and beautiful here, Lord," she said softly. "When I'm by myself like this, I can think and convince myself that you'll sustain me through whatever comes. But, Abba, I'm burdened with feeling where he's concerned. You know the woman I am. You knit me together. Couldn't you have made me a little differently? Lead me not into temptation. Lord, I know I'm a weak vessel. Atretes speaks, and I take his words to heart. He looks at me, and I melt inside. He touches me, and I burn for him."

A soft night breeze caressed the leaves in the tree near the stream bank. The sound was peaceful.

"Lord, may it be your Word that is carved upon my heart, *your* love that I crave. Open my mind and heart to drink in the word Theophilus gives me each morning. Strengthen me for your purpose. Cast out the 'if onlys' and 'what ifs' that plague me when Atretes looks at me. I remember what it felt like to be loved by a man. Sometimes I hunger for that kind of loving again. Help me to see him through your eyes, Lord, and not through the eyes of a fleshly woman. Redeem him, Father. Bring him up out of the pit and set his feet upon the Rock."

Insects chirped around her and the soft burbling of the stream soothed her.

A strong sense of peace overwhelmed her, and she fell silent, too choked with emotion to speak. *Music, Lord. All around me is the music of your creation.* She let the sounds flow over and around her in sweet harmony, thinking of all the times the Lord had sustained her and provided for her, and her heart rose and swelled, renewed.

O Lord, you are with me always. I can rest in your promise. I will let my confidence rest in you.

Unburdened and renewed, she drew up her tunic and knotted it so she could wade in the stream. Hands outstretched, she turned slowly, basking in the moonlight. Bending down, she cupped the icy water and flung it high into the night sky, an offering of sparkling jewels to the one who had quenched her thirst with living water.

Her heart sang out within her, overflowing.

The Soil

★

Atretes sat grimly by the fire, waiting. It seemed hours had passed before he saw Rizpah come up from the stream. He lowered his head slightly so she wouldn't know he'd been watching and waiting for her return. When she came close, he glanced up and noted the damp curls around her face. Had she bathed in that frigid stream? She was looking at Caleb, who was still playing on the packs, and then at Theophilus snoring. She smiled in amusement, and Atretes' chest tightened.

She glanced at him almost shyly and sat down wearily on her own blanket across the fire from him. Why was she so still, that beatific look on her face? He wanted to ask her what had taken her so long.

"Mama," Caleb said and crawled toward her. When she put him on her lap, he rubbed his eyes with his fists. She kissed the top of his head and stroked his dark hair. He rubbed his face against her breasts, his eyelids heavy. Shifting him gently, she lay down and tucked him close to her to keep him warm. She drew her shawl up to cover herself before opening her clothing and nursing him to sleep.

Atretes watched her boldly, willing her to look at him. When she did, his blood went warm at the softness in her eyes. No woman had ever looked at him like that before. Her face was pure gold in the glowing embers of the fire, which he'd let die down as he sat there, wondering how long it would be before she came back.

"Good night, Atretes," she said softly and closed her eyes.

He ached with a profound longing. Disturbed, he added several more thick branches to the fire, then his gaze drifted back to Rizpah. She was asleep already. It annoyed him that she could be so at peace when he was in such turmoil. Was it her Christ again that had brought her this peace?

Atretes' gaze rested on Caleb.

How could this god have such power and yet allow his son . . . *his son* to die at the hands of his enemies? Where was the power in such an act?

He looked again at Rizpah's face and clenched his fists. He wanted to awaken her . . . and then what? Admit his doubts, his questioning, his interest in her infernal god? Admit the longing,

235

the gnawing emptiness that ached within him whenever he saw the peace she and Theophilus shared?

Fool. *Fool!* They'd be traveling miles tomorrow, and instead of resting in preparation, he was sitting here, staring across the fire at a woman, and he couldn't seem to help himself.

He sat a long while watching her sleep. He studied every contour of her face and body. How was it possible for a woman to become more beautiful every day? Stretching out on the ground, he lay staring up at the starry blue-black sky.

Willing himself to sleep, he closed his eyes. Even as he drifted off, her words echoed softly.

"However much you want to protect your heart, it's already too late, isn't it?"

24

They traveled the road through the ancient Etruscan city of Tarquinia, with its painted tombs, and went on to Orbetello near the base of Mount Argentarius. Crossing the bridge over the Albegna, they continued north for the Umbro River and Grosseto. They walked no more than twelve miles a day, for any more than that was too much for Rizpah.

The weather turned cold and wet.

"We'll make it to Grosseto in another hour," Theophilus said as a company of soldiers rode south past them.

Rizpah looked down the road. Though she said nothing, Atretes saw her weariness. The clouds opened, pouring a heavy driving rain down upon them. Long before they reached the edge of the city, she was soaked through, the hem of her tunic muddy.

"This way," Theophilus said, leading them through the streets past a bazaar where the merchants were still carrying on trade within their tent booths.

Atretes grew uneasy as he saw more soldiers down the street ahead of him. "Where do you take us?"

"I know of an inn near the fort," Theophilus said. "It's been ten years since I passed through this city, but if it's still there, we'll find good food and shelter."

The inn was owned by several retired Roman soldiers and had expanded since Theophilus' last visit. The tariff for overnight lodgings had gone up as well, but Theophilus paid it gladly to get Rizpah and the baby out of the cold rain.

Atretes was tense and watchful as he stood within the courtyard. Legionnaires were coming and going from every direction. Many had women of easy virtue with them.

Caleb fussed as a young soldier passed by with a woman clinging to his arm. The legionnaire smiled at the babe, reaching out to chuck him lightly under the chin. "A wet night for travel, little one," he said and fell silent as Rizpah looked up at him. The young man's brows rose slightly in surprised pleasure. "My lady," he drawled, giving her a slight bow and annoying his lady companion.

Atretes stepped closer and pushed the cape back from his hair. "Move on."

The woman stared, openmouthed. Her gaze moved over him in stunned admiration. She smiled, eyes bright.

The soldier straightened slightly, insulted that a civilian would think to command him. He took in Atretes' height, breadth, and the cold look in his eyes.

Atretes took Rizpah's arm. He said nothing more, but the message was clear. The soldier heeded it. He took the woman's arm and headed toward the stairs. She whispered something to him as they walked away. They rejoined the others of their group. As they spoke among themselves, two others glanced back at them.

"He meant no harm," Rizpah said softly. "People always notice babies."

"He was looking at *you*."

Theophilus turned from having paid the proprietor.

"We will not stay here," Atretes said, and Theophilus saw his burning look and where it was directed.

"Lower your hackles. They're leaving." He had forgotten the other amenities the establishment boasted. "We've been given a chamber down that corridor. I've arranged for food to be sent to us."

They entered a huge inner courtyard with a marble fountain. The rain pattered down as they walked along the portico. Rizpah shivered, the chill seeping in through her wet clothing. Their room was large and comfortably furnished with several couches and small tables. A servant followed them in and took hot coals from a bucket to start the fuel in their brazier burning.

Dumping his wet cloak on the floor, Atretes took Caleb and put him on the floor. He stripped the sodden cloak roughly from Rizpah's shoulders. "Warm yourself." He nodded toward the brazier. She started after Caleb, but Atretes caught her arm, giving her a push. Catching up with Caleb, he stripped his son's tunic and wraps, tossing them as heedlessly aside as he had their cloaks. Flopping his son on a couch, he rubbed him dry with one of the woven blankets. Caleb cried at the rough handling and didn't stop until he was wrapped in warmth and held close by his father.

Theophilus had fared better in the rain with his thick woolen cloak, leather cuirass, and tunic. He took a blanket from the foot of another couch and draped it around Rizpah's shoulders. Shivering, she thanked him as she picked up her cloak from the floor. She shook it and draped it over the curled wooden end of the couch, hoping it would dry before morning.

Hugging the blanket around herself, she stood as close to the brazier as she could. Steam rose from the wool. Atretes came near, Caleb peering up out of the blanket bundle in his father's arms, spikes of dark hair sticking straight up on his head. She laughed and tapped his nose, thankful he was dry and warm.

"We'll rest here a day," Theophilus said. "No one will bother us."

"Perhaps the rains will let up," Rizpah said, almost hoping they wouldn't. She desperately needed a day of rest.

A servant brought a tray of delicious foods. Theophilus broke up the braised chicken cooked in honey and mead spiced with coriander and sliced onions. Cooked eggs were sliced and topped with roe on a bed of lettuce and sliced mushrooms. Meatballs in a spicy red sauce were also on the platter along with loaves of bread and ripe winter apples.

"Manna from heaven," Rizpah said, feeding bits of chicken to Caleb before eating any herself. He preferred the cooked eggs with roe.

While her attention was on Caleb, Atretes filled a goblet with strong wine and set it before her. Her tunic was still damp, her skin pale. The wine would warm her and give her a good night's sleep. He looked over her soiled tunic and the worn sandals. She'd freeze in the mountains.

"Wonderful food, a warm place to sleep," Rizpah said, looking around the beautifully furnished room. "All I need is a bath and I'd feel I was in heaven."

"The baths aren't far from here," Theophilus said. "There's no reason not to go."

"She's too tired," Atretes said, his mouth full of pheasant.

"I'd love to bathe."

He tossed the leg bone onto the floor. "You bathed in the stream last night."

"I washed my face."

Atretes glowered. "What about the baby?"

"I'll take him with me, of course."

"We'll go with her," Theophilus said, curious about Atretes' attitude.

"And the gold? Who'll watch it?"

"We'll take turns. I'll keep it on me while you bathe. Then you can do likewise."

"Perhaps we can wash our clothes as well," Rizpah said hopefully.

"There'll be a laundress on hand," Theophilus said. He rose from the couch and crossed the room, rummaging through his pack. He took a bathing set of strigils and an oil flask from his gear. "I'm afraid I left mine in Ephesus," Rizpah said. "We had no time...."

"We can purchase what you need there," Theophilus said.

Atretes looked between the two. Clearly any objections he might make would be overruled. He wasn't about to tell either one of them he had never been in the public baths before, but had heard plenty about them. He drained his goblet of wine and stood, resigned. "Let's get it done."

Theophilus showed them the way. The baths weren't far away from the inn, which was probably another reason the inn was so popular. There was a line of patrons at the door. Atretes queued up with Rizpah and Theophilus, who paid the few copper coins for all of them, and they went in.

Atretes entered the echoing antechamber with misgivings. He hated crowds, and the place was bustling with men and women.

Rizpah glanced up at Atretes. He seemed uncomfortable and out of sorts. He passed the doorway to the changing rooms and stood near the archways, peering into the tepidarium. Several half-clad women came out of the changing room and passed by him into the baths.

Rizpah turned for the women's changing room, then started as Atretes' hand clamped on her arm. "No," he said gruffly.

"No?" she said, confused. "I don't understand." He headed for the main bath chamber, hauling her along with him.

"Atretes!" she said, embarrassed and confused. People were staring. "What are you doing?"

Theophilus followed, suspecting what the matter was. He should have realized earlier.

They entered the huge chamber containing the tepidarium. Atretes stopped and stared. The pool was filled with people, most naked, a few wearing short tunics. Several women lounged on couches near the pool, towels carelessly tossed over themselves. Two men, stark naked, sat on the edge of the pool talking to them. The steamy environment smelled of sweet spiced oils and incense. Atretes looked around in disgust. For the most part, men, women, and children seemed to lack all modesty. Several boys ran past him and dove into the pool. Atretes forgot he was holding onto Rizpah as a curvaceous young woman came up the steps. Like Venus from the sea, she wrung out her long hair as she walked right in front of him, smiling up at him as she did so. She took a towel from the shelf nearby and dried her hair, her gaze gliding over him. She reminded him of Julia.

Rizpah saw his attention fixed on the young woman. Her heart sank. "Please let go of my arm, Atretes." He did so without a word.

Theophilus gave her several coins. "There were bath sets for sale in the hall," he said. "Pick whichever one you want."

"Thank you," she said as a group of young men with towels wrapped around their waists walked by. They were laughing and talking together. Two glanced at Rizpah as they passed by. Atretes grabbed her arm again.

"You stay with me."

"I prefer to bathe with Caleb alone."

"Alone? In this place? Don't make me laugh."

"You've never been in public baths before, have you?" Theophilus said as two women walked by, towels loosely draped over their shoulders. They paused to talk to the two men sitting by the edge of the pool. Several naked girls scampered by and jumped into the tepidarium, coming up and splashing one another. "No one will bother her."

"If anyone gets near her, I'll kill him."

Rizpah's eyes went wide. She had no doubt he meant it.

"There are unspoken rules of proper behavior in a place like this," Theophilus said grimly.

"I think it better if I go back," she said. "You both stay. I'll come later when there are fewer bathers." Another woman walked by and glanced at Atretes with open interest.

"I'm not bathing with a bunch of gawking women around," Atretes said loudly enough to be heard. The woman blushed and averted her gaze. "I had enough of that in the arena." Others close by glanced at him with unveiled interest.

"We'll see Rizpah back to the inn and then go to the fort," Theophilus said. "You'll be in the company of men only in the baths there."

"Ha! Bathe with Roman soldiers? I'd rather my skin rotted from my bones!" His voice carried further this time and drew glances from several young men.

"Not even if you smell like a jackal?" Rizpah said and went back through the archway.

"A jackal?" Atretes said and followed her.

"Excuse me," she said without pausing. "A *goat*. A bleating, foul-tempered goat." She plunked Caleb in Atretes' arms. Ignoring his protest, she went to the vendor of bath sets and purchased two. She turned and saw that Atretes had come into the antechamber after her.

"Don't do that again," he growled.

She tucked the strigil into his belt, leaving the other strigil and oil flask to dangle. She took Caleb. "It won't hurt you to bathe. Don't worry about all those women. I'm sure Theophilus will make sure you're not molested."

Theophilus suppressed a smile at the look of consternation on Atretes' face as she walked away with the baby.

"Where are you going?" Atretes called after her, his voice echoing.

"Back to the inn." She walked across the antechamber and disappeared through the doorway as half a dozen people entered.

"I have a feeling I'm not going to have a relaxing swim," Theophilus said dryly. "You want to bathe first, or shall I?"

Swearing under his breath, Atretes yanked the strigil from his belt. Clamping it between his teeth, he strode back through the archway to the main baths, stripping off his belt as he went.

"Atretes, wait a minute!" Theophilus said, going after him. He grunted as Atretes slammed the belt and money pouches in his stomach. "The changing room is . . ."

Atretes stripped off his tunic and tossed it at him as well. Taking a couple of steps, he dove into the tepidarium. He came up in the middle and shook his hair back. The place seemed quieter. He struck out, swimming for the far end and, when he reached it, planted his hands on the side and lifted himself out of the water. Men and women paused in their various activities to stare as he strode along the portico. He entered the *calidarium*.

For a man who despised being the center of attention, he certainly knew how to become just that. Amused, Theophilus sat on a bench and leaned back to wait. It wouldn't be long.

Inside the calidarium, Atretes opened the flask and poured

scented oil into his palm. He rubbed the oil rigorously on his chest, shoulders, beneath his arms, and down his legs in a hurry to quit the place.

A man approached him. "Would you like me to massage that in . . ." The words dried up as Atretes' head came up. The man held up a hand and retreated quickly.

Muttering under his breath, Atretes scraped the oil briskly from his skin and shook it off the strigil. As soon as the deed was done, he headed into the frigidarium and took a quick cold plunge.

Theophilus saw Atretes striding toward him, a towel wrapped snugly around his waist. Atretes snatched his discarded tunic from him and donned it. "Done," he said and took his belt. As soon as it was on, he took the money pouches, tucked them securely in place, and jerked his head in dismissal. "Take your time."

He strode through the archways.

Laughing, Theophilus followed him out the door into the street and fell into step beside him. "I've never seen a man so eager to forgo the pleasure of a relaxing bath."

"Go and take your bath, Roman. I can find my own way back to the inn," Atretes snarled without breaking stride.

"Like you, I feel less comfortable with women around. I'll bathe at the fort. Besides, this old mule of Marius could use a good massage," he said, making reference to the name often attached to legionnaires for the amount of gear they carried.

They walked along the stone street. White pebbles had been set between the larger cobbles to reflect the moonlight and give illumination to show the lay of the street ahead.

"How far to the mountains?" Atretes said grimly.

"There are mountains all the way. Even following the coast road to Genova isn't easy for someone not conditioned to hard travel."

"She hasn't complained."

"She won't."

Atretes took note of the pictured plaques suspended above several shops along the street. He saw two of interest. "We'll rest *two* days instead of one."

Theophilus' brows rose slightly, but he nodded. "So be it." Whatever Atretes' reasons, Rizpah needed the rest. And it would give him more time to ask questions at the fort and learn what trouble may lie ahead. Last he heard, there were brigands working the road through the Graian Alps. Perhaps there was another, safer way. By sea to the Rhine or through another pass. He needed to find out.

"I leave you here," he said. "The inn's at the end of that street. I'll take my time. Perhaps my absence will give you and Rizpah the opportunity to shore up the breach between you. Whatever happened the other night is eating at both of you. Sort it out."

Atretes' eyes narrowed as he watched the centurion walk down the street toward the west gate of the fort. A guard was posted, and Theophilus paused to speak with him.

When Atretes entered the chamber, Rizpah glanced up in surprise from where she was on the floor playing with Caleb. "That didn't take long," she said and looked past him. "Where's Theophilus?"

Jealousy gripped Atretes without warning. "He went to the baths at the fort." Tossing his cloak onto a couch, he looked at her grimly. Caleb was clutching the front of her tunic as he tried to stand on his own. Her expression was one of bemused question.

"I won't ask if you enjoyed your bath," she said. "You didn't take long enough." She caught Caleb before he fell, holding him up until he found his balance again.

"He's getting too heavy for you to carry."

"For long distances, yes."

"I'll carry him from now on."

"Does that mean I get the gear?"

"No," he said, not amused. "You wouldn't last a mile."

"You needn't add Caleb to what you're already packing on your back."

"You're weak."

It was said so coldly, she almost dismissed his original concern on her behalf. "Weaker than you, yes, but not so weak I can't carry my share. And Caleb," she kissed the baby's neck, "is my share." She picked him up and stood. "Maybe by the time I reach your homeland, I'll be as robust as any German woman."

As she carried Caleb over to the couch, Atretes saw she was barefoot. Her feet looked dirty and sore from days of walking. He noticed other things as well. "How did you tear your tunic?"

"I caught it on a briar when I was coming back from the

stream last night." She sat on the couch, a little less relaxed than she'd been a moment before. She was dirty and felt unkempt. And why was he staring at her like that? She sat Caleb on her knees. "I'll go back to the baths later when it's quieter."

"Over my dead body."

"If you insist." The look he gave her lacked all humor.

"Atretes, I *need* to bathe. So does Caleb. I'll wear my tunic, if it puts your mind at ease. I might as well wash it while I'm washing myself."

He saw she was determined and, looking her over again, he thought she was right. "How long before the throng leaves?"

"Most of them will be gone in a couple of hours. There's a small room reserved for nursing mothers. I would've gone in there."

"You should've told me."

"You didn't give me the opportunity. Would you please sit down? You're making me nervous pacing like that."

He paused to pour himself some wine. His heart was beating fast. He was nervous, though he couldn't quite figure out why. He wished Theophilus had returned with him. Whatever he might feel about the Roman, his company offered distraction from his feelings about Rizpah. Being alone with her now made him remember what he had done in the hypogeum. Was she remembering as well?

"Don't Germans bathe?"

He turned and glared at her. "Yes, Germans bathe, but not in mass, men and women together. Germans have a sense of *decency*."

She thought it best to change the subject. "What was Ania like?"

"Ania?"

She hadn't meant to ask, but now that the question had come without forethought, she pursued it. "Your wife. You said her name was Ania."

"Why do you want to know about her?"

"It might tell me what you were like before Rome made a gladiator out of you."

"She was young."

"Just young? That's all you remember?"

"I remember. I remember everything about her. She was beautiful. Blonde. Fair skin. Blue eyes."

She blushed at his pointed perusal. She had never been so aware of her black hair, olive skin, and dark eyes.

"She died in childbirth," he said and drained his goblet. "My son died with her." The pitcher was empty. He slammed it down.

She closed her eyes, wishing she hadn't asked him anything. She thought of Shimei and Rachel and how her heart still ached for them. She opened her eyes and looked up at him. "I'm sorry. I shouldn't have asked."

The compassion in her eyes made him soften and relax. "It was a long time ago." The truth was, he had lied. He couldn't even remember Ania's face. Worse, the pain he'd once felt over her death was gone. Not even a twinge remained. They had been together in another time and in another world—one far removed from Rome. He cocked his head toward her. "Tell me about your husband."

Her mouth curved and she stroked Caleb's hair, putting him down again so he could move about at will. "He was kind, as kind as John and Theophilus."

Atretes' jaw tightened. He reclined on the couch, forcing himself to appear relaxed. "Just kind? That's all you remember?"

"Baiting me with my own questions?"

"If you like. You've never said anything about him. I'd like to know what you were like before you became the mother of my son."

He was in a strange, pensive mood. She wished she had kept silent, for there were currents of emotion running between them that could suck her down. "He was a master mason and worked very hard at his trade. Everything he did, he did for the Lord."

"I suppose he was handsome and built like Apollo."

"He wasn't beautiful at all, not by most people's standards. He was short and stocky and losing his hair. But he had beautiful eyes. That was one of the things that struck me about him when he first spoke to me. Have you ever had people look at you and there doesn't seem to be anything behind their eyes? They look *at* you without ever really seeing you?"

Atretes had. Many times.

"Shimei was different. When he looked at me, I felt loved for who I was."

Something about the way she said it piqued his interest. "Who were you that people looked at you without seeing you for who you were?" When she lowered her eyes, he frowned. Whatever she had been before marrying, it was something she was hesitant to share with him. "Maybe I should ask *what* were you?"

"Alone."

His eyes narrowed on her. What was she hiding? "A safe answer that says nothing. I'm alone, which doesn't say the half of what I am."

"Perhaps we should talk of other things," she said, heart beating dully. *O God, not now. He'll never understand. Not in his present mood or state of mind.*

Atretes stood, agitated. "You gave a vow you'd never lie to me."

"I haven't."

"Then tell me the truth."

She said nothing for a long moment. "How much truth do you want, Atretes?"

"All of it."

She looked up at him for a long moment. She was tempted, sorely tempted, to fall back into old patterns of self-preservation. But if she did, wouldn't she be turning away from the Lord as well. *O God, let him be satisfied with a little of the truth and not demand all of it.*

"My father drank," she said slowly. "Heavily. Sometimes to the point where he didn't know what he was doing. He would go into black rages like you and break things, sometimes people. My mother was one." She took a shuddering breath, remembering. She didn't want to talk about her father any more than Atretes wanted to discuss the arena. Clasping her hands together, she tried to keep from shaking. She watched Caleb crawling around the legs of the couch on which his father had just been reclining. "I ran away shortly after she died." She didn't want to remember what had happened then.

"How old were you?"

"Eleven."

He frowned, thinking of a small girl fending for herself in a city like Ephesus. "Where did you live?"

"Where I could. Under bridges, in empty crates by the docks, in deserted insulae, in doorways—anywhere I could find shelter, that's where I lived."

"And food?"

"I stole whatever I could get my hands on and lied my way out of it when I was caught. I became very skilled at both. I survived like one of those rats you see living on whatever they can find.

The one thing I didn't do was beg." She gave a soft, bleak laugh of remembered despair. "I was too full of angry pride to do that."

He said nothing for a long moment. "Did you ever. . . ?"

Her hands whitened. She looked across the room at him. Her dark eyes filling with tears and pain. She knew what he wanted to ask. Even after Shimei and redemption and salvation, the things she had done still filled her with shame and anguish.

"Did I sell myself?" she said for him. "Yes. When I was so hungry and cold I didn't think I could live through the night."

He felt sick. "How many times?"

"Twice."

"Shimei?"

She shook her head. "He found me unconscious in the doorway of the insula where he lived. He took me to Claudia, an old woman of deep faith who lived alone. She fed me and cared for me until I was well. Shimei came often. He taught me how to read. They both loved me. I'd never been loved like that before. They took me to the body of believers in Christ. And they loved me, too. Just as I was, wretched and lost. Ruined. Forever, I thought. When Jesus redeemed me, he became my Savior, and Shimei asked me to be his wife."

"And that made you virtuous by their standards," he said dryly.

"What virtue I have comes from the Lord and not from me, Atretes. When I asked Jesus into my heart, he washed me clean—"

"In the river," he said, almost sneering.

"God made me whole again. I felt resurrected." She saw his struggle as he took in all she had revealed about herself. He didn't want to believe her. She wished it wasn't all true. "I have not lied or cheated or stolen or sold myself since I entered Claudia's house. On my life before God, Atretes, I will not do so ever again."

He believed her, but what did that matter?

"I hoped you'd never ask certain questions," she said, her voice choked with tears. She searched his face. "I'm sorry the truth hurts you so."

Anguish filled him, twisting his insides. And anger, too, though at what or whom he didn't know. He didn't know what he felt other than at war with himself and with what she had just told him. But some things were very clear.

"Do you know what they do to women like you in Germania?" he said hoarsely. "They shave off their hair and throw them in the bog. That's the quick way. Most of the time, the girl's father or husband cuts off her nose and whips her. If she survives, she's cast out of the village and left to fend for herself."

Rizpah said nothing. Caleb crawled back to her and sat at her feet, flapping his arms happily. "Mama . . . mama . . ." She bent forward to pick him up.

"Don't touch him!"

She flinched and drew back slowly, her hands clenched in her lap, her eyes shut. Caleb started to cry.

Atretes scooped him up, knocked some tasseled cushions from the couch, and set him among them. Momentarily distracted, Caleb was content.

"How many others know about your past?" Atretes demanded, pacing again.

"Everyone in the church of Ephesus."

He stopped and stared at her, the muscles in his face jerking.

"Were you *proud* of it to tell so many?"

Her eyes welled with tears. "No! I shared my testimony when I accepted Christ, and then whenever the Lord called upon me to do so."

"*Why?*"

"To help others find their way out of the same kind of darkness I lived in."

Anger surged through him. "Why did you tell me? Why in Hades did you tell me *now*?"

"You asked. I said I'd never lie to you," she said very quietly.

"Better had you done so!"

"Better for whom?"

"What am I supposed to do about it?"

Dear Lord, is this what it comes to? She looked into Atretes' blue eyes and saw death staring back at her.

"What do you expect me to do now that I know all about you?"

God, still my trembling heart. He's hurt and angry, and it's within his rights to take my life. Your will be done. I will trust you. I will trust Caleb to your keeping. Only, Lord, please . . .

"Tell me!"

"You'll do whatever you feel you must."

Was she challenging him? Did she dare? Atretes drew his dagger from his belt and crossed the room. He caught her by the throat and pulled her to her feet. "What I must." Her eyes flickered and then became calm, accepting. When his fingers tightened, she didn't raise her hands to defend herself. "What I must." He could feel her pulse racing beneath his thumb, but she made no plea.

Unbidden, the memory of his last meeting with Julia came to him. She had been hysterical, clinging to him, swearing the child she carried was his. Had she not been pregnant, he would've killed her for being unfaithful. Later, he had told Hadassah that even if Julia laid the babe at his feet, he'd turn and walk away, even knowing the child was his.

Lies, lies . . . Julia, Rome, all the rest, lies.

He looked into Rizpah's dark eyes and knew she had told him the truth about everything. *"I will never lie,"* she had said shortly after arriving at the villa in Ephesus. *No matter the cost.*

He saw no fear in her eyes, only sadness. She stood before him, her life in his hand, and said not a word in self-defense. *"I will give you a solemn vow, Atretes. I will never lie."* His heart beat faster. One thrust of his dagger and it would be finished. Or he could squeeze. . . .

The palm of his hand grew clammy with sweat. "I should kill you." The room was silent except for his own harsh breathing.

"I deserve death. I know that. A hundred times over."

His chest tightened at her words and at the look of grief in her eyes. His mind filled with the faces of men he had killed.

"It's by God's grace my life is different," she said.

He let go of her. Gritting his teeth, he shook his head, trying to deny everything she had told him.

"I'm sorry, Atretes," she said, trying not to cry and make it worse for him. "I never thought the choices I made mattered. My mother was dead. My father . . ." She lowered her head. "I didn't care what happened. It was painful enough staying alive without thinking about how I did it. But I was wrong, so wrong."

She put her hand on his arm. When he drew back sharply, she tensed instinctively, expecting a blow. His eyes narrowed darkly and he stepped back, his hand clenched.

Whatever he meant to do to her, she had to finish.

"Jesus shed his blood so that I could be cleansed of what I'd done. He forfeited his own life for every one of us, forgiving us all our sins. He opened a new path for any who choose to take it, and I did. And I will continue to do so, no matter the cost. I cling to Christ with all my heart. And I won't let go."

Atretes remembered Hadassah standing in the corridor of the dungeon. *"Though he slay me . . ."*

"He offers you new life, Atretes," Rizpah said, "if you but receive it."

All her concern seemed to be for him rather than herself. "So, like this unseen god of yours, I'm supposed to forget everything you've done. I'm supposed to *forgive*?"

"You won't forget any of it any more than I can," she said quietly. "Remembering how I lived and what I allowed myself to become makes me that much more grateful for what Jesus has done for me."

"I'm happy for you," he said with a sneer. "But don't expect anything from me." The dagger felt like lead in his hand. He slipped it into the sheath tucked in his belt. "I forgive *nothing*."

The muscles in her face jerked, but she didn't speak. She didn't protest or argue or plead, all of which he'd expected her to do. "I need to think what I'm to do now," he said flatly.

"What about Caleb?" she said, and her voice trembled slightly.

"Wean him. Starting now."

She closed her eyes, and he saw his words had been harder to bear than any blow he might have given her.

He went to the door. "Don't leave this room. Do you hear me? If you do, I swear by Tiwaz, I'll hunt you down like a dog and kill you."

*

Theophilus returned and found Rizpah sitting on the floor, Caleb asleep in her arms. He could tell things hadn't gone well with Atretes. "Where is he?"

"He was here earlier and then left."

"Did he say where he was going?"

She shook her head.

Considering Atretes' disposition, the German might do any number of things to get himself into more trouble. Get drunk. Pick a fight with some Roman soldiers. Or worse. He'd find himself a harlot and spend the night with her, very likely breaking Rizpah's heart.

"I'll take you back to the baths."

"Atretes told me to stay here." Her voice broke and she looked up at him bleakly. "I told him about my past. I told him everything." Her eyes welled and spilled over. "Everything."

"God help us." He knelt down beside her and put his arms around her, feeling her body shaking with sobs.

25

Atretes wandered the streets of Grosseto until he found an inn at the northern end of town, far from the fort and legionnaires. He ordered wine and sat at a back table. It was a mean place, a far distance from the fort, which drew dockworkers and wagon drivers who wanted quantity rather that quality in their drink. They were loud and profane, but no one bothered him.

Rain pounded the roof, adding to the din. He drank heavily, but couldn't seem to drive what Rizpah had said from his head.

Liar, thief, harlot.

He kept seeing her eyes, dark with grief as she told him. She bore no resemblance to the person she had described. She had left all she knew to go with him to Germania for his sake and Caleb's, and not once complained over the physical hardships. She had saved his child from death. She withheld herself from him despite his efforts to make her compromise her morality.

Liar? Thief? Harlot?

He groaned, pounding his fists on the table.

The place grew quiet and still. He lifted his head and saw everyone was staring at him. "What are you looking at?" They turned their backs, pretending interest elsewhere, but he could feel the tension in the room. No doubt they thought him mad. He could feel the hard, heavy beat of his heart, the heat of his blood. Maybe he was mad.

He ordered more wine. It was brought quickly by the proprietor himself, who didn't dare make eye contact before departing. Atretes filled his goblet and clutched it in his hand.

What was he supposed to do about what Rizpah had told him? In Germania, he would have killed her. It would have been demanded of him by the elders. He broke out in a cold sweat just thinking about it and veered off from why he reacted that way.

Liar, thief, harlot. It kept repeating in his mind.

He buried his face in his hands. And what was he? A butcher of men.

He wanted to go home, home to Germania! He wanted to go back to the life he had known before he had ever heard of Rome.

He didn't want to think about anything else. He wanted life to be simple again. He wanted peace.

But was life ever simple? Had he ever known peace of any kind? From the time he was old enough to hold a knife and then a framea, he had been trained to fight. He had gone to war against other German tribes who entered their territory and then against the Romans who thought to enslave them. And hadn't they?

Ten years he had lived with their hand around his throat, fighting for his life, all the while entertaining them.

Shoving the stool back, he got up and headed unsteadily for the door. The rain was pounding outside. As he went out, he stumbled over something and heard a soft groan. Swearing, he braced himself against the door frame and looked down. Someone small and thin scrambled out of his path. A young girl. She huddled against the wall, staring up at him with wide, dark eyes. Her face was pale and thin, her dark hair tangled and unkempt. He judged her no more than ten or twelve and grimaced at the dirty rags she wore.

"*I lived where I could. Under bridges, in crates near the dock, in doorways . . .*"

He shut his eyes and opened them again, thinking his wine-sodden brain had concocted Rizpah as a child. But the girl was still there. She was shivering violently, whether from cold or fear, he didn't know. Perhaps both.

When he moved, she cowered back, seeming to grow smaller before his eyes. "I won't hurt you," he said and took a coin from the money pouch in his belt. "Here. Buy something to eat." He tossed it at her.

She tried desperately to catch it, but her cold fingers wouldn't close around it. The precious coin dropped with a small plunk into the muddy puddle. With a soft cry of despair, she dropped on her knees in front of him and felt around in the mud trying to find it.

Atretes stared down at her, his heart twisting in disgust and pity. No human being should live like this, especially not a child! He shut his eyes again and saw Rizpah on her hands and knees in the mud.

"*Did I sell myself? Yes. When I was so hungry and cold I didn't think I could live through the night.*"

The girl's weeping was like salt on an open wound.

"Leave it," Atretes said gruffly. Hungry and desperate, she paid him no heed. "I said, *Leave it*!" She scrambled back again, frightened. When he stepped toward her, she raised her arms to ward off a blow. "I won't hurt you." He took another coin from his pouch. "Here." She didn't move. "Take it." He held it out. She looked into his face and then at the coin. "Take it," he said quietly, as though coaxing a frightened, hungry animal with a morsel of food. Still distrustful, she watched him warily while her muddy fingers closed around it. "Hang onto it this time."

"An *aureus*," he heard her say as he walked into the rain. "You give me an *aureus*! The gods bless you, my lord. Oh, the gods bless you!" she said, weeping.

Atretes kept walking, hardly feeling the cold wind. The effect of the wine gradually lessened, making him feel even more raw. He reached a narrow bridge crossing a stream just north of Grosseto. The sky lightened as dawn came. He was tired and depressed. His head was pounding.

He wondered if Rizpah had stayed in the room the way he had commanded her or if she'd gone to the baths. Considering what she had told him and his frame of mind when he'd left, he could expect her to be gone by the time he returned.

What about his son?

What a fool he was! He headed back into the town.

Roman legionnaires passed him. The sound of their hobnailed sandals made his muscles tighten. He saw the gates of the fort. The tabernacles lining the street in front of it were opening for business. There were things he had wanted to buy yesterday, but he doubted they'd be necessary now.

The inn was quiet when he reached it. He strode along the corridor and stopped at the door of their chamber. He put his hand on the latch and then paused. Instead of going in, he stood outside, listening, tense. There was no sound from within. It was well past dawn. So much for her obedience! Swearing under his breath, he opened the door and entered. He'd rest before he went looking for her.

Rizpah was standing near the window. She turned, relief filling her face. "You're all right! Thank God."

She still wore the same torn, dirty tunic. She hadn't even washed her feet. "You didn't go to the baths."

"You said to stay here." When he said no more, she walked to the couch and sat down, her knees too weak to hold her.

He wondered if she'd been standing at the window all night, waiting for him. She looked it. He turned away from her, disturbed by the emotions churning inside him. She hadn't run away. She'd done as he commanded and waited for his return.

No matter the cost.

He looked around and saw Caleb wrapped in a blanket and sleeping comfortably among the pillows he had tossed on the floor the night before.

"Where's Theophilus?"

"He went out to look for you a few hours ago."

He looked at her again and knew that whatever she had been, she was someone else now. He couldn't see that other person in her, no matter how hard he tried. And he knew something else. He trusted her. It was a piercing realization and one that filled him with a sense of peace such as he hadn't known in years. He didn't care what she'd been; he knew what she was.

"You never killed anyone," he said simply. Nothing she had done to stay alive was worse than what he was.

His words amazed her, for in them she knew he exonerated her for everything she had done. Thankfulness and joy filled her and then softened as she realized he had also revealed something deep and dark and painful about his own life. He condemned himself. She rose and came to him. "Your sins are no greater than mine, Atretes. The Lord doesn't measure the way man does. He—"

"We won't talk of any of it again," he said and stepped by her.

She turned, watching him cross the room and pick up the wine pitcher. Finding it empty, he swore and set it down. He looked around, distracted, undecided, restless. She'd never seen him look so tired and drawn. "Rest, Atretes," she said gently. "We'll continue on when you're ready."

He stretched out on the larger couch and put his arm up behind his head. He stared at the ceiling, his body tense.

She took a blanket from her couch. He studied her as she came to him, taking in each feature as though he had never seen her before and was trying to read who she was by the way she looked. She put the blanket over him. He caught her wrist as she started to turn away.

"You said there was a room at the baths where you could wash in private."

"Yes," she said, heart racing.

He let her go. Removing his belt, he dropped it with the money pouches on the floor beside the couch. "Take what you need and go. Take Caleb and bathe him as well."

She was taken aback with surprise. "Th-thank you," she stammered softly, wondering silently at his reasons. Was his decision a test or sign of trust? Either way, what did it matter? She knelt down and took a few copper coins from the pouch. Rising, she went and picked up Caleb from the pillows. Opening the door, she glanced back and saw Atretes watching her.

"We won't be long."

There were few patrons at the baths in the morning and most were women with children. For a second copper, a bath attendant washed her tunic while she bathed with Caleb. He loved playing in the water. When she finished, she rubbed the scented oil on her skin and scraped it off with the strigil.

On the way back to the inn, she used the last few coins to purchase enough bread and fruit to feed them all. Water would have to do for she hadn't enough money to buy wine, but then, perhaps Atretes had had his fill the night before.

She entered the room quietly, certain that Atretes would be asleep. He wasn't. He lay on the couch as she had left him. Theophilus had returned as well and was asleep on the couch nearest the wall. Atretes relaxed as she entered the room. He moved, making himself more comfortable, and fell asleep even as she watched.

A test, she thought and wanted to brush the hair back from his face.

Rizpah longed to sleep as well, but there was Caleb to tend. Having slept all night, he was wide-awake and in a mood to play. She made sure there was nothing on the floor or within reach to harm him and sat with her back against the door, trying to keep watch. Caleb was content, entertaining himself among the cushions.

*

The tot's baby chatter awakened Atretes. Rolling over, he watched his son push a cushion across the floor. Sunlight streamed in the window revealing an hour well past noon. Rizpah lay curled on her side against the door. Atretes studied her, taking pleasure in the sight of her. He rose and crossed the room quietly.

As he lifted her, he felt the slight dampness of her tunic from having been washed the night before. He laid her on her couch and stood over her, letting his gaze take in every curve and plane of her body. He curled a strand of dark hair around his finger, rubbing it between his fingers. To look at her, no one would guess she'd lived in the streets of a city like Ephesus, stealing and trading her body to stay alive. She looked young and unsullied. He let the strand of hair uncurl. She shivered slightly, curling on her side. He looked for her blanket and realized she had given it to him.

He saw his cloak hanging near the brazier. He had dumped it on the floor upon their arrival at the inn and forgotten it when he left. He had been too intent on getting out of the room and having time to think about what she had told him. The heavy garment had been soaked anyway and would have been of little use to him. He took it up now and found it dry and warm.

He covered her with it. Brushing his knuckles lightly against her cheek, he stood amazed that her skin could be so soft.

When Rizpah awakened late in the afternoon, Atretes was gone.

Caleb was nowhere to be found.

26

"I'll borrow a horse from the fort and follow the road north," Theophilus said. "Atretes knows enough to go that way. You stay here and wait in case he changes his mind and comes back."

"And if he does return?"

"Start out. Camp near a milestone. I'll find you." He left enough money for her to pay for two days' lodging.

Rizpah paced, praying fervently that Atretes would come back, sure he wouldn't. *Lord, you are my rock and my shield, my everpresent help in time of trouble. O God. Caleb. Caleb!*

Her breasts filled with milk until she hurt with heaviness. With the physical pain came doubt, gripping her heart with taloned fingers.

"Wean him. Starting now."

O God.

"I forgive nothing!"

Lord, please.

She sat weeping in the growing darkness, arms crossed over her breasts, pressing against the pain.

Your will, Lord. Give me the heart to accept your will.

She lit the lamp. Pacing again, she murmured words Shimei had taught her, clinging to them with determination while fighting against the doubts assailing her. "You have plans for me, plans for my welfare and not for calamity to give me a future and a hope. Lord, you found me and restored me. You gathered me to your bosom. You brought me out of the pit." Tears coursed down her cheeks. "Lord, your will . . . your will . . . Lord . . ."

The door opened.

She swung around as Atretes strode in, Caleb in his arms.

"You're awake," Atretes said with a smile, shrugging off a heavy bundle and dumping it on the floor.

Rizpah stared at him.

Atretes looked back at her, his smile turning down in a perplexed frown. "What's wrong?"

"Wrong?" she said faintly.

"You look . . ." He shrugged for want of a word. "Upset."

"What's wrong?!" Her blood went hot. "You take Caleb and leave without a word, and you ask me *what's wrong*?"

"You were asleep, and someone had to watch him," he said with appalling logic. "Here." He dumped the child into her arms. "He's hungry." He headed across the room for the table. "And so am I."

She stood, mouth agape.

"There's nothing here," he said, seeing a piece of stale bread. He glanced back at her.

"Theophilus took the bread that was left."

"And there's nothing else?"

"I had no appetite," she said through clenched teeth, certain she had the strength to kill him with her own bare hands. Shaking with anger, she presented her back to him, sat on the couch, and opened her clothing so that she could nurse Caleb.

"Are you sick?" Atretes said.

"No."

Atretes frowned. She wasn't acting like herself and it made him nervous. "I'll get us something to eat," he said and went out.

Rizpah didn't care if he ever came back, and then was afraid he wouldn't. When he finally did, he brought bread, grapes, two roasted chickens, and two skins of wine and roused her deeper ire with his jovial mood.

"Where's Theophilus?" Atretes said. "At the baths or the fort with his bloody comrades?"

"Neither. He went looking for you. *Again.*"

"Where does he think I went?"

"North."

Atretes stared at her. "North?" He laughed. He laughed harder as he thought about the Roman trying to catch up with him. "North," he said and broke a chicken in half. How long would it take the Roman to figure out he hadn't even left Grosseto? Grinning, he ripped off a hunk of meat with his teeth.

Caleb was replete and asleep in Rizpah's arms. She put him on her couch and covered him with Atretes' cloak. Straightening, she glared at Atretes, incensed by his mirth. "How can you laugh about it?"

"He'll have to walk a long time to find me."

"He was going to get a horse."

"Riding then. Ha! Even better. I like having plenty of distance between us." He laughed again and tore off another hunk of meat with his teeth. He waved the carcass, indicating she join him.

She crossed the room, sat down opposite him, picked up the other half of roasted chicken, and debated hitting him across the side of the head with it. "You could have told us," she said, pulling the leg off instead.

"I said you were sleeping."

"You shouldn't have left."

Atretes' eyes narrowed. "I don't answer to you, woman. And I sure in Hades will never answer to *him*."

"He's showing you the way home."

"Someone else could tell me the way," Atretes said with a shrug.

"If your insufferable pride would let you ask."

He froze for an instant and then tossed the chicken onto the platter, good humor gone. "*My* pride?"

"What was I supposed to think?" she said, anger dissolving into exasperation. "'Wean him,' you said. 'I forgive nothing,' you said." She threw the chicken leg at his head. His reflexes were as good as ever, and she missed. She had never seen him look surprised—until now.

"I thought you left and took Caleb with you!" She dissolved into tears. Humiliated by her lack of restraint, she stood up quickly and left the table.

There was a long silence behind her.

"I covered you with my cloak," Atretes said quietly as though that explained everything.

She turned and looked at him, uncomprehending. Atretes looked back at her as though she had sprouted horns. Perhaps she had.

He felt uncomfortable. Why was she staring at him like that? Mouth flattening, he picked up his chicken again. "Sit down and eat, woman. Maybe you'll *think* better with some food in your stomach."

Rizpah came back and sat down. "*I covered you with my cloak.*" She waited for him to look at her again, but he seemed intent on eating his dinner and pretending she wasn't even in the room. "I thought you forgot your cloak again," she said quietly.

"I didn't forget it." He tossed the bones onto the platter instead of the floor. His manners were improving.

"I'm sorry I threw the chicken leg at you."

How could a woman be on fire with anger one second and serenely calm the next? "Be glad you didn't hit me." He reached for a bunch of grapes.

"I shouldn't have assumed—"

"Eat!"

Smiling, she picked up the chicken and broke off a wing. They ate in silence, his tense, hers tranquil. Atretes finished first and wiped his hands on a blanket. He seemed to want to get away from the table and her as quickly as he could.

"What instructions did Theophilus give you?"

"To head north and camp near a milestone. He said he'd find us."

Atretes went over to the pack he had dumped on the floor. He untied the ropes and opened the blanket. He tossed a heavy ball of cloth to her. As it fell loose in her hands, she realized it was a thick woolen tunic. "You can wear the one you have under it." He tossed her a wool-lined boot similar to those soldiers wore in cold weather. As soon as she caught it, he tossed her the second. The soles of both were made of thick leather and studded with hobnails.

"Your feet will stay dry and warm in those. I had them rubbed with beeswax." He pulled out a heavy woolen cloak and stood. "This'll keep you from freezing in the snow, and there'll be plenty where we're going."

Dropping the boots, she pressed her face into the woolen tunic and cried.

Atretes stood silent, embarrassed. He listened grimly to her sobs and wanted to comfort her. He knew he couldn't. The baby was asleep, Theophilus miles away, and they were alone in this bedchamber. What he felt was too strong. And he knew she felt it, too. If he touched her, he might not listen to any protest she might utter. He didn't trust himself where she was concerned. His baser instincts had been honed to reign too long. He didn't want any more regrets. He lived with enough already.

"If you put those things on *now*, Rizpah, we *might* make a couple of miles before it gets dark."

Sniffling, Rizpah stood and loosened her sash. She pulled the heavy woolen tunic over her head. It dropped in loose comfortable folds down to her ankles. She tied her sash and sat down again, pulling on the boots. She looped the leather laces and pulled them snug before tying them and folding down the tops so they fit midcalf. She stood and thanked God she wouldn't have to walk another mile in her worn sandals.

"Thank you," she said simply, trying not to cry again. "They're a perfect fit. How did you know?"

He came and put the cloak around her. "I took one of your sandals with me." He held onto the edges of the garment, staring into her eyes, his pulse pounding. A fierce tenderness filled him, and a desire to protect her. He didn't like what she made him feel and let go of her.

"When we get to Germania, you will tell no one what you told me," he said, rearranging his gear for easier carry. When she said nothing, he picked the pack up and turned to look at her. "Give me your word."

"I can't. You know I can't."

He couldn't believe she refused. "I told you what they'd do to you. My people don't give second chances." There was a time when he wouldn't have either. She was making him weak.

"I won't lie."

He stared at her. "They'll kill you if they find out."

"It doesn't matter."

No matter the cost, she had said before and she was holding to it. She wouldn't compromise. A part of him was glad. A part of him felt safe in her answer because he knew he could trust her. But another part knew fear. She mattered to him already far more than he cared to admit, and the Chatti showed no mercy.

"All right. Let it be as you say. Don't lie. Just don't say anything." He slung the pack onto his back.

"The way I said nothing to you. I should've told you all about myself when you first began asking questions instead of giving you information piecemeal."

He crossed the room and leaned down to speak straight into her face. "If you'd told me everything the day you arrived, you wouldn't be alive right now! I would've killed you without blinking an eye and been glad of it." She stood uncowed, not even flinching. He straightened. "I wouldn't have had the months of living with you to learn what sort of woman you are *now*."

"So I'm *good* now, Atretes? I just threw a chicken leg at your head."

He grinned. "And missed."

"I still struggle against the flesh. Every day, sometimes every hour."

"And you think I don't?" he said, his gaze moving down over her.

She blushed, feeling hot all over. "That's *not* what I meant."

"Get the boy and let's go." He had to get out of this room, *now.*

She did as he said. They went down the portico and out through the main courtyard to the antechamber. Soldiers were everywhere, a good many of them noticing Rizpah. Ignoring them, Atretes clamped his hand on her arm and headed straight for the wide doorway into the street, eager to be out in the open.

"You're hurting me," Rizpah said and let out her breath when he let go of her. He was walking fast, too fast. She had to make two steps to his one and was quickly out of breath. "I can't keep your pace, Atretes," she said, hating to complain.

He slowed. "This way," he said and started down a main thoroughfare that headed north. They passed through the gates, crossed a bridge, and headed up the road into the growing darkness. They passed one milestone, then another. Stars were beginning to appear. They passed another milestone. Arms aching, Rizpah shifted Caleb.

When they came upon the fourth milestone, she stopped. "It's almost dark."

"We can make another mile."

"I thought you wanted distance between you and Theophilus," she said and walked off the road. She sat down wearily against a tree trunk. Caleb was still sleeping. His day with Atretes must have worn him out. She placed him on the grass and then lay down beside him, curling around him to keep him warm.

Atretes dumped his packs, clearly annoyed to be stopping.

"I'll try to do better tomorrow, Atretes," she said.

He moved about restlessly and then sat a few feet away, knees drawn up, forearms resting on them. He looked at the sky. "We could've made another mile."

✱

They left as the sun was coming up, and Rizpah had nursed Caleb. Atretes bought bread and apples as they passed through a village. Rizpah fed Caleb bits of both as he rode contentedly on her hip. She helped him drink from a skin holding watered wine.

Near noon, a company of soldiers rode toward them. Rizpah saw Theophilus among them and called out to him. They paused as the Roman dismounted and untied his pack from the horse. Slinging it over his shoulder, he spoke cheerfully to the others before heading toward them. One of the soldiers grasped the reins of Theophilus' mount and they continued on down the road.

Theophilus looked Rizpah over, noting the new cloak, tunic, and boots. "So that's where you went," he said to Atretes.

Glowering at him, Atretes started off again.

Theophilus fell into step beside Rizpah. "Have you two been getting along well without me?" he said, his mouth tipping up.

"Well enough," Atretes answered for her and kept walking.

Theophilus grinned at Rizpah. "At least you're glad to see me."

They made good distance over the next days, passing through Campiglia Maritima, Cecina, Livorno, Pisa, and Viareggio. They camped each night near the road. Theophilus purchased more supplies in La Spezia. Atretes insisted on taking the shorter route along the mountainous coastal road rather than the one that went inland.

When they reached Genova, Theophilus arranged lodgings again, this time at an inn not frequented by soldiers and farther from the public baths. Atretes entered the baths this time without comment. When Rizpah asked permission to leave his side, he gave it without hesitation. She took Caleb into a bath chamber with other young mothers while he followed Theophilus into the main chambers.

Fewer people bathed naked in this place. Atretes decided the further one got from Rome, the more provincial the morals. He found himself relaxing in the environment and even enjoying it. He took his time while Theophilus waited, bearing the money pouches and talking with some men who appeared, by their bearing and build, to be soldiers.

"The roads are safe through the mountain pass," Theophilus told him when he returned for his clothing.

"Good. We will make better time." He donned his tunic and belt and took the pouches.

Theophilus wondered if Atretes realized his German accent got thicker the further north they went. "We're not going to be able to keep the same pace," he said, stripping off his tunic.

"It's a hard climb to Novi. Then we can pick up the pace again through Alessandria and Vercelli. We'll be following the Dora Baltea from there to Aosta, and that's a harder climb. Crossing the mountains to Novi is going to be difficult on Rizpah, but nothing compared to what's ahead. We've got the Graian and Pennine Alps to go over."

"We could buy a couple of donkeys. One can carry the gear and the other, Rizpah and Caleb."

"I can get us a good price at the fort."

Atretes' expression darkened. "It's bad enough suffering your company without doing commerce with Roman soldiers as well!"

Theophilus refused to take offense. "An army donkey is as good as a civilian donkey. And cheaper." He tossed his tunic on the stone bench and dove into the pool. When he came up, Atretes was gone. Shaking his head, Theophilus gave the barbarian up to God. Nothing he could say or do was going to change Atretes' opinion of anything. All the German could see was his enemy, Rome, standing in front of him. He was blind and deaf to all else.

Lord, if I can't reach Atretes with your gospel now, how am I ever going to reach the Chatti? he wondered sadly.

Of one thing Theophilus was certain. Atretes' Germanic practicality would win over his insufferable pride. Their money wasn't inexhaustible, and they still had a long, long way to go. Army donkeys would have to do.

27

The two donkeys Theophilus purchased from the army made mountain traveling much easier. One carried the gear that had burdened the Roman and Atretes; on the other, Rizpah fashioned a seat for Caleb with packs, blankets, and leather straps. She walked alongside, holding a lead rope and carrying a stick. Caleb was delighted with the bouncing gait of the small beast, and with such a light load, the animal needed little prodding.

Winter was over and spring was coming on, swelling the rivers with melted snow. The steep roads were grueling and the air grew progressively cooler. Beech and birch gave way to spruce, pine, and fir as they followed the Roman road upward.

Rizpah filled her lungs with the wonderful scent, giving thanks to God. She loved the majesty of the mountains around her, though there were places of fearsome heights and sharp drops. The way was treacherous, for the rule of Roman road building was to connect cities and territories by the shortest route, and that was not necessarily the easiest. By noon each day, her legs ached, and by the time they made camp, her muscles trembled with exhaustion.

They found a sizable contingent of soldiers in residence at Aosta. Theophilus said the number was evidence of trouble ahead and went to the fort to find out whatever he could about the conditions they would be facing going over the Pennine Alps. Rizpah remained at the camp with Caleb and Atretes.

The mountains around them were sheer and white, the air crisp and chill. "I've never imagined a place so beautiful and merciless." She looked at Atretes sitting across the fire, and she felt, in some small way, she was beginning to understand him.

"We go down from these mountains into the forests of my homeland," he said without raising his head to look at her. "The air is not so thin, and there are no mountains like these."

"Do you remember all this from when you were brought to Rome?"

He looked up at the immense mountain to the northeast. Yes, he remembered. "We go down from here to the Rhone

River. We follow that to the Rhine. From there, I can find my own way."

Rizpah felt a chill at the way he said it. "Theophilus is our friend, Atretes."

"He is Roman."

She had never seen eyes so cold. "All this time, all this way, and still you can't trust him?"

"Why should I trust him? What reason does a Roman centurion go to Germania?"

"He wants to give the Good News to your people."

He gave a sardonic laugh. "A soldier wants to know an enemy's strength and weakness so he can report back to his commander."

"He's no longer part of the Roman army."

"So he says." He jerked his chin. "He was with Titus before we left Rome. And he never passes through a city without going to the fort, does he?"

"You're wrong to suspect him, Atretes. Theophilus goes to the forts to learn what lies ahead, to be prepared for our sake."

"You're a woman. What do you know of war?"

"You're right, Atretes. I know nothing of war. But I do know Theophilus. I trust him with my life. I trust him with Caleb's." She heard footsteps and saw him coming toward them.

"Brigands," Theophilus said grimly, crouching near the fire. "A Roman official was robbed and murdered a few days ago."

"Should we wait before going on?" Rizpah said, worried for Caleb's safety.

Atretes threw a stick into the fire and rose. "We go on." Nothing was going to stop him from getting home, not Romans, not brigands, not even the gods. Only when they were over the mountains and down into the black forests of his homeland would he breathe the air of freedom. And once there, he would decide what to do about Theophilus. He leaned down and took the wineskin and went out into the darkness.

Theophilus saw Rizpah's distress and offered what reassurance he could. "Extra patrols are traveling the road."

"It gets harder the further we go. Sometimes I think the closer we get to Germania, the further we go from God."

"God is with us, Rizpah."

"It's so cold." She drew the cloak Atretes had given her around herself. "He still doesn't trust you."

"I know."

"He knows his way from the Rhine."

Theophilus nodded. "You and I both know if it's God's will we reach Germania together, we will reach Germania together."

Rizpah prayed fervently that Atretes' eyes and heart would be opened to the truth.

They left at daybreak.

28

Rizpah's breath came out in soft cloud puffs as she trudged through the snow on the narrow mountain road. Caleb had finally stopped crying after she bundled him beneath the heavy tunic against the warmth of her body. Every muscle in her body ached. Her lungs burned. Her feet felt numb. They had reached the summit two days before and were winding their way down from the glacial heights, but it was slow going. Each day was more difficult, more physically trying.

The valley lay like heaven below, and she drank in the sight of a crystalline lake surrounded by evergreens and sloping meadows. "Tomorrow's the Sabbath," Theophilus had said. A day of rest.

Thank God, she thought. A week wouldn't be enough, for the long journey was wearing down her strength. She paused to shift Caleb's weight. He was growing steadily, adding to her burden. Atretes stopped as well, glancing back at her. She smiled and started off again, praying as she did so that she would have the strength to make it down the mountain.

"Is that Germania?"

"Not yet," Theophilus said, his breath coming out in a puff of white. "A few days more and we'll reach the Rhine. Two days farther and there's a fort."

Atretes glanced at Rizpah again and she felt the force of his look. *You see,* it said, *and I should trust this Roman?*

"Do we need to stop there, Theophilus?"

"The *foederati* may be able to tell us about the Chatti."

"Foederati!" Atretes sneered, unable to believe there were any Germans who would willingly join the Roman army. "German *slaves*, more likely."

"Not all Germans see Rome as the enemy."

"*Ja!* Those who are fools and traitors."

"It's been eleven years since you were home. Much has changed."

"Not *that* much."

"The rebellion has been subdued."

"Rome can build a hundred forts, and this land will still not belong to the Empire!"

"I agree," Theophilus said, unintimidated by Atretes' wrath.

Atretes glared at him distrustfully. "You agree," he drawled in disbelief. "You, a Roman centurion, sworn to serve Rome."

"Gaul was subdued and absorbed, but the Germans are still feri," he said, using a word that encompassed savagery. "They'll be quiet for a while, perhaps a long while, but they're not conquered. It's my hope to win them to the Lord. If they turn, all the strength of their attributes will be for the Lord."

Atretes gave a contemptuous laugh. "No Chatti will accept a god who let his own son be crucified. What good is a god who is weak and useless." He made a sweeping gesture toward the forests beyond. "This land belongs to Tiwaz."

"But was created by almighty God," Theophilus said.

"Then let him try to take it back." Atretes turned his back and headed down the road again.

They camped beside the crystalline lake. Theophilus and Atretes headed for the shore to try to catch fish while Rizpah collected pinecones. She removed the nuts from them while keeping an eye on Caleb as he toddled about the camp. The child was delighted with everything around him, tottering from rock to tree to patch of snow.

When she finished, Rizpah used the dry cones to fuel the small fire Theophilus had built. The centurion returned with three large fish and placed them beside her. Spitting one, she set it over the fire to roast.

The sun went down, and the colors splashed a spectacular reflection across the smooth surface of the waters. She had never seen anything so beautiful.

Atretes appeared, a black shape against the colorful sunset. He walked up the slope empty-handed. Rizpah removed the third fish from the spit as he entered camp, and Theophilus knelt to pray.

"Lord, we give thanks for this food which you have provided for us. May it renew the strength of our bodies and open our hearts to your constant presence and mercy upon us. Bless the hands that have prepared this food for our bodies' use. We pray in the name of your blessed Son, Jesus. Amen."

A muscle jerked in Atretes' jaw as he joined them in the meal. It hurt his pride that Theophilus caught fish without effort while he caught nothing. He ripped the skin from the fish and pulled a hunk of succulent meat from the bones. It tasted like sand in his mouth, and he knew it was pride he swallowed.

Theophilus spooned grain gruel into a small bowl and sprinkled pine nuts over the top. He set it before the silent barbarian. "I'd like to hear about the god you worship, Atretes." He took his own bowl and reclined against the packs, eating his meal in silence, waiting.

Atretes debated saying anything. Thinking about Tiwaz opened old rifts of doubt. Rizpah sat with Caleb in her lap, feeding him pieces of fish. She looked so tranquil. How tranquil would she be when she faced the *Thing*? Sensing his perusal, she lifted her head and smiled at him. The soft glow in her eyes eased his mind, but quickened his senses. Could he bear to lose her?

"Will you tell us about Tiwaz?" she said, searching his face in question. She lowered her head again and spooned more gruel into his son's mouth.

"Tiwaz is the supreme sky god," he said, tossing the stripped fish skeleton into the fire. "His consort is Tellus Mater." Mother Earth. "He's the god of battle and presides over the Thing."

Theophilus frowned. "The *Thing*?"

"The assembly of my people. The men gather to settle disputes and establish laws. No man can be flogged, imprisoned, or put to death except on word of the priests in obedience to Tiwaz, who presides over battle. Tiwaz is the god of the wolf and raven, the god of the dead, and supreme master over magic."

Atretes' description filled Rizpah with misgivings.

"He is a god of valor, as well. Tiwaz was the only god brave enough to face the wolf, Fenrir. He fed the beast his own hand in order to bind him. There's no god in Rome or elsewhere with more courage."

"If that's so, why did your god allow your people to fail in their rebellion against Rome?" Theophilus said.

Atretes hesitated and then was compelled to answer frankly. "Tiwaz is also known as the Arch-Deceiver." He had come to think of Tiwaz more in that way over the past years in Rome and Ephesus. Tiwaz had been his battle cry in Germania, and Rome had been victorious over him. In fact, every time he had cried out to Tiwaz in jubilation or anguish, some further disaster befell his life. "He metes out victory and defeat with the indifference and arrogance of an earthly tyrant or any other god."

"Then why worship him?" Rizpah said.

Atretes gave her a dark look. "I don't. Not anymore. But I will pay him honor when I return home. He is more a god than yours. Tiwaz may be capricious, but he's *powerful*. He'd never let his son die on a Roman cross or leave his believers to be food for beasts."

"He left you a slave of Rome for ten years," she said and saw she had roused his temper. "There is no Tiwaz, Atretes."

"You forget the adversary," Theophilus said, surprising them both. "The enemy of God goes by many names, but his purpose is the same: to blind men to the truth and keep them from fellowship with Christ."

Atretes tossed his empty bowl aside. "Why would anyone want fellowship with a dead man, or with a god who lets his own son die?"

"Christ is alive," Rizpah said fervently.

"Your Jesus Christ was crucified!"

"Yes, and he arose."

"So some say, woman, but I've never seen him. Nor have you, if you're honest."

"Not in the physical sense, no, but I know he lives," she said with conviction. "I feel his presence in the very air I breathe."

"Jesus died in order that all of us might live, Atretes," Theophilus said. "He obeyed the Father and was crucified in atonement for all our sins. When Jesus arose from the tomb, he removed every barrier, including the fear of death, between God and man. Our faith in Christ Jesus sets us free from anything man can do to us. Jesus is the Way and the Truth and the Life. There is no death in him. Through Christ, *in* Christ, we overcome the world."

"So," Atretes said, smiling sardonically, "if I were to kill you right here, right now, you believe you'd still be alive by the power of this god of yours."

"Yes."

Amused, Atretes drew his gladius casually and turned the blade. "Perhaps I should test your faith."

"It may come to that," Theophilus said, well aware Atretes still hated and distrusted him enough to plot his murder.

"Why do you press him?" Rizpah said in alarm to Theophilus, frightened that he should issue such a challenge. She looked at Atretes' cold face, her heart beating frantically. Turning Caleb toward her lest he witness his father committing murder, she clutched him close. "If you kill Theophilus, I'll take my son and return to Rome," she said in a trembling voice.

"He's *my* son, and you're never going to see the other side of the mountains again," Atretes said, his hand going white around the handle of his weapon.

"You want to kill me, too?" she said, angry at his obduracy but not surprised by it. "Go ahead, if it pleases you."

"Be still, Rizpah," Theophilus said quietly. "Atretes doesn't seek to harm you. He intends to keep you with him." He looked at him. "He thinks he has cause against me."

Atretes was startled that defense should come from that quarter. "I *know* I have cause against you."

"Because I'm Roman."

"That, and other reasons."

"He thinks you're making reports at every fort we pass," Rizpah said in great distress and earned a blistering glare from Atretes.

"If that were so, Atretes, you'd already be apprehended," Theophilus said to him, looking straight into Atretes' eyes for he had no motives to hide.

"Not if your intent was to learn Chatti weaknesses and strengths," Rizpah said.

"Woman, you talk too much!"

"Perhaps you should talk more," Theophilus said. "I could've gleaned what information we needed elsewhere and not roused unnecessary suspicions on your part. I apologize for my lack of sensitivity. I have one purpose, Atretes, and one purpose only in showing you the way back to your people. I want to give them the gospel. I'm called by God to do so, no matter what. If it will set your mind at rest, we won't stop at any more Roman forts."

Oddly, Atretes believed him and was even more perplexed.

"What about supplies?" Rizpah said. "We have little grain left."

"The forests are full of game," Theophilus said, relaxing back against the packs. "And we're coming into spring. We'll find plenty that's edible growing all around us."

Atretes studied him. The Rhine was only days away, and it was still a great distance beyond that before they entered Chatti territory.

Sliding the gladius back into its sheath, he reclined and stared into the flames. He would wait to kill Theophilus.

After all, what better sacrifice could he offer Tiwaz upon his homecoming than the blood of a Roman centurion?

29

When they reached a bluff overlooking the Rhine, Atretes raised his fists in the air and gave a bellowing roar that raised the hair on the back of Rizpah's neck. Theophilus laughed, sharing in Atretes' joy.

They traveled north along the high bluffs and then cut inland, to avoid entering the territory of the Vangiones, the Triboci, the Nemetes, and the Ubii tribes who lived near the river. They camped near warm springs, and Rizpah bathed with Caleb in comfort while the men went hunting. When they returned, Atretes was carrying over his shoulders a roebuck dressed and ready for roasting.

Night fell quickly in the forests of Germania. Wolves howled. Shadows moved. Sounds were unfamiliar. Rizpah couldn't rid herself of a gnawing apprehension, even with the sunrise. The land bristled with forests, and she felt enclosed by an oppressive darkness. It was as though someone watched them and kept pace silently among the trees.

A raven lighted on a branch above her, and Rizpah felt herself being pulled back into darker times and beliefs. The huge bird was a bad omen, wasn't it? She had to remind herself that the raven watching them was created by God, as were the mountains that separated her from the civilization she knew, and the forests through which she walked—even the very air she breathed was brought into being by God's hand.

O Lord God, the earth and all that's on it is your creation. You are sovereign of all I see and even that which I cannot see. What have I to fear?

"What's wrong?" Atretes said, noticing her tension.

"I don't know," she said. She looked at Theophilus. "I feel the shadow of death around us."

Frowning, Atretes looked around. He had been raised to believe women had prophetic powers and acute intuition. He wouldn't discount Rizpah's instincts simply because she was Ephesian.

Nothing moved. The stillness made Rizpah's stomach tighten and her heart pound.

No birds sang. No animals moved. All were in hiding. It had been eleven years since Atretes had fought Romans in these forests, but memory returned and with it full realization. The silence warned him what was coming. He drew his gladius and shouted in German to identify himself. It was already too late, for the *baritus* started before he'd opened his mouth. The spine-tingling war cry rose in the trees around and above them.

The hair stood on the back of Rizpah's neck. "What is it?"

The harsh, intermittent roar rose like an unholy chant, made louder and reverberating as the warriors held their shields to their faces, shouting into them and banging them fiercely. The resulting sound was horrendous. Terrifying. Darkly ominous.

As Atretes listened to the rising sound, he knew he had made a mistake, possibly a fatal one. They were standing in a small glen with no protection. "Over there!" he shouted at Rizpah, shoving her hard toward a fallen log. "Get down and stay down!" He stepped into the open road and raised his arms, the gladius in one hand, the other a fist, and shouted louder. "I am Chatti!"

"It'll do no good," Theophilus said and drew his sword. The war cries brought back memories of long-ago battles. He knew what to expect, and his heart fell. The contest wouldn't last long, and if they survived at all, it would be by the grace of God.

The roar abruptly stopped, and they could hear the pounding of heavy, running footsteps. "They're coming," Atretes said.

Theophilus listened, grim faced.

German warriors surged into the road ahead and behind. Arrows and spears flew. Dodging a framea, Atretes sliced through the first man to reach him. Bellowing his war cry, he charged over the fallen man. Caleb was screaming. Atretes plowed into two warriors, not even feeling the point of a sword graze his side as he cut them down.

Theophilus blocked blows and used the hilt of his gladius to down one of his attackers. Ducking sharply, he narrowly missed being decapitated as a sword swished over his head. He brought his fist up into the solar plexus of the younger warrior.

Atretes snatched up a framea from the ground and threw it. It went through a warrior who was coming at Theophilus from behind. The man let out a harsh cry and went down.

As quickly as the attack came, it ended. The Germans melted into the forest and silence fell again.

Atretes was breathing hard, his blood on fire. He gave a jeering shout.

One of the young warriors Theophilus had dropped moaned as he regained consciousness. Atretes strode toward him, face flushed and sweating from exertion, his intent clear. Theophilus stepped in his path. "There's been enough killing."

"Get out of my way!"

Theophilus blocked Atretes' gladius with his own. "I said *no*!" he shouted into Atretes' face.

"They're Mattiaci." Swearing, he rammed Theophilus with his shoulder and made another swing. Theophilus blocked him again and hit him in the side of the head with his iron fist.

"I cracked your skull once," he said as Atretes staggered. "God help me, I'll do it again." He clamped an iron hand on Atretes' throat. "I didn't come to Germania to kill." He shoved him back. "Or stand by and watch you do so!"

The hot blood pounding in Atretes' head slowed and cooled. Breathing heavily from the battle, his lungs still burning, he faced the Roman. "I should've killed you when I saw the Rhine," he said through his teeth. He stepped forward. "I should kill you *now*!"

Theophilus slammed him hard in the chest, knocking him back. He took a fighting stance. "Go ahead and try if you think you have to. *Go ahead*!"

Caleb's screaming penetrated Atretes' haze of rage. Frowning, he stepped back, lowering his gladius. "Where's Rizpah?"

"You told her to get down behind that log."

When Atretes couldn't see her, he strode toward it, wondering why she wasn't seeing to his son. Was she cowering behind that log in fear? Had she run off into the forest, forgetting the boy and leaving him behind?

"Rizpah!"

Putting his hand on the log, he swung himself over. He landed with perfect balance.

Caleb sat in Rizpah's lap. He was covered with blood and screaming. Atretes' heart gave a sharp flip. "How bad is it?" he said hoarsely as he saw Rizpah touch the child's face in an effort to calm him. "Where's he wounded?" He stepped over and lifted his son from her lap.

It was then he saw the arrow protruding from her chest and realized it was her blood covering Caleb. The child was unharmed.

Theophilus heard Atretes' guttural cry and left the two Mattiaci where they lay. He sprinted across the small clearing and came around the log where he saw Atretes on his knees, face ashen, touching Rizpah's cheek tenderly. He was speaking to her in German. Stepping closer, Theophilus saw the wound. It was a mortal one.

"Oh, Jesus," he said softly.

Atretes put his left hand against Rizpah's chest, bracing her as he extracted the arrow with his right. In shock, she made little sound. Blood poured from the wound as he tossed the arrow aside. He pressed the heel of his hand against it to stop the flow, but it did little good. Gripping Rizpah's white face with his bloodied hand, he pleaded with her. "Don't die. Do you hear me? *Don't die.*"

She rasped for breath, blood bubbling from her parted lips and trickling from the corner of her mouth.

"Jesus, O Jesus," Theophilus said, going down on his knees.

"Rizpah," Atretes said, stroking her cheek. "*Liebchen*, don't . . ." Her eyes changed subtly. Atretes saw and knew what it meant. *"No!"* Fear such as he had never known filled him.

He was going to lose her. What would he do when he did? "Call upon your god!" he said raggedly, tears pouring down his cheeks. His fingers bit into her pale face. *"Call upon your god now!"* He had seen death too many times not to recognize it had come to take her.

Her breathing changed. The harsh and rapid rasping for air slowed and eased.

"I need you," he said hoarsely.

Her hand fluttered as though she wanted to touch him and hadn't the strength. She gave a long, soft sigh and was silent. Her body relaxed, and she was completely still.

"No," Atretes groaned and put his hand to her throat. There was no pulse. *"No!"* he said in an agony of grief. German words poured like a flood from him, feelings he had kept hidden, feelings he had fought against. He cupped her face with both hands. Her eyes were open, dilated and fixed, unseeing, her lips softly parted. The blood that had been trickling from her mouth ceased. The wound in her chest stopped bleeding.

Rising, Atretes spread his hands palms up, covered in her blood, and bellowed out his anguish. Over and over, he cried out while his son screamed, untended and forgotten.

Theophilus moved to Rizpah's side and laid his hands upon her. While Atretes poured out his grief and hopelessness, Theophilus poured out his faith in prayer to Christ.

Nothing is impossible for God. Nothing.

No words came from his lips, no clear thoughts filled his head, but his soul cried out to God that Rizpah be returned to them. For the child. For the man still lost in the darkness.

Atretes stumbled away. He couldn't get his breath. He felt as though someone was choking him. He couldn't breathe. His mind filled with visions of every life he had ever taken, every loved one ever lost. He sat down hard, his forearms resting on his knees. Head down, he wept.

Theophilus continued to pray.

Caleb pushed himself up and toddled toward his dead mother. Flopping down, he put his head in her lap and began to suck his thumb.

When Caleb's crying stopped, Atretes raised his head and looked for him. When he saw where he lay, he shut his eyes. How was he going to raise him alone? Theophilus was on his knees, hands firmly covering Rizpah's wound. What did the centurion think he could do now? What good were his prayers?

"Leave her alone. She's dead." Theophilus remained as he was. "She's *dead*, I tell you," he said, shooting to his feet. "Do you think I don't know it when I see it come?"

His angry words hung on the cold air as a sudden stillness fell over the forest. For a heartbeat it was as though all of creation had stilled, then came a soft whisper of wind. Atretes looked around apprehensively, his skin prickling as the wind whispered around him . . . and he began to shake, afraid of whatever forces moved around them.

A gasp drew his attention sharply, and his eyes widened in disbelief as Rizpah drew in a deep breath, her eyes opening wide as she looked beyond Theophilus. "Jesus," she said softly in wonder, and Atretes was knocked from his feet. Clutching the earth, he lay flat, face down, trembling violently.

Theophilus lifted his hands from Rizpah and brushed her cheek lightly with trembling hands. "Praise be to God," he said in a choked voice, overcome. He touched her again, amazed.

"He was with me," Rizpah said, eyes shining. "I felt him touch me."

Whatever force held Atretes down lifted as quickly as it had come, and he clambered to his feet. Heart pounding, he came closer, awestruck. "She was dead!" he whispered.

With a victorious cry, Theophilus stood and moved aside, excitement pouring through him. Laughing and crying, he gripped Atretes' arms. "Tell me now Christ has no power! Tell me he doesn't live! He was in the beginning, is now, and ever shall be. Our God *reigns*!" He released the German and raised his hands in jubilant thanksgiving. "Lord Roi!" His voice rose, carrying through the dark forest, reclaiming it. "*El Elyon*, God Most High!"

Shaking, Atretes knelt down in front of Rizpah, unable to believe what his eyes saw. Swallowing hard, he reached out to touch her and then drew his hand back. The hair on the back of his neck rose, for her face was aglow as he had never seen it before and her eyes were shining. She was alive, more alive than he had ever seen her. A radiance shimmered around her.

Her eyes met his. "He was here with us."

"I believe you."

"Don't be afraid," she said and reached out to him. "There's nothing to fear." She placed her hand tenderly against his cheek. "God loves you."

His throat closed with emotion, and he couldn't speak. He grasped her hand and kissed the palm, tears coming. He touched her face in wonder. He noticed then how her tunic was drenched with blood. He wanted to see to the wound lest the bleeding continue. Taking his dagger from its sheath with shaking hands, he cut the wool carefully. When he peeled the cloth back, he found her skin smooth beneath. Frowning, he searched for the injury.

Awestruck, he touched her skin, feeling gooseflesh rise over his entire body as he did so. The only evidence there had ever been a wound was a small circular scar just above her right breast, close to her heart. No one could have survived such a wound.

Rizpah *had* been dead. He knew it as well as he knew she was now alive. And as well as he knew that Theophilus had not worked this miracle. Nor had Tiwaz. Only one god had done this. Hadassah's God. Rizpah's God. The God he had so confidently dismissed as being weak and ineffective had done the impossible.

Atretes took his hands from her and drew back. He did not understand the way this God worked, but he could not deny the power he had felt and seen. His voice was filled with certainty when he spoke. "Your God is a God of gods and a Lord of kings!"

Theophilus turned. "The only God, Atretes. The *only* God."

Atretes looked up at Theophilus. All his animosity toward the Roman was forgotten in his wonder at what he had just witnessed. "I give him my sword!"

Theophilus knew such a vow to a German meant his honor and life. "As I gave him mine when I came into his kingdom." He held out his hand.

Atretes grasped it. "Baptize me," he said. It wasn't a request, but a demand. "Baptize me so I can belong to him."

Theophilus clasped his shoulder. "And so we begin."

THE GROWTH

"The seed grew...."

30

"I baptize you in the name of the Father, and the Son, and the Holy Spirit," Theophilus said, baptizing Atretes in the first spring they found. Atretes knelt. Giving the German support, Theophilus leaned him back. "Buried in Christ," he said, submerging him, "and raised up in the newness of life." He drew him up again.

Dripping wet, Atretes stood. Turning, he saw Rizpah standing ankle-deep in the water, holding his son, and made another decision that would affect the rest of his life. "I claim Rizpah as my wife."

Rizpah's gaze lost its dreamy haze. *"What?"*

"You said you love me!"

The look in his eyes as he slogged through the water toward her sent her pulse racing and made her want to run. She retreated from the spring onto the bank. "I love Theophilus, too, as I loved Timon and Porcia, Bartimaeus, Camella, Tibullus, and Mnason and—"

"You said you'd never lie to me," Atretes said, his eyes pinning her where she stood.

"I'm not lying!"

He came out of the water and stopped in front of her, putting his hands out. "Give me the boy."

"Why?"

"Give me my son."

She did so with trepidation. Atretes took him, kissed his cheek, and set him on his feet. As he straightened, he smiled slightly. Her stomach dropped and she took a step back. Retreat gained nothing for he caught hold of her. When he drew her into his arms, she had only enough time to utter a soft gasp before he kissed her. It was a long time before he loosened his embrace, and by then she couldn't think clearly.

"You love those others," he conceded, equally affected, "but not the way you love me."

"I'm not sure marrying you is a good idea," she said shakily, alarmed by the power of the sensations he aroused in her. "For you or for me."

Theophilus stood in the spring, laughing. "It will be a blessed relief!" He strode toward them, grinning. "Or have you forgotten God himself put the two of you together in Ephesus?"

"Not as husband and wife!" Rizpah said, trying to put some distance between her and Atretes. She needed time to think, and she couldn't with him holding her the way he was. Was it proper to want a man so much? Was it *Christian*? She looked at Theophilus for help, but he seemed pleased.

Atretes had no intention of letting her go until she capitulated. "We're mother and father to the same child. It makes sense we be man and wife as well. Say yes." When she stammered, he cupped the back of her head. "Say yes. One word. *Yes.*" He kissed her again, as soundly as the last time.

"Theophilus!" she gasped when Atretes finally let her take a breath.

"Say yes, Rizpah," Theophilus said, amused. "There's one thing you should've learned a long time ago about this man. Once he makes up his mind, it takes an act of God to change it!"

Atretes held her at arm's length, his expression somber as he searched her face. "Why do you hesitate?"

"What brought you to this pass?"

"What brought me? Your *death* opened my eyes. I need you, not just because of Caleb, but for myself."

She couldn't look in his eyes without weakening. Closing them, she prayed wildly, her heart crying out to the Lord. *Is this what you want for us? Or is it our own flesh yearning?*

It is not good for a man to be alone.

The words came so softly to mind she thought someone had whispered them.

She felt Atretes' fingertips touching her throat tenderly and shivered. Opening her eyes, she looked into his and saw a softness and vulnerability she had never guessed existed. It wasn't just desire that drove him to this decision. He loved her. Truly loved her.

Lord God, don't let me be a stumbling block. Don't let him be one. Help me light his way. You know how my tongue gets away with me.

Again, the soft whisper came.

Trust in me with all your heart and lean not on your own understanding.

She took his hand. "Not for Caleb only, Atretes, but for

myself, I will marry you," she said. Tears filled her eyes when she saw joy leap into his. Did she really matter so much to him? She had never thought it possible for this hard, violent man to have such tender feelings and deep needs.

More the fool I, Lord. Will I ever see him through your eyes and with your heart?

Theophilus came out of the spring and walked toward them. When he reached them, he held out his hands to them both. Atretes took his right, Rizpah his left.

"Lord God, we stand before you this day to join Atretes and Rizpah in marriage. Be with us, Jesus, in the making of these bonds." He looked at Atretes. "In a Christian marriage, Atretes, the husband is the head of the wife, as Christ also is the head of the church, he himself being the Savior of the body. But as the church is subject to Christ, so you will be subject to Christ, and so also Rizpah will be subject to you in everything. Love her, just as Christ also loves you and gave himself up for you. Sacrificially, willing even to die for her. Love her as you love your own body. Sustain and protect her in all circumstances."

"I will."

Theophilus looked at Rizpah and smiled. "Be subject to Atretes, beloved. Be subject to him as to the Lord. And respect him as your husband."

"I will."

Caleb stood in the middle of their small circle, looking up at them as Theophilus brought his mother's and father's hands together over the child's head.

Atretes clasped Rizpah's hand possessively. Theophilus put one hand over theirs, and another beneath. "Be subject to one another in fear of Christ. There is neither male nor female; for you are one in Christ Jesus, called to live according to God's will and not your own. Remember our Lord Jesus Christ who died on the cross for us and arose on the third day. Our God is patient and kind. He is never jealous nor boasts nor is arrogant. Jesus never sought his own nor was provoked nor took into account a wrong suffered. The Lord never rejoices in unrighteousness. Christ Jesus bore all things and endured all things for our sake. His love never fails.

"Therefore, beloved, remember and follow in his way. Walk as children of light. Cleave to one another. Submit to one another in the love of Christ, and live in a way pleasing to Jesus Christ our Lord."

Releasing their hands, he asked them to kneel before God, then did so with them. Quiet and wide-eyed, Caleb hugged Rizpah's side as Theophilus laid one hand upon her head, the other on Atretes'.

"Lord God, creator of all things, creator of this man and woman, I ask your blessing upon them as they go forth as man and wife."

"Please, Lord," Rizpah said softly, head bowed.

"May they raise up their son Caleb to praise your name."

"We will do so," Atretes vowed.

"Put angels around them and protect them from the enemy who will come against them and try to drive them apart."

"Please protect us, Lord," Rizpah murmured.

"Give them children to raise up in your name."

"Sons and daughters," Atretes said boldly, and heat filled Rizpah's face and body.

Theophilus grinned and then went on. "Lord Jesus, may Atretes and Rizpah serve you with gladness and come into your presence daily with thanksgiving, knowing you alone are God. You have made them in your image and have a divine purpose for their lives. You are their shield and their strength. May they never lean on their own understanding, Lord, but trust in you, acknowledging you in all their ways, so that you will make their paths straight."

"May we please you, Lord," Rizpah said.

"Lord Jesus," Theophilus said, "in whatever circumstances may arise, may your infinite grace and mercy be extended to others through each of them. Amen."

"Amen!" Atretes said and stood, drawing Rizpah up beside him. His blue eyes were alight and he was shaking. Heat poured into her cheeks. She was afraid he was going to haul her into his arms and start kissing her right in front of Theophilus again.

Instead, he lowered his head to kiss both her hands, then released her. "You should wash the blood out of your tunic," he said and hunkered down before his son. "Come on, boy. You need a bath." Lifting him, he stood and tossed the child high in the air. Caleb squealed with thrilled laughter. Atretes caught him and ran into the spring, while Rizpah stared dumbfounded after him. Disappointment and relief warred within her. She would never understand the man. Never!

"Tell Atretes I'll make camp and keep watch," Theophilus said, as he hefted the men's gear onto his back.

She glanced at him, embarrassed that she had forgotten his presence. He grinned wryly. "It's been quite a day."

"Thank you," she said, quick tears of gratitude filling her eyes. She flung her arms around his neck and kissed his cheek. "Thank you for praying for me," she said hoarsely, unable to say more.

Dropping his burdens, he held her briefly. "I've been praying for both of you for a long, long time." As she settled before him, he patted her cheek as he would that of a daughter. "Your husband gave you a command to wash your tunic."

"And I will obey," she said, eyes shining. She took one of his hands in both of hers. "I love you, Theophilus, and thank God you're my brother. What would have happened . . ." Her voice trailed off.

"Go, beloved. Your husband is waiting."

Blinking back tears, she smiled and turned away.

*

Theophilus shouldered the provisions and watched her walk down to the spring where Atretes played with Caleb. She waded in, and Atretes came to meet her. Bending down, he kissed her.

As he watched, Theophilus felt an inexplicable loneliness. There were times when his solitary life chafed, like now, when he felt cut off from Rizpah and Atretes because of the holy bond that would change their relationship to one of intimacy. He had watched these two burn for one another from Ephesus to Germania and prayed they wouldn't be drawn into sin. God knew their natures and their needs. He had given them their desires and made provision for them. They were married.

For himself, soldiers weren't allowed to take wives. The restriction had rubbed on occasion. Before he had been saved by Jesus, he had burned and given in to sin. Women had been a primary pleasure in his life.

All that had changed when he had become a Christian.

Now that he was retired from the army, life would be different. He could take a wife, but he didn't think it was in God's plan for him. The desire to do so had actually diminished. Twenty-five of his forty years had been spent fighting battles and building roads, from Rome to Germania to Ionia. He had few years left upon this earth. Those years he did have, he wanted to dedicate to the Lord.

But there were times . . .

Atretes set his son upon his shoulders and bent to kiss Rizpah again. Theophilus watched and felt a swift and unexpected pang of envy. She was a remarkable young woman. It was clear from her response that they would have little difficulty adjusting to one another. Atretes' life had been hard and bleak till now, but God would give him joy through her.

"Lord, bless them with a quiver full of children," he said. Turning away, Theophilus walked up the hill to lay the camp and prepare a meal.

*

Hours later, Theophilus saw Atretes and Rizpah walking between the scented spruce and fir toward him. Caleb was sleeping against Rizpah's shoulder, Atretes' arm was about her waist. Theophilus had never seen them so relaxed with one another and knew God had blessed their afternoon together. When Rizpah looked up at Atretes and said something to him, he stopped and touched her hair lightly. She lifted her chin, and he kissed her, his hand gliding from her shoulder down her arm in a tender and natural gesture of possession.

Theophilus looked away, sorry to have intruded on such a private moment.

They approached the fire almost reluctantly. He glanced up and smiled in greeting. "Help yourself to the rabbits." He knew Rizpah would be self-conscious and tried to put them both at ease. "There's plenty of bean stew in the pot and berries in that small basin."

Atretes removed his arm from around her shoulders and took his son. Theophilus looked at her and saw her color rise. Atretes put Caleb down amidst the packs and covered him with a blanket. "Sit," he said when he saw Rizpah still standing at the edge of the firelight. As she came forward, Atretes glanced at Theophilus. He gestured for him to eat.

Squatting down, Atretes removed one of the three roasted

rabbits from the spit and put it on a wooden plate. He spooned bean, lentil, and corn mush beside it. "Sit over here," he said to Rizpah and, when she obeyed, he handed it to her. He brushed her cheek lightly and then served himself. When she bowed her head to pray, Atretes watched her and waited until she finished.

Atretes was as ravenous for food as he had been for Rizpah all afternoon. He ate quickly, tossing bones into the fire. He finished the rabbit before Rizpah was half finished with hers.

"You can have the other one on the spit, Atretes," Theophilus told him, amused. He had never seen Atretes so hungry. "I've already eaten."

Atretes raised his brow at Rizpah. She nodded. "There's plenty here for me and Caleb when he awakens."

"I'll hunt tomorrow," Atretes told Theophilus as he slid the last roasted rabbit from the branch spit. "There are plenty of deer."

Theophilus laughed despite his resolve not to do so. It would seem married life demanded added nourishment, but he curbed the temptation to remark on it. Atretes might appreciate manly humor, but Rizpah would be even more embarrassed. He leaned back, making himself comfortable against his pack. "I thought you were in a hurry to find your people."

"We wait," Atretes said decisively and flung a leg bone into the fire. "We stay here until you tell me everything you know about Jesus Christ."

Theophilus could not have been more pleased by Atretes' demand, but he was a soldier and bent to the practical. "What about the Mattiaci?"

"We're on high ground," Atretes said, not the least concerned.

"They attacked once. They could attack again."

"They attack an enemy in a low clearing like the one we were in today. You wounded two. I killed four. They won't come looking for us." He tossed the last of the bones into the fire. "The Mattiaci are cowards."

Atretes dismissed further discussion of tribal disputes with a return to his earlier demand. "Tell me about Jesus. Hadassah told me of his crucifixion and resurrection. I thought he was weak. Now, I know better. He is the true God, but I have questions. You say God sent Jesus. Yet you say Jesus is God. Explain."

"Jesus is God, Atretes. God the Father, God the Son, and God the Holy Spirit, who dwells within you now, all are *one*."

"How is that possible?"

"Some things are too wonderful for man to understand," Theophilus said, spreading his hands and wishing Atretes had asked an easier question. "I'm a simple soldier for Christ and as clear an understanding as I have is that there is God the Father, awesome and unreachable because sin came into the world. And there is Jesus Christ, God the Son, sent to atone for sin and remove the veil from the Holy of Holies so we can go before the Almighty and have an intimate relationship with him as Adam and Eve had in the Garden of Eden."

He saw a frown flicker across Atretes' face, but plunged ahead. "The Holy Spirit comes to dwell within us when we believe in Christ and are redeemed. It is through the Spirit that God reveals mysteries to us, for the Spirit searches all things, even the depths of God."

"And I have this spirit living inside me now?"

"The moment you accepted Christ, the Holy Spirit came to dwell within you."

"Then I'm possessed by this spirit."

"'Possessed' is not a word I'd use to describe it. The Holy Spirit abides in you at your invitation and acts as your helper."

"I didn't invite it in."

"Do you believe Jesus is the Christ, the Son of the Living God?"

"Yes. I believe he is the Living God."

"And you accept that he is your Savior and Lord?"

"He is my God. I have sworn it."

"Then know that Jesus has also given you the Holy Spirit. He told his disciples after his resurrection and before his ascension to the Father that they would be baptized with the Holy Spirit. He said they would receive power when the Holy Spirit came upon them. You're a partaker of the promise because you believe."

When Atretes asked who the disciples were, Theophilus told him.

"Perhaps they were more than men also," Atretes said.

"They were ordinary men. Several were fishermen, one a tax collector, another an insurrectionist like you. There was nothing special about any of them except that Jesus chose them to be his followers. God chooses the ordinary and makes them extraordinary." Theophilus saw Atretes' confusion and felt insufficient for the task of answering and discussing spiritual questions. The German's troubled frown was clear indication he was baffling rather than enlightening him.

God, help me. Give me your words.

"I'm a simple man, Atretes, with simple thoughts and simple faith."

Atretes leaned forward, determined to understand. "Who are Adam and Eve, and where's this Garden of Eden of which you spoke?"

Theophilus felt relief. *Ask in my name and it will be granted you.* The answer had come: Start at the beginning. He laughed softly, rejoicing. God answers. Let the Scriptures be known.

"Let me tell you the *whole* story, not just the finish." His face shone in the firelight, angelic and carved in strength, holding Atretes' full attention.

Rizpah listened as Theophilus told the story of the creation of the heavens and the earth and all that was on the earth, including man. Like music, the Roman's deep voice drove back the sounds of enveloping darkness, making her aware of the stars in the heavens and the hope of God.

"And then man was created in the image of God, and woman was fashioned from his rib to be his companion and helper."

Rizpah marveled anew. God *spoke* and all things came into being. The Word was the very breath of life in the beginning, as it would be to the end of time.

Theophilus told of Satan, God's most beautiful creation, an ancient of ancients who was cast out of heaven because of pride, who entered the Garden in the form of a serpent and tempted Eve to eat the fruit of the tree of knowledge with the promise that she would become like God. Deceived, she ate while her husband stood silent beside her, and sin was conceived and born. Eve gave of the fruit to her husband, who also ate, and because of their disobedience, God cast them out of the Garden. They would no longer live forever nor be in the presence of the Lord, but would live out a life span of years and struggle for existence. And thus, death, the consequence of sin, came into being.

"Adam and Eve bore sons who carried the seed of sin within them. Sin took root and grew in the jealousy of Cain, who murdered his brother, Abel. As men multiplied upon the earth, their wickedness increased until every intent of man was evil.

"The Lord was sorry he had made man and decided to blot him out as well as the animals and all creeping things he had created," Theophilus said. "Only one creature found favor in God's sight, a man named Noah."

Atretes sat enthralled, absorbing every word and feeling faint stirrings within him, as though some deep part of him that had slumbered was now awakening. He listened as raptly as a child to the story of Noah building the ark, of the animals entering into it two by two, male and female, and then of the rains coming to flood the earth and destroy all life upon it.

"Every living thing died except those in the ark. And then God allowed the waters to recede and set the ark upon a mountain where he made a covenant with Noah. God said he would never destroy man by flood again, and set a rainbow in the sky as a sign of his promise. And so Noah and his wife, and his sons and their wives, left the ark and began to populate the earth again."

Caleb awakened hungry, and Rizpah rose to sit with him and feed him the nourishing gruel with bits of rabbit meat mixed into it.

Theophilus went on. "Now, the whole earth used one language and the people gathered together to build for themselves a tower of brick and mortar to reach heaven. Seeing what they were doing, God confused their language and scattered them abroad from there across the face of the earth. Thousands of years passed before God spoke to man again. Then he came to one man, Abram, whom he told to leave his country of Ur and his relatives and his father's house and go to the land he would show him. God promised to make of Abram a great nation through which all the nations of the earth would be blessed."

Theophilus prodded the fire, spreading the glowing coals and adding more thick branches as he spoke.

"Abram did go forth as God told him for he believed God, but he took with him Sarai, his half sister who was his wife; Lot, an ambitious nephew; and Terah, his father. He also took with him all of his possessions, including the slaves he had acquired. When he reached the land God showed him, a dispute broke out between him and Lot, and he gave his nephew the choice of land. Abram settled in the land, and Lot settled in the cities of the valley and lived in Sodom.

The Growth

"God told Abram again that he would make of him a nation, great in numbers. Abram believed God, even knowing that his wife, Sarai, was barren. Sarai believed for a time, but lost patience and took it upon herself to convince Abram that he should beget a child with her Egyptian handmaiden, Hagar. Abram did as she suggested, and Hagar bore a son, Ishmael. Trouble came immediately. Hagar became proud; Sarai, jealous.

"When Abram was ninety-six, the Lord came to him and made a covenant with him. God changed Abram's name to Abraham, which means 'the father of nations.' The sign of this covenant was circumcision. Every male eight days old was to be circumcised. Abraham, Ishmael, and all the boys and men in his tribe were circumcised in obedience to this covenant. As for Sarai, God said she would bear Abraham a son in their old age, and they would call him Isaac, meaning 'laughter.' "

A cool breeze rustled the trees as Theophilus went on, telling of the animosity between the women and their sons. Atretes nodded in agreement as he heard how Hagar and Ishmael were cast out, for it was through Isaac that the promised nation would come forth.

"God tested Abraham, for he told him to make of Isaac a burnt offering. Abraham rose early, took his son and wood, and went to the place the Lord had told him to go. There he built an altar, arranged the wood, bound his son, and laid him upon it. But when he took the knife to slay him, an angel of the Lord told him to stay his hand. Abraham believed, and it was reckoned to him as righteousness. God provided a ram for sacrifice and renewed his covenant with Abraham, telling him yet again that through his seed all the nations of the earth would be blessed."

Theophilus leaned forward, face glowing. "For it was through Abraham that a people of faith came into being, and from them, God promised all mankind the Messiah, the anointed one, who would overcome the sin in the Garden of Eden and give those who believe in him eternal life." He smiled. "But I'm jumping ahead."

Retracing, he told Atretes how Isaac married Rebekah, who bore him twin sons, Esau and Jacob. Esau, the elder, sold his birthright to his younger brother for a bowl of food, and Jacob later stole his brother's blessing by trickery and deceit. Enmity arose between the two brothers, and Jacob fled to Laban, his mother's brother. He fell in love with Laban's younger daughter,

Rachel. Through Laban's trickery and deceit, Jacob married Leah and then Rachel and was bound to his uncle for more than fourteen years. From these two women and their two handmaidens, Jacob fathered twelve sons.

"The favorite son was Joseph, son of Jacob's beloved wife, Rachel. Joseph was a dreamer of dreams and prophesied a time when he would rule over his brothers and his own father. His brothers despised him and, in their jealousy, plotted against him. They threw him into a cistern and sold him to a traveling caravan that took him to Egypt, where he became a slave of Potiphar, an Egyptian officer of the pharaoh. Joseph was a handsome young man, and Potiphar's wife wanted him for her lover, but Joseph refused. When she tried to seduce him, he ran away. Scorned and angry, she told her husband that Joseph had tried to rape her, and so Potiphar cast Joseph into the dungeon."

Atretes gave a cynical laugh. "Women have been causing trouble for men from the beginning," he said, stretching out on his side.

Rizpah glanced up from where she was changing Caleb's linens. "That's true," she said, smiling. "When men are weak and given to passion rather than obedience to the Lord, they usually do run into trouble head-on."

Atretes ignored her observation and raised his brow at Theophilus.

Suppressing a smile, Theophilus continued, telling of Joseph's God-given ability to interpret dreams and how this gift brought him into the palace of Pharaoh and made him second in power in all Egypt. When the prophesied famine came, Joseph's brothers journeyed to Egypt for grain, thus fulfilling the prophesies of his youth that he would rule over them as well as his father.

"Joseph forgave them, telling them that what they had done for evil, God had turned to good."

Rizpah settled Caleb in a nest of packs and blankets and came back to sit near Atretes.

"Another pharaoh rose who didn't know of Joseph's deeds. He saw a threat in the increasing number of Joseph's descendants and made them slaves. When their number continued to grow, Pharaoh became alarmed and commanded that all male newborns were to be killed. Moses, a descendant of Abraham, was born and placed in a basket and hidden among the reeds of the Nile. Pharaoh's daughter found him and raised him as her own son. When he grew to manhood, he went to his brethren and looked upon their hard labors. He saw an Egyptian beating a Hebrew and struck him down. When word spread among the Hebrews of what he had done, he fled to Midian. There, after years in exile, God spoke to Moses from a burning bush."

Theophilus smiled slightly. "Now, Moses was an ordinary man and terrified that God was speaking to him. When God told him he wanted him to return to Egypt and lead the Hebrew slaves out of bondage, Moses was more afraid of the mission than of God himself. He pleaded, saying he was nobody. God said he would be his spokesman. Moses said he didn't know God's name and the Hebrews wouldn't believe him. God told him to say that I AM had sent him. Moses still resisted, insisting they wouldn't believe him. God told him to throw his staff on the ground, and when he obeyed, the Lord turned it into a serpent. Moses ran from it, terrified, but God called him back and told him to take hold of the tail. When he obeyed, the serpent became a staff once more.

"Still Moses was afraid, insisting he had never been eloquent, that he was slow of speech and slow of tongue. God said he would teach him what to say, but Moses asked him to send someone else."

Atretes snorted. "God should have struck him dead."

"God is patient with us," Rizpah said, smiling.

"Indeed," Theophilus agreed. "And we are grateful. God said that Moses' brother, Aaron, was well-spoken and that God would give the words to Moses, and Moses would give them to Aaron, who would speak them to Pharaoh. He also said he would harden Pharaoh's heart, and signs and wonders would be performed before the Hebrews as well as the Egyptians."

"Why would God choose such a coward to lead his people?" Atretes said, disgusted.

Theophilus laughed. "I wondered that myself when I first heard the story. But had Moses been a mighty warrior, vastly intelligent, and with the charisma of an orator, who do you suppose would have received glory for what was to come?"

"Moses."

"Exactly. God chooses the foolish and weak things of the world to shame the wise and the strong, to show his power and our weakness without him. God's power is perfect in our weakness, for it's only through his strength we accomplish anything of value."

Theophilus went on, telling of Moses and Aaron going before Pharaoh and demanding that he let God's people go. Pharaoh refused. When Moses dropped his staff upon the floor and it became a snake, Pharaoh's magicians used their secret arts to make their staffs become snakes also. But Moses' snake swallowed the magicians' snakes. When Pharaoh still refused to let the Hebrew slaves go, Moses touched the Nile River with his staff, and the water became blood. Still Pharaoh refused.

The Lord brought plague after plague upon Egypt: frogs, gnats, swarms of insects, pestilence on Egyptian livestock, boils, thunder and hail, locusts, and darkness. During each plague, Pharaoh relented, then, when the crisis passed, hardened his heart once again.

Atretes sat up. "The man was a fool!"

"The man was proud," Theophilus said. "Proud men are often foolish."

"Nine plagues! Frogs, gnats, boils? What does it take for him to bow down before God?"

"How many plagues have you suffered in your life, Atretes? Defeat. Slavery. Beatings. Humiliation. Degradation. Betrayal. What did it take for you to bow down before God and accept the truth that he is sovereign majesty of all creation?"

Atretes' eyes narrowed coldly, his face hardening.

Theophilus saw and wondered if he had spoken too freely, offending rather than teaching. He retracted nothing, nor softened it. Rather, he waited, leaving the choice to Atretes as he had so often done before.

Atretes thought of Julia. He thought of the hundreds of things that had happened to him from the time he was a young man fighting for his people. He remembered all he had experienced as a grown man fighting to stay alive in the arenas of Rome and Ephesus. Through it all, Tiwaz had remained silent and uncaring. And still it was this god's name he cried out, not that of Jesus. Even after he had been told the gospel by Hadassah.

"You speak the truth," he said. "I was as much a fool as the Egyptian pharaoh."

"God is already at work in you, Atretes," Theophilus said, warming to the barbarian.

Atretes gave a bleak laugh, feeling no vital change within him, only a burning curiosity to hear everything about God. "Go on." It was more a command than a request, as humble a capitulation as he would allow himself.

"God told Moses that he would send the angel of death upon Egypt and all the firstborn in the land would die, from the child of Pharaoh who sat on his throne to the children of slaves in the kingdom down to the young of the cattle in the field."

"Revenge."

"Retribution. And hope. He told Moses that Pharaoh would not listen to him so that his wonders would be multiplied in the land. God also told Moses what to tell the people to do to have death pass over them.

"Moses gathered the Hebrews and told them that each household was to take a male lamb, unblemished and one year old, and kill it at twilight. The blood of the lamb was to be put on the two doorposts and the lintel of the house in which they ate. When God saw the blood of the lamb, he would pass over and no plague would befall them when he struck the land of Egypt with death. The meal prepared from the lamb was, and still is, called Passover."

Theophilus spread his hands. "As God did fifteen hundred years ago for the Hebrew slaves held in cruel bondage, God did again for all of us through Jesus Christ our Lord. Jesus is our Passover lamb, Atretes. When Christ shed his blood for us upon the cross, he broke the chains of sin and death and gave us eternal life."

Atretes felt his flesh tingle at Theophilus' words. "Why didn't Jesus come then instead of waiting so long?"

"I don't know," Theophilus said frankly. "I'll never have all the answers I want. If I did, I could put God into a wineskin or an amphora. And then what sort of God would he be except one smaller than my own limited mind? God chooses the perfect time. Over and over in Scripture, we see how God teaches and tests man. From Creation to this moment, God offers salvation to any who wish it. A gift by grace, not something we earn."

"Or appreciate," Rizpah said quietly. "It struck me as you spoke, Theophilus. Jesus left his heavenly throne, his glory and honor, took the form of humble man. He suffered and died. For me." She put her hand over her heart. "And what do I do? More often than not, I take my salvation for granted. I fill my mind with unimportant things, such as how long it'll take to reach

Atretes' people and what they'll think of me when we get there." Her eyes grew moist. "Oh, that God would put it in my head and heart what he has done for me every morning as I awaken."

"So be it," Theophilus said, his voice gruff with emotion. How many times had he found himself caught up in plans for serving the Lord in the future, rather than praising him *now*. Too often, of late, they had arisen early, said a perfunctory prayer, and hastened on. It had taken Mattiaci warriors and Rizpah's death to slow them down!

Atretes brushed Rizpah's cheek, drawing her attention. "We will praise God first thing every morning." She put her hand over his, her eyes shining with so much love that he felt the warmth of it spread through his entire body. He wanted her close against him and moved so that he was sitting behind her, legs drawn up on either side. He put one arm across her. She snuggled closer to him, her head back against his shoulder.

Theophilus continued his story. "The plague came at midnight and not one household in Egypt was left untouched by death. Pharaoh called for Moses and Aaron and told them to get out, to go and worship God, and take their flocks with them. The Egyptians urged them to hurry, afraid all would die if the Hebrews didn't go. They even gave them gifts of silver and gold as well. Six hundred thousand men on foot, aside from women and children, followed Moses from Rameses to Succoth, and a mixed multitude went with them, along with flocks and herds and livestock."

"Egyptians?"

"Yes. Anyone who believes is God's child," Rizpah answered.

Theophilus smiled at her, then went on. "God told Moses that if any foreigner sojourned with them and was circumcised, they were to be treated as a native, for they had become part of the covenant. And God went before them, a pillar of cloud by day and a pillar of fire by night to give them light. For Pharaoh was hardened again and pursued them. When they came to the Red Sea, the people were terrified. Moses cried out to them, 'The Lord will fight for you while you keep silent.' But God told him to go forth and to stretch out his staff over the sea, and when he did so, the ocean divided. The Hebrews crossed over on dry land, and the pillar of cloud moved behind them. Pharaoh and his army tried to follow, but the moment the last Hebrew stepped on dry land, the water descended, destroying the Egyptians and their horses and chariots, thus giving glory to God in all of Egypt."

Theophilus told of how the people grumbled as they traveled and God gave them manna from heaven to eat, and quail by the thousands when they complained about the manna. God was angered by the people, but Moses pleaded for them. Moses went up onto Mount Sinai and received the Ten Commandments. Atretes listened intently as Theophilus listed each and then went on to tell of the establishing of law, the sabbaths, the feasts, and the firstfruit offerings. He told of the making of the ark of the covenant, in which was placed the testimony of God and a portion of manna as well as Aaron's staff that budded.

"Below the mountain, the people sinned mightily and made graven images of the gods they had worshiped in Egypt." He told of the grumbling, of God's patience and provision, and also of his justice in punishing the people. Still there was rebellion. Aaron and Miriam spoke against their brother, Moses, questioning his right to leadership. God made Miriam leprous, healing her when Moses cried out to God on her behalf.

"When they reached the Promised Land, still the people didn't change. Twelve spies were sent into the land, ten reporting the people who inhabited it were giants and too strong to conquer. Only Joshua and Caleb said they should obey the Lord and go up and take possession of the land."

"Caleb," Atretes said, smiling. "A good name."

"Even Moses, who spoke face-to-face with the Lord, took the counsel of the ten who were afraid. Rebellion arose, led by Korah, while others, unconsecrated, were burning incense. God swallowed up many in the earth and sent fire to consume others.

"Because the people refused to believe and trust God, he made them wander for forty years in the wilderness. When all of the unbelieving generation had died, Moses spoke to the people. He gave the people the Law again and went up on the mountain, where he died. Joshua and Caleb, who believed God wholeheartedly, led the sons and daughters of the old generation into the Promised Land." He prodded the fire, adding more fuel.

"God divided the Jordan River as he had the Red Sea, and the Hebrews crossed over with the ark of the covenant. Through God's counsel, Joshua and the Israelites brought the walls of Jericho down and overran the city. From there, they conquered many cities, dividing the land, south to north, and then settled in it. The land was divided up among the twelve tribes, and for four hundred years God spoke to the people through judges."

He grinned at Atretes. "One of them you would understand very well, for you share similar weaknesses. His name was Samson. But I'll save his story for another time." He tossed another branch on the fire.

"All during this time everyone did that which was right in his own eyes except Ruth, a Moabitess, and Samuel, who was promised to God before his birth. The kingdom was united for one hundred and twenty years and then the people told Samuel they wanted a king like the nations around them. The people rejected God and insisted they be like everyone else. God told Samuel to give them what they wanted, so Samuel anointed Saul, a tall, handsome, and well-formed young man who had no heart for God. Saul was proud and jealous as well as something of a coward. As the kingdom faltered under his rule, God told Samuel to anoint another, a humble, young shepherd named David. David was a man after God's own heart. As a boy, he killed Goliath, the champion of the Philistines, with a sling and stone. The people loved him. That was reason enough for Saul to want him dead. Every attempt he made to kill David met with failure. Even his own son, Jonathan, loved and protected David. When Saul was killed in battle and Jonathan with him, David became king.

"He was a valiant warrior and the leader of a group called the mighty men. Their feats in battle are nothing short of miraculous. David secured the nation, but he fell into sin with the wife of one of his friends. Because of it, his family and kingdom were plagued with trouble from then on. Even his children were beyond control. They committed rape, murder, and even rebelled against him to try to take the throne. David's one great dream was to build a temple for the Lord, but God denied him the privilege because he had blood on his hands. His son, Solomon, who reigned during a time of peace, had that privilege.

"When Solomon became king, he asked God to give him wisdom to rule the people. Because of his humility, God gave him not only wisdom but great wealth as well. Solomon is reputed to be the wisest and richest king who ever lived, in any kingdom, but even Solomon in all his earthly glory proved foolish and halfhearted toward God. He married women from the very nations God told the Israelites to destroy: Edomites, Hittites, Amorites, Egyptians. They set up their own altars and pulled him away from the Lord. He didn't repent until he was an old man, and by then it was too late.

"The kingdom fell to his son Rehoboam, who refused the wisdom of the elder counselors of his father in favor of spoiled friends who had been raised in the palace. The people turned away and the nation was divided by civil war, Israel to the north, Judah to the south. There were nineteen kings of Israel, and not one had a heart for the Lord. There were twenty kings in Judah, and only eight sought God."

Atretes was amazed. "After all God had done for them, they still turned away."

"And God still loved them."

"Why?"

"Because God's love never changes. He's faithful and trustworthy. God doesn't think like man, Atretes. The Israelites were still his children, disobedient and proud, but still his. As they are today. Just as we all are by the fact of his creation. He set the Jews apart so that the rest of the nations might see God working through them, but his chosen people wanted to be like the rest of the kingdoms. God sent prophets to speak for him, warning them to repent or be judged, but they scorned and murdered every one of them."

"He should have destroyed them."

"We all deserve destruction, don't we? And some of us are destroyed on occasion. God used Assyria to scatter Israel, and Babylon took Judah into exile. The exile lasted seventy years, long enough for an unbelieving generation to die, and then God worked upon the heart of the Persian king, who allowed Zerubbabel to return to Israel with a remnant of believers to begin rebuilding the temple. Esther became queen of Persia and saved the Jews from annihilation. Ezra and Nehemiah restored the temple, rebuilt the walls of Jerusalem, and celebrated Passover."

"So the Hebrews returned to God."

"For a time. It's well to remember one thing, one thread that moves through the entire narrative of the Scriptures: God's love never changes and his will prevails. There always have been and always will be those who love the Lord wholeheartedly, through slavery, hardship, famines, war, exile, persecution. His people. You and Rizpah and I. God salts the earth with the faithful because those who cling to the Lord in faith through all circumstances preserve the rest from complete destruction. However, to my knowledge, the last Scriptures were written four hundred or more years before our Lord came to walk among us, and the prophet Malachi was appealing to God's people to repent *again*. The Scripture says they had hearts of stone."

"And so, this time, God sent his own son to call them back again."

"Yes. Jesus shed his blood for us during Passover."

"Ah," Atretes said, feeling as though his mind had filled with light. "And death passes over those who believe and obey him."

"And for everyone who has the eyes to see and ears to hear, the barriers between man and God were removed for all time. The way is open to the Lord through Jesus Christ. Any man, woman, or child who seeks the Lord with heart, mind, and soul *will* find him."

Atretes was filled with excitement. "My people will understand this. It is not far removed from our own religion. One man sacrificed for the many. Such rites have been performed in the sacred grove for centuries."

Rizpah was chilled by his unexpected and appalling words. Theophilus said nothing. She looked up at him in horror and saw he wasn't the least surprised. Perhaps he had always known.

"Let's hope they not only understand, Atretes, but that they embrace salvation through Jesus Christ our Lord as well."

THE THORNS

"Other seed fell among thorns, which grew up and choked the plants...."

31

Atretes was eager to find his people, but for reasons far different from when he had set out from Ephesus. He was on fire with the good news of Jesus Christ, anxious to impart it. He wanted his people to know Jesus, born of woman, declared the Son of God by the resurrection from the dead. He wanted them to know God had poured out his life for them, that they could be one with his power and glory and might. If God was for them, who could come against them? Not even Rome could stand against them with God on their side!

"I will make them embrace Jesus!" he said as he walked alongside Rizpah.

"You can't *make* your people embrace anything," Theophilus said, seeing the way of sin.

"They have to know the truth."

"And the truth they shall know. Have patience, beloved. Did you come to the Lord by force or revelation?"

"I'll tell them how God raised Rizpah from the dead. They'll accept my word." It never occurred to Atretes that it might be otherwise.

Evenings, around the campfire, Theophilus nourished Atretes' hunger by continuing to tell him all he knew. He told Atretes of Mary, the chosen one of God, a virgin, who was to bear the child Jesus. "She was betrothed to Joseph, a righteous man who was a carpenter. When she told him she was with child by the Holy Spirit, he had to decide what to do. By law, it was his right to have her stoned to death for impurity."

"The Chatti have that in common with the Jews," Atretes said. "We don't tolerate impure women. Their heads are shaved and they're driven out of the tribe or drowned in the bog. Only virgins marry." He saw Rizpah look at him, eyes wide. "You are different," he said firmly.

Different how? she wondered. Was it because God had raised her from the dead that Atretes had felt he could marry her? She was afraid to ask, and doubt about his love tore at her.

I will trust in you, Lord. I will trust in you.

Theophilus told of an angel appearing to Joseph and telling him that Mary was with child by the Holy Spirit. Joseph was to call the child Jesus, because the babe would save his people.

Caesar Augustus called for a census. As was the custom of the Jews, Joseph took Mary, who was heavy with child, and returned to his birthplace, Bethlehem, to be counted. Jesus was born there, but in a stable because there was no place in the inn.

Wise men from the east who had followed a new star came and gave gifts of gold, frankincense, and myrrh to the child. King Herod, well aware of the prophesies of the Messiah, tried to find Jesus also, but for far darker reasons. When he couldn't, he ordered all children born in Bethlehem and under the age of two be murdered. An angel of the Lord came to Joseph in a dream and warned him, so that he took Mary and Jesus and fled into Egypt.

When Herod died, an angel came again to Joseph in a dream and told him it was safe to return. Joseph brought Mary and Jesus to Nazareth in the region of Galilee. There, Jesus grew in wisdom and stature and in favor with God and men. It wasn't until a prophet named John the Baptist came along, a man who preached the repentance of sin on the banks of the Jordan River, that Jesus began his public ministry and proclaimed the kingdom of God was at hand.

"Jesus was thirty years old when he came to John and was baptized. John resisted, recognizing Jesus was the Messiah. Jesus insisted John baptize him in order to fulfill all righteousness. That's why we follow his example and do likewise. Our lives are to be a reflection of him. We decide for the Lord and act in obedience. And therein comes the difficulty, Atretes—living in accordance with God's will and daily sacrificing our own. It was after Christ's baptism that Jesus was sent by God into the wilderness where he fasted for forty days. At the end of it, when he was weak and hungry and most vulnerable, Satan tempted him."

Atretes' brows rose in disdain. "But this was God, so Satan was no real threat."

"Satan is the enemy of God."

"An enemy without power. Can he raise the dead?"

"As a warrior, you know better than to underestimate an enemy," Theophilus said. "It's true we aren't to fear anything or anyone except the Lord. But now that you are a Christian, the real battle begins. Satan is a master deceiver, Atretes. Remember the subtle lie he told Eve and the consequences of it? Sin and death. Adam and Eve walked with the Lord in the Garden. They spoke with God face-to-face. If they could be deceived under such circumstances, do you think it impossible that you or I or Rizpah could be deceived as well? Satan is an eternal being, like God. He may not know all things as God does or have God's power, but he knows our weaknesses even better than we do. He knows us intimately. He knows the evil desires of our heart and mind. He knows where and when to attack to gain the best advantage. Satan schemes and plays upon those things in order to separate us from God and bring about our destruction. *Never* underestimate him. Without our armor, we're vulnerable."

Atretes felt the intensity of Theophilus' warning and heeded it. "What armor have we against this being?"

"The truth, the righteousness of Christ himself, the gospel of peace, salvation, our faith. Remember the arena, Atretes. You weren't sent in to face an opponent without training and practice, without protection and weapons. Likewise, God will not send us into battle without the tools we need to stand against the enemy."

He smiled grimly. "Gird up your loins with the truth God is revealing to you. Put on the breastplate of righteousness, shod your feet with the gospel of peace, and wear the helmet of salvation. Your faith in Christ *is* the shield against Satan's arrows, and the Word of God is your sword. Without faith, without the Word of God, we're defenseless against the powers of darkness. The battle is for your mind; the goal, the destruction of your soul."

"We must never forget the power of prayer," Rizpah said. She took her husband's hand in both of hers. "At all times, pray in the Spirit, for Theophilus, for our son, for me, for your people, for yourself."

"I will do as you say."

"Do as the Lord says," Theophilus told him, seeing a reverence for Rizpah that was misplaced. He knew the Germans thought women had spiritual abilities above and beyond men. But the miracle of Rizpah's return from death was God's doing, not her own. "Walk in all his ways and love him. Serve the Lord our God with all your heart and soul, and keep his commandments. We must all be on the alert, Atretes, for we are going to a place of darkness, territory now held by Satan."

"Then we'll do battle for it!"

"Not in the way you think. We will *stand firm* in faith and love, so that God himself will battle for us."

※

They passed several small villages and entered the country of the hercynian forest. The tree-covered hills ran on, sloping down toward the plains. Atretes led Theophilus and Rizpah around a swampland and through a forest of spindly pines with black trunks. It was an eerie place filled with the sound of frogs and insects, with shadows, and with the dank smells of decay.

"Do I smell smoke?" Rizpah said, wondering if it came straight from the fires of hell. The scent was brief, acrid, possibly imagined.

"*Rodung,*" Atretes said and kept walking.

Theophilus fell into step beside her. "The Germans slash and burn sections of forest to release land for raising crops. The wood ash enriches the soil for several years, and then they let it go wild again."

"We're close," Atretes said. "I know this place." The familiar smells of forest, swamp, and burning brought back memories. He felt at home for the first time in over ten years. He wanted to run through the forest, framea in hand, shouting. He wanted to strip off his clothes and dance over the swords before the fire, crying out to the heavens as he had as a youth.

When Rizpah came up next to him, he pulled her close.

"Home," he said, his fingers combing into her hair. "We're almost home!" Laughing, he kissed her, opening her mouth, giving release to his excitement.

Rizpah gasped when he released her, falling back a step, her cheeks bright red. She looked startled and uncertain. Grinning down at her, Atretes took Caleb and sat him on his shoulders as they went on. "I used to hunt in those hills. Over there is swampland and a bog. Beyond that, just over that hill, is my village." But when they came to the clearing, only charred and decaying remains of a long-ago burned village remained. Atretes walked out into the open, looking around. A portion of a huge longhouse remained, grass growing up between the broken-down beams and collapsed walls. Beyond, he saw the burned timber roofs of the *grubenhaus*. The sunken huts had caved in, leaving shallow hollows in the earth.

The old anger stirred in him. Rome!

Eleven years ago, he and his mother had laid his father in a funeral house not twenty feet from where he stood. Many other funeral houses had burned that night, but the village had been intact. A few months later, his people were scattered or dead, and he, a captive, had been chained in a wagon and on his way to the Roman ludus.

Several hundred people had once lived here. Where were they now?

Throwing his head back, Atretes gave a shout that reverberated. Frightened, Caleb started to cry. Atretes swung the boy down from his shoulders and half tossed him to Rizpah. Walking away from her and his son, he shouted again, louder, the sound of his deep voice carrying into the forest. If his people were anywhere near, they would hear and know he had returned.

The sound of his battle cry was so much like that of the attacking Mattiaci that Rizpah shuddered. Theophilus came and stood beside her. "I never made it this far north, but I can guess what happened." He kicked at a burned and rotting piece of timber.

"I'm afraid," she said. "And I'm not even exactly sure what frightens me." She looked up at him. "Do you think Atretes understands, really understands, what it means to be a Christian?"

"No. But then, neither did I in the beginning."

"Nor I. Did you see the look on his face when he walked into the clearing?"

"I saw."

"O God, help us. I love him so much, Theophilus. Maybe too much."

"He has given his life to God. The Father won't let him go."

"But what can I do?"

"Walk in the Lord's way and pray. Pray, beloved, and don't stop." Leaving her, he walked toward the German. "Do you want to camp here for the night or go further north?"

"Here. And we build a big fire."

Theophilus felt the German's anger like a black force. "I'll gather wood." He removed his packs, took a small ax from one of them, and headed for the woods.

Atretes gave another shout.

No answer came.

A few minutes later, the sound of Theophilus chopping wood echoed softly. Swearing, Atretes turned.

Rizpah's heart broke at the look on his face. All the years of dreaming, all the months of travel and hardship, and they came to this: a burned out, deserted village. She set Caleb down and went to her husband. "We'll find them," she said, wanting to instill hope in him. "We won't stop looking until we do."

"They're all dead."

"No. We smelled smoke. You said rodung, and Theophilus told me fire is used by your people to release forest lands."

Theophilus strode across the clearing and dumped an armload of wood near the collapsed longhouse. "They wouldn't leave their sacred grove," he said with excitement, as though it had just occurred to him.

Atretes looked half startled. "You're right." Grabbing up his pack, he headed across the clearing, framea in hand. Rizpah ran for Caleb while Theophilus shouldered his share of the gear.

They walked quickly, weaving their way through the trees. The wind changed, and Rizpah smelled smoke again, stronger this time.

Atretes stopped beside a gnarled pine. A ring of black bark had been cut away and runes carved into the smooth surface. "This marks the boundary of the sacred wood. The grove is a mile from here. That way."

Theophilus shrugged off his pack. "We'll wait for you here."

Atretes glanced at him in surprise. "You're afraid of Tiwaz?"

"No, but your people wouldn't listen to me about the Lord if I desecrated their sacred wood by entering it."

Atretes' respect for Theophilus grew. Even so, he knew the only thing that would keep the Chatti from killing the Roman would be God himself. Theophilus knew this as well. With a nod, Atretes left them. Rizpah set Caleb down to play. The child found an acorn and tried to eat it. "No, no," Rizpah said, stooping. She took it from his mouth and tossed it away.

"No, no!" Caleb said, mouth quivering.

Rizpah brushed his hair back from his face and kissed him. "The fire is to the northeast of us," Theophilus said, leaning against the trunk of the border pine.

Rizpah approached and looked at the symbols carved there. Wolves surrounded a three-headed man with breasts and distended male genitals. In one hand, he held a scythe, in the other, a sword. A horned male figure stood beside him holding a framea. Runes were carved between. Frowning, Rizpah leaned down and touched one. "Atretes wore a pendant with this symbol on it." She had seen it when he removed his clothing beside the spring.

"Does he still wear it?"

"No. When I asked about it, he took it off and threw it away." She straightened up, then took Caleb's hand and moved away from the tree. She didn't want her son near it.

"He's coming back," Theophilus said.

Atretes ran toward them, weaving between trees with the grace of a born athlete. "I saw the white horses," he said, hardly out of breath. "A new path heads northeast. The village must be that way. Two miles, maybe three from here if we go straight across."

"We go around," Theophilus said. "I'll put no stumbling blocks in the way of the gospel. When the Chatti accept the truth, Atretes, Tiwaz will lose his hold upon them and this wood will have no more importance than the land around it."

"Then we'll have to push hard to make it before nightfall."

32

They found the outer reaches of the village at dusk. Several men in coarse woven tunics and trousers were herding cattle into a longhouse for safekeeping. Atretes' shout scattered the cattle and brought the men at a run. When they came closer, their war cries changed to boisterous greetings.

"*Atretes!*" Without releasing their weapons, they buffeted him joyfully while he laughed and gave as good as he received.

Rizpah stood by, staring, alarmed by their violent greeting. She had never seen men so rough looking and boisterous. When she glanced at Theophilus, she was relieved by his calm amusement. When the men's excitement eased, they took full, bold notice of her and then looked at Theophilus. A tense silence fell.

"You bring a Roman with you?"

When the man stepped forward, Atretes made a swift movement, bringing the tip of his framea just below the man's chin. "Theophilus doesn't come as a Roman."

"And that makes a difference?"

"I say it does."

The man's eyes narrowed, but he lowered his weapon. Atretes withdrew the framea, his own manner changed. "See to your cattle."

The three men walked away, cold but subdued. Atretes watched them for a long moment and then glanced at Theophilus. Jerking his head, he took Rizpah's hand and started down the road again.

Theophilus saw that the settlement wasn't *rundling* style as he had expected, with homesteads grouped in a ring about a center space. It was a *sackgassendorf*, with buildings arranged on both sides of a central street. He counted eight large longhouses and more than twenty smaller dwellings, not including the grubenhaus, the meeting house. The far end of the street was blocked off for defense purposes.

Their arrival was noticed immediately, and news spread rapidly as adults sent children on the run from longhouse to longhouse. People came out of their homes and poured into the street, surrounding Atretes, talking and shouting all at once while he laughed and embraced one after another.

A blonde woman pushed her way through the crowd. "Marta!" Atretes cried out, and she flung herself into his arms, weeping. Atretes held her close while a man pounded his back. Laughing and crying, Atretes held her at arms' length. Seeing someone else, he let out a shout and pushed his way through the crowd to a tall, powerfully built man who limped toward him. "Varus!" The men embraced.

Men, women, and children were talking excitedly, words rolling over one another, nothing understandable, and then a hush fell. Atretes and Varus still talked rapidly, not noticing as people moved aside for a woman in white. She walked sedately, nodding as people touched her lightly and moved back in respect. Her gray hair was braided and wound into a thick crown held by gold pins, and she wore a large amber stone encircled with gold and suspended on a thick gold chain.

Varus saw her first and clasped Atretes' arm. Atretes turned and released his breath in surprise. "Mother," he said and reached her in two long steps. Going down on one knee, he embraced her, his head resting against her breasts.

Weeping, Freyja stroked her fingers into his hair and tilted his head back. "My son," she said, tears pouring down her pale cheeks. "My son has come home!"

Atretes was too filled with emotion to speak more and held tight to her. All this time, he had thought she was dead or a slave.

She kissed both his cheeks and then his mouth. "I knew you would return." She stroked his hair back from his face tenderly. "Even when all those around me gave up hope, I *knew* Tiwaz would protect you and bring you back to us."

As Atretes rose, she put her hand on his arm. Her gaze swept the crowd as though searching for someone and came to rest upon Rizpah.

Rizpah saw recognition flicker in the beautiful blue eyes so much like Atretes'. The woman smiled at her and said, "She is with you."

"My wife, Rizpah," Atretes said.

"And the child?"

"My son."

A murmur went through the crowd, whispers of surprise and

curiosity. "So dark," someone said. Atretes took the boy from Rizpah and held him high so all could see. "His name is Caleb."

"Caleb!" all shouted, and Rizpah expected Caleb to start crying from the boisterous, frightening sound that rose. Instead, he gave an excited laugh, reveling in the attention. Grinning, Atretes handed the child back to her. She held him close. She could feel everyone staring at her and heard those words again, "So dark..."

Freyja looked at the man standing beside her son's wife and knew only that he was Roman. He looked back at her, eyes warm and without subterfuge. Fear gripped her, unreasoning and inexplicable. "Who is this man?"

Theophilus stepped forward and bowed his head in respect. When he spoke, it was in flawless German, even his accent matching that of the Chatti. "My name is Theophilus, my lady, and I come in peace as an ambassador for Jesus Christ, son of the living God."

Freyja felt a tremor. She glanced up at her son. "Who is this Jesus Christ?"

Astounded, Atretes stared at Theophilus.

Theophilus answered, "Jesus is the image of the invisible God, the firstborn of all creation." He held his hands toward the stars beginning to appear in the sky. "'For by him all things were created, both in the heavens and on earth, visible and invisible, and in him all things hold together.'"

Rizpah's heart raced as she realized she, too, understood every word spoken in German. What was more, she knew she could speak as well. "My lady," she said, joy filling her as she came forward to stand beside Theophilus, "mother of my husband, I beg of you on behalf of Christ, be reconciled to the God who created you, the God who loves you and calls you to repentance."

The people drew back in fear, their whispers louder.

Atretes stared at her, awestruck. "You're both speaking German."

"Yes," she said, eyes alight. "Yes! The Lord has given us the gift of tongues that we might bring the good news. Oh, Atretes, God is with us!"

Freyja recoiled inwardly at the words. Fear filled her as she looked from Rizpah's shining face to Theophilus, who stood so calm beside her. She sensed power, terrifying, awesome power, and her hand tightened upon Atretes' arm.

"You speak of repentance?" came a woman's mocking voice,

and silence fell again, heads turning. A current of deep emotion spread through the gathered crowd, and the people parted like a sea, opening a way before a beautiful young woman who stood just outside the door of one of the longhouses.

"*Ania,*" Atretes breathed in shock, his heart jumping.

Rizpah glanced at him, recognizing the name of his first wife, and her joy evaporated. Overcome by shock, she looked at the young woman, who was more beautiful and sensual than any she had ever seen. And young, so young, not more than twenty. How could this girl be his first wife? Long, flowing blonde hair curled about her face and shoulders and spilled down over her back to her waist. She was dressed in white like Atretes' mother and wore a similar pendant. Her mouth curved as she walked toward Atretes with a singular grace that drew his attention to the lush, perfect curves of her body. Many bowed their heads as she passed by, but no one touched her as they had Freyja. The silence pulsed, and she didn't stop walking until she stood before him. Her gaze drifted over him provocatively.

"Ania is dead," she told him, her voice cool and melodious. "I'm Anomia. Do you remember me?"

"Her little sister," Atretes said. He gave a surprised laugh. "You were just a child."

Anomia arched one brow. "You've been gone eleven years, Atretes. You've changed, too." She lifted a slender hand with long, elegant nails and placed it lightly over his heart.

Rizpah saw his eyes flicker in reaction.

Theophilus watched Anomia, feeling the darkness within her like a palpable force repelling him. As though sensing his perusal, she turned her head slowly and looked straight at him with cold, opaque blue eyes. Without blinking, her gaze drifted smoothly from him to Rizpah. She smiled contemptuously, dismissing her, and gave Atretes her full attention again.

Theophilus looked at his friend's face. It was clear to anyone looking that Atretes felt the potency of Anomia's seductive charms.

Heart sinking, Rizpah prayed fervently that God would give her husband discernment and wisdom—as well as the strength to avoid temptation.

Anomia laughed softly, basking in her power. "Welcome home, Atretes." At last, at long last . . . the way to what she had always wanted was standing before her.

33

"We will talk," Varus said and dismissed the villagers with promises that Atretes would speak with them on the morrow. He gestured toward the great longhouse built of rough-hewn timber and smeared over with clay so that it looked as though it had been painted with colorful designs.

Almost as an afterthought, Atretes turned to Rizpah and put a protective arm around her. He nodded to Theophilus to go ahead of him. Freyja and Anomia entered the dwelling first, followed by Varus. Marta and her husband, Usipi, entered last with their four children.

Rizpah was surprised at the immensity of the house and even more surprised to hear cattle lowing within. The long rectangular building stretched out before her. The front portion, where the family lived, was simply furnished with benches, beds, and chairs covered with otterskin. The greater part toward the back was divided into stalls for the cattle, horses, and pigs. The ceiling was high and beamed with rough-hewn timbers. It was warm and permeated with the strong odor of manure.

Varus poured a sparkling gold fluid into a horn. "Beer!" Atretes said, laughing and removing his arm from Rizpah as his brother offered him the horn. He drained it. Wiping the back of his hand across his mouth, he let out a gusty sigh of contentment.

Anomia sat in an otterskin chair, her elegant hands resting gracefully on the carved arms. She looked like a queen reigning over her subjects as she watched Atretes with a catlike smile.

Atretes glanced at Theophilus and saw he was empty-handed. He looked at Varus coolly. "Is it no longer a Chatti custom to show a guest hospitality?"

"He looks like a Roman pig to me."

Rizpah's heart stopped at the insulting words. Atretes went rigid beside her, his face flushing with anger.

"Theophilus is my friend."

Varus frowned.

"You don't deny he's Roman?" Anomia said smoothly, stirring the currents of animosity. "Have you forgotten so easily what Rome has done to your people? To you?"

Atretes glanced at her and then returned his hard gaze to his brother. "Three times this man saved my life. Without him, I wouldn't be here."

Rizpah put her hand on Atretes' thigh, thanking God that he hadn't forgotten everything in his joy of being among his people again. Atretes put his hand over hers as though to reassure her and make a proclamation. Anomia's eyes narrowed at the gesture.

"Then we are all thankful to him," Freyja said, instilling more warmth into her voice than she felt. She came close and crouched down before Rizpah. Holding her hands out to Caleb, she smiled. "May I hold my grandson?"

"Of course," Rizpah said, drawn to her. She released her son, but Caleb turned in her arms and clung to her, hiding his face between her breasts. Embarrassed, she spoke softly to him in Greek, trying to ease his fears.

"He doesn't speak German?" Anomia said in disdain.

"No," Atretes said. "I was the only one who spoke German until this night."

"How very odd," she said with the faintest inflection of skepticism.

Rizpah stroked Caleb's hair and felt him relax. She turned him around in her lap so that he faced his grandmother. When Freyja spoke to him again, Caleb pressed back.

"Give him to her," Atretes said impatiently, and when Rizpah started to comply, Caleb began to cry. Freyja shook her head and rose.

"No, Atretes. I'm no more than a stranger to him now," she said, her eyes moist with tears. "Let him come to me of his own accord and in his own time."

Rizpah ached for her.

Eyes cold, Varus waved his hand and watched as a horn was filled and handed to Theophilus. A slave girl served Rizpah a small goblet of wine sweetened with honey and herbs. Varus limped to a large otterskin chair and sat down. Glaring at Theophilus, he rubbed his crippled leg. "How is it you owe a Roman your life, Atretes?"

"Once, aboard ship, he blocked a sword blow that would have killed me. The second time, he pulled me from the sea when

I was unconscious. The final time, he got me out of Rome before Domitian could send me back into the arena."

"We saw you taken and thought they would sacrifice you in a Roman triumph," Usipi said.

"The Roman commander sold me to a slaver who dealt in gladiators," Atretes said grimly. "They chained me into a wagon and took me to Capua." He could almost feel the brand they had burned into his heel in that foul place. The beer turned sour in his mouth. Grimacing, he rolled the empty horn between his hands. "I fought in Rome and then in Ephesus. I earned my freedom there."

"It's a testimony to the power of Tiwaz that you're still alive," Anomia said.

Atretes gave a cold, derisive laugh. "Tiwaz deserted me long before I reached Capua. All your god offers is death."

"Atretes!" Freyja said, astonished that he would speak so and dare the powers that had sustained their tribe's very existence.

"I speak the truth, Mother. Tiwaz is powerless compared to Jesus Christ, Son of the Living God. Tiwaz can kill. Christ raises the dead." He looked at Theophilus, his eyes fiery with excitement. "Tell them!"

"Tell us nothing, Roman," Anomia said, in a voice cold with authority.

Incredulous, Atretes looked at her again. His face reddened with anger. Who was this girl to speak thus in his own home? "Theophilus will speak and you will listen or leave."

"You are no longer chief of the Chatti, Atretes," she said smoothly, in complete control. "You no longer command."

Atretes rose slowly. Anomia merely smiled, seeming almost pleased to see his anger flaming higher.

"You're in my home, Anomia," Freyja said.

Anomia turned her head. "Do you wish me to leave?"

It was a quiet question, spoken in feigned surprise, but Rizpah felt the atmosphere grow cold. She sensed the subtle challenge.

Freyja raised her chin in grave dignity. "He is my son." She put her hand over the pendant she wore, meeting Anomia's cool look with studied intensity.

Anomia gave a nod. "So he is." She rose gracefully from the thronelike chair. "As you wish, Freyja." She looked at Atretes again, noticing with satisfaction the way his gaze moved down over her body and back up again. He was a man of earthly passions, and those passions could be used to cloud his thinking and serve her purposes. She smiled at him.

Atretes watched her leave. The sway of her hips conjured lustful thoughts and roused strong memories of times with women in the cold stone ludus cell. He frowned, disturbed, then turned and sat down again. Varus was staring after Anomia with hungry eyes, his gaze lingering on the door she closed after herself.

"Isn't she a little young to be a priestess?" Atretes said dryly.

His mother looked at him in faint warning. "Tiwaz chose her as a child."

"She's a seer?"

"She hasn't experienced visions as I have. Her gifts lie in sorcery and the black arts. Pay her respect, Atretes. She has great power."

"You mustn't challenge her," Marta said, clearly frightened of the younger woman.

"She hasn't the power of God," Atretes said disdainfully.

"She has the power of Tiwaz!" Varus said, his emotions still running high.

"Our people revere her as a goddess," Freyja said, her slender hands loosely folded on her lap.

"A goddess," Atretes snorted. "You want to hear of power? Rizpah was killed by Mattiaci warriors. I watched her die, Mother. With my own eyes." He saw their doubts, felt them. "If there's one thing I've seen in plenty the last eleven years, it's death." He pointed to Theophilus. "This man laid his hands upon her and prayed in the name of Jesus Christ. I watched her awakened from death. The wound sealed. I swear on my sword, it's the truth! Nothing I have ever seen in the sacred grove matches Jesus Christ. Nothing even comes close!"

Filled with anxiety, Freyja stared at her son. What was it about this name, Jesus, that made her insides shake? "There are many gods, Atretes, but Tiwaz is and has always been the only true god of our people."

"What has Tiwaz brought the Chatti other than death and destruction?"

Marta gasped, eyes wide with fear. Even Usipi drew back. Varus' eyes flamed.

"You must not speak so," Freyja said. "You offend our god."

"Let him be offended!"

"Atretes," Theophilus said softly.

He ignored the appeal for silence, giving vent to his rising anger. "Where was Tiwaz when our people cried out to him in battle against the Hermunduri? In your father's time, Mother, did the Chatti win the battle for the river and salt flat? No. The Hermunduri butchered us. They almost wiped us out, by your own telling. Where was Tiwaz then? What power did he show? Where was this great god when Father and I fought against Rome? Did he or Dulga or Rolf or a hundred others achieve victory over the enemy? No! They fought valiantly and died while crying out the name Tiwaz. And I was put in chains!"

"Enough!" Varus said.

Atretes ignored his brother, his gaze riveted to his mother. Her face was stark white. Atretes calmed, regretting his harshness, but he would not be silenced. "I believed, Mother. I was his disciple. You know of my devotion. I bled for him and drank the blood from the sacred horn. I sacrificed. I killed for him and proclaimed his name aloud in every battle I fought from Germania to Rome to Ephesus. And all I've ever known is death and destruction. Until seven days ago."

Varus stood. "You are here and alive by the power of Tiwaz!"

Atretes looked at him. "Not because of Tiwaz, brother. Jesus Christ kept me alive so that I could come home with this man and this woman and tell you the truth!"

Varus' face reddened. "What truth? The truth this Roman has fed you?"

"You doubt my word?" he said in a dangerous tone.

Varus, incensed, still reeled with jealousy over the way Anomia had looked at his brother. "You're a fool if you believe what any Roman says!"

"Enough," Freyja said.

Atretes rose.

Rizpah grasped his arm. "Atretes, please. This isn't the way." He shook her hand off and stepped forward.

Freyja stood between her sons. "Enough, I say! Enough of this!" She held her hands out. *"Sit down!"*

The two men sat slowly, glaring at one another.

"Atretes has been gone for eleven years, Varus. We will not quarrel on his first night home."

"He will bring a curse upon us with his talk of forsaking Tiwaz!"

"Then we will speak no more of gods this evening," she said, giving Atretes a look of anguish and appeal.

Atretes wanted to convince them and glanced at Theophilus for help. Theophilus shook his head slowly. Annoyed and feeling deserted, Atretes glanced at Rizpah, expecting encouragement from her. Her head was bowed, her eyes closed. Their silence angered him. Shouldn't they be proclaiming the name of Jesus Christ? Hadn't they done so the moment they arrived? Why were they silent now? Why weren't they shouting the truth for Varus to hear?

"Please," his mother said, beseeching him, "no more quarreling tonight." She had waited so many years to see her son again, expecting peace to follow, and within an hour of his arrival home, her family was at war within itself. She looked at Rizpah, beautiful and dark. What of the vision all those years ago? Had she been wrong?

"As you wish," Atretes said, mouth set. He gestured impatiently for one of the slaves to fill the horn again. When it was, he held it between both hands. He let out his breath and glanced at his brother. "Are you chief?"

Varus' mouth curved bitterly. "With my crippled leg?" he gave a harsh laugh and looked at Theophilus. "I've Rome to thank for it." Atretes saw hatred as dark and violent as his own had ever been.

"Rud leads," Usipi said when Varus volunteered no further information. "And Holt stands as his under-chief."

"They are good men," Atretes said. Though older than he, both men had been loyal to him in the past. "I didn't see them outside."

"They left a few days ago to meet with the Bructeri and Batavi chiefs," Usipi said, mentioning two tribes that had been allied with the Chatti against Rome.

"Another rebellion?" Atretes said.

"The Romans burned our village last year," Usipi said. He started to say more but Varus gave him a quelling look. Usipi ruffled his son's hair and fell silent. Varus made a point of glancing at Atretes and then looking straight at Theophilus before he drank from his horn. They would not discuss Chatti matters before a Roman.

Theophilus knew enough from past experience with Germans to see the way of things. These men had more courage and pride than common sense. Domitian lacked the military glory of his father, Vespasian, now dead, and his brother, Titus. He lusted for any opportunity to prove himself. If the Chatti were foolish enough to join with other tribes and start another rebellion against Rome, they would play right into Domitian's hands. He wanted to warn them, but held his tongue. Anything he said now would merely rouse further suspicions.

He had come for one purpose: to present the gospel of Jesus. Before he could warn Atretes, the man had taken the sacred bull by the horns, proclaiming Christ with all the grace and love of a warrior slashing his blade. It would take a long time to overcome the damage done this night.

Caleb slid from Rizpah's lap and toddled over to a cousin not much older than himself. Plopping down before the little girl with blonde braids, he flapped his arms and let out a gusty cry. Marta laughed.

Freyja turned the conversation to the children and then on to the simpler things of life. They reminisced about better times, retelling stories about Atretes' childhood. The laughter lessened the tension. The slaves kept Varus' and Atretes' and Usipi's horns full. Theophilus set his own aside. He was well aware that Germans like their beer and mead. He had been told once by a fellow centurion that some tribes debated only after they were so drunk they were incapable of pretense, but reserved their decision making for a time when they were sober.

Rizpah felt Freyja studying her and smiled at her mother-in-law. Though the woman was high priestess for a pagan god, Rizpah did not feel the misgivings she did when she had looked upon Anomia. She saw no enemy when she looked at Atretes' mother. She saw instead a woman who was deceived by a cunning adversary.

Lord God of mercy, help us to open her eyes.

"Sunup comes early," Usipi said. "The burning is over and we've fields to plow." He embraced Atretes. "We have need of you," he said quietly, his words full of hidden meaning. "We'll fight as we did in Hermun's time." Marta gathered the children, who didn't want to leave Caleb. She kissed Atretes and let him hold her for a moment, then followed her husband from the longhouse.

Varus rose. Supporting himself with a walking stick, he made his way to a sleeping bench. "Let the Roman sleep in a stall."

Atretes took offense, but it was too late. Varus sat heavily on his sleeping bench and fell back. Freyja covered him with a blanket. "You can sleep over there," she told Theophilus, nodding toward a far corner.

"A stall will do, my lady." He took up his pack and slung it over his shoulder. Pushing open the gate dividing the animal shelter from the family's quarters, he entered the corridor.

Freyja watched him close and latch the gate. She was surprised by his mild manner. He looked at her before turning away. There was no threat in his look, but she felt a sudden certainty that this man would turn her life inside out.

She didn't look away until Theophilus went into a back stall. "Your Roman friend walks like a soldier."

Atretes looked at her but said nothing. Telling his mother that Theophilus had been a centurion and a personal friend of Emperor Titus up until a few months ago would make an already grim situation deadly.

Everyone settled for the night. Crickets chirped. Mice scurried in the hay.

The fire burned low, casting soft flickering light. Atretes lay for a long time, staring up at the beamed ceiling, watching the shadows dance as he had when he was a boy. He had imagined then that they were spirits sent by Tiwaz to guard him.

He breathed in the smell of dirt, straw, manure, and wood ash. Rizpah moved closer, her body curved into his side. He turned and took a handful of her hair, breathing in her scent. She moved at his touch, and he knew she was awake. Smiling, he raised up slightly and pressed her shoulder back. "What are you thinking about?"

"I couldn't sleep," she said.

"Tell me what's bothering you."

"Anomia. She's very beautiful."

He had looked overlong at Anomia, he knew. It would have been impossible not to look at her, and foolish now to deny it. "She is beautiful," he conceded.

"And she looks like Ania."

"She's more beautiful than Ania."

"Oh."

He turned her face toward him. "And within, she is like Julia."

Rizpah thanked God. "I love you," she murmured, tracing his

face in the darkness. "I love you so much I think I'd die if I lost you."

He slipped an arm beneath her and drew her close. "Then close your eyes and rest easy," he said softly. "For you'll never lose me."

34

Theophilus awakened with the dawn's light coming through a narrow break in the roof. Rizpah and Atretes were still sleeping. He shook Atretes' shoulder, awakening him. "I'll be out in the woods, praying."

Atretes sat up and rubbed his face. His head ached from too much beer, but he nodded. "Give us a minute, and we'll go with you."

Theophilus, Atretes, and Rizpah with Caleb in her arms walked out into the forest and prayed together as the sun came up. The air was crisp, dew heavy upon the grass. Theophilus surprised Atretes by praying for Varus. "He gives you a stall near the pigs, and you pray for him?"

"I prayed for you from the day of our first meeting, Atretes, and you hated me no less than your brother. When Varus looks at me, he sees Rome, just as you did."

"When he insults you, he insults me."

Theophilus' mouth curved. "A man who is slow to anger is better than the mighty, Atretes, and he who rules his spirit is greater than any warrior who captures a city. You did battle with your brother last night. What did you win by it?"

"I told him the truth!"

"You beat him over the head with the gospel, and he heard and understood none of it."

"All the while you sat silent," Atretes said through his teeth. *"Why?"*

"You were saying too much," Theophilus said as gently as he could. "Listen to me, friend. Lay aside your pride or it will entangle you in sin. Anger is your worst enemy. It served you well in the arena, but not here. When you give in to it, you're like a city without walls. A man's anger doesn't bring forth the righteousness of God."

"What would you have me do?"

"Fix your eyes upon Jesus, the author and perfector of faith. Be zealous, but be patient. It was love that made the Lord give up his heavenly throne to walk among us as a man. It was love that held him on the cross and raised him from the dead. And it is love that will win your people to him."

"My people don't understand love. They understand *power*."

"There is no power on earth that can overcome the love of God in Christ Jesus."

Atretes exhaled a derisive laugh. "This from a man who once used the butt of his sword on the side of my head." He sat down on a log and thrust his fingers through his hair in frustration.

"I'm not perfect," Theophilus said with a rueful smile. He hunkered down. Noticing a pinecone, he picked it up. A few pine nuts fell into his hand. "I will give you words Jesus said." He cast the pinecone away and held the seeds in his palm.

"Behold, a sower went out to sow; and it came about that as he was sowing, some seed fell beside the road, and the birds came and ate it. And other seed fell on the rocky ground where it did not have much soil; and immediately it sprang up because it had no depth of soil. And after the sun had risen, it was scorched; and because it had no root, it withered away. And other seed fell among the thorns, and the thorns came up and choked it, and it yielded no crop. And other seeds fell into the good soil and as they grew up and increased, they yielded a crop and produced thirty, sixty, and a hundredfold."

He scattered the pine nuts. "You and I and Rizpah will sow the Word of God among your people." Brushing off his hands, he stood. "Whether the seed takes root and grows or not isn't up to us, Atretes. It's up to the Lord."

*

Freyja and Varus were standing in front of the longhouse when they returned. Freyja's worried frown turned to relief when she saw them. She stretched out her hands to Atretes as he came near. "I awakened, and you were gone."

He took her hands, bending down to kiss her on each cheek. "We pray each morning as the day begins."

"So early?"

Atretes looked past her to Varus, grim and withdrawn. He released his mother's hands and went to his brother. "You trusted me once, Varus. You followed me in battle. You fought beside me. No brother ever showed more courage than you." He held out his hand. "I want no animosity between us."

"Nor do I," Varus said, taking the proffered hand, yearning for the old times when they had laughed and gotten drunk together. Eleven years had passed, and his brother had finally returned . . . bringing with him a dark, foreign wife and son, a Roman he called friend, and a new god. How could he think things would be the same?

"The cattle have to be pastured." It occurred to Varus as he said it that the land he now held would revert to his brother as well. Resentment and jealousy filled him.

"Theophilus can help us."

"Keep him away from me, or I swear by Tiwaz, I'll kill him."

As he turned away, Atretes started after him. Theophilus caught his arm. "Leave him be. It wasn't many days ago when you felt the same way."

Atretes jerked his arm away, but breathed out slowly, forcing his temper down. Theophilus was right. Patience . . . he had to have patience.

"It will take time for me to make a place among your people."

"A place!" Freyja stared at Theophilus in horror. She swung to her son, appealing to him. "You cannot mean to let him stay here among us. Not after all that has happened at the hands of Rome."

"Theophilus is here at my invitation, Mother," Atretes said, tight-lipped as he saw she, too, was fighting him. "As a brother, not as a Roman."

"I am thankful he saved your life, but last night should have made it clear this Roman has no place among us."

"Would you fight me as well? He stays!"

"What's happened to you? Romans killed your father! They killed Rolf and Dulga and half our tribe. There isn't one person among us who hasn't suffered tragedy at the hands of Rome! And you would dare to bring this man here to make a home among us?"

"I dare."

She turned to Theophilus. "They will kill you."

"They'll try," Theophilus conceded softly.

Surprised, she saw he had no fear of death. "Do you think this god of yours will protect you? Every man among the Chatti will plot to murder you."

"If anyone touches him, they'll contend with me!"

"You will contend with all if he remains! You will have to set yourself against your own people." Neither man was swayed by her warning. Atretes' jaw was set; the Roman looked at her with compassion. She knew her son's stubbornness and so appealed to Theophilus for reason. "Atretes calls you friend. What will happen to him if you stay?"

"It would be worse for him if I left."

Freyja was greatly disturbed by his words, for she sensed powerful forces moving. "What power do you have over my son?"

"None, my lady."

Despite his reassurance, she was afraid. She felt a warning tingle and coldness as the spirit came upon her. Not now, she thought desperately, fighting it. Not now! Her vision narrowed and darkened, and images appeared, unclear and moving. "No," she moaned, her soul struggling and weakening as the force took hold. She saw Rizpah sitting on the forest floor, weeping as she held a man in her arms. She saw blood.

"Mother," Atretes said, chilled. He had seen her look like this before and knew what it meant. "What do you see?"

"Lady Freyja," Rizpah said, alarmed and wanting to help her.

Atretes shoved her back. "Leave her alone!"

"She's ill."

"She's having a vision. You must not touch her when she's like this."

Freyja was fighting and losing against whatever possessed her. Her eyelids fluttered, her eyes rolling back as she trembled violently.

"It's never happened like this before," Atretes said, afraid to touch her lest he bring worse upon her.

"Death." Freyja clutched the pendant over her heart, terrified. "I see death!" She groaned. But whose? She couldn't see the dying man clearly. The vision intensified with terrifying power. Someone—or some*thing*—else was in the forest with them, something dark and malevolent.

"We must help her," Rizpah said, her spirit moved by the woman's anguish.

Theophilus felt the presence of some dark force holding Freyja. Compelled, he stepped forward. "In the name of Jesus Christ, leave her!" he said in a quiet, firm voice.

The vision ended so abruptly, Freyja gasped. Disoriented, she sagged forward. It was the Roman who caught hold of her and gave her support. "Do not be afraid," he said gently, and warmth flowed through her at his touch. The coldness within her fled.

Alarmed, she drew back from him, eyes wide. "Do not touch me. It is forbidden."

Seeing her eyes were clear and focused again, Theophilus released her. She stepped back from him, eyes wide. He wanted to reassure her, but knew nothing he could say at this moment would allay her fears.

Time. Lord, I need time and your help if I'm to reach these people.

Still trembling, Freyja turned to her son and took his hand between hers. "Walk among your people, Atretes. You must find yourself again before it's too late." She let go of him and hurried away.

"My lady," Rizpah said, snatching up Caleb and starting after her.

Atretes grasped her arm, keeping her at his side. "Let her go."

"But she looked ill, Atretes. She shouldn't be alone."

"You can't follow. She's going to the sacred wood."

*

Anomia was out gathering herbs when she saw Freyja walking hurriedly through the forest. Her eyes narrowed. "Mother Freyja!" she called in greeting, affronted when the older woman didn't pause until she called again. It was clear Freyja didn't want to be disturbed by anyone, not even another priestess. As Anomia came near, she noticed the pallor of the woman's skin and the torpidness of her blue eyes. Jealousy gripped her as she read the signs that the spirit had come upon Freyja again.

Why do you deny me, Tiwaz? Her soul cried out in anger as she greeted the elder priestess with a kiss. "You look distressed, Lady Freyja," she said, pretending concern. *Why?*

"I've had a vision," Freyja said, wary of the younger woman. She had never fully trusted her. "I must be alone."

"Tiwaz has revealed the future to you again?"

"Yes."

"What did you see?"

"Rizpah in the forest, holding a dying man."

"Atretes?" Anomia said in alarm.

"I don't know," Freyja said, shaken. "The man wasn't clear, and there was someone or something else with them."

"Perhaps Tiwaz will reveal more to you if you sacrifice."

Freyja put a trembling hand to her forehead. "I'm not sure I want to know more," she said, looking ill.

Anomia hid her contempt. As a child, she had been in awe of Freyja, for she was the chosen one of Tiwaz. Now, she saw her as weak and foolish. Freyja didn't welcome the power that came upon her. She didn't use the hold it gave her over the Chatti.

It had been four years since the spirit had last possessed Freyja and she had prophesied. She had said Marcobus, chief of the Hermunduri, would be murdered by a woman. His death would bring anarchy and bloodshed to the under-chiefs as each strove to lead. The Chatti had rejoiced at Freyja's vision. Why shouldn't they? The Hermunduri had once triumphed over them and stolen a river salt flat.

Freyja, however, had not rejoiced. She had gone into seclusion, distressed by the violence of what she had seen. Foolish, gentle Freyja. Anomia wondered why Tiwaz would use such a weak vessel when she herself was so much more worthy. She had sacrificed and prayed to Tiwaz that he would set Freyja aside in her favor. She had held the sacred horns and spoken the vows before the priest, Gundrid! She had given herself to Tiwaz. Since then, her powers had eclipsed those of the older woman, and even of Gundrid. He was afraid of her, and though Freyja wasn't, her powers had seemed to decrease, for no further visions came.

After a year, Anomia had begun to think Tiwaz had finally discarded Freyja. After four years, she had been certain of it. Surely the dark lord had chosen her now, for her powers and beauty had increased greatly during the long silence. The Chatti men held her in awe, the women in fear.

But now . . . Tiwaz spoke again through Freyja!

Why? She wanted to scream. *I've given my soul to you! Do you give her the vision to taunt me? Do you mock my devotion? Why do you come upon this poor, pathetic creature who has the effrontery to look ill after being blessed by your possession? Take me! I would be triumphant! I would exult in it! Only I am worthy among these pitiful people! Why won't you take me?*

And all the while her mind rebelled, she smiled and spoke softly. "Rest, Mother. I will see to the services this evening. You needn't worry about anything."

Her mind whirred. How had she displeased Tiwaz that he would betray her with Freyja? Didn't she devote herself to sacrifice and service to him? Didn't she perform the rites in the moonlight? Didn't she use her magic to bring people into submission to him? Why did Tiwaz still speak through this pathetic weakling?

"I must go," Freyja said. She wanted to escape Anomia, for she sensed the dark undercurrents swirling around her. "We'll speak later." Anomia's brow arched slightly at being so summarily dismissed, but Freyja was too distraught to care. She left the young priestess standing among the trees, fingers white upon the handle of her basket.

✶

Freyja knew Anomia coveted her long-held position among the Chatti. She often prayed that Tiwaz would give Anomia what she wanted. For herself, she had never wanted to have the spirit take hold of her and open her eyes to the things that were to come. It had never sat easy with her. Each time it happened, she felt more of herself draining away.

The first time the god had come upon her, she had been a child. She was sitting in her mother's lap when everything around her faded and other things had taken their place. She had seen a woman having a child. The vision only lasted a moment and had not manifested itself in any unusual way. When the vision ebbed, she was still sitting on her mother's lap before the fire in the longhouse. Everyone was talking around her. Her father was laughing and drinking mead with his friends.

"Sela is going to have a baby," she said.

"What's this you say?"

"Sela is going to have a baby," she said again. She liked babies. Everyone rejoiced when they came. "A baby will make Sela happy, won't it?"

"You've had a dream, *Liebchen*," she said sadly. "Sela would be very happy to have a baby, but she's barren. She and Buri have been married five years."

"I saw her have a baby."

Her mother looked across at her father, and he lowered his drinking horn. "What's Freyja saying to you?"

"She said Sela is going to have a baby," her mother said, perplexed.

"A child with a dream," he said, dismissing it.

No one thought much about the vision. Only Freyja knew the truth of it. She sought out Sela and told her what she had seen. The dream only seemed to increase the woman's sorrow, and so she stopped talking about the baby, though continuing to spend time with the woman.

In the fall of the following year, Sela conceived, to the amazement of everyone in the tribe. She bore a son in early summer. Everyone treated Freyja differently after that. When she had visions, they listened and believed.

The early visions were good. Babies were born. Marriages took place. Battles were won. When she foresaw Hermun, only a few years older than she, would be chief one day, her mother and father had arranged her marriage with him. It was only later that the visions became dark and foreboding.

The last portent of good had come in the wake of disaster. Rome had destroyed the alliance between the tribes, crushing the rebellion. Hermun was dead; Atretes, the new chief of the Chatti. She had seen her son's future. He would become known in Rome. He would fight as no other Chatti had fought, and he would triumph over every foe. A storm would come that would blow across the Empire and destroy it. It would come from the north and the east and the west, and Atretes would be part of it. And there would be a woman, a woman with dark hair and dark eyes, a woman of strange ways whom he would love.

It was when all others had thought Atretes dead that she had had another vision prophesying his return . . . and that he would bring peace with him.

Now, she was confused and torn. Part of the vision had already proven true. Atretes had achieved fame in Rome. He had fought as a gladiator and had triumphed over every foe in order to earn his freedom and return home. And he had brought with him a woman with dark hair and dark eyes, a woman of strange beliefs whom he clearly loved.

But peace? Where was the peace she had seen with his return? He brought rebellion and blasphemy and heartache. In one night, her family was being torn apart before her very eyes. A new god? The *only* god. How could he say such things? How could he believe them?

And what of the storm that would blow across the Empire and destroy it?

Freyja reached the sacred grove and went down on her knees on hallowed ground. Clutching the pendant, she bowed down before the ancient tree that held the golden horns. "I am unworthy. I am unworthy of your possession, Tiwaz." Prostrating herself, she wept.

*

Anomia found Gundrid in the meadowlands to the east of the sacred wood. He was leading one of the sacred white horses in a circle, speaking softly to it, and listening intently to whatever snorts or neighs it uttered.

"What does she tell you?" Anomia asked, startling him. He untied the rope from around the mare's neck, giving himself time to think before facing the young priestess with an answer. In truth, he had just been enjoying the animal, speaking his affection for her. Running a hand down her side, he patted her haunches and sent her galloping toward the other two white horses grazing in the sunlight.

"Holt will bring back good news," he said. Whatever news Holt brought with him, he could interpret to fulfill his statement, be it rebellion against Rome or a time of waiting.

Anomia smiled faintly, suspect. "Freyja has had another vision."

"She has?" He saw Anomia's blue eyes flicker and knew he should have hidden his pleasure at the news. "Where is she?"

"She's praying before the sacred emblems," she said. "And weeping." Her tone turned acrid.

"I'll go and speak with her."

She came closer so that he would have to go around her to depart. "Why does Tiwaz still use her?"

"You must ask Tiwaz."

"I have! He gives me no answer. What of the sacred horses? What do they tell you, Gundrid?"

"That you have great power," he said, well aware of what she wanted to hear.

"I want *more*," she said with unveiled discontent, then added with less vehemence, "that I might serve our people better."

Gundrid knew Anomia lied. He was well aware she craved the power for her own purposes and not for the benefit of her people. "Tiwaz will use you as he wills," he said, secretly hoping the god would continue to speak through Freyja, who longed for the good of her people and not power for herself.

Anomia watched him walk away, the carved staff in his hand. "Atretes returned last night."

"Atretes?" he said, turning back in surprise. "He's here?"

"Did not the sacred horse tell you that?" She walked toward him with measured steps. "He brought a Roman with him and a dark woman he calls his wife. Both spoke of another god, a god more powerful than Tiwaz."

"Sacrilege!"

"Is it any wonder Freyja sees blood and death in the forest?"

"Whose death?"

"She didn't say." She shrugged. "I don't think she knows. Tiwaz only revealed a little to her, a hint of what's to come."

Perhaps the god would reveal the whole of it to her if she gave him blood sacrifice. She looked at the old priest and wished she could offer him. He was a fraud, currying the sacred horses' hides rather than their spirits. He saw nothing. He knew nothing!

"I will see him after I've spoken with Freyja," he said and left her.

∗

He found her, still kneeling, in the wood.

Freyja rose in respect as he approached her. She took his hands and kissed each in deference to his position as high priest. His heart warmed toward her. Freyja never set herself above anyone, though she could easily have done so. The people revered her as a goddess among them. Yet it was Freyja who often brought him gifts, a woolen blanket in the chill winter, a bowl of roasted pine nuts, a skin of wine, herbs and salves when his bones were aching.

Anomia never showed him reverence. She condescended to show him respect only when it served her purposes.

"I've had another vision," Freyja said, her eyes red from weeping. She told him everything from her waking dream. She told him of her son's return.

"Anomia has told me of these things," he said solemnly.

"I couldn't see the man clearly. It could've been Atretes or the Roman or even someone else."

"In time, we will know."

"But what if it's my son?"

"Have you no faith in your own prophesies, Freyja?" he said gently. "Atretes has returned and brought the woman with him, just as you said he would. He will lead our people to peace."

"Peace," she said softly, craving it with all her heart. "And what of the Roman with him?"

"What does one Roman matter?"

"Atretes calls him friend. My own son stands for him and swears to protect him. You know how Varus is. He's bound to hospitality for the moment, but his anger is so great the hospitality won't last. My sons almost came to blows last night. I'm afraid of what will come of this."

"Nothing important will come of it. They quarreled. What young men do not? And they made amends. They'll stand together as they always have."

"Atretes speaks for a new god."

"A new god? Who will listen? Tiwaz is all-powerful. All that we know is his dominion, Freyja. The sky itself belongs to Tiwaz."

Doubts assailed her. When she had been caught in the vision, the Roman had merely spoken the name of Jesus Christ, and the spirit that Tiwaz had sent upon her had fled her body. She considered telling Gundrid what had happened, but she held her silence. She didn't want to be the cause of anyone's death, even a Roman's. She needed to think. She needed to watch and consider. Atretes was involved with this man and she would do nothing that would jeopardize her son's return to his rightful place as chief of the Chatti. And she prayed fervently that he would do nothing to destroy the people's confidence in him.

Seeing her distress, Gundrid took her hand and patted it. "You're worrying overmuch about this Roman, Freyja. He is one man against many. He will leave."

"And if he doesn't?"

"Then he will die."

35

Atretes took his mother's advice and spent most of his time renewing friendships with the villagers. Theophilus accompanied him, but in deference to Chatti feelings he quietly absorbed conversations without speaking. The villagers tolerated his presence for the sake of Atretes, but their animosity and distrust was felt by both. Theophilus ignored the numerous barbs about Romans, and his calmness lent Atretes the strength of will to allow the insults to pass.

Many of the younger men had gone with Rud and Holt to meet with the Bructeri and Batavi chiefs. Those too old or too young to fight remained. A small contingent of warriors had been left behind so that the village wouldn't be undefended. Should trouble arise, word would be sent to the others. Usipi was eager to relinquish his home-guard leadership responsibilities, despite Varus' misgivings and those of the three men who had greeted Atretes on his arrival.

"You are chief of the Chatti by proclamation of the Thing," he said, encouraging Atretes to take his rightful place.

Atretes declined, no more eager than Usipi to lead. And he did not want to take his previous position of leadership for granted. "That was years ago. Rud is chief now and may think differently." Eleven years was a long time to be away, and he wouldn't usurp the man who had held the Chatti together during his captivity.

While others might covet the power of the chief, Atretes didn't want the responsibility of leadership again. When his father had died and the warriors pressed him, he had submitted to their will for the sake of his people. Not one man had stood against him. Now his own brother wouldn't stand with him.

Atretes wondered how it was possible, in the space of a few short weeks, to feel closer to the Roman than he ever had to his own kin. The bond between him and Theophilus grew stronger with each day. No matter where they were or what they were doing, the Roman spoke of the Lord. Atretes had asked to know everything, and Theophilus was eager to impart all he knew.

Each moment was a precious opportunity, and he made use of it. Whether they were sitting, standing, or walking, Theophilus taught him Scripture, often reading from the scroll Agabus had copied on board the ship.

Rizpah treasured up everything Theophilus said, pondering it when she was away from him. The time they spent together was precious for it was peaceful. Elsewhere things were not.

Varus flew into a rage when Theophilus asked to buy a piece of land on which to build a grubenhaus for himself. "I'll see you dead before you ever own a piece of Chatti land!"

"I don't ask for land within the village boundaries, but on the outskirts of it," Theophilus said, making no mention of the document in his possession giving him the right, by Roman law, to any frontier land he wanted as payment for his years of service in the army. He wanted to gain these people's respect, not their continuing enmity.

"The only land I'd give you is the dung hill."

Atretes lost his temper and interfered before Theophilus could stop him. "By our law, Father's full portion falls to me as the eldest son!"

Varus' head jerked toward him.

"Atretes!" his mother said. "You can't do this!"

"I can and I will. It's within my rights to take back everything, no matter how hard Varus has worked to protect it. And he knows it!"

"Take nothing for my sake," Theophilus said, seeing the breach a few words could make between the brothers. "He has reason not to trust Rome, and you'll add cause to injury."

"Do not defend him!" Atretes said, incensed.

"He's no different than you were when we first met," Theophilus said with a wry smile.

Varus' face reddened. "I don't need the defense of a Roman pig!" He rose and spit in his direction.

Atretes took a step after his brother. Theophilus blocked his way. "Think," Theophilus said under his breath. "Think from his side before you say another word."

"You've been gone eleven years!" Varus shouted back. "All that time, I've held Father's inheritance together. And now you come back and think you can give it away to this Roman dog and *leave me with nothing?*"

Atretes started to step past Theophilus, but the Roman

grasped his arm. "Your anger will not bring about the righteousness of God," he said so only his friend could hear.

Clenching his teeth, Atretes strove to calm himself.

As he did so, reason came. It was true—Varus had cause for resentment. He had lost as much as he himself had, and held onto what was left. It was not in Atretes' mind to strip his brother of all his possessions just because he had the right to do so, and yet he knew his words had implied just that. His anger had only caused more strife rather than bringing some semblance of reason into the discussion.

"I make a gift to you of the eastern half, Varus, as well as all the cattle," he said with impulsive generosity. "Theophilus' portion will come from my half. Will that satisfy?"

Varus was stunned into silence.

"You're giving him the richest portion of farmland," Freyja said, equally stunned.

"I know that. The eastern half also has the best grazing for the cattle," Atretes pointed out, still looking to his younger brother for an answer. "Well? What do you say?"

Varus took an unsteady step back. Wincing, he sat down and stared at his brother as though he had never seen him before. *Half* the land and *all* the cattle? Atretes could take everything and no one would argue his rights to do so. Instead, his brother gave him the best of his inheritance. It was within Atretes' rights to leave him with nothing, no matter how hard he had worked to retain it. In truth, that was what he had expected to happen if Atretes ever returned and one of the primary reasons he had hoped he wouldn't.

"You have a son, Atretes," Freyja said, astounded by such thinking. "Would you give his inheritance to an outsider?" What had happened to her son? Had this Roman cast a spell upon him?

"The land will remain his, my lady," Theophilus said, wanting to allay her understandable concerns. Atretes had surprised him as well. "If it'll set both your minds at ease," he said, glancing at Varus, "I'll pay an annual fee for the use of it."

Varus frowned, wondering where the trick lay in his words. Romans took; they didn't give.

Theophilus saw his distrust and understood it. "My desire isn't to take anything from you or your people, Varus, but to earn my own living while I'm here. I have been grateful for your hospitality, but I think you will agree, it's time for me to leave."

Varus uttered a cold laugh, hiding how the Roman's words troubled him.

Freyja searched Theophilus' face, but saw no sign of subterfuge.

Atretes' mouth tipped sardonically. "Do you agree to the division of land or would you prefer I hold to tradition and take it all?"

"I agree," Varus said.

"Come." Atretes jerked his head at Theophilus. "I'll help you choose your portion."

When they selected a suitable site for Theophilus' house, Atretes gave in to his own curiosity. "What'll you do with the land? You have no cattle. We'll have to raid the Tencteri and Cherusci herds to get you a few head."

Theophilus knew thievery was practiced among the tribes, but had no intention of following the custom—or of encouraging Atretes to do so. "I intend to grow corn and beans."

"You, a farmer?" Atretes laughed. It was so ludicrous.

Theophilus smiled, undaunted. "I'm going to hammer my sword into a plowshare and my spear into a pruning hook."

Atretes saw he meant it. "You'd better wait," he said grimly. "If you do it too soon, you may not live to break the soil."

*

Atretes was helping Theophilus fell trees for the grubenhaus when they heard jubilant shouting from the village. The warriors had returned.

Burying his ax in a stump, Atretes headed for the village. "Stay here until I send for you!" He ran through the woods and between two longhouses, coming into the main street. A throng of warriors mulled around, greeting wives and children. Only a few were on horseback.

"*Rud!*" Atretes shouted, seeing the older man who had been his father's best friend.

The gray-haired man turned sharply on his horse. Raising his framea in the air, he gave an ecstatic war cry and rode toward Atretes, sliding from the animal's back at the last moment and embracing him in a body-bruising hug. "You have returned! Tiwaz is with us!" He embraced him again, pounding his back as the others surged toward them, shouting war cries and all talking at once.

Rizpah watched from the door of the longhouse, Caleb in her arms. The men surrounded Atretes, buffeting him in welcome. Atretes was laughing, shoving several back and taking a good-natured swing at another who dodged and then embraced him. They were rough men of deep feeling and even deeper pride.

Across the street, Anomia emerged from her dwelling. After dismissing Rizpah with a cursory glance, she fixed her gaze upon the returning warriors. Her eyes glowed as she saw how they worshiped Atretes, clamoring around him like excited boys in the presence of their living idol. What power he could wield over his people—and she would teach him how to do so.

The Chatti had never stopped talking about him. Over the past years, he had become a legend, his feats in battle against the Romans retold at hearth and home around the ceremonial fires. How easy it would be for him to yank the reins of power from any who tried to withhold them. Rud would not. He was old and tired, though loyal to her. He had only agreed to the meeting with the Batavi and Bructeri because she wanted it and the younger warriors demanded it. Nor would Holt stand in Atretes' way, for he had long ago sworn allegiance to Hermun's son.

She had been a child of twelve when she had hidden herself in the dark shadows of the trees and watched the rites in the sacred grove that made Atretes chief. She could still remember him holding the golden horns above his head, his naked body bathed in firelight. He had looked like a god to her then. He still did. Soon she would stand beside him.

She had always known what she wanted: to be high priestess and wife of the chief of the Chatti. Had her sister, Ania, lived, she would have stood in the way of her ambitions. Anomia believed her death had been an act of Tiwaz, preparing the way for her to be with Atretes.

When he had been taken by the Romans, she had been confused and angry. Why would Tiwaz allow such a thing to happen? Freyja had foreseen his return, and she had clung to the prophecy, awaiting the unfolding of it, setting her intellect to achieving the fullness of her powers in readiness for him. In part, she had done just that, though she still craved more. Together, she and Atretes would make the Chatti the mightiest tribe in

Germania. They would take vengeance on all those who had thought to make them slaves. They would destroy the Hermunduri and take back the sacred river and salt flats. They would take retribution for the yoke Rome had tried and failed to put upon them. And as they did these things, other tribes would join with them, until the whole of Germania was driving south to the very heart of the Empire: Rome herself!

Nothing would stand in her way, not the Roman Atretes called his friend, not Freyja, not anyone else—especially not the black-eyed, black-haired Ionian witch who stood in the doorway opposite her.

For your glory, Tiwaz, I will take Atretes from her! Together he and I will rule these people and use them for your purposes.

"Ask him about the Roman he brought with him!" someone shouted, and the din of greeting died down.

"What is this you say, Herigast?" Holt said to the accuser. "What Roman?"

Atretes looked at the man standing at the outer edge of the warrior's circle. Long ago, Atretes had been forced to make a judgment against Herigast's son, Wagast. The young warrior had dropped his shield and fled the battlefield, a crime demanding execution. The vote of the Thing had been unanimous, leaving Atretes with no choice but to order Wagast be drowned in the bog. The young man's father had aged greatly in eleven years. Though still robust, his hair was white, his face deeply lined.

"My wife just told me," Herigast said and put his arm around the woman beside him in a gesture of protection, his expression challenging.

Rud turned to Atretes. "Is what he says true?"

"Yes."

Rud's face tensed in anger. "We make an alliance against Rome, and you bring one of the murdering dogs among us!"

"He comes in peace."

"Peace!" a young warrior said and spit on the ground with as much brass and pride as Atretes had ever possessed.

"We want no peace with Rome!" another shouted. "We want blood!"

Men shouted angrily.

"... burned our village ..."

"... killed my father ..."

"... took my wife and son for slaves ..."

Rizpah closed her eyes and prayed as Atretes shouted them down. "I have as much cause to hate Rome as you. More! But I tell you this! If not for Theophilus, I'd be fighting in an arena or hung up on some foul cross for Domitian's entertainment! *Three times* he saved my life. He led me home!"

"No Roman can be trusted!"

Others shouted agreement.

"Where is he?"

"Let's get him and throw him in the bog!"

"Make him a blood sacrifice!"

Herigast's wife pointed. "The Roman is building a grubenhaus just beyond those longhouses. He intends to make his home among us."

One of the warriors started in that direction. When Atretes blocked his way, he took a swing at him. Atretes ducked and brought his fist up into his chest, knocking him from his feet. Before the warrior hit the ground, Atretes had his gladius in his hand and at the fallen warrior's throat.

"Stay down, or by God, you'll never get up again!"

The maelstrom died as quickly as it had erupted.

The warriors moved back slightly, staring while the young warrior gasped for air. "You will all listen," Atretes said, glaring down at the young man, whose eyes had widened when he felt the sword beneath his jaw. One swift jerk and his jugular would be laid open. Atretes raised his head enough to look from face to face around him. "Kill my friend and you will answer to me!" He looked down again, the blood pounding hot in his veins. "Do you want to be first to die, boy?"

"Let him up, Atretes!"

The men turned and saw a tall man striding toward them.

Atretes didn't move, but cursed under his breath.

"Look!" Herigast's wife said. "The Roman comes, gloating over the trouble he's brought upon us!"

Theophilus walked toward them calmly, his demeanor one of authority and purpose. "Put your sword away, Atretes. Those who live by it, die by it."

"As will you, if I listen," Atretes said, not moving the blade an inch.

Theophilus heard the threatening rumble that went through those gathered. There was no time to dissuade Atretes. He needed to speak now while he still had opportunity. "I'm not here as a Roman or for Rome!" he addressed the men. "I ask your forbearance until I can prove myself trustworthy. If I play you false, do with me as you will."

"You look like a soldier," Holt said, measuring him with burning eyes.

Theophilus looked at him squarely, without fear. "I served in the Roman army for twenty-five years and held the rank of centurion."

A stunned silence fell. Holt gave a surprised laugh of derision. What man would admit to such a thing in the midst of a hundred Chatti warriors? He was either very brave or very stupid. Perhaps both.

Theophilus stood his ground calmly. "I fought here twelve years ago when the German tribes rebelled against Rome."

"He fought against us!" one of the men shouted for all to hear.

"Roman dog!" Other names far more profane and insulting were hurled at him.

"I know the Chatti to be a valiant people!" Theophilus shouted over them. "But I know this as well: If you rebel against Rome at this time, you will fail. Domitian waits for an opportunity to send the legions north. A tribal alliance for war will give him exactly the excuse he needs to do it."

"He speaks for Rome!"

Atretes withdrew his gladius and turned slightly.

Theophilus saw doubt flicker in his eyes. "I speak the truth, Atretes. You know the lengths to which Domitian will go to get what he wants. He covets the power and prestige of his father and brother, and the only way to get it is to fight a military campaign and win. This is the only frontier where Domitian had relative success."

Theophilus' reminder of the battles eleven years ago didn't sit well. Atretes put his sword into its scabbard, ignoring the young warrior as he jumped up from the ground.

Anomia saw an opportunity to destroy one adversary and grasped it. "Let Tiwaz reveal his will for our people!" she called out.

The warriors turned as she walked toward them with the full confidence of Tiwaz on her side. They held her in high esteem and waited for her to speak further. She let them wait until she was close enough to see into their eyes, and then she gestured derisively toward Theophilus.

"Tonight is the new moon. As he speaks for Rome, let him fight for Rome. Pit him against our champion. Let Tiwaz tell us what to do. If this Roman survives, we wait. If not, we pursue the alliance."

"Don't listen to her," Atretes said, glaring at the young priestess.

"If your Roman friend is right, Atretes, he'll prevail," she said. "And if not . . ." She let the words hang.

Rud looked at Theophilus and measured him again. "Anomia's words have merit." Her suggestion offered a quick solution to the problem Atretes had created by bringing this Roman home with him. "Have him bound."

"I've never run from a fight yet," Theophilus said before anyone sought to touch him. "Tell me when and where you want the contest, and I'll be there."

Rud was surprised that the Roman showed no fear. But then, perhaps the fool didn't know what he faced. He smiled coldly. "Make peace with your gods, Roman. An hour after nightfall, you'll be dead." He looked at Atretes. "The Thing will meet tonight in the sacred grove. Make sure he's there." He walked away, followed by a contingent of young warriors in his service.

The others dispersed, joined by wives and children.

Anomia smiled disdainfully at Theophilus and turned away, ignoring Atretes' look of fury.

Atretes didn't take his eyes off of her until she disappeared inside her small house. Swearing under his breath, he went after Theophilus who had headed back to the woods.

"Are you out of your mind? You're forty years old! They'll pit you against a warrior half your age and twice your strength!"

"You think simple reason would've swayed them otherwise?" Theophilus said, yanking his ax from the stump where he had left it.

"If you think I can get you out of this, you're wrong. That witch made it a point of augury." Atretes knew all too well that the Chatti put great store in this practice of trusting signs and omens for making decisions.

A loud crack echoed through the woods as Theophilus chopped a deep cut into a spruce. "I'm not dead yet, Atretes."

"You don't understand. It's not going to be a contest of strength. It's a fight to the death!"

"I know." He brought the ax around again and sent a thick chunk of wood flying.

"You know?" Atretes wondered how he could be so calm. "What am I supposed to do?"

Theophilus smiled as he brought the ax around again. "You could start praying."

36

The whole village was eager for Theophilus' blood, and more than a few were celebrating his death before it was accomplished. Only Freyja was distressed at the news of a contest between the Chatti champion and Theophilus.

"You must stop this, Rud. If you kill a Roman centurion, you'll bring war on us."

"We're already at war with Rome."

"What of Atretes?"

"Yes! What about Atretes?" Rud said, angry. "What's happened to your son that he'd bring this Roman cur home with him?"

"The man saved his life."

"So he said, but that doesn't change the blood that runs in his veins. Romans killed your husband. They killed my brothers. Don't defend that centurion dog to my face."

"I don't speak for him. I'm afraid for our people if he dies. You must think of the consequences."

"We've been living with the consequences of Roman domination for decades and will continue to do so until we can drive every one of them back over the Alps! Except for Atretes, there isn't a man in this tribe who doesn't want to see Rolf hack this Roman cur to pieces. For myself, I'm going to enjoy watching it!"

She spoke to Gundrid, but Anomia had already convinced the old priest augury would settle important questions. "The outcome of this fight will decide many factors," he said, dismissing her objections. "Tiwaz will speak to us through Rolf."

"And what if Rolf fails and dies?"

"He won't."

Desperate, she sought Theophilus, hoping to convince him to leave before it was too late. She found him in the forest, on his knees, his hands outstretched, palms up. A twig snapped beneath her foot as she approached, and he rose and turned to her, perfectly at ease. "Lady Freyja," he said and inclined his head in respectful greeting.

"You must go. Now."

"Atretes told you about the contest."

"He didn't have to tell me. The whole village knows. You won't survive the night if you stay here."

"If it's God's will I die, then I die."

"And what of my people? Will they die also because of your Roman pride? How far will you drive us into the forest? How many lives will you take before you relent and leave us to live in peace?" She struggled for self-restraint. "Why did you ever come here?"

"No one knows I'm here among the Chatti. When I resigned my commission, Titus suggested Gaul or Britannia. I didn't inform him otherwise."

She was perplexed. "What are you trying to say?"

"I'm saying if I die tonight, no one will come to avenge me."

She was troubled by his words. Did he welcome death? "Have you forgotten my son? He calls you his friend and has sworn to protect you. Your death will set Atretes against his own people."

Theophilus had considered that and had spoken with Atretes. He had also spent the afternoon praying for him. "Atretes' battle isn't against his people, but the power that holds you all captive."

She didn't understand and shook her head. "You speak in riddles. The only power that tries to hold us captive is that of Rome."

"It's not the power of Rome of which I speak, Lady Freyja."

"I don't understand you."

"Stay with me for a time and I'll explain."

"How much time will it take?" she said, wary of him.

He held his hand out toward an inviting patch of sunlit green. "I'll keep you no longer than the time it takes for the shadows to come across the glade." *An hour. One hour, Lord. Please.*

She sat in the sunshine and listened to him tell of beginnings, of earth and man created by God, and of an arch deceiver who entered a garden.

Freyja began to tremble. She broke out into a cold sweat at his words, her heart pounding out a warning. "I can't listen to you," she said and rose.

He rose as well, looking at her with kind eyes. "Why not?"

She clutched the pendant between her breasts. "*You* are the serpent in our garden, not Tiwaz."

"I never spoke the name Tiwaz."

"Veil your words as you will, I know you speak against him."

"You tremble, my lady."

"Tiwaz is warning me not to listen to you."

"Indeed, he would, for the good news of Jesus Christ will set you free."

Her knuckles whitened on the pendant. She drew back further from him. "You will die tonight. Tiwaz will rain his wrath down upon you for trying to turn me against him." She turned, wanting to flee the glade and him, but forced herself to walk with dignity.

"And if I live, Lady Freyja?" Theophilus called out to her before she reached the edge of trees.

She turned, her face pale and strained. "You won't."

"If I do, will you listen to me then? Will you hear me out to the end of what I have to tell you?"

Conflicting emotions warred within her. "You're asking me to betray my god."

"I'm asking you to listen to the truth."

"The truth as you see it."

"The truth that *is*, my lady. The truth that has been and always will be."

"I won't listen to you! I won't!" She turned away again and hurried through the woods, putting as much distance between herself and this Roman as she could.

Closing his eyes, Theophilus lifted his head. "Jesus, help me."

*

Atretes came for Theophilus at dusk. "I've prayed as you asked," he said grimly, "but I think you'll be with Jesus before this night is through."

"Your confidence instills me with hope, my friend," Theophilus said with a dry laugh.

"Rizpah won't eat. She said she'll pray until it's over."

Theophilus wondered where Freyja was, but didn't ask. He took up his belt and put it around his waist, adjusting it so that the gladius was at the proper angle. "I'm ready." He said no more as he strode through the woods, Atretes at his side. With every step, he sent a prayer to heaven.

The men were gathered at the boundary of the sacred wood.

Some were drunk and shouted insults at his approach. Others laughed, excited at the prospect of seeing Roman blood let. Theophilus could feel Atretes growing more and more angry the closer they came. The men saw and felt it also, and the gathering grew quieter because of it.

Young Rolf stood beside Rud, eyes as blue and fierce as Atretes'. His long red hair was partially covered by a *galea*, a leather cap, as well as the metal *cassis* that covered it. The helmet bore runes of victory, carrying the name Tiwaz. Rolf held a long, broad slashing weapon called a *spatha* in his right hand, and in his left hand, an oval shield made of wood on which was carved the image of the god he served. The horned, twofold being, bearing an ax in one hand and a scythe in the other. The pagan god, Tiwaz.

Youth and strength were clearly on Rolf's side, and there was no lack of intelligence in his direct, assessing gaze. His bearing was proud, his mocking grin full of self-confidence and disdain. He reminded Theophilus of Atretes.

The Roman felt dismissed. He knew what Rolf saw: a man twice his age armed with a shorter sword and bearing no shield. An easy kill. "At least we know one thing for certain," he said with a faint smile at Atretes. "If I win, it'll be by the grace of God."

"What did he say?" Rud demanded, taking offense, for Theophilus had spoken in heavily accented Greek.

"He fights in the name of Jesus Christ," Atretes said loud enough for all to hear.

"And he'll die in the name of his god as well," Rud said, giving his under-chief a nod.

Holt tossed Atretes a rope. "Bind him," he said and turned his back on them.

"Do they think I plan to run away at this late hour?" Theophilus said under his breath as Atretes tied his wrists.

"Only the chiefs enter the sacred wood unfettered," he said quietly and Theophilus noticed then that others were being fettered. "It's a reminder that Tiwaz binds us to him," Atretes said under his breath and gave the ropes a hard tug making sure they were secured properly. "Don't fall."

Theophilus raised his brow at Atretes' low, ominous tone. "What happens if I do?"

Atretes glanced around at the others and lowered his voice.

"If they're feeling merciful, you'll be allowed to roll to the sacred grove. If not, they'll string you up by the ankles and send for my mother or that blonde witch to slit your throat and drain your blood into a bowl as libation for Tiwaz."

"Jesus, preserve me." Theophilus looked around at the Chatti warriors. He had always known the Germans were a bloodthirsty race, but he never guessed the extent of their religious practices. "I don't see anyone in a particularly merciful mood, do you?" he said, smiling wryly.

Atretes gave a humorless laugh. "No, but then they'd rather see Rolf put an end to your life than give that honor to a woman." He hobbled Theophilus' legs.

Rud and Holt, bearing torches, led the procession into the woods. Warriors fell in behind and in front of Theophilus and Atretes. Theophilus kept pace with difficulty. The small steps within the confines of his rope hobbles made him feel clumsy. He looked around at the warriors near him and felt compassion for their plight. Their spirits were bound as surely as were their bodies. His concentration focused on them, he tripped over tree roots and barely managed to keep his balance.

Atretes swore under his breath.

Theophilus felt his tension. "Friend," he whispered, "whatever happens tonight, remember this: The Lord is sovereign. God causes all things to work together for good to those who love God and are called according to his purpose. Whether I live or die doesn't matter."

"It matters. This is murder," Atretes said darkly. "You won't stand a chance against Rolf. Holt would've taught his son everything he knows, and he was champion in my father's time. I swear your death will be—"

"Listen to me, Atretes. Do *God's* will. Do not be conformed to your people, but be transformed by the renewing of your mind that you may prove what is the will of God, that which is good and acceptable and perfect. Remember what I've taught you."

"I'm not like you."

"You're more like me than you know. You must listen. There's little time. Christ's divine power has granted to you everything pertaining to life and godliness through the true knowledge of Jesus Christ who called you. Be diligent to present yourself approved as a warrior who doesn't need to be ashamed."

"I am a warrior and will act as one."

"You're speaking as a man, Atretes. Live for God."

"So I'm to do nothing?"

"Everything. Love your people."

"Love them!" he snarled, casting a dark look at those around them. "After this night?"

"Despite it."

"I was chief."

"Just so. And as such, were you ever part of these rites?"

Atretes gave him a bleak look. "You know I was."

"Then remember the life out of which Christ called you. Remember what it felt like to live in darkness." He saw his friend's stubborn pride. "Atretes, listen to me for God's sake. Let these people see the fruit of the Spirit at work in you. Let the Lord break Tiwaz's hold on your people. Give yourself wholeheartedly to God and let *him* produce in you the love, joy, peace, patience, kindness, goodness, faithfulness, gentleness, and self-restraint that proclaims him almighty God. No law, no empire can stand against these things."

"I will think on it."

"Don't think on it! *Do* the word I've taught you. Walk in a manner worthy of Jesus Christ. Please God in all aspects of your life."

"I could easier die for him myself than stand by and watch you butchered!"

"Satan knows that better than you. You've got to resist him. Hold to your faith and rest in Christ. If I die tonight, *rejoice*. I will be with our Lord! There's no power great enough to separate me from Christ Jesus. You know death cannot."

The men in the forefront stopped. Holt came back to them, the torchlight revealing his anger and fear. "Be silent!" He glared at Atretes. "You know the law."

Atretes stiffened at the reprimand, but Theophilus nodded and said no more.

As they came to the sacred grove, Theophilus saw a fire was burning in a protected casement. An old priest was waiting for them, his heavy white linen tunic interwoven with purple designs. An ancient oak was at the center, and when all were seated, he removed the emblems of Tiwaz hidden within its trunk.

Reverently, Gundrid held up the golden horns for all to see. He always relished this moment and the power he felt come with it. He chanted and swayed as he placed them upon a rough stone altar near the fire that was kept perpetually burning.

Atretes untied the rope from around Theophilus' wrists and ankles. Rolling it up, he set it to one side.

Taking a dagger from his belt, Gundrid cut his own arm and let his blood drip over the sacred horns. Rud came forward and did likewise, then passed the ceremonial dagger to Holt. When Holt finished the rite, Gundrid took the dagger. Placing it flat on both palms, he turned and held it out expectantly to Atretes.

"We have waited long for your return. Atretes, son of the great Hermun, high chief of the Chatti, Tiwaz awaits the renewal of your vows."

Atretes remained sitting. He looked at Gundrid and said nothing.

The old priest stepped closer. "Take the dagger from my hand." Anomia had warned him Atretes had lost faith. "You are a man of honor," he said, wanting the glory of bringing him back. "Remember your vow."

Atretes stood slowly. "I recant Tiwaz," he said loud enough for all to hear.

Gundrid drew back from him. Clutching the dagger's handle, he held it at his side. "You dare speak thus before the altar of our god?" he said, his voice rising with each word he uttered.

"I dare," Atretes said calmly, his countenance as fierce as any other man present. He looked from face to face, seeing men who had been his friends and who now looked at him with wary distrust, anger, and fear. "I dare more. I proclaim Jesus Christ is Lord of all!" he shouted, his voice carrying through the sacred wood.

A dark wind blew, shaking the leaves and branches as it came on like the approach of a malevolent being. Fear filled Gundrid, and he called out a frantic prayer, beseeching Tiwaz to withhold his wrath from them. Even Atretes felt dread as the frogs and insects went silent in the woods around them, and a coldness crept into the circle that had gathered before the eternal flame. He felt a presence, one so cold that it was hot.

Gundrid cast something into the fire, and colors exploded around him, sparks flying upward. The smell of burning sulphur drifted on the air, mingling with other stranger smells. His eyes rolled back in his head as something seemed to take possession of him. Words, incomprehensible, came pouring from his lips, his voice deeper and guttural, a savage growl.

"Tiwaz speaks," Rud said, and all those watching sat in terror, banging their weapons against their shields and shouting. The baritus rose, filling the darkness. "Tiwaz! Tiwaz! *Tiwaz!*" The name sounded like a drumbeat, building until the priest uttered a scream that made Atretes' stomach tremble and his hair stand on end. Whatever had come upon Gundrid departed.

The men fell silent, watching and waiting.

Dazed, Gundrid looked at Atretes standing before him. He saw with keener insight the doubt and fear flickering in the younger man's eyes. Tiwaz had not lost his hold entirely.

"You have been deceived, Atretes," Gundrid said and pointed an accusing finger at Theophilus. "Tiwaz has revealed this man's hidden motives to me!" He looked around at the warriors gathered. "The Roman speaks peace," he shouted, "but brings to us lies and a false god in an attempt to weaken our people!" He spread his arms, encompassing all present. "If you listen, you will be destroyed!"

The Chatti warriors shouted vows to Tiwaz. Gundrid listened, raising his hands again and encouraging them to shout even louder. He was triumphant as he looked at the Roman sitting beside Atretes. He knew a more fitting end for the Roman's life than an honorable contest with a Chatti warrior.

Righteous anger filled Theophilus as he looked into the gloating eyes of the old priest. He saw with a clarity that came from the Holy Spirit that Gundrid didn't want the match to take place. He intended to circumvent it by making the warriors believe Tiwaz craved a human sacrifice instead.

Lord, I'd rather die fighting than on an altar to Satan! And what of these men? If they make a tribal alliance and revolt against Rome now, they'll be annihilated like the Jews.

The baritus was deafening.

Theophilus stood abruptly. "I was brought here to fight your champion over the matter of a tribal alliance!" he shouted in challenge. The deafening roar quieted as he stepped boldly into the center of the circle and faced Gundrid. "Or is your god afraid of the outcome?"

Men began to shout against their shields.

Young Rolf jumped to his feet and strode into the circle, eager for the battle. "You will die, Roman!"

"For Tiwaz! *For Tiwaz!*"

Theophilus removed his belt. "Christ Jesus, be with me. Give me strength and endurance," he said and pulled his gladius from its sheath. "May this battle be for your glory, Lord." He heaved the belt out into the darkness.

The sword as well, came a still, quiet voice.

Theophilus felt as though the air had been punched from him. His palm went slick with sweat, his heart pounding.

"Lord?" he whispered in disbelief.

The sword.

"Jesus, do you want me to die?"

The young Chatti warrior advanced on him, grinning savagely, eager to use the deadly spatha in his hand.

Those who live by the sword, die by the sword.

Theophilus inhaled a lungful of air through his nose and then released it out his mouth. "So be it." He flung the gladius out into the darkness.

Rolf stopped in surprise and straightened, frowning.

"What are you doing?" Atretes cried out as what little hope he had had died. Theophilus paid him no heed.

Lord, Lord! Theophilus prayed. *Do I just stand here and die? Do I let him cut me to pieces like a lamb for the slaughter? I thought I came to stop a war.*

Joshua. Samson. David. The names became like a drumbeat in his head. *Joshua. Samson. David.*

"Kill him!" Gundrid screamed, the spirit within him full of fear. *"Kill him now!"*

The warriors rose en masse as Rolf charged, crying out, "Tiwaz!" He swung the spatha with enough force to split Theophilus' body in half. Theophilus dodged left, turned sharply, and brought his fist down hard on the back of Rolf's head. He dented the helmet and sent the young warrior staggering to one knee.

Theophilus stepped to one side of the circle and waited. Atretes stared in disbelief. *"Finish him!"*

But Theophilus didn't. Rolf rose, shaking his head. Theophilus didn't move. Rolf turned, eyes unfocused. He was breathing hard, his face flushed. Before his head cleared, he brought the spatha up and lunged forward.

With the agility of a seasoned athlete, Theophilus dodged, dipped, and punched him hard in the sternum. Rolf staggered back, but didn't go down. Exhaling hard, Theophilus punched him again with his full strength. The young champion went down like a toppled tree. He fought for breath and, after a few seconds, sagged back and lay still, arms and legs splayed.

Not a Chatti warrior moved or breathed. The battle hadn't even lasted a minute and their champion lay as though dead on the ground.

"All glory to you, Lord God," Theophilus said aloud. He raised his head and turned, looking squarely at the priest.

Gundrid shook with fear. No one breathed.

Theophilus went down on one knee beside Rolf and put his hand against the young warrior's neck. He felt a strong pulse. He put his hand on Rolf's chest and felt it rise. He was breathing again. Theophilus took the spatha from Rolf's hand and rose. He glanced at Atretes and saw his friend's emotions were torn. It was a Chatti warrior lying helpless, after all, a kinsman.

Theophilus' gaze moved slowly around the circle of men standing. He could see in their faces how they tried to harden themselves for Rolf's death. Holt closed his eyes, for it was his dead brother's son who lay at Theophilus' feet. Not a warrior present would move to stop the Roman from taking Rolf's life. It was a matter of honor.

He tossed the spatha on the ground before Rud.

Surprised, the high chief searched his face. After a moment, he gave a stiff nod. "There will be no alliance."

37

Though the men and women still avoided Theophilus after that night, it wasn't long before all noticed the children had no fear or distrust of him. He sang as he worked, and the younger children came to listen. At first they kept their distance, hiding behind trees or climbing up into them and peering at him from the branches. Gradually, they lost their timidity. One brave little soul called out a question from a high branch, and Theophilus paused to answer. His manner was warm and friendly, and so they came down from lofty perches and out from behind trees, and sat on the grass in the sunshine to listen to him.

Theophilus told them stories.

An anxious young mother came looking for her son. "You shouldn't be here. Anomia told you we were to stay away from this man. Do you want the wrath of Tiwaz to fall upon us?"

The child balked and whined. "I want to hear the end of the story."

"Obey your mother," Theophilus said gently from where he sat. "The story can wait for another time."

"You others," the young mother said, waving her hands. "Go home and leave this man alone before Anomia finds out you're here. *Go!*"

Theophilus sat by himself for a long while, his head down. With a sigh, he rose and went back to his work stripping bark and splitting lumber for his grubenhaus. He sensed someone watching him. Pausing, he looked around and saw a man standing in the shadows some distance away. He couldn't make out who he was, and the man made no move to approach him. Theophilus returned to his work. When he glanced up a moment later, the man was gone.

*

Rizpah was tired of hearing Varus and Atretes shouting at one another. Her head ached. It seemed to be the Chatti custom to drink before carrying on a serious debate. Other men had joined them until the longhouse was crowded with warriors, most drunk on beer, some on honeyed mead. Even the young warrior Rolf was in attendance, sitting near the wall, his expression morose, his blue eyes glittering as he listened, but he didn't join in.

Varus' stubborn refusal to listen met head-on with Atretes' stinging sarcasm. Rizpah cringed inwardly as his remarks succeeded only in driving Varus into a towering rage. Had Atretes forgotten everything Theophilus had taught him?

She wished Freyja was present, for Atretes' mother would've known how to soften this maelstrom into rational debate, but she was in the sacred woods, meditating and praying to Tiwaz.

God, help her to see!

Rizpah wanted to cry out for them to stop, but she knew it would be to no avail. Whenever she spoke, no one listened, not even Atretes when he was this caught up in his emotions. At first, she thought it was because she was a woman. Yet others were treated with respect. They were heard. Their words were heeded.

Atretes told her Chatti men brought a dowry of livestock to the woman, and the woman gave the man weapons. Marriage was a partnership made for a lifetime, and the woman shared in the man's adventure. She carried supplies of food to the battlefield and even remained to encourage her husband and sons in the fighting. Chatti men believed there resided in women an element of holiness and a gift of prophecy, which explained why Freyja and Anomia were held in awe.

It wasn't until Rizpah accidentally overheard a conversation between Freyja and Varus that she understood why no one listened to what she had to say. Anomia made sure no Chatti would listen, for the young priestess had warned everyone that she was an Ionian witch who had come to deceive them.

Rizpah said nothing to Atretes about this for fear of what he would do. Anomia roused passions in him that were best left untapped, and the less he had to do with her, the better.

Rizpah could do nothing but accept the situation. She listened as they shouted back and forth, praying with quiet dignity and perseverance all the while she served them.

God, show me what to do. Show me how to do it. Give me your love for these people. Let me hide myself in your peace and not let the storm shake my faith.

Even as she served food to the men debating with Atretes, she meditated on the Scriptures Shimei and Theophilus had taught her. Around her, other men filled their horns with honeyed wine and beer. She went over psalms that spoke to her of God's sovereignty, his provision, his love—all while the men argued.

The Lord is my Shepherd, I shall not want. Over and over, she said the words in her mind, slowly, to calm her nerves, then even more slowly, to savor and treasure them as they brought forth the peace she craved, a peace beyond understanding.

She didn't think anyone noticed.

"Guilty! How am I guilty?" Varus raged, standing on his good leg, his face contorted.

"Sit down and hear me out!" Atretes shouted.

"I've heard enough! Bow down to this weakling god of yours, but I won't. Forgive? I'll never bend my neck to him."

"You'll bend your neck or *go to hell*!"

Frightened, Caleb put his hands against his ears and started to cry. She picked him up and held him close, speaking quietly to allay his fears. Atretes became impatient. "Take him outside! Get him out of here!"

She left the longhouse, thanking God for the respite. She let her breath out in relief and nuzzled her son's neck. He smelled so good to her. "He's not angry with you, little one," she said, kissing him. "He's angry at the world."

Marta's children ran to her, eager to play with their little cousin. Laughing, she put Caleb down. Most of the children in the village ran about naked and dirty. Other than to make sure they didn't wander off too far, the mothers left them to roam and play at will. Caleb delighted in their exuberant company, as did she. What a blessed change from the gathering of angry men in the longhouse.

"Elsa! Derek!" Marta called from where she worked at her loom just outside the doorway of her longhouse. "Come away from Rizpah and stop bothering her."

"They're no bother, Marta," Rizpah said, smiling.

Marta ignored her. "Derek! Come here!"

Rizpah's smile faded as the children walked glumly back to their mother. Others were called away until she stood alone in the street, Caleb bobbing up and down and chattering excitedly. Marta spoke to her children briefly and nodded toward the woods. They argued, but were quickly silenced and sent on their way. Elsa looked back at Rizpah, her expression poignant.

"Go, Elsa!"

Caleb wanted to go with them. "Sa! Sa! Sa!" he said, toddling after his older cousin. Crying, Elsa started to run. Caleb fell. Pushing himself up, he cried. "Sa . . . Sa . . ."

Hurt, Rizpah knelt down and set him aright. Brushing off his linen tunic, she kissed him. Straightening, Rizpah lifted Caleb and looked across at Marta. How could she do this?

Pressing her face into Caleb's neck, she prayed. "God, take my anger away," she murmured, fighting back tears. Raising her head, she saw Marta was sitting with her head down, her hands still in her lap.

Her anger toward her sister-in-law evaporated. Marta wasn't cruel. She was afraid. When she looked up again, Rizpah smiled at her gently to show she held no ill will against her. She remembered what it was like to live in darkness and be afraid.

"We'll go for a walk and visit Theophilus," she murmured to Caleb and started down the street again.

"Theo . . . Theo . . ."

"Yes, Theo." She set him down and took his hand, pacing her steps to his much smaller ones.

Theophilus' grubenhaus was almost finished. A small fire was burning in the open area in front of it, but their friend was nowhere around. Curious, she stepped down into the sunken hut to see inside. He had done more digging since the last time she came to see the house. The hollow was five feet deep and ten by twelve feet in size. In the far corner was a pallet of straw and two thick, woolen blankets. Nearby was his gear, neatly stacked.

A simple timber structure was erected over the sunken room, the superstructure comprised of a gabled framework of slanting poles tied to a ridge pole that was held aloft on six uprights. The walls were made of rough-hewn planks, the roof was covered with thatch, the floor was beaten clay.

The grubenhaus smelled of clean, rich earth. It was cool inside now, but she knew in the winter with a small fire burning, it would be comfortably warm.

"What do you think?" Theophilus said from the doorway above and behind her. Startled, she glanced back at him. He rested one arm against the lintel and leaned down, smiling at her.

"It feels more inviting than Varus' longhouse." She immediately regretted her remark. She hadn't meant to criticize.

As she came outside into the sunshine, Theophilus took Caleb from her and lifted him in the air, jiggling him and getting him to laugh. She smiled as she watched him play with her son. Atretes was so busy arguing with his kinsmen, he had no time for Caleb.

She noticed the dressed rabbit Theophilus had spitted and set over the fire.

"A good, fat one," Theophilus remarked. "Stay and share a meal with me."

"I'd love to stay, but share with Caleb. I'm not very hungry."

He assessed her face and saw she was deeply troubled. "Things aren't going well?"

"Well enough under the circumstances, I suppose," she said evasively and saw his look. "He's sharing the gospel. In fact, he's shouting it to the very rafters. And Varus and the others shout right back about the power of Tiwaz." She sat down and rubbed her temples. "He's not listening to them. They're not listening to him. No one's listening to anyone or anything."

"God works through people in spite of their shortcomings, beloved, and often through them." He put Caleb down and gave him a pat on the behind.

She looked up at him bleakly. "I want to believe that, Theophilus, but when I watch Atretes and listen, I can't see the difference between him and all the others, except that I love him. I wish he would bridle his tongue."

Caleb sat down beside her and played with the grass. She ran her hand tenderly over his dark hair as she went on. "Varus and the others are stubborn and proud and fierce beyond all reckoning. So is Atretes. There are times when he looks ready to grab Varus by the throat and throttle him if he won't believe in Jesus as Lord."

"I've felt that kind of frustration before." Theophilus grinned. "It was a *long* road to Germania."

She smiled. She remembered as well—far better than he—and she didn't want to see Atretes revert to the kind of man he had been.

Her head was aching. She rubbed her temples again. "It took a miracle to change Atretes' mind about Jesus."

"Miracles are happening around us every day, Rizpah."

She rose, agitated. "You know the sort of miracle I mean. It would take the sun going down at noon to convince these people."

"Sit," he said gently, and she did so.

"Atretes hasn't changed, Theophilus. He's as angry now as he ever was. I've never seen a man so determined to have his way. And if he does, he'll drag his people kicking and screaming into the kingdom of God, whether they want to be there or not."

Restless, she got up and turned his rabbit.

His mouth curved in amusement as she sat down again. She was full of nervous energy. If she'd been in the army, he would have ordered her to run it off.

"Do you remember when you told us the Word of God is the sword of truth?" she said.

"I remember."

"Well, Atretes has taken that to his heart. He slashes at his kinsmen with words. He batters them mercilessly with the truth. The gospel has become a weapon in his hands."

Theophilus sat and clasped his hands between his knees. "He will learn."

"After he's driven these people back into the arms of Tiwaz?"

"They never left."

"And this will make them want to leave? I fear for all of them, Theophilus. I fear for Marta and the children. I fear most for Atretes. He's on fire for the Lord, but what of *love*?" She wondered sometimes if Atretes was more concerned with saving his pride than saving souls.

"What have you to fear, Rizpah?" Theophilus asked quietly. "Do you really think God's plan will collapse over the frailties of one man's temper?"

His quiet calm stilled the riotous thoughts whirling in her head.

She knew what he was really asking. Did she believe God was sovereign? Did she believe God had a plan for Atretes and her and these people? Did she have faith enough in Jesus to believe he would complete the work he had begun?

One question stood before her, stark and simple: *Where lies your faith, Rizpah? In others? In yourself? Or in Me?*

Tears pricked. "My faith is weak." *O Lord, my God, I'm such a poor vessel. Pathetic. Ridiculous. Why do you put up with me?*

"You have what God has given you."

"It's not enough."

"Who knows better than God what you need, beloved?"

She raised her face, letting the sun warm her. She wanted to hold onto his words, hold them tight. She lowered her head and closed her eyes. "In the mornings, when we all pray together,

Atretes is so calm. He's happy. In the morning, I believe nothing will stop the Lord from fulfilling his purpose in our lives. I'm filled with assurance and hope."

She looked at her friend, wishing she were more like him. "It's later, when I listen to all the angry shouting, that I wonder who's really in command."

She looked up at the blue sky and the drifting white clouds. "Sometimes, I wish Jesus would come back now, this minute, and set things right. I wish he'd shake the earth and open all their eyes to Satan's schemes. Then Varus and Freyja and Marta and all the rest who live in fear of Tiwaz would know." She thought of the look on Marta's face. The poor woman was afraid and ashamed. "I wish they could see Jesus and all his majesty and glory coming down from heaven. Then they'd know Tiwaz is nothing. Then they would be free."

"Not everyone who saw the signs and wonders Jesus performed was convinced he was the incarnate Son of God."

"Atretes was convinced."

"Atretes was ready to be convinced. Someone had planted the seed before you met him."

"Hadassah."

"He was hungry for Christ. Miracles are no guarantee faith will follow and never more important than the message of salvation."

"Yes. We wait and hope. And we pray."

He smiled and said nothing.

She sighed. "Patience has never been one of my virtues, Theophilus."

"You'll learn."

"It's how I'll learn that concerns me sometimes." She gave him a wistful smile. "Don't you wish Jesus would come back *now* and save us all this trouble?"

"With every breath I take."

She laughed. "Thank God I'm not alone. I have an idea. Why don't we build a house honoring the Lord and go inside and close the doors and never come out again."

Though she jested, he saw the desperate unhappiness in her eyes. "What light can shine from a closed house, beloved? God wants us *in* the world, not hiding from it."

Her smile fell away, her own frustration revealed. "Atretes isn't hiding. He's standing in the center of an arena again, lashing out at any who oppose him. He lambastes brother, kinsmen, and friends alike." She waved her hand toward the village. "When I left, he was in the midst of a *yelling* match with Varus about the *peace* of God and what it could mean to the Chatti. Peace, Theophilus. How will they ever understand when this is the way he tells them?"

"He will learn, Rizpah. He *will* learn. We need to be patient with him."

"As he's patient with them?"

"No, as God is patient with us. Contrary to what you're thinking right now, Atretes shouldn't be your first concern. Our first obligation is to the Lord."

"I know, but . . ."

"You know, but are you acting according to what you know or what you feel?"

She sat down, feeling bereft. She had always been quick to speak and slow to listen. It was one of her failings, like Atretes' quick, hot temper and long, seething memory.

Theophilus stood and turned the rabbit. "Look upon Atretes as a child in faith. He's learning to walk by faith, the way Caleb learned to walk on his two legs. Remember how he stumbled and fell over and over at first. Sometimes he hurt himself. He was clumsy. He went where he shouldn't go. And often he cried in frustration." He straightened and nodded his head toward the sunny meadow. "Look at him now." Caleb was toddling happily after a butterfly. "Every day, his feet are more sure."

He smiled at her. "We're the same way. We're learning to walk with Christ. It's a process, not a finished act. We make a decision for the Lord and are saved, but it doesn't end there. We have to apply ourselves diligently to our own sanctification. What Scripture I know, I'll give to you. You apply God's Word in day-to-day practical living. The truth itself will witness to these people."

"But look around you. There's so much here that is contrary to what God tells us is right."

"Our work isn't to change the way these people live. It's not to fight against a pagan idol any more than it's for Atretes to try to beat into their heads a belief in Christ. Our work is to devote our own lives to pleasing God. It's that simple. We're to devote our efforts to learning to *think* as God thinks, to *see* ourselves and others through his eyes, to *walk* as he walked. That's our life's work."

"You're saying I shouldn't correct Atretes?"

"Gently. In private. And only if he'll listen."

"I've tried. I have things straight in my head and then I open my mouth and it comes out wrong. Sometimes, even when I have it right, he takes it wrong."

"I've talked with him, too. And I rest in this: The Holy Spirit will work within Atretes without our help, perhaps in spite of it." Unless Atretes ever decided to silence the still, quiet voice that had called him in the first place. Theophilus prayed unceasingly that would never happen. "Atretes is faced with a greater battle now than he ever faced in an arena."

Rizpah knew and wanted to weep. "He's losing the battle," she said bleakly. *God, hasn't he had to fight enough?*

Theophilus watched her stand and catch up with Caleb. She took a rock out of his mouth and tossed it away. Wiping the dirt off his face with the hem of her shawl, she spoke to him gently, gave him a pat. She smiled as he headed for the mound of dirt Theophilus had piled up while digging out the grubenhaus, good rich dirt he would spread soon in order to prepare a field for planting.

She returned. It was a warm day, and yet she drew her shawl around her shoulders. "Atretes doesn't listen to me anyway."

"He listens. More important, he watches. For as long as I've known him, he's had his eyes on you."

She gave a short laugh. "Not because I was a Christian."

His grin made her blush. "True, he watched you with less than honorable intentions in the beginning, but what he saw was a beautiful young woman practicing her faith. Your walk with the Lord has had an impact upon him. It'll continue to have impact."

"My walk has been less than perfect, Theophilus." How many times had she said words she regretted?

"That's why I'm reminding you. The sin we need to be concerned about is the sin in our own lives. It's the root of all human woe, the source of anguish. Let God deal with Atretes."

She rose and caught up with Caleb again, bringing him closer.

When she came back again, he could see his words were troubling her. "He doesn't seem to *see* what he's doing. Or what's happening around him. Anomia has such influence over these people. Varus hangs on every word she says. She has no fear of God at all, not even of Tiwaz, whom she worships."

Theophilus was well aware what Rizpah was saying was true, but he didn't want to talk about the young priestess.

"God speaks to these people every day. The Chatti are from the same root stock as we are. They're descendants of Adam and Eve. Look around you, beloved, and rest assured all creation proclaims God's glory to them. And even when they resist, even when they refuse to see, the Lord gave them another gift besides: a conscience."

Theophilus leaned forward, intent to set her mind at rest. "Atretes' conscience knew his inner motives and true thoughts before he was redeemed by Jesus and received the Holy Spirit. No matter how hard he tried to justify himself and his actions, the conscience God gave him wouldn't allow it."

He nodded toward the sacred wood. "Have you watched Freyja? Really watched her? She *struggles* against the forces holding her. She's troubled by them. There's no rest for her. Just as Atretes suffered his demons, she suffers hers. His conscience warned him instinctively of God's judgment and hell to come, just as hers warns her now. His conscience tormented him because he had sinned, just as hers is doing now. Sin produces guilt."

"But neither of them is responsible for what's happened to them. It wasn't Atretes' fault he was made a gladiator."

"Everything we do, we do by choice. Circumstances don't alter right and wrong."

"They would've killed him."

"Maybe."

"Maybe? You know they would have, and he'd have died *unsaved*."

His mouth curved wryly. "You've seen Rolf. I should be dead right now. I *assumed* I would be dead when I stepped into the circle with him. I *assumed* it was time for me to die for the Lord. Rolf is younger, stronger, quicker, smarter. I had no shield the night I faced him, and God told me to get rid of my sword. Who prevailed?"

"You did."

"No, Rizpah." He smiled tenderly. "*God* prevailed."

He took the rabbit from the spit and called Caleb to come eat with him. Rizpah watched him cut the rabbit in pieces and peel some of the meat away from the bone to cool for Caleb. While he waited, he played with the child as easily as he talked with her. Watching the man, her heart swelled with love for him.

Lord, what would we have done without him? Father, we never would have made it if you hadn't sent him to us in Ephesus. Why can't Atretes and I be more like him? The evidence of his faith radiates to everyone around him. My faith is paltry at best, and Atretes drives people away. O Lord, what would we do without Theophilus' wise counsel?

And even as she thought these things, a sharp inexplicable pang of fear struck her.

She could feel the darkness closing in around them, trying to obliterate the light.

38

Atretes left the longhouse, blood pumping hot and fast with anger. If he'd stayed another minute, he would have pummeled his brother and taken on the rest. Let God rain brimstone on their heads! They deserved it.

He saw Marta sitting at her loom across the street and strode toward her. "Have you seen Rizpah?"

"She went along that way," she said, avoiding his eyes, her face pale.

"Have you been crying?"

"Why would you think that?" Marta said, pushing the shuttle between the threads.

"Because you look it. What's the matter?"

"Nothing. Nothing's the matter." Her hands trembled as she worked the loom. She kept seeing the look on Rizpah face when she'd called Elsa and Derek away. Surprise. Hurt.

She felt ashamed.

"Is she with Mother?"

"No."

He glanced at her sharply. "Why do you say it like that?"

"Say it like what?" She tilted her head, defensive.

"Don't take that tone with me, Marta." Was she going to set herself against him also?

"Why not?" she said, her own emotions playing havoc. "Because you might start yelling at me, the way you've been yelling at Varus and Usipi and the others?" She stood up. "Don't ask what's the matter with me, Atretes. What's the matter with *you*?" She fled into her longhouse, weeping.

He stared after her, baffled and even more frustrated.

"She'll be all right," came a sultry voice from just behind him.

Turning his head grimly, he looked at Anomia. She was the last person he wanted to see right now.

She watched his gaze move over her as he turned and faced her. She had chosen her tunic carefully, well aware how the white linen fell smoothly against the lush curves of her body.

Atretes noticed. He couldn't help himself. She savored the

moment, breathing in softly, inhaling triumph. His eyes darkened in a telltale way. *Good.* She relished his lust, even more so because he fought his attraction to her. Let him fight it. His inner struggle would make the consummation so much sweeter. And fierce.

"We should talk," she said.

"About what?"

So terse. His emotions were high. "I've been listening to what you've had to say. The god of whom you speak sounds . . . interesting."

"Indeed," he said dryly.

She smiled up at him. "Do you doubt me?"

"Should I?"

He was not like Varus, but that was good. Varus was boring, weak, and predictable. "Are you afraid to discuss this Jesus of yours with a high priestess of Tiwaz?"

His mouth tipped. "I'm still having trouble seeing Ania's little sister as a high priestess of anything."

She didn't show how his words angered her. How dare he mock her like some foolish, weakling child? Concealing her true feelings, she pouted for him, feigning amusement. "Are you worried I might ask a question you can't answer?"

His eyes flickered at the challenge. "Ask."

"How can you or I be held responsible for what one man or one woman did thousands of years ago?"

He explained about Adam and Eve's encounter with Satan in the same way Theophilus had explained to him, but she laughed.

"A neat but ludicrous story, Atretes. No wonder the men won't believe you."

"What's ludicrous about it?"

She pretended surprise that he would even ask. "You can't be so easily swayed," she said, widening her eyes in dismay. "Think about what you're telling us. Why should we feel guilty for the choice made by a man and woman thousands of years ago in a place you've never seen or even heard of? Were you there? No. Was I? No. Would you have stood by while your wife was being seduced? I have a hard time imagining it, but then . . ." She paused deliberately as though something unpleasant had occurred to her. She let her gaze drift toward the woods where the Roman was finishing his grubenhaus.

Glancing up, she saw Atretes' gaze drift as well. He was a

passionate man and a possessive one. It wouldn't be too difficult to arouse his suspicions about his Roman friend and the fidelity of that little black-eyed Ionian witch.

Atretes frowned. Where was Rizpah? He had sent her outside, expecting her to return when Caleb calmed down. She had been gone for more than an hour. He didn't like the idea of her being alone with a man, even Theophilus.

Anomia saw with growing irritation that she was forgotten. When he started to walk away, she reached out quickly and placed her hand lightly on his arm. "Where are you going, Atretes?"

"To find my wife."

She saw how much he wanted to find her, and a surge of jealousy heated her blood. What did he see in that olive-skinned foreigner? "She's in the woods with that Roman friend of yours," she said, planting a seed.

Atretes didn't like the way she said it. What game was she playing?

"One more question, Atretes, about this idea of some vague sin of which we're supposedly guilty. Why do you think a Roman would want you to believe such things?" she said, pouring water on the seed she had planted. Looking up into Atretes' handsome face, she offered up a silent prayer to Tiwaz that doubt would take root and spread.

Let Atretes turn from that outsider and come to me! Bring your minions to bear upon him. Make him mine!

Atretes patted her hand distractedly. "We'll talk another time," he said and walked away.

Anomia stared after him, lips parted, hands curling into fists.

*

Atretes strode down the village main street.

"She's in the woods with that Roman friend of yours."

He was annoyed that one remark could set his thinking on such a dark path. Rizpah had given him no reason to doubt her fidelity, nor had Theophilus. Yet one blatantly false comment sent his imagination flying! He knew what Anomia was trying to do, but knowing didn't help. In the space of an instant, he had seen his wife in Theophilus' grubenhaus, lying on the earthen floor, entangled . . .

A growling sound came from deep in his throat. He shook his head, trying to shake the thought out. Rizpah was nothing like Julia. It would never even occur to her to marry one man and have another as a lover. Yet he felt an urgency to find them, to set his mind at rest.

Nothing had gone the way he'd thought it would when he returned home. He had expected resistance to the new faith he brought, but he hadn't expected other feelings to creep in. He looked around the village of rough-hewn buildings, dirty children running naked in the streets, and remembered the cobbled streets and marble halls of Rome. He sat in the longhouse, smelling the unwashed bodies of his kinsmen and remembered the pristine Roman baths filled with the aromas of scented oils. He listened to Varus and the others, drunk and shouting for the sake of argument, and thought about the long hours of quiet, yet invigorating discussion he had with Theophilus. Eleven years! Eleven long, grueling years he had dreamed of coming home. And now he was . . . and he didn't belong.

He was more comfortable with Theophilus, a Roman, than he was with his own kinsmen. It disturbed him. It made him feel he was betraying his people, his heritage, his race.

He walked along the path and saw the clearing ahead. Theophilus sat near a small cook fire, sharing a meal with Caleb. He was talking, Rizpah, sitting opposite, listened intently. It was an innocent enough scene, two friends sharing a meal together, carrying on conversation, comfortable with one another. It shouldn't bother him, but it did.

Theophilus saw him first and called a greeting.

Rizpah turned her head and rose. She smiled at him, and he felt the punch of desire, like a fist in his gut. And he felt something more. He knew, without a doubt, that he could trust her. He took her hand and kissed her palm. "I wondered where you were," he said roughly.

"Dada . . . Dada . . ." Caleb waved a partially chewed rabbit leg at him.

He laughed, relaxing, Anomia's words completely forgotten.

"Isn't this nice?" Rizpah said. "It's so quiet, you can hear the birds singing. You have to see the inside of Theophilus' house." She wove her fingers with his. "Come look."

Atretes had to duck his head to enter, but could stand straight once inside. Theophilus' grubenhaus was larger than the others in the village, the structure overhead strong. "Good work, Theophilus!" he called back through the doorway. "You build like a German!"

Theophilus laughed in response.

"Wouldn't it be nice to have a home like this ourselves?" Rizpah said, letting go of him and turning full circle. Atretes glanced at her and saw a longing he hadn't noticed before. The quiet enfolded them again. All he could hear were the birds outside and the beat of his own heart in his ears.

Atretes watched her move around the sunken room. It *would* be nice to get out from under Varus' roof, even if all they had was a canopy of sky over their heads. Just so they could be alone again.

I'll have to do what I can about our own home, he thought, watching her. A smile quirked his lips. *And soon.*

*

"I think you're right," he said, propping his head up on his hand. When she made no answer, he smiled and brushed his fingertips lightly over her lips. "Don't go to sleep, *Liebchen*. We have to go back soon."

"I know. I was just enjoying the quiet."

Leaning down, he kissed her tenderly. "Were you dreaming about a grubenhaus of our own?"

She touched his hair, a faint frown settling. "It would hurt your mother if you left."

He noticed she didn't include herself.

But again, she was right. He lay on his back, staring up through the canopy of pine branches. His mother would be hurt. "Things would be better if Varus would listen to me."

"Or if you would listen to him."

He turned his head sharply. "To what? His blind, pigheaded foolishness about Tiwaz?"

"No," she said gently. "Listen to his fear."

He snorted. "Varus has never been afraid of anything," he said, dismissing the possibility.

Rizpah could feel his anger ease slightly. She didn't want to rouse it again, but had to speak. "The other evening when Theophilus won the match against Rolf, you came back exultant, didn't you?"

He gave a slight laugh. "Of course. God showed his power is greater than Tiwaz's."

"Think what your people must feel." She turned to him, propping her head up and looking at him. "Weren't you afraid when the Lord brought me back to life?"

"Terrified," he said, his mind suddenly clearing with understanding.

"And you were prepared."

"Prepared?"

"You'd been hearing the gospel from the time we left the Ephesian port, to the catacombs, and along the road over the Alps." She smiled. "Against your will, most of the time."

He laughed ruefully. "I couldn't get away from it."

"You laugh now, my love, but you weren't laughing then."

"No," he said, remembering. "I didn't laugh then." He'd done everything he could to keep from hearing the gospel. The Word had struck raw nerves, sunk deep, and worried him.

She put her hand on his arm. "Varus and your mother and all the others had never even heard the name Jesus until a few weeks ago." She watched his face tighten. She gently brushed her fingers across his brow. "God was patient with you, my love. Be patient with them."

He sat up. "Varus insults God. He mocks him to my face."

She uttered a quick, silent prayer. "And you didn't?" she said, reminding him as gently as she could.

Sighing, Atretes closed his eyes and rubbed the back of his neck.

Rizpah rose and knelt behind him. Combing her fingers through his long hair, she kissed him and then began to knead the taut muscles in his neck and shoulders. "Love them, Atretes."

"It doesn't come as easily for me as it does for you."

She thought of Marta calling her children away and Caleb crying because he wanted to play with them. "It's not easy for me, either, but if we allow anger to reside in us, we're more guilty than they are because we know the better way. Anger doesn't achieve the righteousness of God, nor will it open their hearts to hear his Word. Anger stirs up strife. You've got to put your anger aside, Atretes. Otherwise, you'll never hear what Varus and the others are saying to us and what stands in the way to their acceptance of Christ."

"I can't sit and say nothing like you do."

"Speak then, but speak from love."

"From love," he said drolly. Shrugging off her hands, he rose and stepped away from her. "Your way takes too long. My people have to accept the truth *now*, before it's too late."

"It's not my way, Atretes. It's the Lord's way. Remember what we've been taught. 'Love the Lord your God with all your heart, and with all your soul, and with all your *mind*, and love your neighbor as yourself.' Love isn't the easy way. It's an act of will to follow Jesus. If you love Jesus, you *must* do his will. And his will is that we love others as he first loved us."

"I can't."

"No," she said. "You can't."

Atretes shook his head, annoyed because he didn't understand her. "First you say I must, then agree I can't. What do you want from me?"

"I want you to understand, and I haven't the right words to explain. I'm not like Theophilus, so knowledgeable with Scripture. But I know what the Lord tells me."

"What does God tell you?"

"It's not our love that will reach Varus. It's Christ's love. We have to decide to listen to the Lord each time a situation arises where our own pride wants to take control."

"So you're saying I should ignore Varus' insults?"

"Yes."

"Say nothing when he mocks God?"

"Yes."

"Be kind," he sneered.

"Yes."

"Varus needs to learn respect, if not for God, then at least for me as his older brother and a chief of the Chatti."

She saw the anger building in his eyes, the self-defense, the pride. But she couldn't let it go. She couldn't leave things as they were. She was concerned for Varus and Freyja and the others, but more concerned for what she saw happening to Atretes.

"Atretes, how can you hate your brother and still love God?"

He frowned, deeply troubled by her words.

Rizpah saw and prayed, *Let him hear, Lord.* She rose and came closer. "If you hold anger against Varus, you contend with God. The longer you hold on to your anger, the greater it becomes. The more room you give to anger, the less you have for the Lord, until finally there won't be any room for him at all in your life." She blinked back tears. She wanted desperately for him to understand. "Don't you see? You can't serve two masters."

Hearing the tremor in her voice, Atretes looked at her. His heart softened as he saw tears welling in her eyes. He reached out and cupped her cheek. "You're too soft."

"The way before us is hard, but straight." She placed her hand over his. "When you love Varus, you serve the Lord," she said, tears slipping down her cheeks. "When you fight with him, you serve Tiwaz."

"You'd forgive them anything, wouldn't you?"

"The Lord forgave me everything."

As God has forgiven me, Atretes thought, believing his crimes a thousand times worse than hers. He pulled her close. "I'll try," he said softly and kissed her hair. All the tension left him when she put her arms around him. He raised his head and looked to heaven. "I will try."

39

Anomia's heart quickened as she watched Atretes walk down the street. He had been in a dark, unsettled mood when he left her this afternoon. He had been afflicted with the doubts she had planted. Now, barely a few hours later, he returned smiling, his arm draped around that Ionian witch who held their son in her arms!

His laughter set her nerves on edge. Envy poured hot poison through her blood. When he leaned down to kiss the foreigner lightly on the temple, she seethed.

Closing her eyes, she strove for control over the storm rising within her. Her body trembled, cold with jealousy.

Tiwaz, god of darkness! Why do you permit this abomination of a marriage to exist? Atretes should belong to me, not her! The child should have been mine. She watched them again through hooded eyes. He was so beautiful, so powerful, so virile. He should be hers.

Atretes brushed a hand lightly over the Ionian's dark hair and put his arm around her.

Let the woman be racked by disease! Let me rip her heart out and place it on your altar! Atretes belongs to me!

No man she had ever met, among the Chatti or any other tribe, had Atretes' beauty, strength, or personal aura. Her stomach fluttered, her heart pounding a sickening rhythm of lust for something she craved but was yet beyond her grasp.

Give him to me, Tiwaz! Give me my due!

YOU WILL HAVE WHAT YOU DESERVE.

Tell me what you want me to do and I will do it. Anything. Anything!

They stopped to talk with Marta and were joined by Derek and Elsa. Baby Luisa toddled out of the longhouse and headed straight for Rizpah. Anomia waited smugly for Marta to stop her. When she didn't, she drew in a harsh breath of fury. The weakling fool said nothing. She just sat at her loom and watched as her child tugged at the Ionian's skirt. She had warned her!

Laughing, Rizpah stooped and talked to little Luisa. The child clearly had no fear of her. She *touched* her, and still Marta said nothing. Rizpah kissed Luisa's cheek and then let the little girl stroke Atretes' son's hair as he slept.

Now, Marta *spoke*. Not to her daughter, but to the Ionian. She even smiled!

Anomia drew back into the shadows of her house. A low growl rose from her chest. She wanted to scream. She wanted to kill! Grinding her teeth, she tore the white linen robe she wore.

"She'll be sorry she didn't obey me. She'll be sorry." She ripped her garment. "She'll be sorry. I will make her sorry. I'll make them all sorry!"

Yanking the tattered robe off her shoulders, she flung it aside. Kicking the outer garment aside, she went to the dark corner and knelt at the altar where she prayed to Tiwaz.

Rocking back and forth, she beseeched her dark lord. "Reveal the incantation I need to accomplish my aim. Give me your power so that I can make Marta suffer for her disobedience."

And knowledge was given her. It entered her mind with a whirring sound like the wings of a thousand locusts. It rose higher like the keening of hungry bats.

"Yes," she moaned. "*Yes!* Give me more. *More!*"

Charged with the black potency of Tiwaz's instruction, Anomia trembled. She breathed out an exultant laugh and rose quickly to do her master's bidding. She knew exactly how to mix the potion and cast the spell.

She went to her shelf, removing ingredients one by one: nightshade, vervain, baneberries, snakeroot, camas, slips of a yew tree, and finally, a small box. Opening it, she took out a cloth pouch. Inside it was the precious mandrake for which she had traded all her amber. She shook the man-shaped root into the palm of her hand where it glowed softly there in the darkness. She held it possessively, stroking it with her thumb. Mandrake had many uses. It protected against battle wounds, cured diseases, brought luck in love, and promoted fertility.

And it could kill.

She placed it carefully on her small worktable and murmured an incantation as she cut off a small portion, and then replaced the mandrake in its hiding place.

All she lacked was fresh blood, but that was easily obtained.

Taking up a razor-sharp knife, she winced as she made a small incision on her right arm. Her blood dripped into a bowl. She put white thyme on the wound before binding it tightly with a strip of clean linen.

She cut and ground the elements and mixed them with her blood. When the potion was ready, she set it in a pot over her small cook fire. She chanted softly until it began to bubble and then removed it, setting the potion aside.

With a sigh of malicious satisfaction, she sat and waited for her hour of darkness to come.

When the moon and stars appeared and the village slept, Anomia took the poisonous brew and crept to Marta's home. With her fingers she dabbed the potion along the southern base of the dwelling. She whispered the incantation that would give it power. Finishing the task, she hurried back to her own house.

Closing the door behind her, she shut herself into darkness, filled with malicious mirth at what she had done and eager for the horrible results to come.

Tomorrow, Marta would know the cost of infidelity.

But the pain would begin tonight.

Anomia knew Usipi would come, seeking her help, and she would give it graciously. She would tell Marta what was happening to her. Not in words. Just subtle hints that would make the spell more excruciating and terrifying. And delightful. She wanted the undiluted pleasure of watching the pathetic wretch squirm in fear.

O Tiwaz! My god, my god! It feels so good to have power over others. I love it. Give me more. More!

YOU WILL RECEIVE MORE THAN YOU EVER DREAMED.

"Give me Atretes."

IF YOU BUT SERVE ME.

"I will serve you. I give myself to you without restraint. Give me what I want. Give me Atretes."

And her master answered, giving her a deeper craving and darker thoughts that pulled her down further into the vortex of an unhallowed plan. And with it came laughter, softly on the dark wind, mocking and triumphant.

40

Theophilus came awake in darkness. He sat up slowly, so as not to make any noise, and listened intently.

A scuffling sound at the doorway made him peer that way. Squinting, he made out a hulking shape and thought it was the bear he had seen the evening before. Moving slowly, he took his dagger from the shelf he had cut into the wall beside his pallet.

"Roman," came a deep whisper, urgent and demanding.

Relieved, Theophilus put the knife back. "Who is it?"

The man moved back out of sight. "You don't need to know," he whispered.

"What do you want?"

The silence lengthened until crickets began to chirp again. Frowning, Theophilus moved so he could see out the open doorway to the stars. "Are you still there?"

"Yes."

"Then speak as you will, stranger," he said in a calm voice. "I'm listening."

"Shhh!" There was a rustling sound, a restless movement near the doorway. "I want to know about this god of yours," the man whispered.

The voice was indistinct, but vaguely familiar. "Why do you come asking questions in the middle of the night?"

"I don't want to be seen by . . . I don't want anyone to know I'm speaking with you."

"Because I'm a Roman?"

There was a snort of derision. "No."

Theophilus tried to put a face to the voice and couldn't. "Are you afraid?"

"Not of you."

The remark was said with such confidence, Theophilus didn't doubt it. He laughed, until a surprising possibility occurred to him. "Are you a member of the *Thing*?"

The man didn't respond.

Theophilus didn't press for an answer. "What does Atretes say to you about Jesus?"

The man gave a hoarse laugh. "He says too much. And not enough."

"He's new to the faith, but his heart's good."

"I didn't come to hear Atretes praised."

Animosity. Jealousy? An old grudge? Theophilus took the small clay lamp from the shelf above him and set it in the middle of the room. "Come into the light and we'll talk."

"No one is going to know I've been here."

Theophilus frowned slightly. "I won't tell anyone you were here." When the man said nothing, he tried to reassure him. "I give my word what passes between us will be in complete confidence."

"Your word. You're a *Roman*. I'll stay where I am."

Theophilus reached for the lamp, intending to put it away. "Put it beside you," the man whispered sharply.

Theophilus did so, fully cognizant the intruder wanted to be able to see his face. "Will that do?"

"It'll do."

Theophilus waited for the man to ask his questions. The silence lengthened. Crickets chirped. A bullfrog somewhere in the grass near the western wall croaked.

"I want to know the truth about God," the man whispered. "Just tell me everything from the beginning."

✻

"Marta's sick," Freyja said, entering the longhouse and going to her shelves of herbs and oils.

"Sick?" Atretes said, surprised. "Since when? She was fine yesterday."

"Since last night. Usipi came for me early this morning."

"What's wrong with her?"

"I can't be sure, other than she's in pain and has a high fever."

"Probably something she ate." Varus took the bowl of hot grain porridge Rizpah filled for him without looking at her. "You know how she loves berries."

"She said she's eaten no berries."

"If you're not sure what's wrong, have Anomia take a look at her. She'll know."

Varus spoke as though Anomia was an oracle. "Anomia's with her now." She didn't tell her two sons that Marta seemed worse with the young priestess present. Varus was enamored by the sorceress, and Atretes' temper was volatile. He wouldn't hesitate to order Anomia away from his sister, and that would only serve to make the brothers even more antagonistic toward one another.

She looked over her larder of herbs, trying to decide what best to use. Bitter dock tea would purge her system. Ground daffodils would make her vomit. Elderberry would promote sweating. If something in Marta's body was causing the intestinal pain, headache, and fever, a strong draught of these herbs would eliminate it quickly enough.

But what if the sickness was caused by something else, something more malevolent?

She pressed the thought away.

Meadowsweet, white willow, five-fingers, and balm were all useful in reducing fevers. So were basil-thyme, holly, and yarrow. Heliotrope eased pain, and chamomile and red poppy tea would make her sleep.

She took dried daffodil and began to grind it.

Usipi had whispered to her before she left that Marta had been troubled all night by terrible dreams in which winged creatures had swooped down upon her and dug talons into her flesh and bone.

"She said she hurts everywhere the creatures touched."

The fever had risen with the sun.

As Freyja had watched the way the illness manifested itself, she grew afraid Marta was under the attack of spirits.

"How can I help you?" Rizpah said, startling her from her troubling thoughts.

Glancing at the beautiful Ionian, the dark thought gripped Freyja. *What if a curse had been cast upon Marta?*

Anomia.

The name came to mind almost as though spoken, and with it, her own quick denial. Never. Anomia wouldn't lay a curse upon one of her own people. If Marta had been cursed or a spell was cast upon her, it was someone else, an enemy. Or someone who envied her or wanted revenge.

She searched the Ionian's face, using all her powers of perception to try to discern evil.

"What is it, Lady Freyja?" Rizpah said softly without looking away. Why was she staring at her like that, searching her face as though looking for something there? Rizpah came closer. "Tell me what I can do to help you." She reached out and touched her arm.

Freyja saw only kindness and compassion in Rizpah's eyes. Still, in self-defense, she shook off her hand. She was high priestess of Tiwaz! She must remember that. She could not allow herself to trust this young woman, whatever she seemed to be. The fact was that her son's wife was an outsider, a proclaimed believer and servant of a foreign god who sought the destruction of Tiwaz. Freyja knew she couldn't weaken where Rizpah was concerned.

"Look to your child," she said, turning her back on her. "I will look to mine."

Hurt by Lady Freyja's harshness, Rizpah said no more. Turning, she encountered Atretes' look. He had heard his mother's words and was angered by them. "I'll watch my son," he said. "Take Rizpah with you." It was a command, not a suggestion.

"There's nothing your woman can do," Freyja said, grinding herbs, "and her presence would upset Marta."

Your woman? Atretes' offense deepened. "Upset her?" He set his bowl aside and rose. "Why should *Rizpah's* presence *upset* her? She's offered to *help*."

"Atretes," Rizpah said in a tone of appeal to be calm. "It's natural Marta would rather have her mother with her than a stranger."

"You're not a stranger. You're *my wife*. It's time they accepted you."

She put her hand on his arm. "Please," she whispered. "This isn't the way."

Varus set his empty bowl aside. "Let Mother see to our sister." Grasping his walking stick, he rose and limped toward the gate to the animal stalls. "And keep your witch away from her," he muttered under his breath.

Atretes' face went red and then white. "What did you say?"

Varus slammed the gate and glared at him from behind it. "You heard me!"

Atretes took a step toward him.

Rizpah clutched his sleeve. *"Don't,"* she whispered desperately, but Atretes jerked his arm free. "For the love of God, Atretes, *think* what you do," she pleaded softly. "Remember what we talked about."

The interlude they'd shared in the forest came back with a

rush of clarity. *Be angry, but do not sin.* It took his entire will to check the rage that had come upon him like a wild storm, but he stayed where he was.

Varus frowned. Troubled, he looked between them before he turned away and limped down the corridor, banging stalls open as he went.

Freyja's hands trembled as she ground herbs. Fear shivered in her, and she didn't know the cause for it. She poured honeyed mead into a cup. Marta liked the taste. Adding the ground herbs to it, she stirred, beseeching her god to make the brew work. She reached into a basket and took four cloves of garlic to turn back the evil forces of black magic.

Turning, she saw her son looking at her solemnly. He took Rizpah's arm and pulled her in front of him. Putting his hands on her shoulders, he drew her against him. The gesture was deliberate. He was putting his wife before her and all the rest. "If you need us," he said, a muscle jerking in his cheek, "you know where to find us."

Disturbed, Freyja left them without a word. Crossing the street, she entered her daughter's home.

"Lady Freyja's here," Usipi said, and Anomia rose from beside Marta's bed.

"I will go to the sacred grove and pray for her," the young priestess said solemnly, her quiet statement suggesting Tiwaz was visiting this illness upon Marta. She took Marta's hand and patted it. "Your mother will try to make you more comfortable."

Marta looked into Anomia's pale blue eyes and saw no hope. "I don't want to die."

Anomia smiled. "Who said you were going to die?" *You will just suffer. Oh, you will suffer until I'm satisfied you've suffered enough.*

"You're not going to die," Freyja said, determined to instill hope in her daughter. She came closer, so close Anomia had to release Marta's hand and move back from her. Freyja sat down beside her daughter.

"It hurts, Mama," Marta said, gripping her stomach. "It hurts so much. It's as though something is chewing at me."

"Drink this."

"I can't."

She saw how Marta's eyes were still fixed upon Anomia. "Drink it," she said, helping her rise enough that she could. "All of it." She shifted her body so her daughter could not see the young priestess standing nearby. "That's it, *Liebchen*," she said soothingly, brushing her daughter's thick blonde braid back over her shoulder. "The brew will purge you."

"A purge will only make her hurt more," Anomia said tonelessly, moving back, gloating inside.

Freyja glanced back at Anomia in the shadows. "Before you leave, tell Derek to find and pick a bunch of squill." The plant with narrow leaves and bell-shaped blue flowers would ward off evil spells.

"As you say, my lady," Anomia said, her opaque eyes once again on Marta. She was secretly amused. "If you think it can help, I will go myself." She turned away.

Marta shuddered violently.

"Bring pans and cloths," Freyja told Usipi. "Quickly."

Usipi did as he was told and then stood by to help. The purging was swift and fierce, leaving his wife drained and weakened. The cramps and spasms continued long after everything had been eliminated from her body.

"It's not helping, Mother," he groaned, feeling his wife's every pain as though it were his own.

"Ohhh, Mama . . ."

Trembling, Freyja washed Marta like a baby. Sweat poured from Marta's slender body. Surely the impurities were being expelled with it. But the pain, the pain was so intense. "I'm going to brew something to ease your discomfort and help you rest," she said, kissing Marta's brow. She turned to Usipi, his face white and strained. "Try to help her stay calm. And you, as well."

As Freyja left, he lay down beside his wife, drawing her close as she began to shake with chills.

Over the next two days, Freyja brewed teas of cowslip and chamomile to ease her daughter's pain, and chickweed, heliotrope, and devil's bit to treat internal inflammation. Red poppy and wild thyme brought drugged sleep, but still the fever raged. Even teas of sweet coltsfoot, feverfew, and meadowsweet did nothing to cool it.

Marta's skin was hot and dry as the dying leaves of fall that were even now dropping to the ground. Winter and death approached.

Derek climbed high in an ancient oak and cut fresh mistletoe for his father. Usipi hung the sprigs through the longhouse in an attempt to ward off witchcraft. Freyja searched frantically through the woods until she found squill. She hung the the bell-shaped red flowers over Marta's bed to protect her from evil spells. Usipi hung so much garlic, the air reeked of it.

Nothing helped.

"You spoke with the Ionian," Freyja heard Anomia tell Marta quietly one evening. "I warned you Tiwaz would not be pleased, didn't I?"

Freyja went cold listening to her. She looked at Anomia's hand stroking Marta's arm and wanted to tear her away from her daughter. Instead, she moved into the lamplight and saw the start of surprise in Anomia's eyes. Clearly, the young priestess hadn't wanted her close enough to hear.

"I would speak with you, Anomia."

"Of course, Mother Freyja." As Anomia rose gracefully and followed her outside, she brushed her fingers along Marta's arm. "We'll talk more later."

Fury rose in Freyja, but wisdom held her silent. She turned to the younger woman when they were outside the longhouse, keeping her expression calm with effort. "Do you truly believe this illness is brought on by the wrath of Tiwaz?"

Anomia arched her brows, her blue eyes flickering. "Have you heard me say that?"

"I heard enough to know you've frightened Marta into believing it. Why would you do such a thing unless you believe it yourself?"

"I do believe it's true." *And Tiwaz has done it for me, you weak fool. For me!*

"You *believe*. Do you *know*?"

Freyja's tone roused Anomia's pride. How dare she speak to her in this manner?

"Marta is impressionable," Freyja said, seeing the dangerous light in the younger woman's eyes. "Unless you know, without doubt, that Tiwaz is displeased with her, don't even suggest it."

Anomia wanted to say if Marta was so impressionable, she would have heeded her command to not speak to the Ionian, but she held her tongue. "Do you think you're the only one to whom Tiwaz speaks?"

Freyja felt a sudden chill at the look in the younger woman's eyes. She knew instinctively that Anomia was behind whatever was wrong with Marta, but to accuse her would rouse her wrath rather than employ the girl's supernatural powers for the needed cause, to cure Marta.

"If Tiwaz speaks to you, listen. But as a high priestess, you must remember you seek mercy for your people." *And not power for yourself,* she wanted to add.

Anomia sensed Freyja's fear and savored it. "I have listened," she said with a faint smile. "And I do seek what's best for our people." Who knew better than she what the Chatti needed? Certainly not this pathetic soul who wished for peace.

Freyja had known Anomia since she was a small child and knew her greatest weakness. "Then you've failed, haven't you?"

"Failed?"

"If you had the ear of Tiwaz, Marta would be well, wouldn't she?" She watched the dark fire flash in Anomia's blue eyes. "It would seem I've been wrong about you," she said, hiding her anger and fear.

"Wrong?" Anomia said, raising her brows. "Wrong about what?"

"I thought you had power."

The challenge rushed to Anomia's head, a flush of heat spreading down through her entire body. "I *have* power."

"Not enough, apparently," Freyja said. Shaking her head in feigned disappointment, she left the young priestess standing outside the door of the longhouse.

Anomia gritted her teeth to keep from screaming. How dare Freyja doubt her powers? Spinning around, she walked down the street. Varus called out to her, but she ignored him and went into her house. Closing the door, she leaned back against it. Her nails clawed at the wood as she uttered a feral growl in her throat. Shaking with rage, she went to her altar and knelt down. She would show Freyja the power she had!

As night fell, she rose with a blinding headache and mixed an antidote for the spell she had cast. Taking the mixture, she crept through the cold night and anointed Marta's house with it, fully expecting Tiwaz to give her what she demanded by morning.

He didn't.

41

Freyja had never seen Anomia so upset. The young priestess had come into Marta's house without even knocking, fully expecting her to be well. Seeing Marta still in bed, she stared at her in disbelief. "It can't be," she gasped. "He wouldn't do this to me." She came forward a step, her face reddening. Spinning around, she left.

"Where's she going?" Usipi said, his face flooding with fear. "Did you see her eyes?"

"I don't know where she's going," Freyja said, hoping it was well away from Marta. She beckoned her grandson, Derek, and asked him to follow at a distance. When he returned, he told them Anomia had gone to the sacred forest. Too young to enter, he had stopped at the border and come back.

Whatever efforts Anomia had made to appease Tiwaz had had no effect, and that frightened Freyja into desperate measures. Having tried everything she knew, she went to speak with Rizpah.

She found her stirring stew over the cook fire.

"If you can do anything for my daughter, do it and do it quickly."

Rizpah was astonished at the urgent request, wondering at her sudden change of heart. "What's happened?"

"Nothing. Nothing at all has happened. I've tried everything I know. And Anomia . . ." She shook her head. "If you can do something, please help her."

Rizpah was at a loss. What did Freyja think she could do that hadn't been done? She had been praying for Marta since she had become ill, but knew telling Freyja that would bring no comfort at all. More likely it would exacerbate her worry. "I know of no cures, Lady Freyja. I'm sorry. Only the Lord heals."

Freyja swayed, and Rizpah quickly came to her. "Atretes! Come quickly!"

Atretes came at a run from the stall he was mending. "What is it?" Seeing his mother in her arms, he shoved the gate open and strode across the room. Catching his mother up in his arms, he carried her to her bed and laid her upon it.

"Has she a fever?" Rizpah said, greatly concerned.

Atretes put his hand on her head. "No."

Freyja's eyelids quivered and she moaned softly. "I need to go back."

"She's exhausted. She needs to rest."

"She *will* rest. I'll see to it." He looked around and saw Caleb playing with some blocks of wood he had made for him. "The boy's fine and occupied. You see to Marta."

Rizpah took up her shawl and went out quickly. She crossed the street and knocked at Usipi's door. When he opened the door slightly, she was filled with compassion at the weary despair etched into his face. "May I come in?"

Usipi hesitated for a moment, scanning the street quickly before opening the door just wide enough for her to come inside. As soon as she entered, she felt the oppressiveness of their home. It was dark and filled with shadows. She sensed the presence of something malevolent within the confines of the longhouse walls. The odor of garlic made her head swim. If it was difficult for her to breathe without feeling faint, how much worse must it be for Marta and Usipi and the children?

Lord, Lord, drive out the evil I feel surrounding me. I feel devoured by eyes.

"Please remove the garlic, Usipi," she said, taking off her shawl. "It's overpowering."

"It keeps evil spirits away," he said, making no move to do her bidding. He looked worse than Freyja.

"It would drive anything away. At least allow me to open the doors and let air pass through."

He was too tired to argue or even care about garlic. All he cared about was Marta, and he was losing her. Without a word, he went back and sat beside his wife's bed.

Rizpah quickly opened every door and window. Light streamed in, bringing with it a welcome scent of pine and fresh air. She spoke briefly to Elsa, and the girl went out, taking little Luisa with her. Returning to Usipi, Rizpah put her hand on his shoulder. "Sleep for a while, Usipi. I'll sit with Marta."

"No."

Compassion filled her. If Atretes were lying ill, she wouldn't leave him, either. "Then lie down on the bed on the other side of her." She helped him rise and do as she asked. He was asleep as soon as he put his head down.

Marta's eyes opened. Rizpah smiled down at her as she put a blanket over Usipi. She came back around the bed and sat in his place. "Don't be afraid," she said and took Marta's limp hand in both her own. She rubbed it, praying silently that fear would depart. After a few minutes, Marta relaxed a little, and Rizpah praised the Lord.

Rizpah rose and put her palm gently against Marta's forehead. It was hot and dry. "Would you like a cool cup of water?"

Marta nodded.

Pouring some, Rizpah helped her sit up enough to drink it. Marta sipped a little at first and then drank deeply. She lay back weakly. "I haven't been able to hold anything down," she said in a weak, raspy voice.

"Then I pray this time you will." And she did, silently.

Rizpah dampened a cloth. Marta felt all the fear ebb from her as Rizpah washed her face as gently as she would a baby. "Where are my children?"

"Derek is outside, sitting by the wall. Elsa is with Caleb. She took Luisa with her. I hope you don't mind, but I asked if she would help Atretes watch Caleb while I'm with you."

Marta smiled tremulously. "No, I don't mind. She's been pleading with me . . ." A frown flickered. Regret. Shame. She looked at Rizpah and saw no ill feelings, though she had due cause for them. "She'll enjoy it." Why had she listened to Anomia when she had known the moment she met Rizpah that she was kind and trustworthy?

"So will Caleb," Rizpah said as she wrung out the cloth again. She dabbed it gently to Marta's face, smiling. "He adores Elsa, but I think it's Luisa who's stolen his heart."

Casting away Anomia's warning, Marta smiled back. She forgot her fears. She forgot everything but how tired she was. Rizpah's touch was as gentle as her mother's, her voice and manner as soft and loving, somehow even more so. Marta relaxed within it, feeling safe, feeling hope. "I'm glad you're here. I'm so glad." The terrible anxiety that had filled her for days dissipated like a thin mist beneath the warmth of the sun. Just for an instant, she thought she heard a sound like the keening of bats fleeing.

Beads of perspiration broke out on Marta's face. "I think your fever's breaking," Rizpah said, stroking her gently. "All is well, Marta." She sat beside her again and took her hand. "Sleep."

"Will you stay?"

"I'll be with you until you tell me to go." *Lord, be with us. Protect us from the evil I felt in this house when I entered. Put angels around us. Father God, keep us safely in the palm of your hand.*

She prayed silently all the while she watched over Atretes' sister.

And for the first time in many days, Marta wasn't tormented by dreams. She slept peacefully, dreaming of a beautiful garden where she and Usipi and their children walked together in the company of a man who shone like sunlight.

*

"Of course she *cured* her," Anomia said, trembling within at the news that Marta was well and that the fever had broken within an hour after that dark-eyed Ionian witch had been given entrance to the house. "It was probably that woman who cast the spell in the first place." Jealous fury burned within her.

"It does stand to reason that the one who cast the spell would naturally have the power and knowledge to stop it," Freyja said and was surprised by the flash of venomous anger in Anomia's eyes, "but I doubt it was Rizpah who cast it."

"Why do you doubt it?"

"She wouldn't do such a thing," Freyja said.

"How do you know she wouldn't?"

Freyja's brows flickered at Anomia's sharp tone. "Because I've seen nothing but compassion flow from her." She suffered herself to look straight into Anomia's eyes. "Besides, it was *you* who told Marta the sickness was brought on by Tiwaz. It was you who said Tiwaz had revealed this to you in a dream. It was you who said she had been disobedient and had displeased him and that Tiwaz wanted her to listen to you. Are you saying now that wasn't so? Or are you telling me now that you were wrong in your interpretation?"

Anomia felt hot and cold with every word Freyja spoke. She was trapped, and her mind worked furiously to find a way to lay the blame elsewhere. She wanted to insist Rizpah was the cause of all the trouble, but her own proclamations prevented her from doing so. "It was Tiwaz. He did speak to me," she lied and then plowed the ground for more seeds of destruction. "It just seems very curious that Tiwaz would release Marta with an outsider present."

Freyja had thought it curious as well and come to her own conclusions. "Rizpah isn't an outsider. She's my son's wife."

Jealousy wrenched Anomia's heart at her words. *Wife.* The title ripped at her pride. *Atretes'* wife. Her blood sizzled. *Wife!* The word circled in her mind like a carrion bird, mocking her. Used in connection to that woman, it was an abomination. Yet one look into Freyja's eyes and she knew to speak against the Ionian now would bring suspicion upon herself.

"I'm going to the sacred wood to give a sacrifice of thanksgiving," Freyja said. "Would you like to come with me?"

Anomia could think of nothing she would detest more. Give thanks? For what? She had revealed her power in casting the spell on Marta, and no one could know of it. Instead, the foreigner's mere presence in the household was enough to convince the villagers she had appeased Tiwaz in some way. It didn't matter that it made no sense. She couldn't argue without casting suspicion on herself.

The whole thing had turned back on her! *Why, Tiwaz? What game are you playing with me now? That Ionian witch is as much your enemy as mine. And she's being held in higher esteem than before the spell. She's no longer being treated as an outsider. Do you see how she stands in plain view of me, talking with Herigast's wife?*

"Of course I'll go with you," Anomia said, her beautiful face showing none of her inner turmoil.

But Freyja sensed it, and was given further cause to doubt.

42

"Roman!" came the whispered voice. "Are you awake?"

"Awake and waiting," Theophilus said, yawning hugely. He had spent most of the day hunting. The Lord was provident, for he had been hunting for a meal and now had enough meat to last through the coming winter. Even now, the strips of venison were hanging above alder smoke. "I was beginning to think you weren't coming."

"I brought my wife."

A wife. That narrowed the possibilities of who the man of shadows was. His late-night visitor couldn't be Rud as he had begun to suspect. Rud was a bachelor. Nor could he be Holt, who was a widower. Nor could the night visitor be any one of a dozen younger warriors who had not yet taken wives.

"You are both welcome," Theophilus said. "Bring your children next time." He knew he had erred with the remark, for a tense silence followed his words.

He heard the woman whisper something, and the man responded in a sharp whisper, "Do not speak of it. Not a word about it." His whisper dropped again. "He's a friend of Atretes'. . . ." The words became indistinct as the trees rustled from a breeze.

It was cold tonight. Theophilus knew he was far more comfortable in the warmth of his grubenhaus than the man and woman crouching outside in the late autumn night air. His remark had caused them needless alarm. He regretted trying to satisfy his curiosity.

These are your children, Lord. Let them settle long enough to hear your good news. Let love cast out their fear.

"I want you to tell my wife about Jesus."

Theophilus could hear the woman's teeth chattering. "Your wife is cold."

"Then tell her quickly."

"The Word of the Lord isn't something to be rushed. If I put on a blindfold, will you both come inside where it's warmer?"

He heard the woman whispering.

"Yes," the man said.

Taking his dagger from the shelf, Theophilus cut the edge of his blanket and ripped off a strip. He tossed the dagger beside the lamp he had placed in the center of the room to allay other possible concerns. Closing his eyes, he tied the blindfold securely.

He heard them enter and close the door he had finished yesterday. The woman's teeth continued to chatter, perhaps less from cold than tension.

"Be at ease, my lady," Theophilus said, feeling to the left of him until he found the fold of his extra blanket. "Take this and put it around you." He heard movement, and then the blanket was taken cautiously from his hand.

"Go back to the beginning," the man said, no longer whispering. "Tell her about the star in the heavens that proclaimed the birth of the Savior."

*

A party of Bructeri came with goods for trade. They displayed Celtic brooches, pins, shears, and pottery items, as well as silver and gold vessels from Rome. The Chatti bartered with furs and animal skins as well as amber, the fossilized resin much in demand in the Empire's capital markets.

"The merchants who brought this north will hurt from the loss," one Bructeri was heard to say, but few Chatti believed these traders had come by their goods through the honorable means of attack and plunder. Pride pinched less with no questions asked.

Roman traders were infiltrating Germania, seducing tribes with gifts and bribes in order to open commerce. Boats sailed north on the Rhine, carrying goods to Asciburgium and Trier. A brave few brought caravans, tempting death as they followed the Lippe, Ruhr, and Main, entering the valleys of the north by way of the streams of Weser and the Elbe, knowing their lives would be avenged if they failed.

When several Romans had come to the Chatti two years before, they had met with a quick and violent end, and their goods were confiscated. Roman retribution had followed swiftly, leaving the village burned and eighteen warriors, three women, and a child dead. The others would all have been taken as slaves had not they fled to the woods and remained hidden there until the legion had departed.

They only returned once to the old village site, to honor their dead in quickly constructed funeral houses. In the months that followed, the Chatti rebuilt the village on land northeast of the sacred wood.

And now, Rome came again, encroaching ever northward, this time through the representation of the Bructeri, supposed allies to the Chatti cause against Rome. Chatti warriors talked of war when they left.

"We should've killed them while they were here!"

"And have another legion breathing down our necks?" Atretes said.

"We'll take the war south this time."

Despite Atretes' counsel, a band of warriors set off to make their ire known. Atretes remained behind, watching them leave with mixed feelings. He knew enough now of God's way that his conscience forbade him accompanying them. Yet another part of himself longed to ride with them. How long since he had felt that hot rush of excitement in his blood? The closest thing to it was when he held Rizpah in his arms, yet it wasn't the same.

"You miss the thrill of battle," Theophilus said, seeing his restlessness, recognizing it.

Thrill was too feeble a word to describe what he had felt. "Sometimes," Atretes said grimly, "but it's far more than that." As mad as it sounded, he missed the feeling he had had in the arena, staring death in the face and overcoming it by the sheer instinct to survive. His blood had hummed, hot and fast. Sometimes, in a rage, he had a feeling close to it. Exhilaration, a wildness that made him feel *alive*. It was only afterward that the deception was revealed and the cost made known.

Theophilus understood all too well. "You're in battle now, Atretes. We both are, and we're standing against a foe more dangerous and cunning than any we've ever faced before." He could feel the forces of darkness at work around them, closing in.

When the Chatti warriors returned with plunder and good cheer, Atretes' mood grew even more grim. He drank with his friends and listened hungrily to every detail of the battle, part of him coveting their memories of personal exploits during the valorous enterprise.

Theophilus reminded him that what had been done was anything but valorous.

"And Rome's thievery is right?" Atretes snarled, defensive.

"Sin is sin, Atretes. Where's the difference between what Rome did to the Chatti and what the Chatti now do to the Bructeri?"

It was a mark of how much Atretes' heart had changed that he even listened. Theophilus' words made sense to him. But no one else was listening.

Drunk on beer and triumphant, Holt, Rud, and the others were intoxicated with bloodlust and eager for another battle. Peace had no appeal to them, not with victory still racing in their veins and plunder piled up around them. This time, they attacked the Cherusci. Six warriors returned on their shields.

The funeral fires that burned long into the night had a sobering effect on those watching, more so for the mothers who bore those who had died than the fathers who brought them home. Death made the men crave blood even more.

Rizpah prayed for winter snows to cool Chatti tempers and silence the talk of war. And the storms came, one upon the other, until the Chatti had no choice but to remain within the confines of their own borders. Rizpah thanked God, but learned another kind of hardship.

Feeding the cattle was more difficult during the winter months, and, despite Atretes' help, Varus invariably returned exhausted, his bad leg aching past quiet endurance, and in a foul temper. Only Anomia could soothe him. She came to visit often, bringing with her a salve made of arnica, which she massaged into Varus' leg.

Rizpah wondered at her acts of kindness, for when Anomia finished her ministrations, Varus was less in pain, but more restless and short-tempered than before.

"He needs a wife," Atretes said, having watched Anomia. She had looked at him while working her magic on Varus' scarred thigh, and he had felt as though she was stroking his flesh instead of that of his brother with those bold, skillful fingers of hers. The knowledge had sunk deep and hot, rousing him in a way he hadn't felt since Julia.

He unleashed the beast upon his wife, shocking and frightening her with his passion. It wasn't until she uttered a soft cry that he even realized what was happening to him and broke off his mindless race to his own satisfaction.

Atretes was appalled and awash with shame. "I'm sorry," he whispered, burying his face in her hair. He had never hurt her before, and the feel of her body trembling scared him as much as her. *God, forgive me,* his mind cried out. "I'm sorry," he whispered hoarsely and caressed Rizpah tenderly, afraid of the dark forces that had so easily gripped him again.

While lying with his wife, his mind had conjured the image of another. Even now, while comforting Rizpah, memories of lustful encounters came back. They rose like rotting corpses from unclean graves. In an instant, unbidden, those other women were with him, polluting his marriage bed.

Once, long ago in Ephesus, he had seen a man stumbling along the road outside the gates of his villa, the body of a dead man tied to his back. The rotting corpse was strapped to him in a way that he could never be free of it, not until the decay began eating into his own flesh as well. "Why's he doing it?" he had said, and Gallus had answered. "It's the law. He carries the body of the man he murdered."

Put aside the old self.

Atretes had taken him up again. He could feel the weight of sin on his back, the filth of it soaking into him through his pores.

Rizpah uttered a startled gasp as Atretes released her abruptly and sat up. "What is it?" she said with a rush of frightened concern. "What's wrong?"

"Give me a minute," he said, his voice ragged. When she sat up and reached for him, he was harsh. "Don't get close to me!"

That's what he felt, and Anomia had roused it. He couldn't be near her and not see what she wanted, not feel the desire mount in him as well. The realization stunned him. What was worse, he knew it would happen again.

Was it only because she looked so much like Ania?

Raking his fingers into his hair, he held his head. Already, he hurt with what he had started and not finished. And he wouldn't finish, not with what was going on in his mind.

He *loved* Rizpah. He cherished her. He'd die for her. How could he be holding her in his arms and making love to her while thinking of another. It was the worst kind of betrayal. It stank of adultery.

"God, forgive me."

Rizpah heard him mumble something, but not what it was. "God, deliver me."

She heard that and went to him, putting her arms around him. He shook her off and shoved her back from him.

Hear my cry, Lord, Atretes prayed fervently. *Wipe that witch from my mind. Wipe every woman I've ever touched from my mind. Make me clean for Rizpah. Make me clean.*

Calmer, his mind clearing, he turned to reassure his wife. But the damage was already done.

43

Winter agreed with Anomia's cold blood. She chose her time and listeners carefully. Those who were among her chosen carried grudges and unfulfilled desires, discontent and disappointment. She invited them to her dwelling place of shadows and poured honeyed wine into their drinking horns and bittersweet vitriol into their hearts. They went away parched and came back over and over again, thinking she could slake their thirst.

"Atretes speaks of *guilt*. The guilt of *sin*, whatever sin may be," she said, her beauty sharpened by derision. "Why should we feel guilty? The Bructeri betray us by fornicating with Rome, do they not? The Hermunduri stole our sacred salt flats, did they not? He is deceived."

The men readily agreed, their eyes moving over her in ardent fascination.

She smiled, feeling the power she had over them, the power they gave her of their own free will.

"We are the greatest among the German tribes. Chatti led the forces against Rome. We were first into the field and last to leave. And now, this *Roman* and this Ionian woman have worked upon Atretes, the greatest of all our warriors, and turned his heart away from Tiwaz. What would they have us believe about ourselves? That we are nothing. Nothing?"

A growl came from the men, their pride burning.

She fanned the flames of their discontent and added the fuel of ungodly desires.

"They claim we've *sinned*." She gave a derisive laugh and a wave of her hand. "How can I or any of you be held responsible for what one man or one woman did thousands of years ago in a garden none of us have ever known existed? It's ludicrous. It's laughable! Is Herigast responsible for his son dropping his shield in battle? No. Is Holt accountable for the men who died to defend our land? No. None of us are responsible for what someone *else* has done. And we are not responsible for the sin of this nonexistent Adam and Eve."

She moved around the circle, serving them, staying close

enough to see the look in their eyes, to encourage their passions. "It's a fable they tell us, a repulsive little tale with a dark purpose. And I'll tell you what it is."

She saw she held them in her hand and relished their rapt attention to her every word. They soaked each one in like dry earth drinks in rain.

"They want us to believe we carry the sin of this Adam and Eve because by believing it, we become *weak*. They want us to feel like worms before this god of theirs. They want to conquer us without even having to send a legion."

She gave a soft, disquieting laugh. "Are we worms in the eyes of Tiwaz? No. But if we listen to them, we will be worms. Worms in *Roman* eyes."

"Atretes swears on his sword that his wife was raised up from death," one man said, uneasy.

"A trick," she said, dismissing it airily, and poured more wine. She brushed hands as she poured, moving close so the small gathering of men would inhale the scent of sweet herbs she had rubbed on her skin. Let them hunger. Let them thirst.

"They'd like us to swallow this invented religion of theirs. They say they want to *save* you. But do they? Do they really care? From what do you need to be saved? From the pride of being *Chatti*? We *are* Chatti. We are the fiercest, bravest of all the people of Germania. We are a race above all others. Is it any wonder they come to us in the disguise of peace, bringing with them poisonous ideas?"

She filled them with the bile of suspicion and anger, and then told them to keep it secret within them.

"Where we go, other tribes will follow, right over the Alps to rip the heart from Rome. Ah, but if we listen to them and accept this new god as a weak few are doing, Rome will have conquered us without raising a finger. And then we will be low and weak and unworthy, just as they already think we are."

"We should kill them."

"No," she said, seeing her words take root and spread like nightshade and belladonna. "No, we won't kill them. Not yet. We must be as cunning as they in order to win Atretes back," she told them. "The time will come when both will be destroyed, but we must wait for now and be wise.

"When you speak with Atretes, pretend to listen while closing your ears and hearts to what he says. Use the opportunity to *remind* him of the acts of atrocity that Rome has perpetuated upon us. *Remind* him of his father's death. *Remind* him of the countless others who have died or been taken as slaves. Ask him about his life in Rome. He was used as entertainment. Let him remember what it was like to be treated as an animal. Remembering will turn him back to himself. We *need* him. Go cautiously."

She smiled. "We will prevail." She instilled her arrogant confidence into them. "Remember, we are many, they but a few. Now go and do the will of Tiwaz."

44

Anomia's words had a devastating effect. The men followed her instructions skillfully, seeming to listen to the truth while asking questions that stirred up memories Atretes had fought so hard to bury.

Rizpah saw how the questions plagued Atretes. He never talked about his life in the ludus or what it was like to fight in the arena. She had never asked. The men, sensitive to pride, had avoided asking him before. Yet now they seemed unduly curious, intent on knowing.

They weren't satisfied with or sensitive to the brevity of Atretes' answers. They wanted more. "I've heard that . . . ," one would say, prefacing a question that sent Atretes back into slavery.

"What was it like to fight in the arenas of Rome?" a young warrior asked.

"Is it true they dress you up in shiny armor and fancy, colored plumes and make you parade around so the Roman mob can look at you?"

Rizpah would see that look come into Atretes' eyes. "Sometimes less."

"How much less?" Rolf said with a frown.

Atretes turned his head slowly and looked at the younger man. Rolf said nothing more.

But others did.

"I've heard the lanista gives you a woman if you perform well enough."

Atretes' eyes flickered to Rizpah and away.

"Like a bone for an obedient dog," another said softly from the opposite side.

Atretes' face whitened in anger.

The remarks surrounded him like a pack of wolves. They snapped and growled and tore away chunks of his peace of mind. Doubts, like hot coals beneath a camouflage of gray ash, began to surface, their hot breath blowing away the thin blanket and fueling the dark memories underneath.

He tolerated their questions with uncharacteristic control, but the next morning, in Theophilus' grubenhaus, he let his anger show.

"They ask questions about God I can't answer." Closed in the warmth of Theophilus' home, he felt free to give in to his frustration. "Answer this! If God's so merciful and loving, why does he let evil exist? Why didn't he destroy Satan instead of allowing him free reign on the earth?"

Rizpah held Caleb in her lap and watched Atretes. He acted like a caged animal. Last night, he had lain awake for hours, and when he did sleep, he was restless with nightmares. He had cried out once and sat up, but when she tried to talk to him, he told her to leave him alone.

"Sit down, Atretes," Theophilus said calmly.

"'Sit down,'" Atretes growled. "I've been sitting for weeks! I forgot how much I hated winter." He glowered at his friend. "Just answer the questions, if you can."

"God permits evil so that he can demonstrate his mercy and grace through the redemption of sinners. All things work to good purpose—"

"Don't talk to me of good purpose! What good purpose is there in being branded? What good purpose in beatings and constant training? Tell me!"

Theophilus saw what was happening. "It wasn't God who made you a slave, Atretes. It was men. It wasn't God who did those things to you. The heart of man is wickedness."

Rizpah watched the old anger stirring in her husband. Too often, lately, his temper erupted over the smallest incident, the most innocent remark. He would lash out at her over trivial matters after the men had had their long evening together. Even a soft answer brought his temper to the surface.

"Maybe Rizpah's right," Atretes said. "Maybe I should listen to them more." He left, slamming Theophilus' door so hard it banged twice. Setting Caleb aside, Rizpah rose and watched him stride through the snow and into the woods.

"I wish we could go back," she said. "I wish we could take Caleb and go back to Rome and find the others."

"God wants us here."

"Why?" She was as agitated and incensed as Atretes had been. His anger seemed to rouse her own. "None of these people want to hear the truth. You should hear the men each night in the longhouse, going on and on about the battles they've won or want to win. They boast and gloat and they drink until they can hardly stand up to go home. None of them have a heart for the Lord, Theophilus. Not one!"

"Two do," he said, "and probably others, though they haven't the courage to show themselves. Not yet."

She stilled in surprise. "What do you mean?"

He told her about his night visitors. "Trust in the Lord, Rizpah. His Word doesn't go out and come back empty."

"Well, God is taking too long," she said, hugging herself against the cold. "Atretes' faith is crumbling."

"All the more reason for you to remain strong, beloved."

She turned and looked at him. She had hoped for reassurance, but Theophilus saw as well as she did what was happening to Atretes. "Be strong, you tell me." Her eyes welled. "I'm *not* strong, Theophilus, not like you are. If we couldn't come here and speak with you, we'd both fall apart."

Theophilus stood and took her hands in his. "You must listen to me, Rizpah. Look to the *Lord*, not to me."

"I'm afraid of what's happening to him. They won't relent," she said. "They torment him with questions and debate. Sometimes I think they do it deliberately, just to make him hate Rome and the Bructeri and the Hermunduri and everyone who isn't Chatti. They make me so angry. And that woman . . ."

"You know the Word of the Lord. Don't let yourself be moved by their words. God is allowing Satan to sift Atretes, just as the apostle Peter was sifted. Each one of us is sifted. We go through fire."

"For some, it's worse." She took her hands from his and went outside. Drawing the cold air into her lungs, she wondered if she should follow Atretes and talk with him.

"Leave him alone, Rizpah," Theophilus said quietly from the open doorway. "Let him think."

"Sometimes he thinks too much and all about the wrong things."

"He's going to have to choose."

She knew he was right. Atretes needed to be alone. He needed to be away from the clamor of men and her. Everyone was pulling at him. "They want their leader back, Theophilus," she said bleakly. "They want him the way he used to be, a warrior to lead them into battle."

"Atretes put himself in God's hands when he believed in Christ and was saved."

"You don't understand. I think he *wants* to lead them."

"To God."

"That was true when we first came here. I don't know if it is anymore."

"He's learning the hard way that he can't employ the same methods of persuasion he always has used. Strength and pride won't work. Weakness and humility are the only way."

"Atretes doesn't know how to be weak and humble."

"Then let go of him, Rizpah, and let God teach him."

She closed her eyes. "Sometimes I see a look on his face . . ." She looked out at the stark white snow again.

Theophilus came outside to stand beside her. He could see the struggle going on within her and wanted to put his arms around her and comfort her. But there was trouble enough brewing without creating further tensions. Atretes wasn't in a rational mood, and he doubted he had gone far.

Rizpah sighed. "Holt said to him last night that a man feels more alive when he's facing death. Is that true?" When he didn't answer, she glanced up at him. Her lips parted in surprise. "You miss the fighting, too, don't you?"

Theophilus gave her a rueful smile. "Sometimes. Less as I get older." His expression became solemn. "Less as I draw closer to the Lord."

"I wish I could understand."

"You do, in part. You don't contend with Atretes the way you once did. The Lord has softened you."

"Softened my head, perhaps."

He laughed. "Softened your heart, beloved." He touched her shoulder. "Let him soften you more. Pray for these people, especially the ones who are trying to pull Atretes back to the old ways. Even Anomia."

"I do, but I don't see any answers coming on the horizon."

Looking toward the woods where Atretes had gone, Theophilus became pensive. "Give thanks for what's happening." He knew worse was coming. He could feel the darkness gathering force around them. "Tribulation brings about perseverance; and perseverance, proven character. Proven character brings hope." He looked at her. "Hope never disappoints, beloved, because the love of God is being poured out within our hearts through the

Holy Spirit. And it will be *that* love, the love of God, that turns these people to Christ."

"Two, maybe more," she said with a smile.

He felt a bond with her that had grown stronger over the past few months. He had watched her grow in Christ. She said she wasn't strong, but she was stronger than she realized, and the Lord would give her even more strength when the time came to stand. She thought she had no influence, that nothing was changing, that God wasn't working. What other reason had Satan for attacking her from all sides?

Theophilus ran his hand lightly over her hair. He loved her, maybe a little too much.

"Put on your armor, beloved. The battle is coming."

"What should I do to help Atretes?"

"Give him time."

45

Spring came early, bringing with it an exuberance and trembling excitement that swept the Chatti. Hunting was good and feasting lasted far into the night. The younger warriors stripped off every scrap of clothing and danced over the swords and frameas while the men and women laughed and shouted encouragement.

Rolf left the bachelor's longhouse and built a grubenhaus of his own. When he disappeared without a word, some of the warriors went looking for his body, but found no trace of him.

A fortnight passed and Rolf appeared, a Hermunduri girl with him. Her hands were bound in front of her, another loop of rope around her neck. Rolf held it firmly in his hand.

"What's she look like under all that dirt?" Rud laughed.

The men surrounded Rolf and his captive and began teasing him with ribald remarks.

"I'll give you a horse for her," Reudi said, grinning as he looked the girl over from head to foot. "She may be dirty, but she has a nice shape."

Rizpah stood just outside the longhouse, filled with pity for the girl.

Anomia watched as well, gloating over the fruition of her plan. Rolf had glimpsed the girl during the battle with the Hermunduri the spring before, and Anomia had encouraged him to go back and get her. She hoped her father or brothers would come after her. An attack would serve to rouse the winter-lethargic Chatti into fighting spirit again.

"I'll give you two horses!" an older man called out.

Rizpah's anger grew as she listened to the men taunting the poor girl and bidding over her like they would an animal.

Rolf, normally able to take ribbing, was thunderous. "She's not for sale!"

The girl uttered a frightened cry and swung around as one of the warriors took liberties. Rolf knocked the man back, to the loud guffaws of the others.

"Don't be selfish. Share her!"

"Touch her again, Buri, and I'll cut your hand off."

The warrior barked out a laugh. "She looks as dark as Atretes' woman." He caught the front of her tunic and ripped it. "But she's white under the dirty rags."

Rolf lunged at him.

Gasping at the violence of the fight, Rizpah wished Atretes were there to stop the fracas, but he was hunting with Theophilus. Freyja was in the sacred woods gathering herbs, and Anomia, who could have done something to stop it, stood in her doorway, laughing and deriving obvious pleasure from seeing the men pounding one another.

Buri went down amidst shouts and more laughter.

The Hermunduri girl was crying hysterically and slapping at another warrior who sought to fondle her. Rolf made swift work of Buri and turned on him.

Rizpah shifted Caleb and set him on his feet. Kneeling before him, she gripped his shoulders. "Stay right here and don't move." He nodded. "Pray for Mama," she said and kissed him. He nodded again. She left him in the doorway of the longhouse and walked quickly down the street toward the jostling men who were shouting challenges. She was affronted by their crude laughter.

Reaching the back of the crowd, she pushed her way between the men until she faced Rolf. The young warrior's face was red and streaming sweat. He was shocked to see her.

"Enough of this," she said. She stepped by him and untied the rope binding the girl's wrists together.

"What do you think you're doing?" Rolf said, breathing heavily from the fight with Buri and Eudo.

"Exactly what it looks like I'm doing." She untied the rope around the girl's neck and let it drop into the dust at his feet.

"She's *mine*!"

"I know she's yours, Rolf, but would you have her trampled?"

A muscle jerked in Rolf's face as Rizpah took the weeping girl by the hand and walked back through the crowd of men. Not one of them said a word or tried to stop her.

"I want her back!"

She took the Hermunduri girl inside the longhouse, Caleb trailing behind them. Speaking softly to the girl, she tried to calm her fears, wondering what she was going to do if Rolf came, determined to drag her away. She held the girl and stroked her back. The Hermunduri smelled strongly of dirt and nervous sweat. Vermin were crawling in her matted hair.

The Thorns

Freyja returned, her basket full of herbs. "Anomia told me what you did. You had no right to interfere." She looked at the Hermunduri and wondered how many Chatti would die so Rolf could keep her. The young fool!

Rizpah sensed no rebuke. "I know I didn't, but I couldn't stand by and watch the way they were tormenting her."

Freyja had been amazed when she heard. Not a single Chatti woman she knew would have dared interfere as Rizpah had done. Even Anomia knew to stay out of such matters. Marta said the men were shouting and fighting when Rizpah marched down the street and into the midst of them. "She parted them like reeds in the swamp, Mama. She just walked right through them and took the girl away from Rolf. No one's ever taken anything from him before."

Anomia had been livid. Freyja couldn't remember ever seeing the young woman so angry.

"The girl belongs to Rolf by right of conquest, Rizpah. You must understand."

"By conquest. You say that so easily."

"It's not easy. It's *life*."

"The way it was when Atretes was taken and put in chains?"

Freyja paled. "What good do you think you do reminding me of that?"

"This girl is someone's daughter, just as Atretes was your son."

"Rolf built a house for her."

"And so all he needs do now is drag her into it and rape her, and she'll be his wife?"

Freyja turned her back on her, not wanting Rizpah to see how distressed she was. She didn't approve of what some of the men did, but she understood reality. She took the herbs from her basket and laid them upon the counter. She could still hear the girl's weeping, and it pierced her heart. "You don't understand our ways."

"I understand well enough. Your ways are no different from those of Rome."

Furious, Freyja turned. "Over the past ten years, we've lost many of our people. To Rome. To the *Hermunduri*. Some of the men take this way to find wives. Lana is Cherusci, and Helda from the Suebi."

"I wonder if you'd feel the same if Marta had been taken when she was this girl's age."

Freyja turned her back again. Hermun would never have let it happen. She tied the herbs carefully though her hands trembled.

"Where does it stop, Lady Freyja?"

Rizpah's words filled her with discomfort. She hung the herbs upside down to dry.

"Her family will want her back, and that will mean more Chatti will die."

Freyja looked at Rizpah and realized she was concerned with far more than the girl's situation. Rizpah was troubled by the ramifications of Rolf's act just as she herself was. "There's nothing you can do. Rolf wants her. He has no intention of taking her back. If he let her go and she returned, no man among her own people would want her now. She's defiled."

"Rolf didn't force himself upon her."

"How do you know that?"

"Helana told me."

"Helana?"

"That's her name."

Freyja was amazed she had gained the girl's trust so quickly. "It wouldn't matter. She's been with him for several days."

Rizpah rocked the girl back and forth, murmuring words of comfort. Her eyes filled with tears as she looked at Freyja. "At least allow me to bathe her and give her something decent to wear before I give her back to that young wolf."

Freyja was moved by pity. The Hermunduri was young. "Use larkspur. Save some sprigs for her hair. It'll kill the lice and mites on her. As you've been holding her, I suggest you put sprigs in your hair as well."

While Rizpah took care of the girl, Freyja prepared a salve of arnica and thyme. "Rub this into the raw skin around her wrists and neck. I'll tell Rolf you're going to bring her to him before nightfall." She went to the door. Pausing there, she looked back at Rizpah. "Lana and Helda accepted their situation. She will, too."

Rizpah learned all she could about the girl during the little time allowed her.

Freyja returned later. "Rolf said to bring her to his grubenhaus." Rizpah nodded, continuing to brush the girl's waist-length red hair and then braiding it loosely.

Atretes came banging in through the back. He slammed the gate between the animal shelter and the family's living quarters.

Ignoring the girl, he glowered at his wife. "What did you think you were doing?"

"I don't like watching someone in bondage misused." She had had all morning and part of the afternoon to wonder what purpose she had served. The poor girl's situation wouldn't change, and she might have worsened it by angering Rolf. Would he take it out on the girl once he had her in his possession again?

Seeing his wife's distress, and remembering his own captivity, the anger went out of Atretes. He stood thinking for a long moment, and then took his dagger from his belt and offered it to the girl. "For Rolf."

Freyja's hand fluttered to her breast, her throat aching with tears. She had never seen her son perform an act of kindness. It was clear Rizpah didn't understand the significance of what he had done, but the girl did. She took the dagger and clutched it to her breast, weeping again.

Atretes put his hand on Rizpah's shoulder and squeezed gently as he stood up. "Take her to him before there's trouble."

Rizpah did as he commanded. When she left with the girl, Atretes headed back through the longhouse. He took two oxen and a horse from the stalls. "Tell Varus I'll settle with him later," he said and went out the back way.

Villagers came out of their houses to watch Rizpah walk down the street with the Hermunduri captive. Washed, hair braided, and attired in a fresh linen tunic, the girl was lovely to behold, but it was Rizpah who held their attention.

Rolf was waiting outside his grubenhaus. He looked fierce, but as she came close, Rizpah saw he was more captive than the trembling girl beside her.

"Her name is Helana," she told him, the girl hugging her side, her head down. "Her father was killed eleven years ago, fighting alongside the Chatti against Rome. Her mother died of fever this past winter." She wondered if Rolf heard a word she said. He had eyes only for Helana. Rizpah was at a loss as to what more she could do. Clearly, she would be unable to talk the young warrior out of having the girl. But she need not have worried.

Helana let go of her hand and stepped forward shyly. Her gaze flickered to Rolf and color mounted in her cheeks. Trembling, she lifted the dagger in both palms.

A pained expression came into Rolf's face as he looked at the dagger Helana offered him. He seemed suddenly agitated and unsure of himself. Glaring at Rizpah, he made no move to accept the weapon.

Rizpah didn't understand anything other than he was ashamed and embarrassed.

"Rolf!" Atretes called as he came toward him from the woods behind the grubenhaus. He slid from the back of a mare and presented the younger man with the reins. "The two oxen are grazing back in the woods."

Looking confused, but vastly relieved, Rolf accepted the proffered gift. Turning to Helana, he seized the dagger and looped the reins quickly over her hands.

Watching Rolf, Atretes was reminded of himself long ago. Rizpah didn't know what was going on and looked up at him in confusion. He winked at her and smiled.

Helana stepped up to the mare and began stroking the animal's neck in unhurried fashion. Rizpah wondered if the girl was considering mounting the mare and riding away as fast as she could. Apparently, the idea had occurred to Rolf as well, for he moved a step closer, his eyes fixed upon her. Rizpah knew if the girl did try to escape, she wouldn't get far.

*

Helana leaned her head against the mare's neck. Her heart was pounding. She looked back at the woman who had taken her from the men and felt reassured. No one had ever cared what happened to her. She stole a glance at the young warrior who had kidnapped her. Worrying her lip, she studied him. He was tall and powerfully built. He was blushing! She could see his throat work down a swallow.

Amazed, Helana studied him more. She had been terrified of him. And why shouldn't she have been? He had grabbed her near the stream, gagging and binding her and then carrying her over his shoulder through the woods.

He had dragged her along behind him for a hundred miles, tying her to a tree each night to make sure she didn't run away. And now, having exchanged the gifts of marriage, he looked oddly vulnerable, uncertain and embarrassed.

Her fear dissolved. A muscle worked in his jaw, but he was silent, as silent as he had been all during the time he had brought her here. She hadn't known he could even speak until he was shouting at the men manhandling her. Tilting her head, she searched his eyes. After a long moment, she let the reins drop to the ground.

※

Rizpah uttered a surprised sigh as the girl walked into Rolf's grubenhaus without a word of encouragement.

Rolf stared after her. Saying something under his breath, he took a step to follow and remembered Atretes. "I'll . . ."

"You owe no debt. The oxen and horse are gifts." His mouth tipped. "Treat the girl gently, lest my wife take her from you again."

Rolf glanced at Rizpah, his eyes glowing. Tucking the dagger into his belt, he went inside the house he had built for his captive bride.

Atretes took Rizpah's hand and turned her firmly toward the village. "She's his wife now. Considering the way he looked at her, I don't think you need worry he'll abuse her."

"Will the Hermunduri come?"

Atretes considered the possibility and shook his head. "I don't think so. If they'd cared about the girl at all, they would've hunted Rolf down long before he reached us."

His mother came to meet them. "Is everything settled?"

Atretes grinned. "Well settled."

They walked back toward the longhouse together. Freyja saw Anomia and thought to relieve her with the good news. "I'll follow along shortly." Smiling, she approached the young priestess. "Rizpah returned the girl to Rolf. He's married her."

"Married her? How can he with nothing to his name?"

"Atretes gave them what they needed. It's done."

"The Hermunduri will come."

"Atretes doesn't think so. Helana's father and mother are both dead."

Anomia's plan to rouse the warriors from their winter lethargy disintegrated with her words. Freyja touched her shoulder in a gesture of assurance. "I'll tell the others we need not worry."

Anomia fumed silently, hiding her feelings as best she could. The plan had developed in her mind when the young warrior had come to her lovesick and wanting a spell cast to make the girl of his passionate reverie reciprocate his yearning. She had been well pleased with herself when she fired Rolf's lust enough for him to throw caution to the winds and go after the girl he wanted. From his description, she had been sure the girl had to be the daughter of a chief. Instead, Rolf brought back a common village maid, pretty, but not important enough to cause a war.

Her bitter anger grew when Holt and several others passed by, paying her no attention and talking of the Ionian. "I'm beginning to see what Atretes finds so intriguing about the Ionian." It was a bad sign that it was Holt speaking.

Varus wasn't bothered by the loss of the oxen and horse and even declined Atretes' offer of another section of land to compensate. And though Freyja said no more about the incident, it was clear to Anomia as well as others that the high priestess was looking upon her son's foreign wife with growing warmth and curiosity.

Anomia watched Rizpah do her usual chores. The woman seemed unaware of the effect her kindness to the Hermunduri had had upon the villagers, but Anomia knew and writhed inwardly with jealousy. Out of Anomia's heart flowed evil thoughts. A raging river of them raced through her blood. She coveted Atretes, desiring him with an intensity that shook her with burning envy and sensuality. She despised Rizpah, relishing thoughts of harming her, devising schemes to destroy her. For now, she could do nothing.

But a time would come.

46

Several days passed during which Rizpah felt the subtle change in the villagers' attitude toward her. Some greeted her, though they didn't linger to talk. She even found Varus studying her at odd times during the evening.

The men went out hunting, and Rizpah set herself to the task of cleaning out several stalls and taking the manure out to the garden behind the longhouse. Caleb followed her, playing on a patch of grass while she hoed the manure into the soil around the bean plants. She said a psalm of praise and worship that Theophilus had helped her memorize. The joy of the Lord filled her as she repeated the words again and again, the richness of the promises making her heart sing.

"Lady Rizpah?"

Startled, Rizpah turned, brushing a few damp tendrils of dark hair back from her forehead. Helda stood a few feet away at the edge of the garden. None of the women had ever sought her out before. Rizpah smiled and gave her a simple greeting.

Helda approached her shyly. "I made this for you," she said and held out a pile of folded cloth in both hands.

Laying the hoe aside, Rizpah brushed off her hands before accepting the gift. "Thank you," she said, mystified.

"It's a tunic to replace the one you gave the Hermunduri girl," Helda said. "It would've made things easier had someone been so kind to me." She gave a dip of respect and left quickly. Rizpah loosened the folds carefully and gave a soft exclamation of pleasure. The handwoven linen outer garment was ornamented with a lovely pattern of purple. She had never possessed anything so lovely.

Laying it carefully aside, she finished the work in the garden and then put the hoe away. She toted water and heated it for washing. Setting out a few wooden toys Atretes had carved for Caleb, she left him to play while she went into one of the clean stalls to wash. When she finished, she donned the long under tunic. Leaving her own worn outer tunic draped over the wall, she drew on the one Helda had made for her. Tying her belt, she gathered the soiled work tunic to wash.

Varus returned before Atretes or Freyja. He put the horses in their stalls and then herded the cattle into the area at the back. One of his Tencteri slaves remained to fill the mangers with feed while he limped down the corridor and opened the gate to the living quarters.

Rizpah greeted him warmly. Her serenity never failed to irritate him. She continued stirring the thick porridge of beans, corn, lentils, and chunks of salted venison. The rich aroma made his mouth water and his resentment rose even higher. Crossing the room, he sat down on his chair, stifling a groan as he stretched out his bad leg. Atretes was off hunting again, he supposed. He rubbed his leg and winced as pain licked up his thigh into his hip. Hunting was one of many pleasures he could no longer enjoy.

Rizpah poured mead and brought it to him, knowing the strong drink would ease his pain. Varus' eyes flickered to her face and then down over her as he took the horn and drained it. She returned to the cook fire.

Wiping the froth from his mouth with the back of his hand, Varus studied her with a frown. "Where'd you get that garment?"

She was surprised he had addressed her, but before she could answer, Freyja opened the front door and entered.

"She said she's been having the dreams for two days," Anomia said, entering just behind her.

"Did you give her an amber amulet to wear?" Freyja said with a quick smile of greeting to Varus and Rizpah. Caleb forgot his toys and came to her, having long since lost his shyness where his grandmother was concerned.

"I gave my last piece of amber to Reka," Anomia lied, not wanting Freyja to know she had traded for mandrake and belladonna. Freyja bent to pick up her grandson and kissed him.

Annoyed that a child usurped her attention, Anomia glanced balefully at Rizpah. She froze, fury rising in her like a hot geyser. "Where did you get that tunic?"

Rizpah looked between Varus and Anomia. Neither of them ever spoke to her and the fact that they had meant something was wrong.

When Freyja turned and looked at her, her eyes widened as they swept over her.

Straightening, Rizpah touched the neckline of the outer garment. "One of the women gave it to me," she said, wary at revealing Helda's identity.

Anomia stepped forward, fingers curling into fists at her side. "What woman would dare give *you* such a garment?"

Rizpah lowered her hands to her sides. "It was a gift."

Anomia's eyes flashed. "From whom?"

Rizpah said nothing. Freyja set Caleb down and straightened. Anomia took a step forward. "Answer me!"

"What do you mean to do?"

"That's none of your concern! Now tell me!"

Freyja put her hand out for silence. "I doubt any offense was meant by the gift."

"Tiwaz will take offense," Anomia said, trying to regain control. The hot blood pumped through her veins until it was all she could do to curb the rage filling her. This foreigner had no right to such a garment! If anyone was entitled, it was she, not this interloper!

Varus stared at Anomia, glimpsing for the first time the rabid nature hidden beneath the seductively beautiful face and body. Revulsion and fear filled him.

"Tell me who it was!" Anomia said, her voice low and trembling.

Rizpah remained calm, disquieted but not afraid. "Someone who was showing me a kindness."

"Kindness! It's *blasphemy*!"

Surprised at the accusation and not understanding it, Rizpah put a hand against her heart. She looked down over the garment she wore in confusion. "What do you mean?" She looked at Freyja for explanation.

"Take it off!" Anomia screamed, teeth bared.

Rizpah looked at her, repulsed by her arrogance. It was pride and jealousy that burned in her blue eyes. Simple, childish jealousy.

"Do as she says," Freyja said quietly, greatly disturbed. "*Please.*"

Dismayed, Rizpah removed the outer garment. Folding it with care, she held it out to Freyja. Before she could take it, Anomia snatched it away and flung it into the fire.

Rizpah gasped. "How could you burn anything so lovely?"

"You have no right to it!"

"And Mother Freyja did not? I'm sure the woman who gave it to me would have been delighted for her to have it rather than to have it so heedlessly destroyed in a fit of childish temper."

Freyja was astounded that Rizpah would speak so boldly, and to Anomia of all people.

Rizpah let out a sigh and watched the garment burn. The stench of burning linen filled the air. She looked at Anomia again and shook her head. How many hours had Helda put into making that beautiful garment?

"Now tell me who gave that tunic to you!" Anomia said in a low, searing voice.

Rizpah remembered how furtively Helda had come to her, proffering the gift in secret. She saw now in the young priestess' face that Helda had risked a great deal in giving her such a gift. "A friend gave it to me," she said, wishing she understood the full significance. She began stirring the stew again, not wanting it destroyed as well through her own lack of attention.

"A friend?" Anomia said with venomous sarcasm. "You have no friends among *loyal* Chatti," she said, unwittingly setting herself against Freyja who knew her daughter Marta held Rizpah in highest esteem, and with good reason. *"Give me the name of the blasphemer!"*

An inexplicable calmness filled Rizpah as she looked into Anomia's virulent blue eyes. "No."

Freyja and Varus were no less astonished than Anomia.

"No?" Anomia said, her voice trembling.

"Divine the information yourself if you think you have so much power."

Enraged, Anomia took a step toward her, hand raised. Freyja caught her wrist before she could strike. "I'll handle this," she said firmly.

Anomia jerked free, shaking with rage at being defied by a foreigner and then thwarted by a kinswoman. "A curse on you, and your god be cursed!" she snarled at Rizpah, angered all the more because she looked back at her placidly. Casting a rancorous look at Freyja, she left the longhouse.

Freyja clutched the amber amulet between her breasts, her stomach tightening in fear. Varus was no less affected. The power of Tiwaz had radiated from Anomia. It was as though the young priestess was the embodiment of the god.

Rizpah let out her breath softly. "I'm sorry, Mother Freyja. How did I give offense this time?"

Mouth dry, Freyja looked at her, amazed that she was so composed. Didn't she know what she had just faced? "Whoever gave you that garment wove the emblems of our sacred tree into it," she said. "Oak leaves and acorns are sanctified symbols of long life and fertility."

Varus gave a dismal laugh. "It would seem at least one of our tribe wishes you well."

"Varus, please," Freyja said, giving him a quelling look.

Rizpah understood all too clearly how her wearing the garment would bring offense. "I'm sorry," she said, concerned more about the consequences to Helda than to herself. What would happen to her if Anomia found out? "I'm sure the woman meant no offense to you or Anomia, Mother Freyja. As Varus said, she was only wishing me well."

"No," Freyja said, disturbed. "She was doing more than that." She was sure it was the subtle implications of the gift that had caused Anomia to lose control so completely. "Gundrid wears the symbols, as do Anomia and I."

Rizpah was distressed. "But everyone knows what I believe, don't they?" she said in dismay. "Jesus is my Savior and Master, Mother Freyja, *not* Tiwaz. Why would anyone give me a garment meant for a priestess?"

"To cause trouble," Varus suggested.

"I don't think so," Freyja said and knew Anomia shared the same perceptions. "The woman who gave you the gift honors you as a spiritual leader."

THE SACRIFICE

*"I tell you this, unless a seed falls
to the ground and dies, it remains only a single seed.
But if it dies, it produces many seeds...."*

47

"The disease of deception is spreading among our people," Anomia said, looking around at the circle of men sitting in the lamplight of her house before her altar. "Tiwaz has spoken. The hour has come to act."

She had chosen each man carefully, nurturing their animosity and disappointments, stirring their passions until they were enslaved. Some, she knew, came only because of loyalty and not conviction. "You have burned the incense and presented your offerings. You have drunk the blood and eaten the flesh of the sacrifice. Tiwaz has revealed to us what we must do. Now we will learn who among us will have the honor of carrying out his will."

Taking the white linen cloth from one side of the carved altar, she loosened the folds with solemnity. Uttering an unholy incantation, she laid it upon the ground in the middle of the circle. With great ceremony, she made sure all the wrinkles were removed and it was stretched out flat and smooth upon her earthen floor.

Turning again, Anomia took a silver bowl from the left side of the altar. Each man had placed within it a piece of wood inscribed with a rune he held personally sacred. She shook the bowl gently, murmuring another incantation as she did so. Once, twice, thrice, and again. Seven times she shook the bowl. Then she cast the wooden chips upon the white cloth.

Four bounced onto the earth and were quickly taken up by their owners and restrung and hung around their necks. Three others were turned over so that the runes didn't show. Anomia turned these and returned them one by one.

Anomia took the five remaining chips and put them back in the bowl, going through the ritual once again. When she cast the chips onto the white cloth, four were faceup, one facedown. The four were taken up quietly by their owners.

Eyes glowing, Anomia looked at the young man to whom the charge fell. She took up the piece of wood and held it out in the palm of her hand. "Tomorrow. At sunrise." She saw his eyes flicker once and recognized doubt. Her own eyes narrowed and chilled. "Tiwaz has given you another chance to redeem yourself," she said, deliberately bringing up his past failure and raking his pride. "Be grateful."

With a sick feeling in the pit of his stomach, Rolf took the chip and clenched it in his fist. "For our people."

"For Tiwaz," she said and gave him the ceremonial dagger.

*

Theophilus came out of his grubenhaus and filled his lungs with the pine-scented morning air. Darkness was being eased away with the coming dawn, but the stars still shone in the heavens. Raising his hands, palms up, Theophilus praised God.

"Bless the Lord, O my soul; and all that is within me, bless his holy name. Bless the Lord, O my soul, and forget none of his benefits; who pardons all my iniquities, who heals all diseases, who redeems our lives from the pit; who crowns us with loving-kindness and compassion; who satisfies your years with good things, so that your youth is renewed like the eagle."

His heart felt as though it would burst with joy at the new day. Darkness was passing away. Those who had come to him, hiding themselves, had entered into the light, revealing themselves at last and talking with him face-to-face.

"As far as the east is from the west, so far has he removed our transgressions from us."

*

Rolf came out of the woods. He watched and listened, heart pounding. The Roman stood in the middle of the glen, arms raised as he spoke to the heavens. Taking a deep breath to calm his tension, he walked toward him from the woods.

"The Lord has established his throne in the heavens."

Stomach knotting, Rolf kept on, setting his mind to the task he was sent to do.

"Bless the Lord, O my soul!"

Rolf felt the sweat breaking out on the back of his neck. Seven times, Anomia had said. Seven times.

Sensing he was not alone, Theophilus turned. He frowned slightly, wondering what brought the young champion. Then he saw him draw a dagger from his belt and knew.

Now, Lord? O Lord God, now?

The Chatti champion came on, and Theophilus turned fully, facing him as he had in the sacred grove. He made no move to protect himself or escape, and the young man's face filled with distress and uncertainty.

"You can choose another way, Rolf."

"There is no other way," he said bleakly, his throat closing as he looked into the Roman's eyes. He saw no fear, only a deep sorrow and pity.

"Anomia deceives you."

Rolf felt himself weakening, but he knew Anomia was right about the man. He was dangerous. "I failed my people once before," he said and struck the first blow, driving the dagger in to the hilt. "I can't fail them again." As the Roman stumbled back, Rolf caught hold of the bloodstained tunic and held him. Jerking the dagger free, he raised it again. "I can't fail them," he rasped through his tears.

Theophilus spread his arms wide. "I forgive you, Rolf."

Rolf's heart turned over at the look of compassion in the Roman's eyes. Uttering a hoarse cry, he plunged the dagger in again. Seven times, Anomia had said. Seven times, he was to drive the ceremonial dagger into the Roman. But his mind rebelled. Why so many when the first would prove mortal? Was he to strike him over and over for the sake of cruelty? Or to prove his loyalty?

As he withdrew the dagger the second time, blood bubbled from the wound in the Roman's chest. Sickened, Rolf flung the dagger aside and braced the man, sinking down with him on the morning-damp ground. He remembered the night in the sacred grove when the Roman could have taken his life and didn't.

"Why didn't you defend yourself?" His hands fisted the bloody tunic. *"Why?"*

"Turn away from Anomia," Theophilus rasped, "before it's too late."

Rolf eased him back and wept. "Why didn't you fight back? Why didn't you?"

Theophilus saw his anguish and gripped his arm. "Turn . . ." he rasped, "turn to Jesus."

Rolf surged to his feet. He looked at his hands, covered with the Roman's blood. Turning, he fled.

✶

Rizpah reached the end of the path just as Rolf ran into the forest on the far side of the glen. She frowned when she saw him and entered the glen, looking toward the grubenhaus. Surely Rolf was not one of the ones Theophilus said came to him to learn about the Lord?

She had awakened the night before, feeling oppressed and filled with disquiet. The scene with Anomia was still fresh in her mind, and she prayed for Helda and the unknown others who had gone to Theophilus in the night. When she had finally slept, she had tossed and turned, troubled by strange dreams. She awakened abruptly in darkness, afraid for Theophilus for no explicable reason. Distressed, she awakened Atretes and said she was going to him.

"Dawn will be here soon. Wait until then."

"I have to go *now*."

"Why?"

"I don't know, but I must. Please come as quickly as you can."

"What about Caleb?" he said, sitting up and raking his hands through his hair. His head was pounding from the mead he had drunk the night before with Holt and Rud and the others.

"Leave him with your mother."

Now she stood in the cool morning air, the sky sweetening with the hint of sunrise, and scanned the glen for a sign of Theophilus. He wasn't in the grubenhaus and he didn't answer her call. She found him on the far side of his garden, lying on the dew-covered grass.

"No!"

✶

Theophilus rasped in pain, feeling strength flow out of him with each beat of his heart. "Lord . . ." He saw Rizpah above him, the sunrise behind her, and then she was on her knees beside him, pulling him up into her arms.

The Sacrifice

"God, no," she wept. "Oh, Theo."

"It's all right, beloved," he said. "All is well."

"*Atretes!*" she screamed, tears streaming down her pale cheeks. "O God, please." She pressed her hand over one of the wounds, but she saw it was no use. "*Atretes! Atretes!*"

"Keep . . . Caleb away," Theophilus managed, having difficulty breathing.

"He's at the longhouse. I didn't bring him with me this morning. Something warned me not to bring him. I knew I had to come. O God, why didn't I come sooner? Why did Rolf do this to you?"

"Sent," he managed, coughing. "He didn't want to do it."

"But he did. He *did*."

"Forgive him, beloved."

"How can I when he's taken you from us?" She wept.

"Jesus forgave." Theophilus took her trembling hand. "Tell Atretes. Remember the Lord." He coughed. Each breath he took made the wound in his chest bubble red, but he gripped her wrist with surprising strength. "Don't tell Atretes it was Rolf. He's weak. He'll want revenge." The heaviness of his own blood was filling his lungs. "Stand firm."

"Don't try to talk." She saw her husband running toward her. "Hurry!" she called, weeping, cradling Theophilus closer, feeling him slipping away. "O Jesus, please, please don't take him from us. Don't take him. Hold on, Theophilus. Atretes is coming."

And then he was there, going down on one knee, staring at his friend, his face ashen. "Who did this?"

Theophilus gripped his wrist. "Feed the sheep."

"I have no sheep!" Atretes said, wanting to understand the ramblings. "Who did this to you?"

"Feed the sheep." Theophilus said, fumbling until he caught hold of the front of Atretes' tunic and held on.

Grief-stricken, Atretes looked at Rizpah in confusion. "What's he talking about?"

"Feed the sheep." Theophilus' fingers loosened. He let out a long sigh and relaxed in Rizpah's arms, his brown eyes still open and fixed on Atretes.

"He's gone," Rizpah whispered, fear coursing through her.

"Bring him back!" Atretes commanded. "Bring him back the way he brought you back!"

"I can't." Her hand shook as she gently closed his eyes.

"Why not?" he said desperately. "Try." He put his hands against Theophilus' chest, covering the wounds. "Try!"

"Do you think we can command God to give us what we want!" she cried out. "He's gone."

Atretes drew back.

Rizpah shook violently, her breath trembling. *Father God, what will we do? What will we do without him? O God, help us!*

And with a sudden rush of warmth, an answer came to her. She remembered the word Theophilus had taught her and said it aloud as it came back now when she needed it. "The Lord is our light and salvation; whom shall we fear? The Lord is the defense of our life; whom shall we dread?"

Atretes' cry broke her tranquility. She looked up at him, standing above her, his face contorted with grief and rage. She had never seen such a look. He was breathing heavily, as though he had run miles, and his eyes blazed.

"I'll kill the man who did this. I swear before God almighty, I'll find him and do to him as he's done!"

"No, Atretes," Rizpah said, seeing Theophilus knew better than she. "Theophilus told you to feed the sheep. The sheep are your people. Theophilus told me there were two who came to his grubenhaus by night to hear the Word. There may be others hungry for the Lord. We must feed them with the Word."

"Maybe it was one of them who did this to him!"

"No, it wasn't," she said, glancing toward the forest where Rolf had disappeared. Blinking back tears, she laid her hand tenderly against Theophilus' serene face.

"What do you mean?" Atretes said quietly, his eyes narrowing.

"Look at him, Atretes. He's at peace. He's with Jesus." She stroked his cheek, realizing how much she had loved him, how much she would miss him.

"Answer me!"

She looked up and saw the stillness in him, the cold suspicion—clear warning of the violent storm to come. Her heart trembled.

"You saw who did it, didn't you?"

"Theophilus said he didn't want you to seek revenge."

"You think I can let this go?"

"Feed the sheep, Atretes. That's what Theophilus told you to do. *Feed the sheep*. Don't let yourself think of anything else but that."

"Tell me who did it!"

"Love, God says. Love your enemies."

He swore at her, the look in his eyes no less obscene than what she had seen in Anomia's face the day before. He was lusting for blood.

Anomia, came a dark whisper in her mind. *Tell him Anomia is behind Theophilus' murder. Tell him it was her. He'll take her life and rid the Chatti of her influence. He'll never look upon her with desire again. Tell him it was—*

She closed off the thoughts abruptly, shuddering that she had even allowed them entrance at all. *O God, help me.*

She had to protect Rolf, just as she had protected Helda. She had to strive to make every thought obedient to the love of Christ whatever violent feelings churned within her. She had to take her every thought captive to the obedience of Christ and leave no room for anger and jealousy and thoughts of revenge. If she didn't, what would become of her husband?

She knew.

Lord, help me. Help me.

"Be still and know," Theophilus had said so often. "God is with you."

"Beloved, what does the Lord your God require of you?" she said softly, eyes filling with tears as she remembered and repeated another Scripture. "Fear the Lord your God, walk in all his ways and *love* him, serve the Lord your God with all your heart and with all your soul, and keep—"

"He was *murdered*!"

"As was our Lord. Jesus forgave," she said, desperate to call him back to himself. "Theophilus *forgave*. You must—"

"No. Justice *will* be done," he said, a muscle moving in his cheek.

"Justice, Atretes? Your mouth is watering for revenge."

"Better the cur die by my hands than be put in the bog!" When she still said nothing, his temper burst the reins he had tried to put on it. *"Tell me who it was!"* he said, grabbing her by the hair and pulling her head back.

Gritting her teeth against the pain, she looked up at him. She was afraid, not for herself, but for him. When his hand tightened, she gasped in pain and closed her eyes.

Seeing her face drain of color, Atretes released her abruptly and stepped away, swearing vilely. He gave a shout of frustrated fury. He wanted to kill whoever had murdered Theophilus. He wanted to hunt the man down and tear him apart with his own bare hands. He wanted the satisfaction of hearing him beg for mercy. He wanted to plunge a dagger into him over and over again as the killer had done to his friend!

Rizpah wept as she saw the struggle going on within him. He was turning away from God right before her eyes, and she was powerless to stop it. She ached with grief, praying incoherently for God's help.

Atretes turned on her, his face contorted with grief and wrath. "Curse you for protecting a murderer!"

She saw the same pride and wrath she had seen in Anomia's eyes blazing in Atretes. It shook her. "No, I'm not," she said, weeping harder. "I'm protecting *you*."

He strode away, leaving her in the glen alone, Theophilus' body cradled in her arms. She held her friend closer, rocking him in anguish.

48

Rizpah prepared Theophilus' body for burial, but Atretes returned and informed her he was going to cremate him according to Chatti custom. He spent the rest of the day building a funeral house. Freyja came with food and wine, but Rizpah had no appetite, and Atretes wouldn't stop to eat.

"I'm sorry," Freyja said to Rizpah softly, watching her son. "I didn't agree with your friend, but I wouldn't have wished such an end upon him."

"Could you have prevented it?" Rizpah said softly.

Freyja looked down at Theophilus' face and wondered at the peace of it. "I don't know," she whispered. "Perhaps. I don't know." She laid her hand gently on Rizpah's arm. "I'll bring Caleb to you later."

Hours later, the funeral house burned against the night sky. Rizpah stood watching it, weeping softly, Caleb held close in her arms. Atretes stood beside her, not speaking or touching her. He hadn't uttered so much as a prayer. She felt the coldness in him and didn't know what she could do to help him. Glancing up at him, she saw the muscle working in his jaw, his eyes blazing as hotly as the fire consuming Theophilus' body. She felt the distance widening between them.

Pressing her face into the curve of Caleb's neck, she continued to pray even as she had started that morning in the glen. *Lord, turn his heart, incline his ear, let his soul respond.*

A violent burst of sparks and flame shot upward as the funeral house caved in. Just for an instant she glimpsed Theophilus' body lying on the bench before it was consumed in the bright light.

Caleb let out a joyous cry of delight, raising his hands as the embers rose heavenward. Rizpah looked up as well. Above were the stars and the moon as they had always been, reminding her that God had been there even before them and would be long afterward as well. The knowledge filled her with peace and, strangely enough, joy. Theophilus was home with the Lord. His battle was won. It was only she and Atretes who were still struggling with temporal existence and the forces against them.

Lord, Lord, my heart longs for you. You know how much we both relied on Theophilus' sweet spirit. Is that why you took him from us? So that we would have to stand on our own and put all our trust in you?

"Are you going to tell me who murdered him?" Atretes said without looking at her.

She lowered her head and closed her eyes. "No," she said very softly, praying he would relent.

Turning, he yanked Caleb from her arms. "You're not welcome at the longhouse."

She stared at him, lips parted. "What do you mean?"

Caleb started to cry in his father's arms. He reached for Rizpah, she took a step forward. Atretes stepped back from her. "He's *my* son, remember? Not yours."

The coldness of his voice froze her. "And you're my husband," she said shakily, striving for calm and reason in the face of what she saw in his blue eyes.

"Then remember your vows to obey. Tell me who killed him!"

O God, does it have to come to this? "Vengeance is mine, saith the Lord," she quoted. "I can't tell you knowing what is in your heart. I *can't*."

"Do you think the Lord *wanted* Theophilus murdered? Do you think he ordained it? Do you think Jesus sent someone to do it?" He cursed again, his voice rising. "If he did, then where's the difference between Christ and Tiwaz?"

She didn't want to argue. God was sovereign. God *knew*. Her mind worked desperately for reasons. "God permits evil so that he can demonstrate his mercy and grace through the redemption—"

"Is the killer here, begging forgiveness?" Atretes sneered. He shifted Caleb, jarring him. Frightened, the child screamed, but in his wrath, Atretes didn't notice or care. "Do you see the murderer repenting?" he said, glaring at her as though she had done the deed herself. "Do you think he's afraid of God? Do you think any of my people will have respect when they see nothing happens after a man's been murdered in cold blood?"

"Is yours any warmer?"

A red haze seemed to overshadow his vision. "You betray Theophilus with your silence. You betray me!"

"Theophilus told me not to tell you!"

"You're standing between me and justice!"

"I'm standing between you and *revenge*!"

He slapped her before he could stop himself, and the blow was so hard she reeled and fell to the ground. Shock and regret made him take a step toward her, and then the black fury within him held him back. A war raged within him. He groaned with the intensity of the battle. He watched her push herself up, saw how she shook violently from shock, her dark eyes wide with pain and disbelief, her lip bleeding.

A part of him was appalled at what he had done and wanted to beg her forgiveness, but he hardened himself against it. If he gave in, Theophilus' murder would go unanswered. He couldn't let that happen. His very blood cried out against it.

"I don't want to see your face until you're ready to tell me who it was. When you do, I'll allow you back in the longhouse. Not until."

"Atretes—"

"Shut up! Don't come back unless you've had a change of heart, Rizpah, or by God, you'll live to regret it. If you live at all." His mouth twisted in bitterness, even as his heart twisted inside him. "You're no better than a faithless wife, and I'll treat you as such."

With those words, he turned his back on her and strode away, Caleb screaming in his arms.

Drawing her knees up against her chest, Rizpah covered her head with her hands and wept.

Not far away, hidden in darkness among the trees, Anomia watched. She had heard every word Atretes uttered. Her heart had swelled with malicious joy when he had struck the Ionian down. Now she listened with heinous relish to the woman's sobs drifting softly in the still night air.

Eyes glowing, she smiled, triumphant.

49

Rizpah moved into Theophilus' grubenhaus. She covered herself with his blanket, breathing in the scent of his body, grieving over him as she would an earthly father.

Fears attacked her from all sides; nightmares assailed when she slept. Caleb was screaming, and she couldn't find him. Though she searched frantically, she found herself deeper and deeper in the forest, darkness closing in around her. She came upon Atretes entangled in the arms of the young priestess and cried out. He didn't hear her, but Anomia did and exulted.

Rizpah awakened weeping, Anomia's laughter still ringing in her ears. Her heart was racing, her whole body trembling. She covered her face.

"O Lord, you are a shield about me. Be gracious to me and hear my prayer. Make your way straight before me."

She sat in the darkness, praying and waiting for dawn, all the while beseeching God. Surely Atretes would have had time to think and relent and take her back with him to the longhouse. He had loved Theophilus. Surely he would honor his friend's last request. And Caleb would need her. He hadn't been weaned and would cry in the morning, and Atretes would have no patience with him. Varus would be angry.

"He's my son, remember? Not yours."

She held herself and rocked. *His eyes, O God . . . open his eyes*.

Atretes' words cut her heart every time she thought about them, resurrecting other hurtful things from the first time she'd met him. How could she have thought there was any gentleness in him? How could she have thought he ever really loved her? She was still Julia to him, still like a hundred others he had been given in his cell.

"*Let all bitterness and anger be put away from you, beloved, and be kind to one another,*" John the apostle had said so long ago in Ephesus. Was it really only two years since she had left everything she knew to come to this place of desolation? "*Be *kind and tenderhearted, forgiving each other, just as God in Christ also has forgiven you."*

She knew she had to forgive Atretes for abandoning her. She had to lay the hurtful words aside or bitterness would take root in her and grow. Atretes treated her as though she had killed Theophilus, but she couldn't think of that. She couldn't allow his anger and actions to keep her from obeying the Lord.

"Stand firm."

She thought of Rolf fleeing into the woods with blood on his hands. She wanted to tell Atretes and see justice done, but she knew it wouldn't be justice that was served if she gave in to her feelings. Theophilus had spoken plainly. She couldn't pretend she didn't understand. She couldn't convince herself it was all right.

Why did life have to be so hard? Shouldn't believing in a living God make it easier? Did the Lord really expect her to stand against her husband and lose her son in the process? And for what? To protect a murderer?

"Forgive them for they know not what they do."

Dawn came. Atretes didn't.

As the first day passed and then the second, Rizpah despaired, her mind and heart in torment. How had things disintegrated so quickly? Was it possible that one act of violence could obliterate faith? She felt as though her own was crumbling. Was she doing the right thing? She wanted to be with Caleb, not alone in this quiet, cold earthen house. She wanted to talk with Atretes, reason with him, make him understand. But could she? Would any amount of reason reach a man who had given himself over to the desire for vengeance?

She knew him so well. He wouldn't relent, and if she did, he was lost. Rolf would die, and she would have the young warrior's blood on her hands. She would have to live with the guilt of knowing her weakness had opened the way to Atretes committing a murder no less abominable than what Rolf had done.

And so she set her mind on Christ.

She weakened when she found the dagger. It lay half-hidden in Theophilus' garden, the blade glinting in the spring sunlight. She picked it up before she realized what it was. The blade was stained by a streak of dried blood. Theophilus' blood. She dropped it in horror, tears flooding her eyes. Dark, marauding thoughts stole into her mind, making her blood go hot and her muscles tense. What mercy had Rolf shown Theophilus when he plunged the dagger into him? Why should any mercy be shown him? She wished she could plunge the dagger into Rolf herself and give the wretch to the god he worshiped.

But her conscience recoiled at such thinking, and she responded in repentance. Rolf was unredeemed and incapable of understanding the truth. He was incapable of believing in God, incapable of pleasing the Lord or even seeking him. But she was. She *knew*. And still she had found herself indulging in thoughts of violent retribution.

God knew her heart. God knew her every thought. How was she any different from Atretes? The realization humbled her even more.

"Don't tell him," Theophilus had said. *"He's weak. He'll want revenge."*

Hadn't Theophilus' words proven true? And now she found herself as weak as her husband, hungering for retribution, craving a man's death. Atretes had turned away from everything Theophilus had taught him. Theophilus' last words had been a commission, and Atretes had ignored it, too intent on vengeance. Was she going to turn away from the Lord as well?

"God, forgive me. Cleanse me, Lord. Make a right spirit within me," she prayed, filled with compassion for her husband. There was no room for anger and hurt. How much worse must it be for Atretes, having been trained in violence for so many years. He had only just begun to know the Lord. What excuse had she who had followed the Lord for seven years? "God, help him. Turn him back."

When she opened her eyes, her gaze fell on the dagger again. What forces had worked on Rolf to drive him to kill Theophilus? Hadn't Theophilus spared his life in the sacred forest? Theophilus said the young warrior hadn't wanted to do the deed. Why had he? She picked up the dagger. The handle of bone was carved in the shape of a goat's foot, runes etched the length of it. It was no ordinary weapon. She turned it over and saw the carving of a man with horns, holding a scythe in one hand and a framea in the other. Tiwaz.

Had Gundrid sent Rolf? Surely Freyja would not be a participant in such an abominable act. She couldn't believe it of Atretes' mother. Anomia, yes, but not Freyja. Never Freyja.

She thought of the young priestess who had no fear of God, even of the one she worshiped. Rizpah had seen the darkness behind her eyes. She had felt it every time the young woman looked at her. The day before Theophilus had died, she had revealed her true feelings. Anomia was a child of wrath, hostile, inflamed by hatred of the Lord.

Rizpah wondered if she should give the dagger to Atretes. She felt sick at the thought, knowing that more than Rolf would die if she did so. And what if his own mother had taken part in Theophilus' death? What then?

She hid the weapon in the hollow of a tree near the stream.

Theophilus had given a commission to Atretes. "Feed the sheep." But he had given her a commission as well. "Stand firm," he had said. But could she?

"Stand firm."

*

Again and again over the next days, his words came back to her, especially during the hours of darkness when she weakened and wanted to run back to the longhouse and beg Atretes to let her come home, when she wanted to give him the dagger and not think about the possible repercussions.

"Stand firm."

Had Theophilus known she would be left alone? Would it have made a difference if he had?

"Stand firm, beloved."

How many times had he said those words to her over the months of traveling from Ephesus to Rome and from Rome north across the Alps into the forests of Germania? *"Stand firm. Stand firm."*

She lay down upon Theophilus' pallet each night and prayed. *Lord, I am weary with sighing. Every night I make my bed swim and dissolve this pallet with my tears. I am wasting away with grief.*

She could almost hear Theophilus speaking to her. Closing her eyes, she took comfort from the memories of him. She thought of him sitting across the fire from her, smiling that tender smile of his.

Hadn't he stood firm all these months, alone in this grubenhaus?

Other things he had said came to her: "Remember the Lord, beloved. Jesus delivered us from the domain of darkness and transferred us to the kingdom of his beloved Son. Put your armor on. Gird your loins with the truth. Put on the breastplate of righteousness. Shod your feet with the gospel of peace. Take up the shield of faith and the helmet of salvation and the sword of the Spirit. And pray.

"You must be a doer of the Word, Rizpah. Remember the Scriptures. Let God's Word enter your heart and bear fruit.

"Be steadfast. Set your mind on the things above. The mind set on the flesh is death, but the mind set on the Spirit is life and peace. Guard your heart, for from it flow springs of living water. Imitate the Lord. Walk in love."

Scriptures came, flooding her mind.

"Greater is he who is in you than he who is in the world."

"I love my husband, Lord. I love my son."

"I am the Lord your God, and there is no other."

God's Word came like a clap of thunder and then followed with a gentler rain.

"I am sufficient. I am sufficient. I am sufficient."

And she wept, knowing what God asked of her.

"O Lord, you are my Rock and my Redeemer. You hear my supplication. You receive my prayer. You have heard the sound of my weeping. Help me to stand firm in you. Give me strength, Abba, for I have none of my own. Fill me with the knowledge of your will and keep me in the way everlasting. O Lord, my God, I live to worship you."

And as Rizpah poured her heart out in surrender to the Lord, the God of the universe poured back into her love and assurance. She wept, and his Word comforted her. She was weak, and he strengthened her. Scripture upon Scripture came back to her, vital and alive, driving away fear and loneliness, obliterating all doubt. As the days wore on, dark forces closed in around her, but Rizpah clung stubbornly to Christ and her passion deepened.

"We can rejoice," Theophilus had said during a time of tribulation. "We can pray. We can praise God."

And she set her mind and heart upon doing these things, no matter what came against her.

50

"It's been ten days, Atretes," Freyja said and saw the flash of anger in her son's eyes, clear warning he didn't want to speak of his wife. But she had to speak of Rizpah. Ten days was too long for a woman to be on her own at the edge of the forest. And he knew it. She had watched his tension increase with every day that passed. Rizpah had no food other than what little might be growing in the Roman's garden, and how long would that last? She had no protection, and Freyja felt the spiritual forces moving until the air trembled.

"You can't leave her out there on her own."

He was pale, his emotions raw. He continued staring into the fire, the muscle working in his jaw.

"You must bring her back."

"No."

"Caleb needs his mother."

"He has you."

"He misses *her*. *You* miss her."

Swearing, Atretes stood abruptly. "Leave it be!"

She saw the pain behind his fury. He had expected Rizpah to capitulate. When he had returned from the funeral fire, he had thrust Caleb into his mother's arms and sat before the fire. She had asked where Rizpah was, and all he had said was, "She knows who did it, but she won't tell me. Until she does, she's not welcome in this house." He sat before the fire, leaving her stunned and filled with questions. "She'll come," he said, punching his right fist into his left palm. "She'll come before morning."

He had waited all night for her. When morning had come, he was still sitting before the fire, staring so intently into the flames that he didn't even hear the pitiful wailing of his hungry son. She had taken Caleb to Marta who was still nursing Luisa. She had milk enough for two.

Now Atretes looked around the room. "Where's Caleb?" he said, eyes blazing. "Did you take him to Rizpah?"

"I took him to Marta. He hasn't been weaned."

"He's old enough."

"He's confused and frightened enough without doing that to him."

"I don't care," Atretes said, running his fingers through his hair. "Do what you think best, only don't give him to Rizpah. No matter how much she pleads, don't let her touch him."

"She hasn't come to me. She hasn't pleaded. She—"

"Enough! See to the boy and leave me alone!"

Varus spread the word through the village that Atretes had cast Rizpah out because she refused to tell him who had killed the Roman. No one understood her reasoning, least of all Varus, who carried the news. Why would the Ionian set herself in the path of vengeance over a man she had loved as much as Atretes? It made no sense. Her logic defied reason. Had the Ionian gone mad with grief?

Only Atretes knew it was not madness. It was her stubborn will that kept her from giving in. And knowing made him all the more angry.

People could talk of little else, though they didn't dare do so in Atretes' hearing.

On the twelfth day, Freyja waited until Atretes went out with Usipi to hunt. She took the path that had been worn from the back of the longhouse to the glen and Theophilus' grubenhaus. Crossing the open space, she saw Rizpah working in the garden. She looked like any other young woman going about her daily chores, but as Freyja came nearer, she heard Rizpah talking to herself as she loosened the soil and plucked weeds. The poor woman had gone mad.

"Rizpah?" she said cautiously.

She glanced up in surprise, and Freyja saw the ugly yellowing bruise on the left side of her face. "You startled me," Rizpah said and straightened. She brushed back a few loose tendrils of dark hair with the back of her hand. "Did Atretes send you?"

Freyja's heart sank at the look of hope in her dark eyes. "No."

"Oh," Rizpah said softly and looked toward the village. She closed her eyes for a brief moment, fighting back the tears, and then looked at Freyja again. She felt the older woman's discomfort and sympathy and smiled. "How is Caleb?"

"Marta's taking care of him."

Rizpah nodded. "I knew I could depend on you to see to his needs," was all she said, her smile filled with gratitude. She made no protest, uttered no heart-wrenching appeal or angry accusations, but Freyja felt the terrible toll of separation. Rizpah was not mad at all. She was resolved. She had set her course, and no wind would change it. Freyja wished she could understand.

"Why won't you tell Atretes who killed Theophilus?"

"Because he would kill the man."

"Is that so hard to understand?"

"Are you eager for more blood?"

"Of course not, but neither do I condone murder."

"Nor do I, Mother Freyja." She thought of the ceremonial dagger hidden in the tree. She searched Freyja's face for subterfuge and saw none. She thought of showing her the dagger and finding out whether it was Gundrid or Anomia behind Theophilus' death, and then decided against it. Not only Rolf would die. How many others were involved?

"I want to understand," Freyja said.

"Theophilus told me not to tell Atretes who it was," she said simply.

"But why? Surely the Roman would want his life avenged."

"No." Rizpah smiled gently. "Jesus forgave those who crucified him. Theophilus forgave as well. I can do no less."

"Atretes can't."

"He can if he so chooses."

"He won't. It's not in his nature to forgive the way you mean. It's not the Chatti way."

"It's not in anyone's nature, Lady Freyja, but it's the will of God." Her eyes filled again. "In Christ, anything is possible, even changing a man's heart. I pray for that constantly, that God will change Atretes' heart. And mine." She couldn't ask God to do something in Atretes' life that she wasn't willing to have done in her own.

Freyja wished she had brought her something—bread, cheese, a shawl to keep her warm.

Rizpah saw her dilemma and smiled. "The Lord is with me, Mother Freyja."

Freyja felt a shivering warmth within her at Rizpah's words and saw a look of serenity that was beyond anything she had ever felt in her life. How was it possible? "It's not right that you're the one punished."

"I thought that at first, but it was deception. This isn't punishment. It's war. Theophilus battled against the forces of darkness that live and breathe in this place, and now I must stand in his place."

Freyja paled and drew back.

Rizpah saw her fear. "You know what I mean, don't you? I can see it in your eyes that you understand. And you're afraid. But I tell you this: Christ's love casts out fear, Mother Freyja. If you will let Jesus redeem you, you need never be afraid again."

"I didn't come to speak of your god," Freyja said, disturbed by the feelings that gripped her, wondering yet again what it was about the name Jesus that made her shake inside. She clutched the amber pendant to protect herself, praying the spirit would not come upon her again.

It had not since Theophilus touched her.

Rizpah was saddened to see her so afraid. "The Lord will bring to light the things hidden in the darkness and disclose the motives in a man's heart." Or that of a woman. She wondered if Freyja had played an unwitting part in the tragedy, and knew if she had, it would distress them both to know it. "I can't set Atretes' feet on the path to murder. I won't. If he goes that way, he will go of his own free will and not with my assistance."

Freyja knew there was no use in talking to her. The young woman was set upon her strange task. However misguided she was, she sought only to protect Atretes from himself, not hurt him. Perhaps, given time, she would come to understand and accept that feuding and revenge were ingrained in their lives.

"I am sorry your friend was killed," she said with all sincerity. "He was not like other Romans." Seeing Rizpah's eyes fill again, she wished she hadn't spoken. "It wasn't my intent to hurt you more, Rizpah, but to see if I could help bring about reconciliation."

"Blessed are the merciful, for they shall receive mercy," Rizpah said softly, her eyes aglow with love.

Stifling the soft cry that welled within her, Freyja turned and hurried away.

"Tell Atretes I love him, Mother Freyja," Rizpah called out to her. "Tell him I always will."

Freyja paused and looked back. Tears running down her cheeks, Rizpah crouched again and plucked at some small weeds at the base of a small stalk of corn.

"I will tell him."

But when she did, Atretes wouldn't listen. "Even my mother betrays me!"

He took his possessions and moved into Rud's longhouse with the warriors who had no wives.

51

Anomia was vexed by the amount of interest expended on the Ionian, but hid her feelings. She had called together the secret council twice since the Roman had been killed, and each time fewer came. Neither time had Rolf appeared. When she asked where he was, the men laughed about a young man's lust, but Anomia sensed it was more than that.

Rolf should have sought her out. Several times she had seen him in the village since the night the lot was cast and the dagger was given to him. He always avoided her. If he didn't come to her soon, she would have to seek him out. Pride chafed at the thought, but she needed the dagger. It must be returned to the sacred tree where it was kept with the other emblems of faith in Tiwaz. And it had to be placed there before the new moon.

She thought of threatening him with exposure, but knew she couldn't. Just as the sacred vow of secrecy and blood prevented the men from revealing who the Roman's killer was, it bound her, too. If she exposed him, she would lose the others' trust.

She wanted the dagger in her hands again.

Frustrated, she turned her thoughts away from it. It didn't really matter. It was only a matter of time now before everything fell into place and she had all she deserved. Even if the woman revealed Rolf now, Anomia doubted Atretes would forgive her. He was Chatti through and through. It wasn't in him to forgive. She smiled.

She had won already. Oh, if they but knew. The war was almost over. Soon, they would know it. All of them. A few careful hints, and Atretes would take his revenge. Rolf would die in punishment for his lapse. When Atretes killed him, the loosening hold the Ionian and her weakling god had upon him would be broken. Tiwaz would reign supreme in his life again. He would be their warrior chief. No mention would ever be made of the Chatti needing a savior or bowing down to another god. She would see to that.

Anomia laughed in profane delight, reveling in the knowledge that she, and only she, had accomplished the task Tiwaz had set before her. The Roman was dead, the Ionian cast out.

What more could Tiwaz ask of her?

Soon she would have the power she craved, and with it, the man she wanted. Atretes.

*

A tapping awakened Rizpah in the predawn hours.

"Woman," came a gruff whisper, "I've left something for you. You'd best get it before the animals do." She heard running footsteps.

Rising sleepily, she opened the door and went outside to see who had come, but they were already gone. Bread, cheese, a skin of honeyed wine, and a dead rabbit had been left for her on a woven reed mat. She thanked God for the food and for the heart that had been moved by him to give it.

Two, at least, Theophilus had told her. *Perhaps more.*

Were they praying for her? She prayed for them all morning as she made a fire and roasted the rabbit. *Whoever they are, Lord, watch over them and protect them. Let their faith deepen.* She hadn't realized how hungry she was. Green beans and squash had sustained her, but this was a feast straight from heaven.

Needing to wash, she headed for the small stream nearby. She found the place where she always took Caleb to bathe. Wading in, fully clothed, she let the tears come as she bathed. Marta was good with Caleb, and he loved little Luisa. He was safe. She was comforted in knowing that, though she would never stop missing him. He was part of her, just as Atretes was, and the separation was as painful as if flesh had been torn away.

Who will teach my son about you, Lord? If Atretes doesn't turn back, who will teach Caleb the truth? Will he grow up the way Atretes did, trained to be a warrior, schooled in feuding among neighbors and his own people? Will he be like Rolf or Varus or Rud and a hundred others? Lord, please be with him. Make him a man after your own heart. Please, Lord.

When she came out of the stream, she wrung the water from her hair and loosened the folds of her garments. Her mind was so occupied with praying that she didn't hear the man approaching, nor see him standing in the trees. When she did, she stumbled back, fear her immediate reaction, then anger swiftly following.

"Did you come to kill me, too, Rolf?"

He said nothing. He just stood there in the shadows, silent, motionless, but she saw in his face what no words could have expressed. Fear and anger dissolved as she was moved by deep compassion. She came up the bank until she stood within a few feet of him. He looked so young, so wounded.

"You can talk to me. I'll listen."

His throat worked. She waited, tears brimming in her eyes as she saw the suffering in his.

"I was deceived. I . . ." He looked down at the ground, unable to look into her eyes. She saw his hands clench and unclench at his sides. "I *let* myself be deceived," he amended and looked at her again. "He just stood there and let me do it. He said . . ." His face worked. "He said . . ."

"He said he forgave you," Rizpah said in a trembling whisper, when he couldn't finish. She saw clearly how love had broken through his walls.

Rolf started to cry. "He spared my life, and I took his." He hadn't wanted to give in to unmanly tears, but they came, hot and heavy. He couldn't restrain them. Remembering Theophilus' face as he stabbed him the second time, he sank to his knees, his head in his hands, sobs wracking his body.

Rizpah put her arms around him. "I forgive you, too," she said, stroking his hair as she would a hurt child's. "Jesus forgives you. Take your heavy burdens to the Lord, for he is gentle and humble in heart; and you will find rest for your soul. His yoke is light and easy, Rolf, and he will give you rest."

52

Atretes came awake abruptly, breathing heavily as he stared up at a beamed roof. His heart slowed from its racing pace as he realized he lay in the straw of the bachelors' longhouse, surrounded by the rattling snores from the others who lay strewn nearby, blown down by whatever wind of passion had come upon them. Too much ale, too much living.

His body ached and his head throbbed from too much wine. He had drunk until he couldn't stand the night before, but not enough to drive the dreams away, nor fill the emptiness he felt.

He thought about Rizpah. He could still see the look on her face after he had hit her. Something else he couldn't forget. He tried to justify himself. If she had told him who the murderer was, everything would be settled by now. Theophilus' death would be avenged, and they could go on as they had.

The Spirit within him revolted at such thinking. It wouldn't give him peace, plaguing him constantly. He tried to lie to himself, but the truth was there, inside him.

"Feed the sheep."

He groaned. Sitting up, he rubbed his face. The headache intensified, his stomach churning. The dream was still too vivid in his mind, vivid enough to bring physical consequences. Stumbling to his feet, he barely made it out the back of the longhouse before he vomited. When the spasms were over, he leaned heavily back against the building, squinting against the afternoon sunlight. What time of day was it?

And what did he care? He wasn't going anywhere. He wasn't doing anything.

He had forgotten what it was like to live without hope, without love.

The strength of his body was wasting away. He seemed to spend every day lamenting. He felt a heavy hand upon him. His vitality was draining away as though the fever of rage sapped his strength. Not a night went by that he didn't dream of death or of life so painful he didn't want to live it. He saw the countless faces of men whose lives he had taken. He saw Bato dying by his own hand. He saw Pugnax chased down and torn to pieces by dogs. Sometimes he ran with him, heart in his throat, hearing the growls and feeling the snapping teeth behind him.

Then there were the dreams of Julia putting Caleb on the rocks and laughing when he couldn't get to him before the waves did. She always vanished as he ran into the crashing surf, trying desperately to find his son in the cold, frothing water. And then he'd see Caleb, always out of reach, swirling and dipping and sucked under by the dark currents.

Worst of all, he dreamed of Rizpah standing outside the grubenhaus, weeping. "Why didn't you do what he asked of you? Why didn't you feed the sheep?" And everywhere he looked were people he knew, lying dead—in the meadows, beneath the trees, in the longhouses, along the streets of the village, as though struck down during normal chores and living. Rud, Holt, Usipi, Marta, Varus, his mother, the children, all of them, *dead*!

"Why didn't you feed the sheep?" Rizpah would weep as she had this morning before he had awakened. And then she, too, was gone, swallowed by the encroaching darkness, and he was left alone, facing unspeakable terror.

Atretes wanted to shake away the memory of the dream.

"Feed the sheep."

"I tried!" Atretes groaned aloud. Angry, he looked up into the sky. "I tried, and no one listened!"

"Are you talking to yourself now, Atretes?"

He turned sharply at the soft, faintly mocking voice and saw Anomia standing at the corner of the longhouse. She smiled at him, a slow, provocative smile, and came into the open. As she walked toward him, he couldn't help but notice her body, lush and graceful. "A long night of drinking?"

"What are you doing here?"

"Oh. A headache, as well." She dangled a leather pouch. "I have something in here that will make you feel better."

He grew wary at the glowing look in her blue eyes. She came closer, close enough that he could smell the sweet musk scent she had rubbed on her body. Desire stirred. When she looked up into his eyes, he felt the hunger in her, insatiable, dark, beckoning . . . and his flesh responded.

"Shall I make you feel better?"

The temptation lay before him, stark and bold. He struggled

against it. "Where'd you come from?" He glanced back in the direction from which she had come. "It's hardly a beaten path."

Anomia's eyes barely flickered. She still smiled, but he felt her anger as strongly as he had felt her passion and knew the cause of it. "I was gathering herbs in the forest. Every morning about this time I go by myself to replenish my stores. Sometimes I go in the evening as well. Tonight, for instance. It'll be a new moon in a few days. There are things I need to gather in preparation."

"Indeed?" His blood caught fire, though his mind cooled with deeper understanding.

"Indeed," she said, smiling again, a faint, toying smile that plucked his nerve ends. She let the leather pouch swing back and forth on the end of her finger. "Shall I mix a little of this in some wine?"

"I've had enough wine."

"Ale, then, if you like it better. Or honeyed mead."

His head pounded harder. Maybe a little wine would help. Turning, he went back inside the longhouse. When he filled a horn and turned, she was standing in the shadows. "How the mighty fall," she said, sounding amused. He didn't know whether she was looking at him or the others passed out in the hay.

"We were celebrating."

She laughed softly. "Celebrating what?"

"I don't remember. Does it matter?" He brought the horn to her. When her fingers brushed his, his blood stirred. She opened the small pouch with her teeth, and he found himself staring at her mouth. She added the herbs, swirled the brew slowly, moistening her lips before she took a sip of it herself, and then held the horn up to him, her eyes glowing.

"Drink all of it, Atretes."

He drank, his gaze still fixed upon her. He drained the horn. "Not too bad," he said, wiping his mouth with the back of his hand.

"Now, sit."

His eyes narrowed. "Why?"

"You sound like a belligerent child. Are you afraid of me?"

He gave a derisive laugh.

"Then do as I ask. You want to get rid of the headache, don't you?"

He sat cross-legged in the hay. She moved behind him and began to knead his temples.

"Relax, Atretes. I'll do you no harm." She was laughing at him. He forced himself to relax, feeling ridiculous for his hesitance. He crushed the feelings of warning within him.

"Are you having dreams?"

"They never stop," he said, feeling the effects of whatever she had put in the ale. The pain was departing. She smoothed his hair back. Her hands were like magic, strong, yet gentle, knowing just where to press and give. He felt, too, the unspoken intimacy as she explored his muscles.

He heard the hay rustle behind him and felt her warm breath on the back of his neck. His body went hot.

"Does this feel good?"

Too good, he thought, but couldn't bring himself to draw away. How long since he had felt the heat of something besides wrath? Not since he had held Rizpah in his arms the night before Theophilus had been murdered.

Rizpah.

Anomia's hands gripped his shoulders. "I can make you feel better."

Her whisper sent his mind reeling. Sucking in his breath, he closed his eyes, fighting the lust rising within him. Like a sharp bang, he heard a cell door closing, and he was back in the ludus. With an uttered curse, Atretes jerked from her and stood.

"What's wrong?" Anomia said, startled by his retreat. He moved a few feet away from her. She had felt his desire through her fingertips. What had happened to break the mood? "Tell me, Atretes."

"Nothing!"

"Did I do something?" she said.

Atretes glanced back at her. She looked all innocence and hurt confusion. "I don't know. Did you?" His breath still came hard, and he raked a shaking hand back through his hair. His best friend had been murdered. He was estranged from his wife. His child was being raised by his sister. He was living the wild life he had longed for as a youth! And he had just toyed with thoughts of adultery. He laughed mirthlessly. What could possibly be wrong?

"Nothing's wrong," he said bitterly. Nothing other than the fact that his life was in shambles.

What had happened to the peace he had known?

God, if only I could go back to those few weeks after I was baptized and married Rizpah. I was never more happy than I was then. I'll never be that happy again. Was it all a dream, Lord, a chance idyll before reality struck? Were you playing a cruel joke on me? Do you even exist?

Unbidden, other voices came to him.

"She told me to tell you she loves you and she always will."

"I give you a solemn vow, Atretes. I will never lie. Even if it costs my life."

Anomia saw his torment and hoped it was the passion she had roused in him that caused it. She rose and came to him. "Come back to us, Atretes."

"I am back."

"Not the way you were. Oh, I remember you, all passion and fire and strength. You were like a god. Everyone would have followed you to Hades if you'd asked it of them."

He shut his eyes. *Jesus,* his soul cried out.

He could see Theophilus' face and hear his voice. *"Feed the sheep."*

"Leave me alone," he said roughly.

"You're in torment," Anomia said with feigned sympathy, secretly glorying in it. It made him vulnerable. "I can see your anguish. I share it. I can help you. Let me help you. You could be the man you once were, Atretes. I know you can. Let me show you the way."

I am the way.

One of the men roused from sleep. Anomia drew back into the shadows so she wouldn't be seen. She clenched her hands, throbbing with impatience until the man sank back again with a loud groan.

By the time she was able to return to Atretes' side, his mood had changed. Too immersed in his dark reverie, he paid her no heed. She laid a hand upon his arm and felt his muscles tense. "I must go," she whispered, cursing the place and circumstance. "Come out with me tonight, and we'll talk."

He didn't hear her, too absorbed in his thoughts of Rizpah. He ached for his wife, all the while resenting her hold on him with every ounce of his will.

"You act as though you've been bewitched," Anomia said, angry and full of jealousy that he should be so indifferent.

"Maybe I am," he said grimly. "Maybe I am."

53

Atretes spent the day in feasting and nursing his grievances against his wife. She had chosen to stand in the way of justice, hadn't she? She had *chosen* to live without him. Why should he allow the woman to plague his every waking thought? He seared his burning conscience with excuses.

Dulled further by drink, he let his imagination wander. Anomia came to speak with one of the men, and when she looked at him, sultry invitation glowed in her pale blue eyes. When she left, he remembered other women who had been brought to him. Once he had wanted his mind wiped clean of his past so they wouldn't pollute his marriage bed. Now he dredged up the memories, living them again, hoping past pleasures might drive away the present pain. Instead, he fell into a deeper, more confusing despair.

The men around him did not help. After the long months of winter inactivity, they craved action. But until a war was declared, they had little to do but drink and talk about the battles they had won. No one talked of losses. They told bawdy tales, each trying to outdo the other. The laughter grated. Arguments over trivial issues erupted in fights between younger warriors hungry to prove their manhood.

Atretes didn't join in. He sat in a far corner, his expression enough to warn others away. He drank with purpose, to drown his pain. And failed.

The noise grew louder, men arguing over a dice game. His head was spinning from the ale. Rising, he headed for the back door, wanting to be alone.

Pale moonlight cast an eerie glow as he stumbled into the forest. He didn't know where he was going. He didn't care. He heard a soft voice beckon him and his heart jumped. "Rizpah?" he whispered, looking around him.

But it was Anomia in the darkening shadows.

Anguished, he went to her without thinking. She took his hand and drew him deeper into the darkness. "I knew you'd come," she said and was in his arms. She was rapacious, the force of her passion rocking him. "I knew you'd come to me." Her voice was feverish with desire, reminding him of another time, another woman. The memory slashed across his mind, opening old wounds.

Julia. She was like Julia had been, on fire with lust.

"What are you doing here?" he groaned, sluggish from the ale he had drunk.

"You wanted me here. I knew when I looked in your eyes tonight."

"I came out to think."

"No, you didn't." Anomia moved against him, her nails digging in. "You came out to be with me. You want me as much as I want you." Her voice was like an animal growl in the hollow of her throat. "I see it in your eyes every time you look at me. You're burning up with it the way I am."

Her body moved. Her hands moved. He couldn't breathe. "Don't."

"Why are you stopping me? You want this. You've wanted me since the first." She let her head go back, wanting him to press his mouth to the curve of her neck. "Do it, Atretes. Do what you want."

"Rizpah said to tell you she loves you and she always will."

Atretes looked down at Anomia and felt the hot breath of hell in his face. Her throat was an open grave. He shoved her away from him and stumbled back. "No." He struggled against the drink-induced cloud in his head. *"No."*

Anomia came close, her flowing hair drifting with the cool night wind. He felt a strand of it like the gossamer web of a spider across his eyes. "You want me," she breathed, her hands spreading over his chest. "I can feel your heart pounding."

"You're like Julia," he said raggedly.

"Julia? Who's Julia?" Her hands slipped away, her eyes narrowing.

Atretes drew back from her, dizzy from the ale.

"Caleb's mother," he said without thinking, the cold night air intensifying the effects of the ale.

Caleb's *mother*? Anomia's eyes gleamed. She came closer.

He swayed slightly, his laugh bitter. "Julia, lovely wanton Julia. She came to me in the temple of Diana, dressed like a harlot, bells on her ankles. She was beautiful, like you, and as corrupt as decaying flesh."

Corrupt as decaying flesh? Anger flooded her being, cold and calculating. "I love you. I've loved you for as long as I can remember."

"Love," he sneered. "What do you know of love?"

She shook, hot tears moistening her eyes—tears of fury. "I know what it's like to ache for someone and have them be indifferent to you." How dare he treat her this way? She was a high priestess, more powerful than his own mother, more powerful than Gundrid. Half the men in the village were in love with her! Some would give their souls to taste what she was offering him!

Atretes saw her tears and regretted his harsh words. Perhaps she did love him. Vanity blinded him to the cunning heart that lay beneath the innocent facade.

Anomia knew. He was so proud, so full of himself. She put her hand on his arm, her hair floating up with the breeze, strands of it tangling around him. "Other men have wanted me."

"I have no doubt," he said hoarsely.

"I saved myself for *you*. I'm a virgin. No other man has had me. I waited for you."

He looked at her, stunned. It never occurred to him that a virgin could have the mind of a harlot.

His body responded. He knew what she was offering, and the temptation shook him. "No," he said before he could change his mind.

"Why not?"

"Because I've been down this road before, and I won't walk it again." He'd be lost if he did. He knew what it was like to be chained to a woman because of lust.

"You want me," she said again, coming so close her body brushed his. "I can feel how much you want me." Her touch was like fire. "The Ionian doesn't love you the way I do." She slid her hands up, relishing her sense of power when she felt his heart pounding against her palms. "If she did, she would've come to you weeks ago, begging for you to take her back."

Atretes cringed at the thought.

Anomia brushed against him again and heard him suck in his breath. "I've waited so long for you. I'll never hurt you the way she has. Just this once, Atretes." Once and he would never be able to say no again. "Just once. No one has to know."

He would know.

The Sacrifice

Atretes caught her wrists and took her hands from him. "She's my wife, Anomia, and you know the law."

Her eyes flashed and then cooled again. "You have a wife who doesn't want you. You have a wife who's a foreigner and doesn't belong here. You've already come to realize that or you wouldn't have abandoned her."

He stepped back, wanting distance between them, needing it so he could think clearly. *Abandoned.* The word struck like an arrow, piercing him with guilt. With a groan, he stumbled away from Anomia.

Cold rage swept through the priestess. It came over her like an onrushing tide, jealousy in the crashing of waves. She watched him stumble and waited for him to fall. When he did, she approached him stealthily and knelt down beside him.

"You said someone named Julia bore your child," she murmured, brushing his hair back from his face.

"She ordered him put on the rocks to die." He gave a bitter laugh. "Roman women do that. They throw their children away when they don't want them. If Rizpah hadn't taken him, he would've died."

"Don't pass out yet, Atretes," she murmured, pinching him hard in the side. "She took your son? Without you knowing?"

"A slave girl brought him to her." He thought of Hadassah standing in the torchlight corridor of the dungeon, her face serene. *"Though he slay me, yet will I trust in him."* He remembered how she had stood in the mouth of the cave where he had lived after Julia betrayed him. *"The heavens tell of the glory of God, and their expanse declares the work of his hands,"* she had said, looking out at the night sky. It was from Hadassah's lips he had first heard the gospel of Jesus Christ and in her that he'd first seen the peace God could bring into a life.

He could see the stars now, looking up through the branches of the tree under which he sat. What he wouldn't give to feel that peace again.

Forgive your enemies.

Jesus forgave.

Theophilus forgave.

Anomia saw him grimace as though he was in pain. He groaned, his head lolling back and forth. "Rizpah...," came the soft insidious voice that seemed to be worming its way inside his head. "I love her."

"Not that. Did she bring the child to you?"

Troubled and drunk, he didn't think. "No. I had to hunt for him. All I knew was a widow had him."

"A widow?"

"She lost her own child." Atretes rubbed his face, trying to clear his head. "I took Caleb from her, but he wouldn't nurse from anyone else."

"Bewitched."

"As I'm bewitched," he said bleakly. "She bewitched me from the first moment I laid eyes on her. Can't stop thinking about her. Can't stop." All he wanted to do was sink into the void of dreamless sleep. And closing his eyes, he did.

Anomia's mouth curved. He was too drunk to realize the power he had just placed in her hands. She leaned close, nuzzled his neck, and then whispered in his ear. "But you will. Just wait until you realize . . ."

She pulled his head back. The ale he had drunk had rendered him unconscious. She touched his face, marveling at how handsome he was, feeling bitter and thwarted in her desire, hungry for her own revenge at being scorned. If she couldn't have him, the Ionian certainly wouldn't.

"A pity you didn't want me." She pressed a hard kiss to his unresponsive mouth. "You're going to have so much to regret."

She left him sleeping in the woods.

THE HARVEST

"The seed on good soil produced a crop, multiplying thirty, sixty, or even a hundred times."

54

Atretes awakened to someone calling his name. He thought he imagined it. Sitting up, he realized he was in the woods. His tunic was drenched with night dew, the stars still bright against the darkened sky. What was he doing out here?

He remembered leaving the longhouse, wanting to get away from the noise, needing quiet to think.

He vaguely remembered Anomia. He felt unclean, and niggling worry ate at him.

"Atretes!"

He didn't feel like talking to anyone, but the voice was so urgent, he roused himself.

"Atretes! Where are you?"

"Over here," he said, grimacing.

Herigast appeared. He was out of breath from running. "You've got to come with me. Gundrid and the Thing have had your wife taken from the grubenhaus."

"What are you talking about?" Atretes said, shaken by a wave of nausea. "Taken her where?"

"To the sacred grove for trial. Anomia said she's been with other men."

The fog left Atretes' mind and his head snapped up. He'd warned Rizpah never to speak of her past, for he knew the cost if it ever became known. "What did you say?"

"Anomia said *you* told her your wife had been with other men before you."

He swore softly and tried to get up. His blood went cold as he sat down hard again. "Julia!" He remembered rambling bitterly about Julia!

"Are you listening to me?" Herigast said, grabbing the front of his tunic and shaking him. "They're going to kill her unless you tell them Anomia's lying!"

"*I will never lie,*" Rizpah's words haunted him again. He knew she would tell the truth, even if her life was forfeit.

"O God," Atretes said under his breath. "O Jesus, what have I done?" He jerked free of Herigast and ran. As he did, he tried to remember what he had said, how much he had told Anomia that could be used against Rizpah.

Enough to get her killed.

When he reached the gathering, he pushed his way through the warriors to get to the inner circle. Rizpah stood in the center, hands bound. "Don't say anything!" he told her. "Don't answer any of their questions!"

Anomia stepped forward quickly, pointing at him. "Keep him away from her! She's cast a spell on him and can make him say anything!"

Hands fell upon him.

"Let go of me!" He struggled as they dragged him back. "You don't have to answer their accusations, Rizpah! *Say nothing!*" Pain lanced his heart at the look of sorrow in her eyes. He had betrayed her. With his own lips, he had poured out the words that would be used against her.

"Atretes told me himself she bewitched him!" Anomia called out to the gathering, her eyes glittering as she looked at him.

"You're the witch!"

She relished the anguish and rage she saw in Atretes' face, gloating openly. Let him suffer for his indifference toward her. "He said the child isn't even hers."

"Rizpah *is* his mother!"

"You told me yourself the mother's name was Julia! You told me this woman took your child—"

"Don't listen to her!" Atretes fought against those holding him. Others helped, forcing him to his knees.

"And *you said* she cast a spell upon the child so he wouldn't take milk from anyone but her."

Rizpah looked at him, and he wanted to die.

"It's Atretes' word against yours," Rolf said, stunning every warrior present as he entered the circle.

"Betrayer!" Anomia cried out at him, eyes blazing. "*You* dare question *me*, a high priestess of Tiwaz?"

"I dare," he said. "I dare even more!" He pointed at her while addressing the others in a loud voice. "*Anomia* is the one who sent me to kill the Roman! She has a heart for murder. Don't listen to her!"

Atretes uttered a loud cry and tried to fight free of the men holding him.

"*I* didn't send you! *Tiwaz* sent you." She felt Gundrid's look and turned on him. "The lot was cast upon the white cloth, and the honor fell to Rolf. The Roman was a deceiver!" His fear of her made him acquiesce, obliterating that small threat.

"The Roman spared my life!" Rolf cried out to all.

"In order to fool us into believing he came in peace!" Anomia said disdainfully. "He came to weaken us, to make us believe in his god who said to forget trespasses done against us! Should we forget what Rome has done to us? Should we forget those who have died, those who have been taken as slaves, those who have been left crippled?" She looked from face to face, knowing those who were most vulnerable, driving her words into their hearts.

"The Roman came to make us turn away from Tiwaz!" she cried out. "Turn from Tiwaz, and be destroyed! Is it any wonder Tiwaz called for the Roman's execution? Tiwaz saw the truth about him."

She thrust out her hand. "As Tiwaz knows the truth about this woman! She is *unclean*! She is a black-eyed witch! Atretes told me himself. He said she was with another man before him, perhaps more than one. He said she had another child by another man and that child died. He said Roman women cast their children upon the rocks."

Some of the men shouted, "Harlot! Kill her!"

"She's lying," Atretes cried out, fighting with all his strength and gaining nothing.

Freyja pressed her way forward, striving for inward calm as she raised her hands and beseeched all for quiet. "You must have proof, Anomia."

"There is no proof!" Atretes ground out as loudly as he could. "It's her word against mine."

"See how the Ionian has bewitched him!"

The men shouted.

Gundrid raised his arms high in the air. "Mother Freyja wants proof. I will give you proof of other crimes the woman has committed while here among us," he said in his orator's voice. "She practices cannibalism, a crime worthy of death. She eats the rejuvenating flesh and drinks the blood of this Jesus Christ whom she serves. And through witchcraft, she has drawn Atretes into this abominable practice."

"*Kill her!*"

"No!"

"I heard the Roman say they were eating the flesh and drinking the blood of a man named Jesus!" Gundrid cried out, having crept close and spied upon them when they were unaware.

"The evil must be cut out from among us!" Anomia cried out. She saw her time had come. "You already have all the evidence you need. Do you remember the first day the Roman and this woman came to us? They spoke our language by the power of the demons. That is enough to seal her fate. We don't need proof that she stole a newborn baby in order to capture the father. We don't need proof that she slept with other men. We know these things to be true. Have you not seen the pull she already has upon all our children. Ask Usipi about Luisa, who goes to her each time she appears! Ask others how our little ones went into the forest to hear the Roman sing to them. Will you let her live so she can steal your children, too?"

"No!"

"She's an enemy of Tiwaz!"

Freyja could not believe the things she heard, would not believe. "Let her speak in her own defense," she pleaded. "By our law, she has the right."

"She will cast a spell upon us as well," Anomia said in consternation. "She must be destroyed before she destroys us."

"Let her speak!" Rolf shouted. "Or are you afraid she has more power than you?"

Herigast joined him. "Let her answer the charges!"

Filled with wrath, Anomia looked upon the ones who had turned from her. She saw others doubting. She would make them sorry. She would make them pay.

"Let her speak!"

Atretes tried to lunge free. *"No!"*

Hearing what was in his voice, Anomia turned to him in veiled surprise. His fear was like a drug in her system, rousing her senses, making her mind buzz. Atretes didn't want the woman to speak. Why? Turning, she studied Rizpah. At first, all she saw was a beautiful young woman, her enemy, standing before her. Then she saw more. She saw her quiet humility, her dignity, her *integrity*, and she knew why Atretes wanted her to say nothing.

Anomia raised her hand for silence. "Perhaps we should ask her."

"Say nothing to them," Atretes said, struggling with every

ounce of his strength. He gained nothing. "Rizpah!" She looked back at him, face pale but serene, and he knew she would keep her word to him. *No matter the cost,* she'd said.

And the cost would be her life.

Rizpah saw his grief and shame. "I love you, Atretes," she said and saw tears fill his eyes before he shut them.

Anomia struck her across the face. "Do not speak to him or look at him, witch!"

"This is your hour, Anomia, the hour of darkness," Rizpah said quietly and looked straight into her opaque blue eyes without fear.

"You think to frighten me? You or your imagined god?"

"A day will come when every knee shall bow and every tongue confess that Jesus Christ *is* Lord. Even *you* will bow down to him."

"Do you hear what she says?" Anomia shouted with a mocking laugh, her gaze still fixed upon Rizpah. "She would have us on our *knees.* She would have the Chatti, the greatest race on the earth, groveling before a crucified *savior.*" She turned to the others then, spreading her arms. "How long would it take then before Rome killed every last one of you?"

Rizpah bowed her head, praying silently and fervently. *O God, you know my foolish heart and my every weakness. None of my wrongs are hidden from you, Father. Please may Atretes and Rolf and all those who have heard your Word and believed not be ashamed because of me. O Lord God, may those among these people who seek you not be discouraged or dishonored through me tonight.*

"What's your decision?" Anomia cried out.

Men shouted for her death, but some for pardon.

Herigast entered the circle. "Because the woman believes in another god doesn't make her a harlot!"

Warriors shouted more angrily, hearing one of their own speak on her behalf.

"You never forgave Atretes for commanding your son to be drowned in the bog for cowardice!" Holt said.

"I have heard you speak often against him and his wife. Why do you now defend her?" another cried out.

"Because I heard the Word of her God from the Roman," Herigast shouted back, "and it took the hatred and the pain from my heart!"

"And took your strength as well!" Anomia said contemptuously.

"The Ionian has bewitched Herigast as she bewitched Atretes!" Gundrid said, and more men shouted. "How many others has she bewitched!"

Anomia turned again to Rizpah. "Speak the truth, or may your own god strike you dead!"

"Be strong and courageous, beloved," Rizpah could almost hear Theophilus speaking again. And on the heels of that remembrance came the words of God: *"Do not be afraid or tremble at them, for the Lord your God is the one who goes before you. He will not fail you or forsake you."*

"I will speak the truth," Rizpah said loud enough for all to hear. "Hear the Word of the Lord! The Lord is our God, the Lord is one! It is the Lord who pardons all your iniquities, who heals all your diseases, who redeems your life from the pit, who crowns you with loving-kindness and compassion, and who will satisfy your soul!"

Anomia screamed in rage, the words like hot coals upon her mind.

"It is the Lord God who has made us. He is the Good Shepherd, and we are the sheep of his pastures!"

"Speak no more!" Gundrid cried out in fear, looking to the skies. Darkening clouds swirled overhead, thickening. "See how her words have angered Tiwaz!"

"It is the Lord God you have angered!" Rizpah cried out. She saw the night sky blackening and was desperate for them to hear. "Tiwaz holds no power over you but what you give him. Turn away. Turn away from him before it's too late. Turn to the Lord."

"Don't listen to her! Stop your ears!" Gundrid commanded. "Cry out to Tiwaz! Cry out!"

The warriors began the baritus.

"The Lord made the heavens and the earth and the sea and all that is in them!" Rizpah cried out. "There is no one holy like the Lord. There is no God besides him, nor is there any Rock like our God!"

Anomia hit her hard enough to drive her to her knees.

Atretes lunged forward but was dragged back. Other hands fell upon him and he was forced down, face to the ground. Holt's knee was in his back, others held his arms and legs.

The baritus rose louder, a battle cry against the Lord.

"*Put your armor on, beloved,*" Atretes remembered Theophilus saying. "*One man of God puts to flight a thousand, for the Lord your God is he who fights for you.*"

"God," he groaned. "God, fight for her." Bound and helpless, he prayed, crying out with his heart to the Lord. *Jesus, I have sinned. I deserve death, not her. I turned away. Lord God, forgive me, I turned away. There is no one besides you. O Lord, my God, come between my wife and this multitude. O Lord God, my God, forgive me.*

He wept. "Jesus! Jesus!"

God, don't let her be destroyed because of my weak faith and foolishness. O Lord, let them not prevail against you.

The clouds swirled, boiling over and blocking out the stars and the moon so that only the torches cast light upon the sacred grove. An ominous rumble rolled.

"Hear Tiwaz's voice!" Anomia screamed, heart racing wildly.

"Repent!" Rizpah cried out, sobbing in fear for them. "In repentance and rest you will be saved, in quietness and trust. Turn your hearts to the Lord!"

"Cry out to Tiwaz!" Anomia screamed above the din. "Let him hear your voices! Yes! *Yes!* Let him hear you!"

"*Tiwaz! Tiwaz!*" Warriors banged frameas against their shields.

Lightning flashed, the jagged spear of hot light striking the sacred tree. The mighty oak cracked down the middle and fell, shaking the earth on which they stood. Flames shot up from its root.

Men screamed, some fleeing the circle in terror, Gundrid among them.

Anomia remained, ranting at them. "Call upon Tiwaz before he destroys you!"

"*Tiwaz! Tiwaz!*"

Lightning flashed again, striking the altar this time and melting the golden horns.

Rizpah prostrated herself in holy terror. "God, forgive them. O God, forgive them." She wept.

Herigast fell to his face and clung to the earth.

Only Rolf stood arms spread wide, filled with elation. "Justice belongs to the Lord!"

"Silence them before they bring further wrath upon us!"

Anomia screamed, and those of her chosen council moved against them. "*She* is the enemy! Our salvation depends upon her death!"

"No!" Freyja cried out, staring up at the swirling heavens. "Her god comes upon us. Don't touch her!"

"She must die!"

"*No!*" Others screamed.

Anomia saw the terror in those who remained and knew she had to use it. "Better that one should die to save the many!"

Freyja was terrified. "What if what she says about her god is true?"

"You have betrayed Tiwaz with your lips! You have always betrayed him in your heart. I have seen. I know!"

Freyja drew back.

Anomia dragged Rizpah up from the ground by her hair. "What if she's lied about everything else? Speak, witch! Is the child of your body?"

Atretes dug his fingers into the earth and moaned.

"No," Rizpah said.

"And his mother's name was Julia?"

"Yes."

"Did Atretes take his son back from you?"

"Yes."

"Did you have a child by another man?"

"Yes."

"And that child is dead?"

Rizpah closed her eyes. "Yes."

"O God," Atretes groaned softly.

"By her own lips, she has passed sentence upon herself," Anomia said, her fist tightening in Rizpah's hair as she looked around at the circle of stunned faces. "Tiwaz struck the tree and the holy emblems because we are forsaking his law by letting her live! See how the heavens clear now and the stars shine again!"

"Lord, you are my Rock and my Redeemer," Rizpah murmured in complete surrender.

Anomia pulled Rizpah's head back further, exposing her pale throat. "Atretes knows the law! He brought her here, for he knew in his heart that only we could set him free of the spell by which she's bound him and his son. Once she is dead, he'll be the man we used to know. He'll lead us to victory."

Atretes raised his head, his eyes awash with tears. "Kill my wife and I swear before God, I'll lead you all to hell!"

"No, Atretes!" Rizpah said in grief. "No, beloved. Remember the Lord. Remember what we've been taught."

Feed the sheep.

He wept. "They're going to kill you because of me!"

"God is with us. Whom shall we fear?"

"I love you! I love you. Forgive me." He saw in her eyes she already had.

"See the power she has over him!" Anomia cried out. "There is no deliverance for us if we let her live."

"Take her to the bog!" Rud shouted, and as chief, his words were heeded.

"The bog!" Others agreed, until Rolf and Herigast's voices were drowned out in the din and confusion.

Anomia's eyes gleamed with malicious delight as she looked down into Rizpah's face. "See the power I have over you," she hissed.

"You have no power but what God has given you."

"So even *he* heeds my voice," she mocked. She leaned closer. "I thirst to rip out your throat with my own teeth, but they must do it." She released her and stepped back. She called forth Rud to fulfill the law and the custom. "Shave off her hair."

Rud took out his knife and proceeded to shave the left side of Rizpah's head close to the scalp. On the right side, he cut the hair two inches in length, letting the luxuriant dark locks fell to the ground around her.

Rizpah saw Freyja weeping, clutching her amber amulet. "Turn to the Lord, Mother."

Anomia struck her again, dazing her. "Strip her and put the collar on!"

Rud slit the back of Rizpah's tunic and tore it from her. He took the heavy leather collar from Anomia's hand and put it around Rizpah's neck, then dragged her roughly to her feet.

"The Lord will bring to light the truth, if you but ask," Rizpah said, using what time she had left. "Christ died for your sins. He was buried and raised on the third day. Through one man, Adam, death came into the world; and through Jesus Christ, our Lord, we have life everlasting."

"Silence her!" Anomia said, her eyes flashing with fury.

Rud struck Rizpah a vicious blow and then shoved her in the direction of the bog. The others followed.

"Bring Atretes!" Anomia called back to them. "He must watch her die if the spell is to be broken." She looked into his eyes, wanting him to know it was his suffering and not his redemption she sought.

Hauled to his feet, Atretes was taken along. Others, concerned for Rolf and Herigast, brought them as well.

Anomia led the gathering of Chatti warriors by torchlight through the dense forest to the edge of the marshland. She felt an eerie change around her, as though the air itself was charged with power. The hour of darkness was passing away. Dawn would be upon them soon. The deed must be done.

She hurried her steps, urging the others on.

Gray moss hung from the branches of ancient trees. The air smelled of decay. She came to the edge of bog and turned, facing those who had followed her. Atretes wept openly, his eyes never straying from his wife's face.

The priestess looked upon Rizpah with contempt. Atretes' woman, too, was broken, for her eyes were closed, her lips moving as though she had gone completely mad.

"By the power I've been given by Tiwaz, I proclaim this woman unchaste, a foul witch and deceiver, and I pass the sentence of death upon her. Let her be cast into the bog."

Rizpah raised her head and looked from face to face. "My God, whom I serve, is able to deliver me from the pit."

Warriors jeered.

"Deliver you?" Anomia laughed. "You're going to be sucked down into the bowels of the earth, never to be seen again." Stepping back, she spoke loudly to those gathered. "Listen to me and obey! Her name is never to be spoken among the Chatti again. Let it be as though she never walked the face of the earth." They cried out their assent.

Atretes went to his knees, his lips moving as the Ionian's had done. Anomia saw Rizpah smile at him tenderly.

"Take her!"

Rud grasped Rizpah's arms.

"No, Rud," Rizpah said, looking into his weathered face. "Let me go alone, lest you die as well."

His eyes flickered.

"Do you listen to her or me?"

Rud's grip tightened. He pushed Rizpah out onto a wide plank, but as he came near the end, his feet slipped. Releasing her, he tried to save himself. Instead, he lost his balance, and they both fell.

"Throw him a rope!" Holt shouted. Panic spread through the gathering as they saw their high chief in the bog, flaying for a handhold.

"Hurry!" he screamed.

A rope snaked out to him, but he was already going under.

Atretes shut his eyes tightly so he wouldn't have to watch his wife drowning with his friend. "Lord Jesus, God of mercy," he moaned, as men shouted. He heard Rud choking and crying out for help.

The men pulled and pulled and then fell back as the rope was released.

Silence fell, and then another scream rent the air, a woman's scream.

"Look!" Freyja pointed, her face draining of all color. *"Look! Do you see?"*

Restraining hands dropped from Atretes as Chatti warriors cried out and fled or fell upon their faces in terror. Uttering a moaning wail, Anomia stared and still could not believe. And then fear such as she had never known filled her and she ran wildly, disappearing into the shadows of the forest.

"He brought me up out of the pit of destruction, out of the miry clay, and he set my feet upon a rock, making my footsteps firm."

Rizpah kept walking until she was twenty feet beyond the place where Rud had sunk into the bog, and there she stood, in the middle of the bog, as though on solid ground.

Beside her was a man, tall and powerful, shimmering with radiant white.

The sun rose brilliantly behind Rizpah, and for an instant Atretes wondered if he had gone mad and was imagining what he thought he saw. "Rizpah!" he cried out, throwing his hand up to shield his eyes from the brightness, unable to see her. *"Rizpah!"*

Then suddenly, he saw her again. She was running toward him, the dazzling light still at her back. He met her at the edge of the bog and caught her in his arms, pulling her close, holding her tightly against him. He buried his face in the curve of her neck, his hands covering her shaven head, his legs buckling. She went to her knees with him.

Shaking violently, eyes wide, Herigast stared out into the swamp. Sunlight streamed through the distant trees, almost blinding him. He realized he was shouting and crying and laughing all at the same time. The white light faded into softer colors of morning.

Rolf rose from the ground where he had prostrated himself. The few who had remained rose with him. Most had run away.

Atretes rose, drawing his wife up with him. "Jesus is Lord!" he said, a joyous conviction ringing in his voice that hadn't been there before. The sound of it echoed through the forest, driving back the darkness. "He is Lord of the heavens and the earth and all that is within it. Bless his holy name!"

"Bless his holy name," Herigast said, awed, heart still pounding.

Trembling, Freyja rose from the ground where she had prostrated herself. She fumbled with the amber talisman bearing the runes of Tiwaz, removing it from around her neck. With a soft cry, she flung the pendant far out into the bog and watched it quickly sink from her sight. The fear and despair that had so often held her captive melted away.

Rolf waited, uncertain. Not until Atretes turned and looked at him would he would know whether he lived or died. In either case, so be it. Atretes released Rizpah and turned. When he let his wife go and walked toward him, Rolf lowered his eyes, feeling the heavy purpose in each step that brought Atretes nearer.

"Forgive me," Atretes said hoarsely. "I was a fool."

Rolf's head came up. Tears filled his eyes. "Less than I."

Atretes gripped the younger man's shoulder. "It seems to be the failing in all men."

"We must tell the others!" Freyja said, face shining.

But someone else had reached them first.

Marta burst from the forest, thrusting Caleb and clothing in Rizpah's arms. "You must go. Take her quickly, Atretes, or they'll kill you, too."

"Marta!" Rizpah said, reaching for her, but Marta shook her head, backing away.

"Shake the dust of this place from your feet and leave," Marta said, running away as villagers appeared.

"Leave us!" men and women shouted hysterically. "Take your

foreign wife and god and go from us before you bring further calamity."

Theophilus' possessions as well as their own were thrown at them.

"*Go!*"

"No!" Freyja cried out. "The Lord Jesus Christ *is* the true God." She ran into the midst of them, searching for Varus, for Usipi, for anyone who might listen.

Herigast and Rolf ran in search of their wives.

"Their god will destroy us!"

"Go away from here!"

Some picked up clods and stones to throw.

"Leave us!"

"*Leave us!*"

Atretes pulled Rizpah back. "We must go."

"We can't leave them."

Grabbing up the gear, Atretes sheltered his wife and son as he urged them toward the forest east of the village. When Rizpah looked back, he caught hold of her hand and kept walking.

"*Feed the sheep,*" Theophilus had said, but something more impelled Atretes onward and kept him from looking back again: "*And any place that does not receive you or listen to you, shake off the dust from the soles of your feet for a testimony against them.*"

Rizpah wept for the lost, and so did he, but they'd made their choice, just as Rud had the instant before he fell into the pit.

"Wait!" someone called. "Wait for us!"

Atretes stopped and looked back, his throat working as he saw Rolf running toward him, holding his wife by the hand. When they reached them, Rizpah thanked God and embraced them each in turn while Atretes stood to one side, his gaze searching the forest for others, praying fervently more would follow. "Are there others coming?"

"I don't know," Rolf said, out of breath. "I didn't wait. I didn't look back."

Atretes led them on through the forest.

55

They made camp on an eastern hill a far distance from the village.

As darkness fell, Rizpah sat in front of her husband, leaning into him, Caleb in her lap. Atretes put his arms around her, nuzzling her shorn hair, thanking God he hadn't lost her. Then he closed his eyes.

Rizpah knew he was praying. He had said hardly anything all day. She knew what was in his heart and joined him in beseeching the Lord.

A twig snapped and they looked up. Atretes drew in a ragged breath, his heart in his throat. "Thank God," he said in a hoarse voice.

With a soft cry, Rizpah set Caleb quickly aside and jumped to her feet.

Freyja came into her arms and clung to her. "Wherever you go, I will go. Your God will be my God."

Others had come with her.

"Good thing you camped on a hillside," Usipi said, grinning as he came forward, clasping Atretes' hand. Marta set Luisa down and went into her brother's arms, the children around her. Herigast and Anna had come, as well as Helda and her husband, Sig. Everyone was talking at once.

Atretes looked around at those who had come out of the darkness into the circle of light.

So few, he thought and then pressed the sorrow back. There were other things to think of, many things to do, and with the same fierce determination he had always possessed in matters of life and death, he turned his will and life to the task ahead.

"Feed the sheep," Theophilus had said. *"Feed the sheep."*

It was a small flock.

But it was a beginning.

EPILOGUE

Atretes led the small of band of Christians into the northeastern plains where they established a small community on one of the Roman trade routes. Atretes and Rizpah began the task of teaching and guiding those who had left behind all for the glory of the gospel. The small band grew strong in their faith and soon were sharing their testimony with traveling merchants who came to their village. Before long the Word of the Lord spread north, south, east, and west.

Rizpah and Atretes found a new and deeper joy in each other as they grew ever closer to the Lord. And Caleb was delighted the day their family was increased when his sister, Hadassah, was born. She was to be the first child of many born in the small community; the second generation of a people wholly devoted to Jesus Christ.

As for Anomia, within a year of her hasty departure from the sacred grove, she returned to her people and plied them with claims of having received revelation from Tiwaz. Rome would fall, she told them, and they would be the ones to bring her down. They believed her. Alliances were sought and made, warriors gathered.

In A.D. 83, the Chatti led a second rebellion against the Empire. Domitian, the new emperor, sent his legions north. Within two years, the Chatti were destroyed. A few villagers survived, Anomia among them.

They all died as slaves in foreign lands.

When he heard the news, Atretes gathered his people together. "God's promises are sure," he said, his voice ringing out. "As is his judgment. We can be certain both will come, as surely as the dawn will come each day. Now, as we grieve our lost brothers and sisters, let us rejoice in all God has done for us, and let us remember that the only difference between us and those who perish is Christ. Without him, we all fail. With him, we come out of the darkness and into the dawn, for he has given us a future and a hope."

"Amen," Rizpah said quietly beside him.
"Amen," the others responded.

✳

"Rizpah, would you teach me to read?"

She looked up at Atretes in surprise at his question, and he smiled wryly. "Every day I hear you reading the words of God, and I long to do so for myself, to spend time with those words, to carry them to others." He reached down for her hand and held it tenderly. "Please, my love, will you teach me to read?"

Moved by the humility of his words, Rizpah could only nod. With each new day, she had seen more and more of Atretes' pride be put to death, and in its place God was filling the man she loved with wisdom, gentleness, and the fierce determination to follow Christ's example. As she gazed upon his face, she was overwhelmed with a sense of gratitude.

Lord, how good you are!

Within a few months, Rizpah taught Atretes to read the copy of the scroll Theophilus had brought with him from Ephesus, the same scroll Agabus had copied during the long sea voyage years before. The original scroll had been left with the church in Rome.

At last, one early morning, Atretes gathered the believers together and sat before them. Rizpah was beside him, the scroll in her lap. When Atretes reached for the scroll, unfurled it, then began to read to them, a hush came over the room. Those gathered listened raptly to the German's deep voice as he read from the testimony of one who had walked with the apostle Paul, as well as others who had spoken face-to-face with the Christ.

The letter began, "Inasmuch as many have undertaken to compile an account of the things accomplished among us, just as those who from the beginning were eyewitnesses and servants of the word have handed them down to us, it seemed fitting for me as well, having investigated everything carefully from the beginning, to write it out for you in consecutive order, most excellent Theophilus, so that you might know the exact truth about the things you have been taught."

The letter had been written by a physician, a friend of Theophilus', a man named Luke.

At the end of the reading, many came forward to shake

Epilogue

Atretes' hand and clap him on the back. "A true leader never stops learning," Freyja said to her son, her eyes shining with pride. Atretes drew her to him, hugging her fiercely. Rizpah watched them, tears in her eyes.

For as long as Atretes lived, he led such gatherings, teaching and instructing those in the community on the words of the Lord. And every morning, as the sun rose, Atretes and Rizpah went to their knees, praying for their children. Beseeching God on Hadassah's and Caleb's behalf, they entreated God to instill his words within their children's hearts, to create a hunger within them for his Word, and to make them *his* children, not theirs alone.

And God answered. Both Caleb and Hadassah grew up strong in the Lord. Hadassah was a credit to her namesake, for she became known throughout the region as a young woman of wisdom and great kindness. But it was Caleb who seemed especially attuned to the things of the Spirit. He studied the Word of God hungrily, as though he could not get enough of it.

"God has a special purpose for that one," Herigast said one night, watching Caleb where he was bent over the scrolls. Rizpah and Atretes only nodded, smiling.

It was little surprise, then, when their son came in one evening, his eyes alight with excitement.

"God has spoken to me!" he exclaimed.

Atretes sat in silence, waiting for his son to continue.

"Father, Mother, God has called me to take his Word to the Vikings."

Rizpah looked at Atretes in alarm. "The Vikings?" she said. "But, Caleb—"

"Rizpah." Atretes' quiet voice halted her words, and she met his loving gaze. "Not ours alone, remember?"

She nodded and went to embrace her son. *He is yours, Lord,* she prayed. *He has been from the beginning!*

It was a bittersweet moment, as was the morning when the community gathered to bid Caleb farewell. They prayed together, commissioning him in God's name and trusting him to the Lord's care.

And though none of them ever saw him again, they knew he was in God's hands—just as each of them was—and they were at peace.

GLOSSARY OF TERMS

amorata (pl. amoratae): a male or female devotee, or fan, of a gladiator
alimenta: a portion of money set aside to aid the poor
Aphrodite: Greek goddess of love and beauty. Identified with the Roman goddess Venus.
Apollo: Greek and Roman god of sunlight, prophecy, music, and poetry. The most handsome of the gods.
atrium: the central courtyard of a Roman dwelling. Most Roman houses consisted of a series of rooms surrounding an inner courtyard.
augury: the practice of divination; using a sign or an omen to determine meaning or actions
aureus (pl. aurei): a Roman gold coin equivalent to twenty-five denarii and weighing between five and eleven grams
baritus: a fierce war cry used by German warriors. It was made by holding their shields in front of their faces and yelling into them while banging on them with their weapons.
Batavi: a tribe from Gaul that fought with the Chatti and Bructeri against Rome
bibliotheca: library room of a Roman dwelling
brassard: a piece of armor that covers the upper arm
Bructeri: a Germanic tribe that fought with the Chatti against the Romans. The Bructeri apparently warred with the Chatti before being united with them against Rome.
calidarium: the room in the baths that was nearest to the boilers and thus was the hottest. Probably similar to a Jacuzzi or steam room of today.
cassis: a metal helmet worn over the galea that often had runes engraved on it
centurion: an officer commanding a century (a subdivision of the Roman legion)
Chatti: one of the Germanic tribes
cingulum: elaborate leather belts made for members of the Roman army and served as badges of office. The apron of decorated leather strips protected the soldier's groin in battle
civitas (pl. civitates): a small city or village
consul: a chief magistrate in the Roman republic. There were two positions, which were elected annually.
corbita: a slow-sailing merchant vessel
cubicula: underground chamber; nucleus of a family crypt
denarius (pl. denarii): a Roman unit of money equivalent to one day's pay for a common laborer. (See also *aureus, sesterce, quadrans*.)
El Elyon: God Most High

GLOSSARY OF TERMS

Eros: Greek god of physical (i.e., erotic) love. Equated with the Roman god Cupid.

fanum (pl. fana): a temple that was larger than a shrine but smaller than the regular temples

framea: a spear with a long, sharp head; this was a weapon used by the Germanic tribes. It could be thrown like a javelin, or its shaft could be wielded in a manner similar to a quarterstaff.

frigidarium: the room in the baths where the water was cold

galea: a German leather cap

gladiators: gladiators were male prisoners who were forcibly trained to compete in the Roman gladiatorial games. Their prison/school was called a *ludus*, their trainer, a *lanista*. There were several types of gladiators, each of which was identified by the weapons he was given to use and the prescribed role he was expected to play in the games. Except in unusual situations, gladiators fought until one of them died.

grubenhaus: a German longhouse, usually containing living quarters for humans and livestock

Hades: Greek god of the underworld; also, his kingdom

hemiolia: pirate ship having sails and oars; also known as a one-and-a-halfer

hypocrite: an actor

hypogeum: a family burial vault

lanista: a trainer for gladiators. Being the head *lanista* at a *ludus* was an occupation that was both disgraceful and famous. However, owning and hiring out gladiators was a regular and legitimate trade.

lararium: part of a Roman dwelling. The *lararium* was a special room reserved for domestic gods.

Liebchen: German for sweetheart or darling

loculi: individual burial cells in a crypt

Ludi (pl.): refers to the Roman games: *"Ludi Megalenses"*

ludus (pl. ludi): school/prison where gladiators were trained

mandragora: mandrake. A Mediterranean herb of the nightshade family used to promote conception, as a cathartic, or as a narcotic and soporific.

mensor (pl. mensores): a shipyard worker who weighed cargo, then recorded the weight in a ledger

palus: a cloaklike garment worn by Roman women over a *stola*

peculium: an allotment of money given to slaves by their owner. Slaves could treat a *peculium* as their own personal property, but under certain circumstances their owner could take it back.

peristyle: a section of a Roman dwelling (often a secondary section) that enclosed a courtyard and was surrounded by columns on the inside. Often located in the *peristyle* were the bedrooms of the family, the domestic shrine (*lararium*), the hearth and kitchen, the

GLOSSARY OF TERMS

dining room (*triclinium*), and the library (*bibliotheca*). In wealthier homes, the courtyard in the *peristyle* became a garden.

pollice verso: at the Roman games this was the signal of approval to kill. It was usually a "thumbs-down" sign.

praetor: a Roman magistrate that ranked below consul and whose role was chiefly judicial in nature

Praetorian Guards: Roman imperial bodyguards

proconsul: a governor or military commander of a Roman province; answered to the Senate

quadrans (pl. quadrantes): a bronze Roman coin. It took four of them to equal a copper coin, sixteen to equal a sesterce, and sixty-four to equal a denarius.

rundling: homesteads grouped in a ring, surrounding a center space

sacrarii: shipyard workers who carried cargo from wagons and dropped it onto a scale

scimitar: a saber (sword) made of a curved blade with the cutting edge on the convex side.

sesterce: a Roman coin, worth one-fourth of a denarius

spatha: a long, broad sword

statio (pl. stationes): a stopping place along roads where horses could be changed for hire and where garrisons of soldiers who patrolled the roads were stationed. Generally there were *stationes* every ten miles along the roads.

stola: a long, skirtlike garment worn by Roman women

stuppator: a shipyard worker who balanced on scaffolding to caulk ships when they docked

tepidarium: the room in the baths where the water was warm and soothing

Tiwaz: the war god of the Germanic tribes (Chatti, Bructeri, Batavi). Tiwaz was symbolized by the head of a goat

toga: the characteristic outer garment worn by Romans (although its use was slowly abandoned). It was a loose, oval-shaped piece of cloth worn draped about the shoulders and arms. The color and pattern of a toga were rigidly prescribed—politicians, persons in mourning, men, and boys each had a different toga that was to be worn. Boys wore a purple-rimmed toga, but when they came of age, they were allowed to wear the *toga virilis*, or man's toga, which was plain.

triclinium: the dining room of a Roman dwelling. The *triclinium* was often very ornate, having many columns and a collection of statues.

Way, the: a term used in the Bible (the book of Acts) to refer to Christianity. Christians probably would have called themselves "followers of the Way."

DISCUSSION GUIDE

Dear reader,

We hope you enjoyed this story and its many characters by Francine Rivers. It is the author's desire to whet your appetite for God's Word and His ways—to apply His principles to your life. The following character study is designed for just that! There are four sections of discussion questions for each of the four main characters:

- Character Review—gets the discussion going
- Digging Deeper—gets into the character
- Personal Insights/Challenges—gets you thinking
- Searching the Scriptures—gets you into God's Word

When writing this story, Francine had a key Bible verse in mind: "Dear brothers and sisters, be quick to listen, slow to speak, and slow to get angry. Your anger can never make things right in God's sight" (James 1:19-20). Notice the order: First, listen—and be quick about it. Speech is to come slowly, after listening; that is, after getting all the facts. Anger is—or should be—an afterthought. How often do we reverse the order? With this in mind, let me encourage you to get together with some friends and discuss your favorite scenes, characters, and personal insights from this novel. May your insights never end.

PEGGY LYNCH

HADASSAH

CHARACTER REVIEW
1. Discuss how Hadassah was perceived by those in the arena prison. How did Atretes see her?
2. Examine Hadassah's role in Atretes' life.

DIGGING DEEPER
1. Recount the information and advice Hadassah gave Atretes. How effective or persuasive was she?
2. What do you think made this conversation with Atretes so intense for Hadassah?
3. In what ways have you been persuasive or effective in intense situations?

PERSONAL INSIGHTS/CHALLENGES
1. In your opinion, what stands out the most about Hadassah?
2. Do you think Hadassah's sense of peace was realistic? How does your own sense of peace measure up?
3. "Dear brothers and sisters, be quick to listen, slow to speak, and slow to get angry. Your anger can never make things right in God's sight" (James 1:19-20). Describe how Hadassah exemplifies this passage of Scripture.

SEARCHING THE SCRIPTURES
As you recall Hadassah's patience and courage, look up the following Bible verses. They may give insight to the source of her effective life and challenge you as well.

> COLOSSIANS 4:5-6
>
> 1 PETER 4:12-13
>
> PSALM 27:14

ATRETES

CHARACTER REVIEW
1. Select a moving or disturbing scene with Atretes and share any memorable insights.
2. Discuss Atretes' relationship with Rizpah. How did it change?

DIGGING DEEPER
1. Recount the plans Atretes had for his son. In what ways did God change those plans?
2. In changing Atretes' plans, how did God change Atretes?

PERSONAL INSIGHTS/CHALLENGES
1. In what ways do you identify with Atretes? How are you different?
2. What do you think was Atretes' central conflict?
3. "Dear brothers and sisters, be quick to listen, slow to speak, and slow to get angry. Your anger can never make things right in God's sight" (James 1:19-20). What lessons did Atretes learn along these lines?

SEARCHING THE SCRIPTURES
As you examine Atretes' life, look up the following Bible verses. Consider what insights might have led to the changes in his life and may do the same for you.

> We can make our plans, but the Lord determines our steps. It is better to be patient than powerful; it is better to have self-control than to conquer a city. PROVERBS 16:9, 32

> Finally, all of you should be of one mind, full of sympathy toward each other, loving one another with tender hearts and humble minds. 1 PETER 3:8

> When you bow down before the Lord and admit your dependence on him, he will lift you up and give you honor. JAMES 4:10

RIZPAH

CHARACTER REVIEW
1. Discuss your favorite scene with Rizpah. What draws you into it?
2. Compare Rizpah's faith with Hadassah's.

DIGGING DEEPER
1. Describe Rizpah's head versus heart conflict.
2. In what ways did Rizpah's past affect her ability to trust God? How did she change?
3. What interferes with your ability to trust God?

PERSONAL INSIGHTS/CHALLENGES
1. In what ways are you like Rizpah? How are you different?
2. Do you think Rizpah's relationship with God was realistic? Explain.
3. "Dear brothers and sisters, be quick to listen, slow to speak, and slow to get angry. Your anger can never make things right in God's sight" (James 1:19-20). What happened with Rizpah's anger? And your own?

SEARCHING THE SCRIPTURES
As you think about Rizpah and the choices she made as she struggled with her faith in God, try reading the following Bible verses. They may reveal her challenges and victories and provide insights for you as well.

> *For you have been called to live in freedom—not freedom to satisfy your sinful nature, but freedom to serve one another in love.* GALATIANS 5:13

> *A gentle answer turns away wrath, but harsh words stir up anger.* PROVERBS 15:1

> *So be careful how you live, not as fools but as those who are wise.* EPHESIANS 5:15

THEOPHILUS

CHARACTER REVIEW
1. Choose a memorable scene with Theophilus and discuss what makes it unforgettable.
2. Compare Theophilus' relationship with Rizpah to his relationship with Atretes. What differences do you find?

DIGGING DEEPER
1. Describe Theophilus' reputation.
2. In what ways did Theophilus share his faith in God? Was he effective? What would you like to learn from his example?
3. How would others describe your reputation?

PERSONAL INSIGHTS/CHALLENGES
1. How are you like Theophilus? In what ways are you different?
2. Consider Theophilus' wisdom and counsel. How does your own wisdom and counsel compare?
3. "Dear brothers and sisters, be quick to listen, slow to speak, and slow to get angry. Your anger can never make things right in God's sight" (James 1:19-20). Discuss how Theophilus understood the principles in this verse.

SEARCHING THE SCRIPTURES
As you ponder Theophilus' life and reputation, read the following Bible verses. They may reveal his motivations and challenge you as well.

> EPHESIANS 5:19
>
> COLOSSIANS 3:16
>
> PHILIPPIANS 1:12
>
> GALATIANS 6:4-5

Books by Beloved Author
Francine Rivers

The Mark of the Lion series
(available individually or in a collection)
A Voice in the Wind
An Echo in the Darkness
As Sure as the Dawn

A Lineage of Grace series
(available individually or in an anthology)
Unveiled
Unashamed
Unshaken
Unspoken
Unafraid

Sons of Encouragement series
(available individually or in an anthology)
The Priest
The Warrior
The Prince
The Prophet
The Scribe

Marta's Legacy series
(available individually or in a collection)
Her Mother's Hope
Her Daughter's Dream

Stand-Alone Titles
Bridge to Haven
Redeeming Love
The Atonement Child
The Scarlet Thread
The Last Sin Eater
Leota's Garden
And the Shofar Blew
The Shoe Box (a Christmas novella)

Children's Titles
Bible Stories for Growing Kids
    (coauthored with Shannon
    Rivers Coibion)

www.francinerivers.com

Can God's Love Save Anyone?
Redeeming Love
by FRANCINE RIVERS

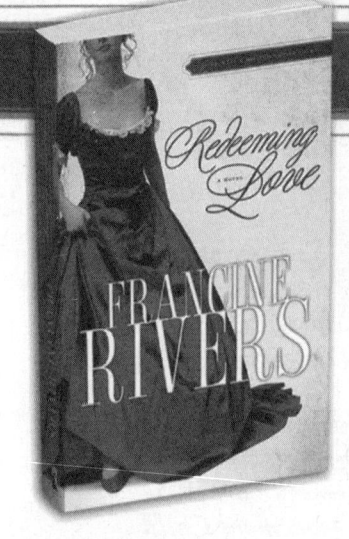

OVER 1 MILLION COPIES SOLD

California's gold country, 1850. A time when men sold their souls for a bag of gold and women sold their bodies for a place to sleep. A powerful retelling of the book of Hosea, *Redeeming Love* is a life-changing story of God's unconditional, redemptive, all-consuming love.

Now available in hardcover and softcover

"The truth that ran through that story [Redeeming Love] absolutely took me to my knees. And I was a changed person when I finished reading that book."

—Amy Grant
(Singer/Songwriter) in an interview with Ted Koppel, ABC News

www.francinerivers.com

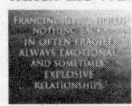

Check out Francine's website and blog at www.francinerivers.com, and visit her on Facebook at www.facebook.com/FrancineRivers.

have you visited tyndalefiction.com *lately?*

YOU'LL FIND:

- ways to connect with your favorite authors
- first chapters
- discussion guides
- author videos and book trailers
- and much more!

PLUS, SCAN THE QR CODE OR VISIT BOOKCLUBHUB.NET TO

- download free discussion guides
- get great book club recommendations
- sign up for our book club and other e-newsletters

TYNDALE FICTION

Are you crazy for Tyndale fiction? Follow us on Twitter **@Crazy4Fiction** for daily updates on your favorite authors, free e-book promotions, contests, and much more. Let's get crazy!